# DEATH OF A POET

*Ancient Egypt Mysteries*
*Book One*

## Keith Moray

SAPERE
BOOKS

# DEATH OF A POET

Published by Sapere Books.

24 Trafalgar Road, Ilkley, LS29 8HH

**saperebooks.com**

ISBN: 978-1-80055-719-2

Keith Moray is represented by Isabel Atherton at Creative Authors.

*For the two Johns, my late father and brother, who were both present
when the germ of the idea for this novel first came to me.*

Hecataeus made this bronze like Philitas in every way,
accurate down to the tips of his toes
in size and frame alike describing this investigator
on a human scale. He included nothing from the physique of
heroes.
No, with the straight edge of truth and all his skill he cast
the old man full of cares.
He seems about to speak — how fully his features are
elaborated! —
alive, though of bronze, this old man:
I stand here dedicated by Ptolemy, god and king at once,
for the sake of the Muses, the Coan man.

The statue of Philitas of Cos
Posidippus (310–240 BC)

# ACKNOWLEDGEMENTS

With grateful thanks to Ahmed Elsayed, my Egyptologist friend and guide, and to Mark Saltveit, the first World Palindrome Champion, who probably knows more about Sotades the Obscene and palindromic poetry than anyone else. Their help was of inestimable value to me. And also to Isabel Atherton, my wonderful agent, and to Amy Durant and all the fabulous people at Sapere Books.

# PROLOGUE

It was a good night for murder.

They were in one of the parts of the city that was never touched by the beams from the Pharos lighthouse and where there was just enough light from a sliver of a moon for them to do what they had to do without being seen. Not that they expected anyone there at that time of night. That was partly why the fool thought he would be safe to meet them. In the shadows he had not been able to anticipate their attack.

But it hadn't been easy. He had come round too quickly after they had knocked him out. Then, even though they had lashed his hands behind his back and shackled his ankles together, it had taken both of them to hold his head under the water in the trough until the very last bubbles broke the surface and his body went limp.

'Let's hold him there for a while longer, just to make sure,' the older of the two said. 'You sit on his back and I'll hold his head under.'

The other guffawed. He punched the body hard in the small of the back three times as if he was making a sack of grain comfortable enough to sit on. In fact, he was just doing what he'd never have dared do if the man was still alive. Satisfied that there was no sign of life, he lowered his weight onto the back. 'You think of everything, don't you?'

'Someone has to. After we got rid of the other one, it was only a matter of time before this bastard started nosing around.'

'*He* won't be happy about this when he finds out.'

'Why not? It was his problem as much as ours. Him and however many of them there are. He may be our boss, but we know he takes orders from higher up. How high, who knows?' He grabbed a handful of hair and yanked the head backwards. Water trickled from the open mouth, and as he shook the head he watched the sightless eyes. They were the eyes of a wooden doll and made no movement.

'A bit longer,' he said dispassionately as he shoved the head under again.

'We'd better shove him completely in to make it look right.'

'Time enough. We'll pour that skin of wine down his throat first.'

'Like I said. You think of everything.'

'It's a good thing I do, or you and I would be dead too.'

# CHAPTER 1

*The Island of Caunus, 10 leagues south of Crete.*
*9th year of Pharaoh Ptolemy II*
*(275 BC)*

Hecataeus liked to sculpt in the nude. After he broke his fast, he would divest himself of clothes and begin his work.

In his studio atop his villa on the tiny triangular island of Caunus that he had retreated to after failing to obtain a sinecure at the Musaeum of Alexandria, he spent his early mornings working on the life-size statue of Tyche, the goddess of fortune. He believed fervently that his artistic creativity was at its height when unfettered by clothing. When it was finished, he wished to send it as a gift to Pharaoh Ptolemy and Queen Arsinoe the Second, in the hope that his talent would be rewarded by an invitation to find glory in Alexandria. He was sure that was where his destiny awaited him.

Drakon, the oldest of his three slaves, had thrown open the shutters when Hecataeus rose and had set out his usual breakfast of goat's milk, figs and bread. As Hecataeus ate and drank he watched the sun rise over distant Crete, simultaneously lifting the shadows on the terraced vineyards of Caunus. The air was calm and full of the hum of myriads of insects that hovered over the flowering shrubs and contributed to the daily chorus of life. The drone of the bees and the high-pitched whirring noise of the mosquitoes merged with the song of the terns, cranes and the various gulls that were in flight enjoying the plentiful food available to them. He found that the rich scent of mint, laurel and myrtle was quite heady in the mornings, especially when the dew on the olives and grapes began to evaporate in the sun. Focusing on the wonders of nature always prepared him for the work ahead. Especially after a night of frolicking in bed had relaxed him.

To the left of his villa the land rose to the island's solitary peak, surrounded by the small forest of poplar and juniper. Looking out to sea he espied a vessel in the distance, coming from the direction of Crete.

*Curious,* he thought. *It does not look like* The Trident, *old Captain Nestor's ship. Although I am not expecting him for some days yet.*

He watched it with increasing interest for several minutes until it gradually became clearer and he could see that it was a trireme. As it slowly approached, the sun glistened on the layers of oars that powered it through the shimmering water. And then it was lost to sight around the headland.

*Hmm, but it is still too far to see its flag. Whither has it come and to whom does it belong? It could be Macedonian, Cyrenean, Greek or Syrian. But if it is from the Pharaoh's fleet, then the time for bravery has come. I must be bold until the last and I must not betray myself to anyone.*

Despite himself, he let out a soft chuckle.

*Betrayal! Apart from my art, betrayal is my greatest talent. Why, this statue that my bedfellow Sotades has seen me carving these last few days would seem the ultimate betrayal to him, which is why I dare not finish it until he has gone.*

With a shiver of excitement at the sight of the trireme, he picked up his mug of milk and drained it before standing and stripping off his scarlet chiton and throwing it over the window ledge. He stretched his muscles and ran his hands through his mane of curly, black hair before pulling back the sheet that covered the statue.

*Well, glorious Tyche, is this a sign that you have smiled on me?*

He smiled at the effigy of the goddess that he had carved from the huge pink marble block. After a year of chiselling and chipping, shaping and polishing, it was nearing completion. He had done well and depicted her as a near naked figure dressed only in a diaphanous robe, bearing what would be a double cornucopia of plenty in one arm, while her other hand held a globe representing the unsteadiness of fortune.

*I cannot yet start upon the cornucopia while Sotades is my guest, for he would realise the level of my duplicity.*

His eyes roved over the voluptuous figure with its perfectly curved breasts and hips, its graceful neck, the beautiful face with the long, straight nose and the faintly pouting lips. He ran a hand over the smooth abdomen and felt that stirring male sensation that made him realise yet again that he had fallen in love either with the goddess or with the untouchable human model that he had used in his mind to depict her.

*Not now, Hecataeus. Breathe deeply. You have spent too long in Sotades's company. Think only of stone.*

Giving himself a few moments to calm down, he turned to his worktable and selected one of the many abrasive rubbing stones that he used to polish the marble and began to apply it to the figure's torso. So absorbed in his work and his reveries did he become that he soon lost sense of time.

Ever since he had been a boy, it had been Hecataeus's dream to one day sculpt for kings and queens and have men say his name with the same reverence that they spoke of Myron of Eleutherae, Phidias of Athens or Polyclitus of Argos, the greatest sculptors of Greece, a band to which Chares of Lindos also belonged.

As a teenager Hecataeus had seen the great Colossus that Chares had created at Rhodes and longed to achieve his fame. But when he reached manhood and inherited his father's estate and fortune and learned his craft from a series of private tutors, he began to despise the weakness of Chares.

The great sculptor, the designer of the Colossus that bestrode the harbour at Rhodes, had been mortified when a minor defect in his work had been pointed out. He had drunk himself into a stupor before slitting his wrists. The cruel irony was that no one noticed that tiny flaw, that one of the sun rays on the enormous Colossus's headdress was three feet shorter than the others.

'As if it mattered, you poor bastard!' he exclaimed aloud, vigorously polishing and adding to the marble dust that settled like a patina on his bare torso.

Laughter from the doorway made him turn round.

'Are you berating poor old Chares again?' asked Sotades, his lover and secret house guest. He was wearing a loose robe, but from his wet ginger beard and hair and the water dripping from him, it was clear that he had been swimming. A decade older than Hecataeus, yet the poet Sotades still had well-toned muscles, despite having spent six months in one of the pharaoh's jails. His high cheekbones and red hair made him stand out in any gathering, as did his sea-blue eyes. Yet that was not what attracted males and females to him so much as his humour and his wit.

Hecataeus saw the goblet and the flask of wine he was carrying.

'Sotades! You were up early,' he said, his tone slightly accusatory.

The other grinned and shrugged his shoulders. 'You know I love to swim by moon and starlight in the company of blessed Artemis, before her brother great Apollo rises from his slumber. Besides, as you have told me often enough, I must not be abroad in the day when people might recognise me —

even here on your estate on Caunus!' He gave a short laugh. 'But you didn't answer my question, my prince. Were you castigating poor Chares again? You seemed in a petulant mood, and when you get into one of those you worry me with the way you send those lumps of stone flying around. You could injure yourself somewhere it would pain those who love you to see you injured.'

He crossed his legs and sucked air through his lips as if suddenly struck in his nether region. Then with a guffaw he raised the wine goblet and filled it from the flask in his other hand. 'Shall I come and dust you down? You begin to look like a statue yourself.' He chuckled suggestively. 'I could polish you and make those muscles glisten.'

Hecataeus looked out the window at the vineyards below, where two of his slaves were already hard at work. Glancing further out to sea, he saw no sign of the trireme.

'No, Sotades,' he replied emphatically. 'You are an insatiable rogue. I have work that needs to be done. I don't need further distractions from you.'

The poet harrumphed and raised his goblet. 'Perhaps it will be your loss. Time to break my fast then, I think.'

'You drink too much, Sotades,' Hecataeus remarked with a shake of his head and a resigned smile. 'You should eat more wholesome food. Why don't you have milk and bread and figs for breakfast? Give your stomach a rest from wine. You know that you have to look after yourself and stay fit.'

The poet placed the flask on a table and took a hefty swig of wine from the goblet. He belched, then grinned and slapped his firm abdominal muscles. 'You don't think I am fit? And you want me to eat better and drink less wine? Why, Hecataeus, I can run like the wind and I swim as fast as Poseidon himself. If I just skulked around and ate, I would soon be as round as that sphere in Tyche's hand. Besides, this fine wine that your slaves make here on Caunus loosens my tongue and frees my mind so I can write and compose. What do you expect when even the great Homer in his tiresomely long *Odyssey* used this tiny island as a love nest where the nymph Calypso trapped Odysseus so she could bed him for eternity?'

He coughed and then went into an impromptu dance.

*'Oh bold Odysseus to Caunus came,*
*ensnared by the Calypso named.'*

He wrapped his arms about himself, turned around and wriggled so that from behind it looked as if he was being embraced. After but a moment he turned about again, his face taking on a leer as he lewdly moved his pelvis.

*'It was on Caunus where bold Odysseus came,*
*and echoing most bold, came and came again.'*

He took a sudden breath, as if in the final throes of rapture.

Hecataeus smiled despite himself and focused on polishing Tyche's cleavage. 'You have an eternally dirty mind, Sotades. But as I said, I must work.'

Sotades pouted in mock disappointment. 'Work, work, work! That is all you think about. You are determined to be a success, aren't you?'

'You say it contemptuously, as if success doesn't matter.'

'It can be a monster, Hecataeus. Look what it did to me. Sotades, one of the greatest poets that has ever lived. I have been a court poet in every major country in the world. I have written masterpieces, given performances everywhere and composed poems that will last through time. And what has it gained me? Some months in Ptolemy Philadelphus's prison, that is what.'

'How modest you are, Sotades.'

'Pah! What is there to be modest about? I have greatness in me, which is why kings and queens listen to my words.'

'Pharaoh Ptolemy and his queen listened to your insults, Sotades.'

'He needed to be told. If I really believed in any of the gods, I would swear by them that it is not done to marry and fornicate with your sister. It isn't the Greek way! My poem merely told them what the Greek subjects of Alexandria and the whole country were thinking.'

'I know, you have told me so many times. The truth is that you revel in all manner of lovemaking and you are a master of mischief-making.'

Sotades chuckled. 'That I do. Just as the great Hipponax of Ephesus did before me, I want to stir the people's minds. Like a stick in a bee's hive, my honeyed words will agitate and sting. Love and fornicating in every which way are meat and drink to me. Literally, I pen my poems about sex and who's doing what to whom, and how and why and how often, and people pay me to eat and drink and live merrily. This is why they call me Sotades the Obscene. Obscenity itself is both my muse and my whole pantheon of gods and goddesses.'

'And it is why you have ended up here, as my secret guest? Your fame has made you a fugitive from the pharaoh.'

'Exactly my point, Hecataeus. This is what success does. My genius has taken me everywhere, from Athens to Antioch and back. I have been court poet to Lysimachus in Thrace, to Demetrius in Macedon, to Seleucus Nicator and to Ptolemy Philadelphus of Egypt.'

Hecataeus stopped what he was doing and turned. 'Court poet to Pharaoh Ptolemy? Is that quite right, Sotades?'

Sotades shrugged and topped his wine up again. 'I was when Pharaoh Ptolemy was married to Queen Arsinoe the First. He liked me well enough then, and the queen and I had a most congenial relationship. Egypt lost much when she was repudiated by Ptolemy in favour of his sister. Yet even when he married his second wife, Arsinoe the Second, and I lost my position as official court poet, he still paid me much when I was reciting poems about his enemies. And there were many in his court who were willing to wine and dine me and accommodate me and my needs. Some at the very top of the court.'

'Until you insulted Queen Arsinoe and Pharaoh Ptolemy Philadelphus.'

'That is true, but mind you, he only became Philadelphus when he married his sister, a most un-Hellenic thing to do. I did not approve of it, but I realised that the Egyptians see it as a means of keeping their dynasties pure. I merely echoed in my poems the feelings of my fellow Alexandrians.'

He took a hefty swallow of wine. 'No, Hecataeus, the pharaoh and his sister were unnecessarily sensitive. Why should I not point out that incest, distasteful as it is to the Greeks, is just normal for Egyptian royalty? They should have praised me for supporting them instead of casting me in prison.'

He chuckled. 'You like talking about truth, don't you, Hecataeus? Well, the truth is that Queen Arsinoe is a woman with a most capricious nature.'

Hecataeus did not see the wistful look that had crossed Sotades' face.

'But you also insulted many of the nobles, didn't you, Sotades?'

The poet laughed again. 'In my time I have insulted many people. It is a brand of humour that is unique to me. Admittedly I am usually careful where I recite particular poems. In Lysimachus's court, I insult Seleucus. When in Antioch, I would make Ptolemy my target. In Macedon, Lysimachus is painted for the fool that he was. I perhaps stretched my luck too much in Alexandria. And as you say, that is why I am here with you, waiting to be rescued.' He drained his wine. 'It is all part of the great scheme.'

Hecataeus gave a short, humourless laugh. 'But it wasn't just Queen Arsinoe the Second that you insulted, Sotades. You insulted the pharaoh's mistress, Bilistiche.'

Sotades sipped more wine. 'A whore who rides horses. I merely wrote about her love of stallions and her ability to get the most out of them. Man or horse, she treats them the same way, by riding them into the ground.'

'And for all of these insults the pharaoh sentenced you to death.'

'Thankfully, I had friends who secured my release.'

'At great personal risk to themselves.'

'And you know that I love my friends for it, Hecataeus. You know that I love you.' Sotades crossed the room and put a hand on the younger man's shoulder. 'I am truly grateful for all that you have given me. Your home, your food and wine, and your company. In exchange, what have I given you? Some sentimental poetry?' He sucked air through his lips. 'It is hard sometimes, skulking here, unable to go to the agora or the Emporium, visit the theatre or give poetry readings to anyone. I am forced to live in hiding in Caunus, ever in fear that Ptolemy's reach will find me, until good Nestor returns to take me to safety.' He patted the younger man's shoulder and added, 'Wherever that may be.' He returned to the table and picked up his flask.

Hecataeus glanced out the window, shrugged his shoulders and lay down his tools. Brushing the marble dust from his shoulders, he picked up his scarlet chiton and put it on. Crossing the studio to the poet, he kissed him on the lips. 'We have lived well these past weeks, Sotades, but all things that are good have to have their end.'

'What do you mean?' the poet asked, his brow beetling.

The sound of hammering on doors below and the protestations of Drakon were followed by raised voices and the sound of many feet.

'It is the end of the good time, Sotades!'

A cacophony of scuttling, sandaled footsteps and the heavy tread of boots sounded outside the studio before the door was unceremoniously thrown open. Drakon entered a moment before a tall, broad-shouldered man with a black beard that looked as if it had been sculpted from obsidian. He was of about forty years of age and was followed by a young man in his early twenties, and then by two heavily armed guards.

'You are Hecataeus of Caunus? Your friend Captain Nestor told us that you were holding Sotades,' said the older man, dressed in a purple chiton with a gold pectoral atop it. 'His Majesty Pharaoh Ptolemy the Second will be pleased that I have finally tracked down this dog poet.'

Sotades stared at the newcomer for a moment before a slow smile came to his lips. Then, as if he was without a care in the world, he raised his goblet. 'Admiral Patroclus, I can honestly say that it hasn't been long enough since last I saw your handsome face.' He drank some of his wine and smacked his lips before turning to Hecataeus. 'And you, my prince, I see that success really does mean everything to you. Give me a moment and I shall compose a poem to this, your sweet betrayal.'

The younger man behind Admiral Patroclus smirked as he clapped his hands against the blonde beard that covered his cheeks. 'Oh, not more of your nonsense, Sotades the Obscene. I have been praying to my mentor Harpocrates, the great god of silence and secrets, that we should not have to endure more of those empty, banal obscenities that you dare to call poems.'

Sotades beamed at him. 'Why, Diomedes, what brings you to Caunus? Are you still doing your soothsaying and writing your pathetic little ditties, or are you now just joined by the rear to the admiral?'

Patroclus instantly dealt Sotades a backhanded blow across the face that made him stagger backwards. The goblet went flying, spraying the rest of the wine across the admiral's chiton. It immediately earned him another strike that burst his lip and sent his head crashing against the wall, knocking him out. He slid down the wall, blood trickling freely down his chin and neck, and quickly soaking his flimsy robe.

Hecataeus snapped his fingers at Drakon. 'Bring fresh clothes for him and a bowl of water for his lip.'

Admiral Patroclus held up a hand. 'No need. His Majesty Ptolemy Philadelphus has ordered that he be taken from here how he is found.' He nodded to the two guards, who picked the poet up by his hands and feet. 'Take him outside and await us.'

Reaching inside his chiton, Patroclus drew out a roll of papyrus and handed it to the sculptor.

'Hecataeus of Caunus, you have served our pharaoh well and this is a pass for you to see me, Patroclus, Admiral of the Fleet and the pharaoh's vizier at the palace when you come to Alexandria.'

Hecataeus bowed and took the papyrus. 'I thank you, my lord. It is my humble ambition to join the Musaeum and offer my meagre services as a sculptor.'

Patroclus looked admiringly at the statue of the goddess Tyche and nodded. 'If this is a sample of your skill, then I think Pharaoh Ptolemy Philadelphus will be pleased to employ you as one of his court sculptors. I see the resemblance to Queen Arsinoe.'

'When it is complete, it will be a gift to Their Majesties.' Hecataeus pointed to the crudely chiselled outline of the cornucopia. 'This is to be a double cornucopia that symbolises the blissful union of the pharaoh and his wife. Of divine brother and sister.'

'Then bring it with you when you come, and I will arrange for Their Majesties to see you themselves.'

The young man identified by Sotades as Diomedes stepped forward and put a hand on the marble statue, stroking the illusion of a diaphanous robe. His eyes appeared to go slightly misty, as if he was in a trance and looking through the statue.

'This statue of Tyche is beauty personified,' he said, addressing the air rather than anyone present. 'I see Queen Arsinoe the Second of that name is herself the model for this image of sacred Tyche. I see that it will become a shrine at the Royal Palace.'

'Diomedes is a poet and soothsayer and often has these insights,' Admiral Patroclus explained. 'He accompanied me on my latest mission to Syria and said that he had been given a message from the god Harpocrates that the fleet should make for Crete. And sure enough, when we arrived we were approached by your friend Captain Nestor. The fleet is making its way slowly back to Alexandria. We came here to Caunus to arrest the poet Sotades and will re-join the fleet shortly.'

The soothsaying poet cried out and blinked rapidly. Then he put a hand to his brow, as if suddenly feeling faint. A moment later he recovered and looked appraisingly at Hecataeus. 'I have just been delivered of a message from Harpocrates, the god of mysteries. You, Hecataeus, will soon become famous.'

Admiral Patroclus clapped Diomedes on the shoulder and nodded sagely. 'You are seldom wrong in your interpretations. I am sure it will be as you say.' He nodded and made for the door. The slaves who had been hovering uncertainly stood aside.

Diomedes spoke. 'Admiral, I would deem it a favour if I could spend a few minutes with our friend, Hecataeus, here. It will help me compose my poem.'

Patroclus nodded. 'It will take us a while to ready the ship. I will leave one of the men on the beach to row you back. Do not take too long. We will make for Alexandria once you are on board.'

When he had gone, Diomedes looked at the goblet on the floor and then at the flask on the table. He raised an eyebrow and pointed.

'Of course, Master Diomedes,' Hecataeus said, turning to Drakon. 'Fetch fresh goblets and more wine for my important guest.'

'Perhaps you should count me your friend now, Hecataeus,' the other replied. 'I can be useful at court. But first, tell me all about the time Sotades has spent here on this idyllic island.' He looked again at the statue, walking round it and stroking the marble body admiringly.

Drakon returned almost immediately and poured two goblets of wine, before vanishing as a good servant should.

Hecataeus told Diomedes the story that he had rehearsed in his mind, should this situation arise. He knew that it had come to pass because his old friend Captain Nestor had either been stopped by a ship from Ptolemy's fleet, or he had made contact with someone in authority on Crete, instead of one of the other contacts they had agreed upon.

Either way, it was a distortion of the truth, which was that Hecataeus's contact at court had been involved in the poet Sotades's escape from his Alexandrian prison. Hecataeus was to provide safe haven for the poet to lie low until he could be transported safely to whichever of the capitals of the known world would offer him sanctuary. Then his poetic and oratorical talents would do the rest.

But the version that Hecataeus gave to Diomedes was that Nestor had discovered Sotades stowed away in a cargo of leopard skins, wine and timber that he was transporting to Crete. Upon realizing whom the stowaway was, he had sailed to nearby Caunus where he knew the villa of Hecataeus the sculptor. Nestor was to say that he knew this because he had often been commissioned to drop off large blocks of marble for Hecataeus to sculpt. They had agreed that Hecataeus would hold Sotades prisoner until Nestor was able to bring authorities to the island to take him into custody again.

They drank some more, like old friends. Hecataeus was shrewd enough to appreciate that Diomedes was pumping him for information, not because he was suspicious of their account, but because he would undoubtedly use it to strengthen his own assertion that he had known where they would find Sotades. It would strengthen his reputation as a soothsayer.

'As a poet, it my duty to write an account of this happening and of the divine message from Harpocrates that led to Sotades the Obscene's recapture,' Diomedes went on as he drank his wine. 'Of course, it will be a real poem, not like the disgusting nonsense that Sotades traded in.' He pointed to the statue of the goddess Tyche. 'I am sure that Harpocrates must have talked with Tyche upon Olympus. She must have told him that you were sculpting a likeness of Queen Arsinoe in her image. This is what Harpocrates told me.'

Hecataeus raised his goblet to the poet. 'I am sure you are right, my friend. The gods see everything and we are blessed that we have soothsayers like yourself who can speak to them.'

'There are no others like me, good Hecataeus. But have no fear, for your part in this great adventure shall be written in my poem. I shall begin composing it and we shall talk further when you come to Alexandria.'

After he left, Hecataeus took some time to consider all that had happened. By rights he knew that he should feel guilty about betraying his lover and friend, to whom he had given refuge for the past few weeks. He had of course been careful about what he told Diomedes, for he dared not tell him the truth.

He felt a pang of remorse, but swiftly shrugged it away. If he was to become a famous sculptor, he had not time for guilt. Besides, now he had reason to go to Alexandria, and with the promise under Admiral Patroclus's patronage of meeting both the pharaoh and the queen. He stared out of the window and saw Diomedes walking swiftly down the hillside path. The soothsaying poet turned and smiled as he waved up at Hecataeus, his new friend. It felt to Hecataeus that a bond had been made between them.

'Poor Sotades. He himself told me many times that he does not believe in the gods and goddesses. The fool.'

He stroked the cold marble breast of Tyche and then bent close and kissed it. 'Thank you, my lady. It seems that Sotades's fortune has run its course and mine is on the rise.'

He reached for a hammer and chisel and began to fashion the double cornucopia.

# CHAPTER 2

Sotades did not regain consciousness until Admiral Patroclus's trireme was on its way to Alexandria. Even then it took a bucket of water to rouse him.

The poet cursed as he spluttered awake, only to find himself leaning against a large ceramic pithos jar with his legs outstretched on the ship's deck, manacled at the ankles. The helmsman was some way off, beating out a rhythm on a large drum and calling orders to the three banks of oarsmen who were propelling the vessel at some speed through the water.

Blinking in the sun, he saw Admiral Patroclus and Diomedes sitting on wooden stools opposite him, each drinking wine.

'Might I have some fresh clothes?' Sotades asked. 'It appears I have been bleeding. And maybe a drink of wine?'

Patroclus nodded to Diomedes, who summoned an awaiting servant. A few moments later, with his robe taken away and a rough blanket over him, he was given a goblet of wine. He winced as he put the goblet to his burst lip before taking a good swig.

'What are all these pithoi for?' he asked, looking round and seeing that the pithos he was leaning against was just one of several huge storage jars.

'Some are full of wine, others of grain, another of ingots and yet more of spices. We took them on board from Captain Nestor's vessel *The Trident*. The one you are leaning against is empty.'

Sotades made no comment, but merely nodded. 'So what shall we drink to? My return to see our great pharaoh and his delectable wife, his sister?' He winked at Patroclus and drank more wine, as if any answer was of no consequence.

'His Majesty, Pharaoh Ptolemy, wants you,' Patroclus said blandly. 'He —'

'I know, he misses my wit,' Sotades said quickly.

Diomedes snorted. 'He missed your presence in the jail he had you thrown into.'

Sotades drank again. 'That surprises me not at all. He used to come and watch me through the bars. He liked seeing me grovel and apologise. Although he would not admit it, he smiled when I told him of the famous inadequacies of Lysimachus, Seleucus and Cassander and all of their woefully unintelligent offspring. Not once did he show any sign of forgiving me, the ingrate.'

'Why should he?' Patroclus asked. 'You insulted the queen. You said he was shoving his peg in an unholy hole.'

'Oh, it was better than that. Get your words right, Admiral Patroclus. Listen.' He shuffled his buttocks to get more comfortable and eased his back against the large earthenware jar.

*'In the land of the Nile where dogs are gods,*
*A King stuck his prick in an unholy hole.*
*In that unholy hole a king's prick stuck,*
*Where gods are dogs to the vile of the land.'*

Diomedes snorted contemptuously. 'Doggerel! Insulting not just the pharaoh and his queen, but the religions of the land. You are lucky he did not have you impaled on a spike.'

Sotades smirked and winked at the younger man. 'You would know about being impaled, would you not, Diomedes? Surely the admiral would agree with that?'

Patroclus glared at him for a moment, then sipped his wine. 'I would say that you are still an impertinent dog, Sotades, and you have wasted much of my valuable time in tracking you down. It is fortunate that Diomedes was sent a message from the gods, telling us where you were.'

Sotades gave a short laugh. 'Ah yes, our famous soothsaying poet, Diomedes. He has made so many predictions about the future that he was bound to be right once. If this prediction was where to find me, it must be the first correct one ever. I will drink to that!'

He drained his goblet and held it out before him. 'Well, Ptolemy wants me, so that means he must have missed me. May I have more wine?'

Diomedes seethed. 'Let me pour it down his throat, my lord. And then I will shove the flask after it like a stopper. I owe him a debt for insulting me and my eels.'

Sotades tossed his head back and laughed aloud again. 'Ah yes, your slithery friends, of whom you have so many — or should that be so few? But why hold a grudge, Diomedes? I made you famous with my little poem.'

The soothsayer gripped his goblet tightly and glared at the shackled poet.

Patroclus put a hand on Diomedes's arm and shook his head. He turned again to the poet.

'Sotades, you must learn to curb your tongue. You must apologise to Diomedes. See how you have upset him with that jibe about his divine-given gift. He came on a mission with my fleet to Syria, and after we had won our battle he had his message about you from the god Harpocrates, which is why we came to Crete.'

Sotades laughed sarcastically. 'But he has no gift, Admiral. He has no ear to Harpocrates the so-called god of silence and secrets, just as he has no gift for poetry. His gift is no gift and it was given freely, because it was given by nothing from nothing. Since nothing is never more than nothing, Diomedes himself is nothing.'

The younger man sucked air through his teeth and shook his head. 'And you wonder why Pharaoh Ptolemy is anxious to have you caught again.'

'As I said to the admiral, he misses my wit. The trouble is he has not the wit to realise that my wit was truly god-given. Given by Apollo, the god of poetry. Or it would have been, if there was such a thing as a god.'

Patroclus harrumphed. 'So you refuse to apologise to Diomedes and now you insult the gods by denying their existence!'

'Why would they be insulted? If I deny your existence, does that stop you being real, if indeed you are?'

'But you never denied my existence, did you, Sotades? You insulted the pharaoh, the queen, the Lady Bilistiche — and you insulted me.'

'You, Admiral? When did I insult you?'

'In that disgusting poem you wrote, parodying the great Homer's *Iliad*. Everyone knows that by insulting my namesake, the great Patroclus, friend of Achilles, you were insulting me. The references to me were as thinly disguised as the ones about Pharaoh Ptolemy Philadelphus and Queen Arsinoe.'

Sotades waved the goblet dismissively. 'Then with respect, Admiral, you did not understand the wit of my poetry. It is unique, as unique as Homer's. I write in what I call palindromes, which no one has done before. If you saw reference to yourself, then you should be honoured to be mentioned in my poetry, for it will shine down through the ages.'

'Not if Pharaoh Ptolemy has anything to do with it,' interjected Diomedes. 'In case you did not know, all of your work has been burned.'

Sotades shrugged. 'Pharaohs come and pharaohs go. When they go, the next one usually claims their monuments and their deeds as their own. Eventually it is as if they have never been. They become nothing. But words and poetry, they are different matters, for they inspire and praise and will last for as long as people speak. Words can be rewritten more easily than monuments can be built.'

'Your poetry neither praises nor inspires, as you well know, Sotades. Your nonsense is meant to injure and insult,' said Patroclus.

The poet shrugged. 'The truth is that I have a fiery mind, and a hot tongue from which the words tumble like cinders. Sometimes they burn when they land on people. But it is all lightly meant — most cinders fizzle out, it is only the ones that reach the sky that become stars.'

'So your words are lightly made,' said Patroclus, standing and tossing his empty goblet to the waiting guard. 'Well then, we must give them some weight.' He snapped his fingers and the two guards who had carried the poet Sotades from the villa of Hecataeus came forward. At a gesture from the admiral, they picked up Sotades and manhandled him by his shackled feet into the large pithos jar so that only his head protruded from the top.

'I will not walk far with this on me,' jibed Sotades. 'Must I crawl like a turtle with this great weight, for I surely cannot make it hop like a frog?'

'Still the comic fool,' Patroclus said. 'But it is true, you will not travel far stuck in there.' He turned to one of the guards. 'Go and tell the helmsman to stop the rowers.'

Moments later the helmsman stopped drumming and called out orders to raise and rest the oars. Gradually the trireme slowed in the water.

'Am I to be treated like a philosopher now? Like the great Diogenes the Cynic, who lived in a pithos in the marketplace of Athens?'

'Diogenes was also one who promoted obscenity,' pointed out Diomedes.

'He did,' Sotades agreed. 'Then as a fellow cynic, I am counted in good company. Am I to be set up in the marketplace in Alexandria, to live in this pithos?'

'Perhaps,' said Patroclus. 'What say you, Diomedes? Shall we take Sotades at his word and have him live like Diogenes?'

Diomedes laughed. 'He said his words were lightly meant, so I say that first we should give his words even more weight.' He pointed to one of the other pithoi jars.

Patroclus nodded and smiled as he took his meaning. He snapped his fingers at the guards and then pointed at the pithos. 'Bring some weights.'

Immediately, the guards began pulling large lead ingots from the jar and one by one started to lower them into the pithoi around Sotades's feet.

'You are making sure that I will not move, but really, if you just asked, I would give my word not to run away — or not to dive overboard and swim away, even though I can swim like any Olympian.'

Patroclus shook his head with a humourless laugh. 'We are just making ready to quench that hot tongue and that fiery mind that you told us you have. Water is needed for that, and you will be able to sing your obscenities to Poseidon. But I do not think you will be swimming far from this jar.'

For the first time Sotades stared at him in alarm. 'No! Ptolemy needs me. He wants to humiliate me in front of his whore Arsinoe.'

Diomedes took up one of the heavy lead ingots and drawing a dagger, he started to inscribe something on the soft metal. When he had finished he showed it to Patroclus, who read it out:

'*Sotades the Obscene*
*Never heard, never seen.*'

With a cruel smirk, Diomedes dropped it into the pithos. 'Let this be my poem written especially for you, Sotades.'

Patroclus laughed, then with a supercilious grin he gestured to two more guards and pointed first at the pithos jar and then at the sea. All four picked up the heavily weighted jar containing Sotades and carried it towards the side of the vessel.

'Sotades, I only said that the pharaoh wants you, but you didn't let me finish. He actually wants your poisonous words finished forever. You were disparaging about the gods, so now go and sing to the fishes — tell your poems to Poseidon. Beg for his mercy.'

Sotades screamed as the guards shoved the pithos jar over the side. It dropped, weighed down with the lead ingots and immediately began to submerge, dragging the struggling poet with it.

Patroclus and Diomedes looked down from the side of the trireme and watched the momentary bubbling of the water before returning to their seats to drink a farewell toast to Sotades the Obscene.

Patroclus signalled for the helmsman to set the oarsmen to work again and set a course to re-join the fleet. Soon the drumming quickened and the trireme picked up pace.

'I liked your poetic touch, Diomedes. A suitable epitaph for the dog, Sotades. It is a pity no one but the fish will ever see it.'

'No, my lord, but they will hear about it.' Already Diomedes was mentally composing a poem of his own. He smiled at the idea of including his own verse, with just one final line added:

*Sotades the Obscene*
*Never heard, never seen.*
*All wish he'd never been.*

Patroclus sat on the stool and picked up his goblet. He held it aloft in the expectation that it would be refilled. 'Come, Diomedes, let us drink a final toast to wash away the memory of Sotades the Obscene.'

Diomedes joined him and their goblets were filled. 'I am going to write an epic poem about Sotades, and how the god Harpocrates led us to him and you sent him to his watery grave in a leaded jar.'

Patroclus tossed back his head and roared with laughter. 'You must dedicate it to Pharaoh Ptolemy and Queen Arsinoe. They will appreciate that. So, let us also drink to your poem.'

'It will be a poem for the age and it will be told for generations,' laughed Diomedes. 'I will have it ready for when Hecataeus comes to Alexandria to give them his statue of noble Tyche.'

They drained their goblets and then lobbed them into the wake of the trireme, which was already some distance from where the last bubbles from the leaded jar had burst on reaching the surface of the water.

# CHAPTER 3

His official appointment by the pharaoh was something that Hanufer would never forget. After all, it was not every day that one was permitted to kiss the toes of both a living god and goddess.

Coming from Crocodilopolis, Hanufer was well aware that Pharaoh Ptolemy Philadelphus and Queen Arsinoe the Second were considered to be the divine embodiments of the gods. Brother and sister had married and become *theoi philadelphoi*, 'brother and sister gods.' The people of Egypt, all the way from the delta to the borders with the land of Kush, had accepted it without question, for it was long considered the way for royal siblings to marry and produce heirs. It was a strange irony that the Greeks who had bestowed upon them this title and who now lived and thrived in Alexandria, the capital of the country founded by Divine Alexander himself, were the most divided.

Incest was not the Greek way and only half of the Greeks of Alexandria, those who followed the pharaoh's example and adopted the Egyptian way of life, accepted and paid them the respect that the divine couple expected. The other half secretly seethed, derided and criticised.

Up until his appointment Hanufer had been the captain of the Medjay police in Crocodilopolis, the ancient city on the west bank of the Nile, south-west of the great Memphis. His work had mainly been to protect property, investigate tomb robbing, pursue petty criminals and solve the odd murder. Indeed, the particularly unpleasant murder of a local businessman and his family had caused mayhem and the outbreak of local feuds that threatened to spread out of control. The Greek nomarch in charge of the district had been so impressed with Hanufer's solving of the case and his handling of the threatened riot that he had sent a letter to Pharaoh Ptolemy Philadelphus himself, who had already made it known among his nobles and officials that he planned to appoint an Egyptian to the office of *Archiphylakites*, or Overseer of the Police in Alexandria. The pharaoh's intention was to further unite the two countries by permitting high-ranking Egyptians to hold important offices. So it was that Hanufer, with his most trusted sergeant Sabu, found themselves in the wondrous city that had been founded by the conquering Alexander.

The great and good of Alexandria were assembled along both sides of the atrium of the palace, along the onyx-colonnaded outer corridors and ultimately between the brightly painted Egyptian papyriform columns on either side of the great hall. Although they were all keen to see, they knew that they must stay at least two paces behind the rows of armed guards whose purpose everyone knew was to protect the royal couple from assassination.

There were few Egyptians among all of the Greek nobles and scholars who were permitted closest access to the royal presence. Hanufer, one of the few Egyptian officials, walked their length, conscious of all the murmurings about him. Finally, he prostrated himself at the foot of the dais, where Pharaoh Ptolemy Philadelphus and Queen Arsinoe the Second sat enthroned.

Many of the Greeks were bearded and had their hair groomed in the Greek style, but some had followed the example of their pharaoh and adopted the Egyptian dress. Others went so far as to wear the traditional wig.

Alexander's general, Ptolemy Lagides who became Ptolemy Soter, Pharaoh of Egypt, had been the first of his dynasty to wear the Egyptian kilt. He had ruled Egypt as co-regent with his son Ptolemy Philadelphus for two years until he died. Ptolemy Philadelphus, the present pharaoh, was clean-shaven, and wore the royal *postiche*, a long false beard made of goat hair that was broader at the base than from the chin. Like his father before him, he was dressed in the traditional kilt, bare chest covered in the pharaonic robes, and on his head was the *pschent*, the combination crown of Upper and Lower Egypt. Beside him on a slightly smaller throne, the stunningly beautiful Queen Arsinoe was also dressed in the traditional Egyptian royal robes, her abundant black hair held up in a fine gold wire hair net, crowned with a Greek gold semi-crescent stephane band with an ornamental Herakles knot at the front. Emerging from this knot was a silver uraeus, the stylised cobra of royalty. Hanufer felt more comfortable seeing them both dressed thus, because although he had chosen to wear a Greek chiton he was clean-shaven and wore his neatly styled, black, shoulder-length wig.

A priest rapped a staff on the floor, the signal that Hanufer had been told signified that he was to crawl up the steps of the dais and kiss the toes of first the pharaoh and then the queen.

He did so, then waited with his head bowed, not daring to look up until spoken to by the pharaoh.

'So, you are the crime-solver and police captain from Crocodilopolis?' Ptolemy Philadelphus asked.

Hanufer looked up and saw the pharaoh gesture for him to rise.

'I am that humble person from Crocodilopolis, Your Majesty. It is my honour to serve you and Her Majesty, Queen Arsinoe.'

'And what think you of Alexandria?'

'I am in awe of it, Your Majesty. Everyone in Egypt knows of the great lighthouse that you have built upon the Island of Pharos, which is a wonder to behold. The statue of the divine Alexander atop it rivals the pyramids of Giza. And they know too of the magnificent library, which I have already visited and hope to do so often. My sergeant and I walked all over the city familiarising ourselves with its landmarks, the different quarters, in order to discover all that may be encountered. I was particularly impressed by the temples to your gods, Your Majesty. You and your father and the Great Alexander before him have created wonders within wonders. The world will marvel at them for centuries.'

Ptolemy Philadelphus, whom Hanufer estimated to be about four decades old, perhaps ten years or so older than himself, laughed with a hint of self-deprecation. 'Yes, we are pleased with our city. Do you know how it was *dreamed up*?'

Hanufer saw the smiles that passed between the pharaoh and his queen when he asked the question. He could see that they were subtly testing him to see if he had done his research.

'I do, Your Majesty. It was the divine Alexander himself who had the dream about the great poet Homer. He saw him, an old, wise man with white hair standing on the ridge between the sea and Lake Mareotis, looking out towards an island. In the dream he heard Homer recite words from his great work, *The Odyssey.*'

'Very good, Hanufer. So you have heard of the greatest of our poets and his poetry?'

'Indeed, Your Majesty. I can speak and read Greek and I have read both *The Iliad* and *The Odyssey*. In particular I wanted to read for myself the exact lines that divine Alexander heard the great Homer recite. They are in the midst of a speech by

King Menelaus of Sparta to Odysseus. If you wish, I could try to speak them.'

Ptolemy looked surprised, then nodded with an encouraging smile. 'It would be enlightening for my court to hear an Egyptian scholar recite what many Greeks have probably never read.'

There were a few involuntary coughs and clearing of throats from one side of the hall, which caused the pharaoh to laugh. He pointed to a group of scholarly-looking men of assorted ages. 'Not including some of the illustrious members of the Musaeum and the Library who are with us today. You will meet them all in time, Hanufer. Now, allow your voice to fly so all can hear.'

As he had approached the dais where Pharaoh Ptolemy and Queen Arsinoe sat, Hanufer had noticed the presence of Callimachus, the Libyan poet, standing with Zenodotus the head librarian and the two physicians and anatomists Herophilus and Erasistratus. They were standing with a group of other Greek scholars whom he had seen, but had not yet met personally. He noted that while several of them were gazing at him and nodding receptively, there were others whose expressions told him that they were less than happy about his presence. At least one had a scornful look about him, as if expecting Hanufer to humiliate himself.

'Then please excuse me if I do not get the words exactly right, Your Majesty. It is kind of you to say, but I am not a scholar, merely a country *epistates phylakiton*, an officer of police.'

'Soon to be *Archiphylakites*, my Overseer of Police. Pray proceed.'

Taking a deep breath and inwardly bracing himself, for he did not consider himself a performer, Hanufer recited:

41

'*Now there is an isle in the sea-surge off the mouth of the Nile, that men call Pharos, a day's run for a hollow ship with a strong wind astern. There's a good anchorage there, a harbour from which men launch their trim ships into the waves, when they have drawn fresh black water.*'

Both Ptolemy and Arsinoe applauded loudly, stimulating a chorus of approval from around the great hall.

Ptolemy raised a hand and silence was immediate. 'And so, what did divine Alexander do after his dream?'

'After he had driven the Persians out of Egypt he came here, to the fishing town of Rhakotis, and then he found the spot where in his dream he saw great Homer stand. He saw that two large spurs of land projected out from the coast and that a crescent shape was formed. Then, as he looked at the Island of Pharos, he realised that if there was a great causeway between the coast and the island, it would form two great harbours.'

'And the birds? Do you know of the birds?' the pharaoh asked, enthusiastically.

'Yes, Your Majesty. Divine Alexander instructed his architects to lay out the ground plans for this city that was to bear his name. The surveyors calculated the angles and the distances, and they were followed by servants who sprinkled barley flour to map out the whole city — its streets, palaces, temples, and main buildings. As you would imagine, the barley flour attracted birds, many hundreds of thousands, of all types. No sooner had lines been laid than the birds descended and pecked the flour.'

Ptolemy leaned slightly forward, enjoying the tale. 'But what think you of that? Surely that was an ill omen?'

Hanufer saw Queen Arsinoe's slight smile and realised again that it was a test that the pharaoh and queen had possibly decided upon together.

'I understand that many did consider it an ill omen, but divine Alexander's own soothsayer, one called Aristander, declared that it was a great omen, for it showed that one day Alexander would feed the world.'

Ptolemy nodded approval. 'Do you have faith in soothsayers, Hanufer? Will you use the services of such an individual in order to detect crimes and uphold the law?'

Once again sensing that he was being tested before the whole of Ptolemy Philadelphus's court, Hanufer was careful in choosing his reply. 'Soothsayers like the great Aristander that I just mentioned have done our people great service. But in detecting crime I consider that my duty is to collect facts, to pick up clues and follow the trail through the use of the mind and logic, as written and taught by the great Greek philosophers, such as Pythagoras, Heraclitus and Aristotle.'

The pharaoh smiled. 'Well, know you that soothsayers are welcome in our court, provided they are truly gifted and have a connection with the hidden mysteries, rather than rogues who pretend they have the second sight. But know also that I am impressed that you know of these Greek philosophers, Hanufer. You are obviously a well-read man.'

'I endeavour to acquire knowledge that may assist me wherever I can, Your Majesty. Which is why I am so excited by the great library of Alexandria.'

A proud smile came over the pharaoh's face. 'It was my father's idea for Alexandria to become the centre of learning in Egypt, and I am determined to build on the foundations that he laid. You may already have heard that our intention is to have a copy of every book or papyrus ever written. Every ship that arrives in our harbours is obliged to hand over any books they may be carrying. These are copied in the eastern quarter by one of the many publishers and copying businesses. That copy is given to the library and then the original is handed back.'

'That must be a monumental task, Your Majesty.'

The pharaoh's eyes twinkled with amusement. 'You must know that we have as many scribes in Alexandria as they ever did in Thebes or Memphis. And you have no doubt heard that my librarian, Zenodotus of Ephesus, has brought seventy-two Jewish scholars from Jerusalem to a great villa on the Island of Pharos to translate their Hebrew holy books into Greek. There are six men from each of the twelve tribes. It will not be long before they are finished. We are calling it *The Translation of the Seventy*.'

Hanufer nodded. 'It will be a wonderful work to unify the Egyptian and the Jewish people, Your Majesty. I have heard that they are fortunate to have the protection of Proteus, who I understand was the local god of Pharos before the city of Alexandria was built.'

'That is correct again, Hanufer. Proteus was the son of Poseidon,' Ptolemy Philadelphus replied with a knowing smile, 'and of course we in Alexandria are now fortunate to have the great god Serapis to look after us. He is local no longer, but to my mind is now one of the most powerful gods of Egypt.'

Once again he gave Queen Arsinoe a knowing smile before continuing. 'Yet the city that you came from is famed for its crocodiles and the god Sobek, is it not?'

Hanufer affirmed the pharaoh's question, knowing full well that the ruler knew this for a fact. He was also aware that the pharaoh, like his father before him, was a shrewd man and was determined that his dynasty of Greek rulers should succeed in unifying the whole of Egypt. He meant to do this by not only putting Egyptians like himself in certain key positions, but also by amalgamating the Egyptian gods Osiris and Apis with the Grecian gods Hades and Dionysus into the new cult of Serapis. Also, since the Egyptian goddess Isis was the sister and wife of Osiris, she was identified with the Greek goddess Demeter.

'Sobek is one of the oldest and most revered gods of Egypt, Your Majesty. Like everyone else from Crocodilopolis I venerate the great protector Sobek, yet I also worship Maat, the goddess of truth. Of course, now that I am in Alexandria, I will also make offerings to the god Serapis as well.'

Hanufer was acutely wary of saying anything that could be construed as an offence to either the pharaoh or the queen. He was aware that their union was a sensitive issue with the Greeks, many of whom disapproved strongly of the pharaoh's marriage to his sister. Looking at the royal couple now, yet without appearing to look too directly, the sibling resemblance between them seemed very strong.

'Yes, we also appreciate the goddess Maat here in Alexandria,' Pharaoh Ptolemy said. 'The goddess of truth and justice is to be venerated everywhere in Egypt. My nomarch in Crocodilopolis informed me of your allegiance and your skills in mob control as well as in crime-solving, which is why I was eager to have you as my *Archiphylakites*, Overseer of the new Alexandrian Police Force.'

Hanufer bowed low. 'I am grateful and honoured, Your Majesty.'

Ptolemy Philadelphus lay a hand on his queen's shoulder. 'One of the handmaidens of my sister-wife, Queen Arsinoe, had relatives who were murdered in Crocodilopolis. It was you who brought the murderers to justice. For this we have decided to rename the city in her honour. From now on, it will be the city of Arsinoe. You, Hanufer of Crocodilopolis, may take some share in that honour. Come closer and I shall put the pectoral of office around your neck. Tomorrow, as my Overseer of Police, you have the honour of keeping Alexandria safe and free from crime.'

Hanufer bowed low, and when he looked up again to move forward to receive his pectoral of office from the pharaoh, he saw that Queen Arsinoe was smiling at him. But he was not sure whether it was a smile of pleasure or of queenly benevolence, or yet simply one of amusement at him, a minor Egyptian police officer given such a daunting task.

And then, to his surprise, she spoke to him.

'It pleases my brother-husband and I that our Overseer of Police is so knowledgeable about poetry. It is our sincere hope that you can tell the difference between a good and bad poet. The heart of a good poet will balance the feather of Maat, while that of a bad one will be fed to the Ammit monster.'

Ptolemy Philadelphus looked at her and laughed loudly. Then he looked around the hall and raised a hand encouragingly. It was a sign for the whole assembly to laugh politely.

To Hanufer it was a strange thing to be laughing at. Every Egyptian hoped that when they died, their own journey to the great Hall of Truths in the *Duat*, as the underworld was known, would be successful. There their heart would be weighed by the god Anubis on the scales of justice against the goddess Maat's single feather of truth. If pure, they would pass on to meet Osiris and enter the afterlife for eternity. If impure, it would be thrown to the crocodile-headed demon goddess Ammit, the devourer of hearts and souls, who was also part hippopotamus and part lion. When their heart was consumed, they would become nothing.

'In case you did not know, Hanufer of Crocodilopolis, my sister-wife has strong opinions on poetry.'

Hanufer dutifully laughed softly.

And then he realised why her smile had puzzled him. It was the enigmatic smile of one who had the power to have life snuffed out if she so chose.

He did not know that there were others present in the hall who were dutifully laughing, but who did not consider the royal couple to be living deities. Or whose hearts they hoped would one day be fed to the Ammit monster.

It was late and the oil lamps had been refilled along the corridor leading to the queen's bedchamber. The Keeper of the Queen's bedchamber tapped on the door as soon as he heard the sound of sandaled feet striding purposefully on the marble floor. Hearing the queen's order from within, he waited until the beaded curtains further along the corridor were pulled open by guards so that the pharaoh did not have to break his step, then he opened the door and lowered his head to avert his eyes from the royal person. Ptolemy marched in and stood at the end of the bed where his sister-wife was reclining on cushions. She wore no clothes and had removed all of her jewellery apart from rings on her ears, fingers and toes.

Ptolemy did not look behind as the door was silently closed behind him.

'I hoped that you might visit me this evening, Ptolemy.'

He smiled and undid his kilt, letting it drop to the floor. Then he took two steps and dived onto the bed, as if plunging into water.

'I played with the children after that audience,' she said with a laugh, encircling his neck and kissing his nose. 'But I would rather play with my brother-husband.'

He laughed and kissed her back. 'Do you remember how we played when we were children? You and me and our half-brother and half-sister Ptolemy Keraunos and Lysandra. How we used to argue because they were older than us and liked to order us about. And then there was Magas, our other half-brother, who disliked how close you and I were.'

'None of us knew how complicated life would be. Ptolemy Keraunos, who should have been pharaoh before you if not for his temper, which annoyed father so much and caused him to be banished. We girls were just pieces in a game, to be married off to either strengthen Egypt or broker peace with the neighbours. Incredible that I should be sent to marry that old lecher Lysimachus in Thrace and my older sister sent to marry his son, so I became her mother-in-law.'

Ptolemy laughed. 'And Lysimachus sent his daughter, the first Arsinoe, to marry me and have our children.'

'They only became ours after you divorced her and married me, Ptolemy.'

'True, which is why our son bears the name of your first husband, her father.'

She heaved a sigh. 'And when Lysimachus died and I fled Thrace, who should I be forced to marry but our half-brother Ptolemy Keraunos.' She suddenly pushed herself away from him and swung her shapely legs off the bed to sit up. 'The murdering bastard who killed my own two children before my eyes.'

Ptolemy shuffled down the bed and swung his legs over to join her. He put a comforting arm about her shoulders. 'But he's dead now, Arsinoe. Thanks to the Gauls. And you are here, mother to my children. Ours now, and they are all happy, just as we were.'

She squeezed his knee. 'As we are, my love.'

He patted her hand. 'And how quickly things change as time flies. Now it will not be long before young Ptolemy can sit in on such audiences as we had today. He will have to learn how to rule, as he will one day succeed me.'

'Succeed us, did you not mean?'

He grinned and touched her full lips. 'Us, of course. Unless the gods decide otherwise and young Lysimachus succeeds instead. Or even our little daughter, Berenice.'

Arsinoe gave a wan smile. 'Our young Ptolemy wanted to know all about the new Overseer. He's only nine years old and he wants to know all that happens in court and in Alexandria. Lysimachus is seven, and all he wants to do is play with throwing sticks and his bow and arrows. Who knows what little Berenice will be interested in?'

Ptolemy laughed. 'They can stay children and dream for a while longer. But tell me, what did you think of our new *Archiphylakites* Hanufer of Crocodilopolis?'

'I think he was too interested in poetry, Ptolemy. If he is to keep the peace and ensure our safety, I would rather someone who is more interested in tactics and plotting so that he could anticipate problems.' She ran her hand up his thigh and turned to kiss him again.

*Yes, someone who knows about plotting*, she thought to herself. *Someone who has had to survive that way. Someone like me.*

# CHAPTER 4

Hanufer was still getting to know Alexandria. From the very start, he knew that he was going to have to prove himself as he was aware that news of his appointment as the *Archiphylakites*, the Overseer of Police, by the pharaoh had been greeted by many of the Greek citizens of Alexandria with disdain. Though he had not yet seen evidence, he was sure that there were people who wanted to see him fail.

Pollio, the police department scribe and office head clerk, was a man in his middle forties who had worked in the police office since the days of Pharaoh Ptolemy Soter. He had the round-shouldered posture so characteristic of professional scribes and clerks. He blinked much and held papyri and ostraca close to his eyes when reading, which suggested that his eyesight had been damaged from straining his eyes over the years. Nevertheless, he seemed to have a pleasing disposition and seemed efficient enough, if somewhat set in his ways.

Hanufer and Sabu spent a morning with him going over the way the administration of the department had always been organised. Pollio told him of the way in which all documents, petitions, invitations and reports came to the office and were viewed and catalogued or copied by him in the first instance. The new Overseer of Police could tell by his demeanour and slight air of anxiety that he was hoping that he would not want to institute too many changes. Hanufer had complimented him on the obvious efficiency of the office, but indicated that he would be making certain adjustments once he had considered it all. Pollio had bowed and replied that all proposals would be accepted without hesitation.

Hanufer had liked the fact that he did not display any churlishness. Yet what pleased him most was Pollio's attitude to the public slave that Hanufer was informed that he had inherited on taking up his position.

'In Cario, we have the most hard-working slave in Alexandria, my lord Hanufer,' he had said. 'I have trained him to help with filing and laying out all the documents. He knows the city like the back of his hand and can be trusted to go on errands anywhere you send him. Indeed, you could not have a better guide to show you the city.' He had added proudly, as if he were the owner of an obedient and well-trained dog, 'He does not loiter, so there should be few occasions when he has to feel the lash.'

The latter remark had not pleased Hanufer, because he did not approve of beating servants or slaves. He had seen too many examples of masters and slave owners inflicting grievous injuries upon those who were not permitted to protest or to defend themselves, sometimes with the most tragic consequence.

The Overseer's office had two desks, a large one for Hanufer and a smaller one for Sabu, his sergeant, who was now appointed as his deputy, officially with the title of *Hyparchiphylakites*. There were various baskets upon the desks with writing paraphernalia. On the floor were several large chests and fixed to the wall behind Hanufer's desk was a large map of the city.

Hanufer was fairly tall and fit, but Sabu was a full hand's breadth taller, with broad shoulders, the long muscular legs of a sprinter and the well-developed biceps of a wrestler. Like most Egyptians, his face was clean-shaven, as was his head.

Hanufer instructed Pollio to send Cario to meet him and Sabu and to tell them about the layout of the city.

Cario was a Greek *demosios*, a public slave attached to the police office. He was a wiry, good-looking young man of twenty years with curly, black hair and an innocent smile, who had been born and bred in Gortyn in Crete, but brought to Alexandria by his master, a scholar, who had been given a minor position at the Musaeum of Alexandria. This learned man, Apollinarus, had no family of his own and had taught the bright son of his favourite female slave to read and write in Greek, and had also instructed him in some of the rudiments of rhetoric and logic. He treated him more like a son than a slave, which brought censure when he took up his post at the Musaeum, for his colleagues believed that Cario probably was his own son.

Unfortunately for Cario, Apollinarus was much addicted to wine and many clandestine vices not considered becoming to a scholar of the Musaeum. He became desperately ill after a few months and ran out of money to pay off his debts to creditors, as well as to the physician for the wine and medicines he needed to curb his increasing pains. Cario had hoped that his master, whom he too suspected was his father, would exert manumission and turn him into a freed slave, but when Apollinarus suddenly died he found himself sold to become a *demosios*, a public slave, to the office of the police.

Without any bitterness he showed them the scar on his shoulder where he had been branded with a delta letter, indicating his status as a *demosios* slave.

He was indeed most willing to please. He answered all their questions candidly and intelligently. When Hanufer asked how Alexandrian citizens felt about the appointment of Egyptian officials like himself and Sabu, Cario told him of the sort of talk that was circulating in the beer shops, the Emporium and the markets and temples of the Greek gods. With Hanufer's permission he did it humorously as well, like an actor taking on different characters.

*'We can't have a provincial Egyptian lording it over us!'*
*'Why has the pharaoh brought a half-educated savage here?'*
*'They probably can't even speak Greek.'*

'They had better not try whispering about us in Greek,' said Sabu, sternly. 'In Crocodilopolis, it was known that I did not take kindly to insults issued in any tongue.'

Cario glanced at the sergeant's rippling muscles and had no doubt that he was capable of cracking heads.

Pointing to the map, he showed how the two large spurs of land projected out from the coast into the sea to form a crescent shape, which together with the Island of Pharos created a natural channel.

'Pirates used Pharos in the old days, my lord. They plundered ships of all the nations and were safe from capture — until divine Alexander's fleet drove them all out. Then he ordered a great causeway to be built between the coast and Pharos, which cut the channel in two and created two great harbours. The eastern one is called the Grand Harbour and within it is the royal harbour itself. The western one is the Eunostos Harbour.' He proudly tapped the mole causeway that linked the land and the island. 'It is called the *Heptastadion*. That means it is seven times the length of a Greek stadium, my lords.'

Next he ran a finger round the city walls and described how in outline it resembled a Greek chlamys, or oblong cloak. It had two huge main streets, each about fifty cubits wide, that crossed to virtually divide the city into quarters.

'They were built like that so that a chariot and horses could turn in them,' Cario explained enthusiastically. 'And see how the streets are laid out in a grid system with parallel streets, exactly as divine Alexander decreed.'

'And where are we now?' Sabu asked.

Cario jabbed a finger at an area with a large square. 'Here, sir. You can see that the police office is well placed in the city. The police barracks is over here near the Gate of the Moon.'

Hanufer pointed to another part of the map. 'And this is where the villa allotted to me is. So, show us roughly the main parts of the city.'

Cario smiled. 'This is easy, my lord. There are five sectors of the city. Each is labelled with a letter of our Greek alphabet, so they are called alpha, beta...'

'...gamma, delta and epsilon. We both know and understand the Greek language, Cario,' Hanufer said, patiently. 'But for what purpose are they so labelled?'

Cario touched his forehead and bowed his head slightly, a gesture that already both Hanufer and Sabu had noticed he did whenever he mentioned or was about to mention the name Alexander. They looked at each other with amusement as they anticipated his reply.

'I am not sure of the exact wording, but the scholars say it is a special phrase meaning "*Built by King Alexander Son of God.*"'

Then on the map he indicated the positions of the five sectors. 'Rhakotis is the alpha sector in the west of the city, where most of the rich Egyptians and many of the people of other races live. There you will find wealthy Syrians, Nabataeans, Nubians and Mycenaeans. Beta is the part nearest the northern coast. This is called the Brucheum, and it covers the area of the Royal Palace, the Library and the Musaeum. Gamma is the area of the Soma in the centre of the city, where divine Alexander's tomb is and where his new temple is to be opened. Then there is delta, over here on the right of the city, which is the Jewish sector.'

'Where do most of the Greeks then live?' Hanufer asked.

'The noble and wealthiest live in the Royal quarter, where of course Pharaoh Ptolemy and Queen Arsinoe and the royal family live in the palaces, of which there are several. I cannot say more about it, for of course I am not permitted to enter that area. But also in the Brucheum there are many great villas, including your own, my lord, where there are many rich people who never seem to leave the walls that surround their grounds. Their needs are all catered for by servants and slaves — like me.'

He smiled wistfully, and Hanufer noticed the moistness that had suddenly appeared in his eyes.

'And what of the last area, this epsilon?' Sabu asked.

'That is the south of the city near to Lake Mareotis, where most of the Egyptian workers and the boat people live and work.' He pointed to two waterways. 'These are the two canals of Alexandria, sirs. This one on the left is the Cibotus canal, which links the western harbour to Lake Mareotis, running through old Rhakotis. This other on the right is called the Canopus Canal, which comes from the town of Canopus in the Nile Delta to Alexandria, and passes right through the Jewish sector into the Brucheum and then into the Royal Harbour.'

The following day Hanufer arranged for Cario to take him and Sabu on a walking tour of Alexandria, so they could familiarise themselves with it properly. The young slave proved to be an enthusiastic and knowledgeable guide to the city and its organization, and he knew much about the rumours regarding the machinations of the various governing bodies, and about the peccadilloes and affairs of the Alexandrian elite. He was also able to tell them about who was of importance in the scheme of things, from the pharaoh and his court, to Patroclus his vizier and admiral of the fleet, to the notable scholars of the Musaeum and the Library.

They began their tour from the police headquarters, which consisted of an annexe of the *Dikasterion*, the Alexandrian court building, which was surrounded by ornamental groves just off the Emporium, the city's main marketplace. The *Dikasterion* was an imposing building with columns either side of large wooden doors, above which was a statue of *Dike*, the Greek goddess of justice, depicted as a slender woman wearing a laurel wreath and holding a balance scale before her.

The other buildings in the Emporium square were almost as imposing.

'There are many wealthy merchants and businessmen in these places,' Cario explained. 'Money-lenders — or bankers, as they call the wealthiest of them. Merchants, traders and many of the town officials have offices here.'

Indeed, as they made their way through the busy square they saw all sorts of people: nobles and officials being carried in litters or palanquins, priests, servants and slaves, bustling about, together with simple peddlers and street traders touting for trade. There was also a veritable army of *demosios* slaves, clearing the streets of rubbish and horse dung and tending the palms and sycamore trees in the boulevards.

Cario pointed to a couple of small urchins who were each carrying a sack on their back. 'They have probably found dead cats or birds, my lord. They take them to the City of the Dead where they can sell them to the embalmers, who will mummify them and sell them in the markets as sacred animals.' He gave a winsome smile. 'Such people have to earn enough money to buy food however they can.'

From there he led them across the *Heptastadion*, where they saw how exquisitely the mole causeway divided the curved bay into the east and the west harbours. They mingled with the crowds of assorted people that came and went across it to the small market town of Pharos on the island, some to ply their trades or conduct business. Others came to worship at the Temple of Isis and still many others to visit and marvel at the incredible Pharos lighthouse at its easternmost tip, overlooking the opening to the Great Harbour.

Returning from there Cario took Hanufer and Sabu around the city, showing them the five sectors he had pointed out on the map.

They walked on to the impressive residential Brucheum and Royal quarter, situated around the eastern harbour. Its most magnificent buildings were the Royal Palaces, which took up the whole long spit of land that formed the easternmost boundary of the Great Harbour, where the naval fleet and royal vessels were moored. Guards stood at the closed gates of the Royal Palaces, but they saw enough of the opulent buildings with their polished marble and limestone façades.

'I do not think I have ever seen so many sphinxes, my lord,' Sabu remarked.

'Nor as many obelisks,' Hanufer agreed as he waved a hand at a particularly tall one set amid a small grove of palm trees.

'That is dedicated to Pharaoh Ramesses the Great. It is a famous landmark in the city. I am told that Pharaoh Ptolemy, like his father, has had many sphinxes, obelisks and pylons brought to Alexandria from Memphis, Thebes and —'

'And from Crocodilopolis,' Hanufer interjected, pointing with interest to a statue of the crocodile-headed god Sobek standing incongruously on its own in one of the many little public gardens that were dotted around the city. Almost automatically, he rubbed one of the two rings on his hand and made a mental note to remember exactly where the statue was.

From there Cario took them to the eastern delta sector, home to the large Jewish community, where he showed them dwellings, businesses and the house of prayer in the middle of the quarter that they called their Synagogue. It had a dome and stood out as the only such building they had seen in the city.

Close to it he entered a large building with a sign outside that had writing in Greek, Hebrew and hieroglyphic script on a sign.

'This is the street of the publishers, and this is Saul Sofer's establishment,' he explained, as they entered a hall with innumerable shelves filled with scrolls and writing supplies. About two dozen men were sitting at desks, busily writing on papyrus. Some were clearly copying from other scrolls while others were preparing ink blocks and paints. A small man with a bushy beard and a headscarf tied round his head with a cord immediately detached himself from a group working at one desk and came to meet them with a beaming smile.

'Ah, you must be our new Overseer of Police,' he said, bowing and steepling his fingers in front of him. 'I see the good Cario has brought you to see my humble establishment. I am Saul Sofer, and here is where I and my modest workers make the finest books and scrolls in Alexandria. I am the prime copyist and publisher to the great librarian, Zenodotus.' His eyes almost twinkled as he added, 'And we have the privilege of copying whatever petitions that are sent to us by your department, sir.'

Hanufer and Sabu returned the greeting and accepted his offer of a drink of palm wine, while the publisher showed them around. Cario went to wait outside.

'I see from your sign that you publish in three languages,' Hanufer casually remarked.

'Or any other that is wished, my lord. We can reproduce any written word in any style.'

'Does the Library of Alexandria collect books in Hebrew?'

Saul Sofer smiled a great deal and was obviously an enthusiast for his work and his business. 'We supply work for many people in the city apart from the Library, sir. And you probably know that we have many Hebrew scholars currently working at the Library at the express invitation of Pharaoh Ptolemy Philadelphus himself. They are translating the holy books of our people into Greek.'

As they chatted further, it was clear that Saul Sofer was considered a person of importance within the Jewish quarter and that he knew everything that went on in his community. Hanufer felt sure that his intelligence could be useful and should be cultivated. Yet he knew enough of the nature of people to realise that the publisher was holding something back. He had been considered in his choice of words and the things he was prepared to talk about. Perhaps it was because it was their first meeting, and he was not yet sure what sort of an Overseer Hanufer was. He determined that later discussions would help them both understand each other's position.

As Cario took them further on their tour of the city, he led them down the two huge main streets, each about fifty cubits wide, that crossed to divide the city into quarters. It did not take long to appreciate the unique grid system with its parallel streets.

Each of these two bustling streets was lined with colonnades along their entire length, and off them they saw parks, gardens, extravagant villas and buildings and temples. The Canopic Way ran west to east, bounded by the Necropic Gate in the west, where the vast Necropolis or the City of the Dead was to be found. There the Greeks, Egyptians and Jews and those of other races disposed of their dead by embalming, cremation, burial in the earth or entombment in cut caves in the rocks. The road was bound by the Canopic Gate in the east, beyond which the dusty road led to what the Greeks called 'Old Egypt.'

The Street of the Soma crossed it from north to south, and was named thus because it contained the Soma, the lavish tomb and the temple of Alexander the Great himself, which had been constructed by Ptolemy Soter and extended and enhanced by Ptolemy Philadelphus. It was bounded by the Gate of the Moon in the Brucheum and by the southern Gate of the Sun, beyond which was the vast glittering waters of Lake Mareotis.

The Egyptian workers and lower classes lived mainly in the Mareotis quarter. In the marshy Lake Harbour the boats and river traffic from the Nile and Lower Egypt brought cargoes of papyrus and textiles, grains and the products of the fertile lands of the Nile, and spices from the east. Workers then unloaded goods for local use or for sale or onward movement across the city, from the Western Harbour to distant Crete and Greece. In the other direction, Greek trading vessels were sent down the Nile.

He showed them Rhakotis, the old town where most of the wealthier Egyptian population lived and where the shops, businesses and temples predominantly retained the Egyptian way of life. And on its southern tip, there were the great stadium and the huge temple complex of Serapis, parts of which were still under construction.

One of the main things that Hanufer gained from the tour, apart from knowledge of the geography of Alexandria, was the insight Cario had given them into the people. Not only had he shown the respectable side of the city, but he had also taken them to some of the less reputable streets and informed them of some of the criminal activities that lurked beneath the surface. Hanufer knew that he was going to be extremely useful in his future investigations.

# CHAPTER 5

It was only two hours after dawn, but the heat was already quite oppressive. Large, bloated blowflies had begun to swarm, as if released into the day by the god Khepri as he rolled the sun disc into the sky, just like the scarab rolled a ball of dung.

Hanufer grimaced at the sight of the battered and torn male body that had been laid upon a trestle table in one of the temple outhouses where the bull's feed was kept, so that he, Alexandria's new Overseer of Police, could see the body and decide whether any further action was needed. It was naked except for a bloodstained, short-sleeved tunic that had been muddied and ripped to pieces.

'Trampled by a fully grown bull,' he mused, bending over the corpse to look at the face that had been reduced to a pulp so that no recognizable facial features were discernible. The skull had been cracked like an earthenware pot and pinkish-grey brain tissue had spilled out, some of which had been turned to a mush. Virtually all of the body showed similar horrific wounds.

With the tips of his fingers and thumbs, Hanufer lifted the remnants of the bloody tunic to view the abdominal injuries. A loop of bowel protruded from an ugly wound. 'He was gored, too.'

'What a way to die, sir,' remarked Sabu.

Hanufer raised one of the hands and inspected it. The fingers were crushed and some stuck out at impossible angles, while others had been denuded of flesh. 'The bones are badly broken, but there are hard callosities on the palms. This man has done hard work in his life.'

'A labourer, my lord?' Sabu asked.

'Possibly,' Hanufer replied slowly. He pursed his lips as he shifted his attention to the feet. 'Although I think not, since on this foot he has worn a cothurnus boot. You can see that the skin is definitely less tanned by the sun on the lower half of his leg, where it would have been covered. A labourer would not have worn those. That means he regularly wore them, so this man could have been a soldier.'

Sabu folded his arms across his chest. 'We should be able to check on that, sir.'

'Or perhaps he was even a slave in a rich house, or a public slave of some sort,' Hanufer continued. 'Who discovered the body?'

'The temple's Keeper of Animals found him early this morning when he went to muck out the bull's pen. He woke the high priest, who ordered him to remove the body and see to the bull before he sent him to report the finding.'

Hanufer harrumphed. *Of course*, he thought, *the priest would naturally have thought that a sacred bull's needs would have to be considered first.*

'After we have finished here, we shall talk to the priest and the Keeper of Animals.' He brushed aside some strands of hair that had fallen across his eyes from his wig. 'First, let me see the man's back. Roll him towards you, Sabu.'

Clasping the corpse's shoulder and hip, the tall sergeant pulled the body over so that the Overseer of Police could scrutinise him from behind.

'The injuries here are very different, Sabu. There is no sign of goring. The skin is greatly grazed, as if he had been moved around a lot on his back.'

'I do not follow, my lord. Does this tell us anything?'

Hanufer pursed his lips. 'I am not sure. I would have expected to see more wounds like those on his front, had he been gored and tossed about, but it looks as if he was sort of shuffled by the bull rather than rolled over. Hence all the abrasions on his back.'

Sabu nodded. 'I see, sir. You always say to build up a picture of the way a man might have reached his death. In this case, there is no doubt he was trampled to death by the bull.'

Hanufer gave a non-committal grunt. 'We are not sure of anything yet, Sabu. Note that there are no old scars or wheals on his back, so that again goes against him being a slave that was ill-used.' He continued to inspect the flesh. 'If he had borne signs of having been abused, it could have suggested that he entered the bull pen through fear of someone who coerced him. But as I said, there is no sign of that.'

Sabu frowned. 'But what was he doing in the pen in any case? Was he trying to do something to the sacred bull?'

'As an Egyptian, I am still learning the ways of the Greeks. Pharaoh Ptolemy Soter, the current pharaoh's father, made Alexandria the capital of Egypt, but it is still a mixture of Greek and Egyptian culture. It is possible that this man was trying to tamper with the beast in some way.'

'You mean poison it or kill it, my lord?'

Hanufer did not reply immediately but ran his fingers up the spine to the base of the skull, where he felt under the mud- and dung-caked hair. He whistled softly and bent closer to part the hair and examine the scalp and the skin beneath. Straightening, he looked grimly at Sabu and shook his head.

'This man was trampled, that is for sure. But that was not the cause of his death.'

Sabu's eyes shot wide open in surprise. 'You don't think the bull killed him, my lord? Then what did?'

'Roll him over onto his front and I will show you.'

Sabu did as he was told.

'This may have killed him!' Hanufer beckoned his sergeant to lean closer as he held the hair away to reveal a small wound at the base of the skull.

He reached into his chiton and drew out his sandalwood writing case. They had both adopted the Greek style of clothing since they'd arrived in Alexandria, except that like most Egyptians of high status Hanufer continued to wear the traditional oiled, kohl-black wig. Opening his writing case, he took out a reed pen and placed it over the puncture wound. Gingerly, he pressed against the tissues and found that he was able to slip it upwards into the wound at an acute angle as deep as four finger widths. 'You see, there is a wound here. A weapon of some sort entered the large hole at the base of the skull, where the spine joins it. His brain would have been punctured.'

Hanufer withdrew the reed pen and handed it to Sabu to clean. 'A narrow instrument like this, or something equally thin and sharp could have been used.'

Sabu wiped the gore from the reed pen on the remnants of the dead man's tunic, then rolled the body back to its original position.

'How is this possible, my lord? Do you mean that he was doing something in the pen and someone else was there? Or he was disturbed? Could it have been the Keeper of Animals or one of the temple priests? Someone who sneaked in behind him?'

Hanufer took his writing case and crossed the outhouse to a stone shelf where various brushes and tools were kept for grooming the bull. He swept an area with the edge of his hand and placed his writing case upon it. Then, taking out a thin roll of papyrus, he broke a small piece off an ink-stone and dropped it into the round pot depression in the sandalwood case. Scooping some water in his palm from a bucket, he dropped sufficient to make his ink. Using a new reed pen, he started to write a note in Greek.

'These are several questions that we must consider, Sabu,' he said as he wrote several lines from left to right. 'There is much that we still need to learn. For that, I want his body to be taken to the Medical School of the Alexandria Musaeum, where I shall ask Herophilus or Erasistratus the anatomists and physicians to examine it. So, ask the two constables who accompanied us here to fetch a cart to transport the corpse there. They must then seek out either of the two physicians and give them this message.'

He leaned forward and took the tip of his pectoral, which held a circular disc of lapis lazuli on which the seal of the *Archiphylakites* was embossed. Pressing it on his ink block, he made the message official.

Having finished, he sprinkled a little powder made from ground shells and then blew it across the ink. Giving it a shake, he rolled it up and handed it to Sabu.

'And then we shall look at the bull, its pen and interview the Keeper of Animals and the high priest.'

Behdet, the Keeper of Animals, was a swarthy Egyptian youth of about sixteen with a thick neck, strong legs and arms and a gentle disposition. He was clearly terrified of Hanufer and Sabu and still in a state of shock after finding the body.

In contrast, Kleitos, the high priest of the Temple of Poseidon, was an arrogant-looking Greek of about fifty-five years with a hairless head and face and a downturned mouth that looked as if it had not smiled in decades.

Both of them stood in front of the bull pen behind the impressive marble temple in the Royal Quarter. A wall surrounded the pen where the bull was exercised and permitted to mate with cows brought to it, as befitted its sacred purpose. Behdet wore a simple kilt and aged wooden sandals, while the priest wore a Greek chiton bared at his right shoulder.

'So, Behdet, after you found the body you went straight to wake the high priest, Kleitos?' Hanufer asked.

The Keeper of Animals bowed promptly, careful to avoid looking the Overseer of Police directly in the eye. 'Yes, my lord. I ... I did not know what to do. I —'

'I instructed him to remove the corpse straight away,' interrupted Kleitos, irritably. 'Such a thing cannot be permitted before a sacrifice. And you must deal with this swiftly and remove the thing from the temple grounds.'

Hanufer did not like the priest's tone or his contemptuous manner, but he let it pass for the moment. 'Did you inspect the body before you gave this order?'

'Of course not! It had to be done straight away.'

Hanufer turned back to Behdet. 'So you removed the body? What state was the animal in? After all, it had just killed a man.'

Kleitos interrupted. 'A man who should not have been permitted to get into the temple grounds. As the Overseer of Police, you should have prevented —'

Sabu clenched his fists and stepped closer to the priest, who immediately cowered back. 'Do not be impertinent, priest! Lord Hanufer is the Overseer of the Alexandria Police. Treat him with respect.'

Hanufer eyed the high priest coldly. 'My sergeant has saved me the trouble of reprimanding you. I am investigating a suspicious death in this temple, and I will ask questions to which you will give me answers.'

'But the fellow was just a slave,' Kleitos protested.

As was his nature, Hanufer talked firmly, but without raising his voice. Experience had long since taught him that to display anger could be counterproductive. 'A suspicious death must be investigated thoroughly, whether the person is a slave, freeman or noble. No life can be dismissed. You say that this person who was unfortunate enough to lose his life in the bull pen was a slave. How do you know this?'

The high priest's jaw fell, and he replied hesitantly, 'I beg your pardon, my lord. I — do not know.'

Turning once more to Behdet, Hanufer asked, 'What state was the bull in?'

'Apis … that is what I call him, my lord,' Behdet replied, 'he was … I don't know how to say it … he seemed upset. He was slavering and stamping his feet.'

Hanufer turned to the bull pen and looked over the wall. The beast was huge. It was pure black with horns that were painted gold, as was the custom with temple bulls.

'He looks settled now, my lord,' said Sabu. 'And clean and groomed.'

'He is, sirs,' Behdet volunteered. 'High Priest Kleitos told me to remove the body and clean him and the pen up. I did so and fed him as usual.'

'Which explains why there is no blood on the ground of the pen,' Hanufer said. 'Is Apis a violent or a difficult beast to look after?'

Behdet shrugged his shoulders. 'He is a bull. They are never gentle creatures, my lord. But he and I are friends. He knows me and I can get close to him with no fear on either his part or mine. He let me take the body out and do my work.'

'So you washed and groomed him?'

Behdet nodded. 'It is my duty to care for him until the day that is soon coming, when he will be sacrificed.' Tears started to well up in the youth's eyes. 'I will miss him, but he will die for the sake of the god, Poseidon.'

'But you are an Egyptian, are you not?'

The youth dropped his gaze to the ground. 'I was sent to Alexandria from my village near Memphis when I was a boy and have lived in Alexandria ever since. My pharaoh's gods are my gods.'

'Behdet has served the Temple of Poseidon for ten years, Lord Hanufer,' said Kleitos, his tone now far more respectful. 'He has looked after many sacrificial bulls and pigs. He has a way with animals. This bull is to be sacrificed to Poseidon when Admiral Patroclus and the Navy fleet return.'

Hanufer nodded. 'Did you find anything unusual when you were cleaning the pen or, indeed, the bull itself?'

Behdet looked uncertainly at Kleitos before looking up at Hanufer, this time straight in the eye. 'Apis had several small bleeding wounds, my lord. On his flanks and his back. I ... I cleaned them and rubbed them with a salve of myrtle and goose fat that seems to help.'

Hanufer raised an eyebrow. 'And how do you think he could have received these wounds, Behdet? Could he have been mistreated by this man whom he trampled?'

'He would have been a foolish man to even go into the pen, my lord. Apis knows me and one or two of the priests, but he would only allow me to get in without showing his annoyance.'

Sabu looked down sternly at the youth. 'Did you wound him?' he snapped.

Behdet looked startled at the question. 'No, sir. I would never hurt Apis while he is under my care. I ... I do not want to see the day when he is to die, but I know that I must.'

Hanufer noticed that his eyes had grown moist again. 'Point these wounds out to me.'

Behdet opened the gate to the pen and entered it, whistling first and then whispering soothingly to the bull, which seemed to respond by grunting, stamping its right forefoot and lowering its head. It stood swishing its tail as Behdet put a hand on its great back and moved slowly round it, all the while stroking the well-groomed coat.

'Here, my lord,' he said, pointing to a scattered number of areas that had been covered with the salve and goose fat that he had applied.

'Had they bled a lot?' Hanufer asked.

'Enough to dribble down his haunches. I cleaned him. At first he did not want me to touch them, as I could see that they pained him, but my salve calmed him.'

'What sort of thing could have made such wounds, do you think?'

Once again, Behdet looked uncertainly at Kleitos the high priest.

'Just answer my questions, Behdet,' Hanufer said sharply. 'You do not have to seek Kleitos's approval.'

The young Keeper of Animals swallowed hard. 'A sharpened stick of some sort, my lord.'

'A long one? Like a spear? Something that could be reached over the pen to prod him?'

'Yes, my lord. Something like that.'

Hanufer nodded. 'And was there any such thing in the pen when you found the body or after you had removed the body and cleaned Apis?'

'No, my lord. I would have told Kleitos if there had been.'

Hanufer considered for a few moments. *Any long stick with a sharpened point could have been used, then easily broken up and disposed of later.*

He did not hold up a great hope of finding it.

'Where do you sleep, both of you?'

'I sleep in my chambers, which are in the building on the other side of the temple, inside the boundary wall,' replied Kleitos.

'And I sleep in a bay by the pigsties,' said Behdet.

'Did anyone hear any screaming? A man being trampled to death would surely make some noise at least before he was either knocked unconscious or killed.'

Both Behdet and Kleitos shook their heads.

'I am a poor sleeper,' replied Kleitos. 'I am of an age when I frequently have to get up to relieve my bladder. I heard occasional noises from the animals. But I am used to that.'

'I heard Apis bellow a few times,' said Behdet, 'but I thought nothing much of it.'

'At what hour was that?' Hanufer queried.

Behdet shook his head. 'I do not know, my lord. I did not properly wake up. I heard nothing unusual.'

Hanufer nodded. He was aware that it had been a full moon the night before, when the god Thoth was at the height of his power. In the bright moonlight, there would have been no need for an oil lamp or torch.

'That is enough questions for now,' he said. 'You may return to whatever duties you both need to attend to.'

Kleitos bowed. 'I must go to pray to Poseidon and supervise the other priests as they prepare the morning offerings. Behdet has to attend to his pigs.'

When they had gone, Hanufer and Sabu spent some time looking about the other outhouses and temple buildings for

71

signs of blood or of a spear or stick that could have been used to prod the bull, but they found nothing.

After the constables arrived back with the cart to remove the body, Hanufer and Sabu left the Temple of Poseidon. They went down the majestic marble steps of the temple entrance, which were flanked by mighty statues of the god, each holding a trident.

'We shall give them time to get to the Musaeum and deliver my message to whichever of the physicians they find first. I also want to walk in the fresh air after seeing that poor wretch's body. So come, we shall take the circular route.'

They walked across the first street of the grid and made their way toward the small public garden with palm trees and the statue of Sobek that they had seen when Cario had given them their tour. Hanufer led the way across and stood for a few moments, silently looking up at the statue of the god of their home city of Crocodilopolis. Sabu said nothing when Hanufer closed his eyes for a few seconds, being well aware of his boss's veneration for the deity.

After opening his eyes and bowing, Hanufer signalled for Sabu to walk on with him.

'So, Sabu,' he began, 'we can say with some certainty that this man, whoever he was, did not die in that bull pen. He was trampled by the bull, that much is clear, but he was already dead. His killer must have brought him here and put the body in with the animal.'

'But why, my lord?'

'To make it look like a foolish accident.'

The sergeant frowned. 'So, you think this was deliberate murder, my lord?'

Hanufer nodded. 'We can say more than that. The bull was prodded and goaded to trample him so as to destroy his features and make him unrecognisable and thus unidentifiable.'

As he spoke, Hanufer put his hands together and stroked the rings he wore. Mentally, he asked the gods for help.

He had seen many violent deaths in his career, but he had a singular sense of foreboding about this one.

# CHAPTER 6

They left the public garden by the far exit and continued south along the Street of the Soma. The large Soma building itself, which was to be a new Temple to Alexander and which also contained his tomb, came into view ahead of them. The Soma had not yet been opened for worship, as it was expected that there would be a grand procession and opening when the pharaoh decided to install the new high priest. It was no secret in Alexandria that this was to be the pharaoh's vizier, Admiral Patroclus.

As expected, the Soma was already surrounded by crowds of people. Many of the citizens apparently made it part of their daily routine to go and touch the walls of the great marble-clad building, which had atop it a gleaming limestone pyramid. They turned right onto the great Canopic Way, which was busy with all sorts of carts, slaves carrying litters with nobles, boys leading asses laden with wares and men riding camels. The wide stone pavements on both sides of the street were decked with stalls where pilgrims to the Temple of Alexander, which stood beside the tomb, could purchase votive offerings to leave on the steps of the temple.

They circumvented the crowd of sellers and pilgrims, took another turn right and walked up the street towards the Library and the Musaeum.

The Musaeum had been one of the first building complexes embarked upon by Pharaoh Ptolemy. It was actually linked to the Royal Palace by a *peripatos*, a long covered walkway. It had been the first Ptolemy's plan to establish a seat of learning such as had never been seen before. He had been inspired to do so by Demetrius of Phalerum, an Athenian peripatetic philosopher and statesman who had stayed at the first Ptolemy's invitation and suggested to him that he should use the model of Aristotle's Lyceum at Athens. Thus they came up with the concept of the Musaeum, a great institution in the centre of Alexandria which would become the home of music, poetry, philosophy and learning. The most learned scholars, artists, philosophers and musicians from around the world would be invited to come and be employed at the pharaoh's expense to develop and advance their areas of learning.

A Temple to the Muses with a high priest was at the centre of this institution, which was allowed to gradually expand, so new buildings were added according to the institution's requirements. Thus it had an *exedra*, a large arcade where the *philologoi*, the scholars, could sit and converse, with study rooms, studios and chambers suited to their particular needs. Attached to it was a large palatial building called the *oikos*, where they ate and were lodged.

As the Musaeum rapidly developed, the number of papyri and books had hugely increased until Demetrius suggested that a great library should also be constructed to house the products of the *philologoi*'s intellectual and artistic pursuits. When Ptolemy Philadelphus was called by his father to share his throne during the first pharaoh's final years, he greatly extended both the scope and aim of the Musaeum and the Library.

The two constables were waiting at the entrance to the Temple of the Muses at the centre of the Musaeum, beyond which was the Hospital and Medical School of Alexandria. Hanufer asked them if they had delivered both the body and the message.

'We did, my lord,' returned Pylyp, the elder of the two constables, a man in his late thirties. 'The Physician Erasistratus himself showed us where to carry the body. He seemed pleased to receive it.'

Hanufer noted the look of distaste on the constable's face and the pallor on that of the younger constable.

'The place we took it to smelled of death, my lord,' Filemon, the younger constable volunteered. 'The priest who took us to the hospital brought us back and told us to wait here for you.'

'Then lead us to him,' Hanufer said.

They followed the constables into a large circular chamber where they were immediately met by a priest wearing only a kilt and a pectoral who had been waiting inside. A high dome with clerestory windows around its rim to let in light seemed to be supported by nine huge statues of women in Greek dress.

Hanufer told the constables to wait for them outside, much to the obvious relief of Constable Filemon.

'Welcome, my lord Hanufer,' the priest said, bowing as they approached. 'I am Pappus, the high priest of the Temple of the Muses.' He stretched his hands upwards and pointed to the statues. 'Behold the benevolence of the Nine Muses, daughters of mighty Zeus and Mnemosyne. They are Calliope, Clio, Euterpe, Melpomene, Terpsichore, Erato, Polyhymnia, Urania and Thalia. Our *philologoi* have all been to seek inspiration from them this morning after they broke their fasts, for each muse governs one of the arts and can give insight to those who venerate her.'

He pointed to several curtained entrances in the circular wall. 'These are special cubicles where one can sit and ponder a question and ask whichever muse seems most appropriate to give an answer.'

Sabu suddenly gave a loud sneeze, which echoed about the circular chamber. He rubbed his nose apologetically. 'Your pardon, my lord. Those incense burners must have tickled my nose.'

Pappus smiled haughtily and pointed to a statue of a muse with a wreath on her head, carrying a comic mask in one hand and a trumpet in the other. 'That may have been blessed Thalia, the muse of comedy and bucolic poetry. She has a mischievous side to her and is given to play jokes on the unwary. She may have tickled your nose, not the incense.'

Sabu looked up at the statue with a mixture of suspicion and anxiety. 'Why, have I offended the goddess? Should I make an offering?'

Pappus smiled, but it seemed to the two Egyptians that it was more condescending than affable. He pointed to an offerings table which was covered in food, fruits, and flowers. 'The Muses always look favourably upon those who ask for their assistance, be they Greek, Egyptian or barbarian.'

Sabu gave the priest a sour look, fumbled inside a pocket of his chiton and drew out two dates. Staring up at the statue of Thalia, he went across and deposited his offering on the table.

Hanufer had noted the exchange, but said nothing. Had the man been more openly offensive, he knew that Sabu would have dealt with him in no uncertain manner. He looked up wonderingly at the nine statues. 'And which Muse is the one who concerns herself with human tragedy?'

Pappus pointed to one on the other side of the chamber from Thalia. 'That is Melpomene, my lord. She bears the mask of tragedy and a wreath of ivy.'

Crossing to the offering table, Hanufer placed a bronze obol coin beside the two dates that Sabu had put down. Bowing his head, he closed his eyes for a moment and silently asked the statue of Melpomene for enlightenment over the tragedy that they had been called to deal with that morning.

Pappus stood patiently with his hands clasped in front of him until Hanufer opened his eyes and nodded to him.

'So now, please take us to see the Physician Erasistratus,' he said, touching his two rings. *Let us see if the Greek Melpomene can aid our great goddess Maat and show us the path to the truth with this dead man*, he thought.

The way to the hospital from the Temple of the Muses was a straight colonnaded path covered by wooden latticework, over which vines had been cultivated. It was, Pappus told them, the way that the *philologoi* went to reach the Medical School, but the citizens of Alexandria could reach the hospital by the main doors that opened into the city's busy Emporium.

A slave was waiting to greet them outside the Medical School and they thanked Pappus, who left them. The slave, a young boy of about twelve, eyes averted so that he did not look directly at them, led the way through several corridors, passing many chambers where patients in beds were being treated by doctors or tended by assistants. The odour of body fluids and the smell of incense wafted after them, accompanied by the curiously mixed sounds of people either in distress or being relieved.

At last they arrived at a pair of large wooden doors. The young slave struck a gong at the side and then stepped back. Sandaled feet could be heard from the other side of the door, then a bolt was slid back and a man of about thirty with a prodigiously thick black beard opened the doors. Hanufer had met the physician Erasistratus of Ceos at a welcoming party at the Library arranged by the palace when he first arrived in Alexandria. Despite his relative youth, Erasistratus had already gained a considerable reputation as both a physician and an anatomist. Hanufer and he had got on well, both having declared a mutual interest in swimming.

Behind him, standing beside a stout wooden table upon which was the corpse, the middle-aged Herophilus of Chalcedon was tying on a leather apron. Like Erasistratus, he was bearded, but his was heavily streaked with grey. He was also bald apart from greying hair at his temples. Unlike the open face of Erasistratus, the older anatomist had deep frown lines etched on his forehead, which conveyed a look of both suspicion and curiosity.

'Welcome to our anatomy amphitheatre,' said Erasistratus, opening the door wider for Hanufer and Sabu to enter. 'Both I and my colleague Herophilus, the dean of our Medical School, were pleased to receive your message when your two *phylakitai*, your constables, delivered this very interesting corpse to us.'

Hanufer and Sabu entered to find themselves in what seemed to be the pit of an amphitheatre with several steep crescent-shaped tiers of benches. Light streamed from vaulted arch windows high above the topmost tier.

'We normally allow our students to watch all dissections of cadavers,' said Herophilus as they approached the corpse. 'But your message said that this was a police matter, so we will conduct this one alone.'

Sabu looked around the amphitheatre and noted that there were many buckets and tanks, some filled with water, others with natron and still others with vinegar. Inside them he saw assorted body parts. A human skeleton had been tied together and dangled eerily from a hook on a wall. The coppery smell of blood and the vague smell of putrefaction so reminiscent of a charnel house made his nose itch, and he sneezed loudly.

'Does the smell of death offend your nose, young man?' Herophilus asked Sabu in a kindlier tone than Hanufer had anticipated from his initial impression of the anatomist.

Sabu recovered himself. 'No, sir, it is just that I have a sensitive nose. My father was an embalmer, so I am used to seeing — and smelling — the way in which dead bodies are prepared for the passage into the afterlife from my early childhood.'

Erasistratus nodded and pointed to the corpse. 'So what is it you wish us to do, Hanufer of Crocodilopolis? You said in your message that you were suspicious about this poor man's death.'

Hanufer described the finding of the body in the bull pen at the Temple of Poseidon and outlined his deductions. 'When I and my sergeant examined the body, I found a puncture wound at the base of the skull.' He drew out his sandalwood writing case from his chiton pocket and opened it to show the reed pen. 'I was able to pass this into the puncture wound as far as the width of four fingers.'

The two anatomists looked at one another and nodded in unison. Without a word Erasistratus began to peel off the remnants of the tunic from the corpse while Herophilus took a sponge from a bucket of water and started to wash the dried blood away from the flesh.

'Why do you and your sergeant not take a seat in that second tier?' the older physician suggested. 'You will have a better view of what we are doing from above.'

Hanufer and Sabu did as suggested and watched as the blood was removed and the extent of the wounds became clearer.

'We always begin with an examination of the body,' Erasistratus explained, 'since there may be features on the body that tell us about the illnesses a man or woman may have had while they were living. For example, there is much that we can tell about the veins — those are the tubes that carry blood in the body. My esteemed colleague Herophilus has in his dissections found that there are different types of vessels that carry blood.'

'Some we have called *arteries*,' Herophilus went on as he scrutinised the hands of the corpse. 'They carry blood from the heart.' He looked up. 'You know the purpose of the heart, I take it?'

Hanufer nodded. 'We call it the *Hati*, and it is where the soul, the *ib* lives. The *ib* is one of the ten parts of a person's body and soul. It is where we feel joy and happiness in one who lives a good life. In the life of a murderer with a bad heart, it may be where hate and cruelty reside.'

Herophilus snorted. 'Ah yes, of course. I have read that you Egyptians have such beliefs. But from our work we know that these arteries are all six times thicker than the ordinary veins. They carry blood from the heart to different organs like the liver, the lungs, the kidneys and the *encephalon*, the brain.'

Hanufer looked surprised. 'But how can you tell this?'

The two anatomists looked at each other as if both aware of what the other was thinking. Herophilus gave a thin smile and fixed Hanufer with his steely regard. 'Because we have been able to witness it in our dissections.'

'But blood cannot flow after death, surely,' Hanufer said.

'We have seen it when we dissected animals like sheep and pigs, but most importantly, when we were given living criminals who have been condemned to death.'

Both Hanufer and Sabu stared back in shock.

'It is permitted by law upon Pharaoh Ptolemy Philadelphus's command,' said Erasistratus. 'It has enabled us to identify the functions of different parts of the body. In my own dissections, I have found that the heart is a pump. It has valves inside it, which control the way the blood flows.'

'Are you shocked, Hanufer of Crocodilopolis?' Herophilus asked, looking up at the Overseer of Police and his sergeant.

From the corner of his eye Hanufer saw Sabu tensing and put a hand on his arm to stop him from reacting.

'Yes, Herophilus, I am shocked that you should experiment on living people, but I am also surprised. I had thought that we Egyptians knew most about the workings of the body. After all, we have many papyri written about medicine and surgery, and we have been preparing bodies and embalming them for centuries.'

'Ah yes, as your sergeant said,' Herophilus returned. 'But I ask why in all that time did your physicians not make these discoveries? The reason is because they were not looking for answers as we are. Our dissections of the living, which we call *vivisection*, have taught us much. Between us, Erasistratus and I have written six books on anatomy so far.'

The two anatomists returned to their study of the corpse, from time to time whispering together and nodding in agreement. After some moments, they both straightened up.

'From our examination of the wounds, it is clear that this body has injuries consistent with being trampled upon by the cloven hooves of a bull,' Herophilus announced. 'We agree with your assessment that from the pattern of tanning, he at some time wore cothurnus boots. He also was a slave, as indicated by this branding on his shoulder.'

'I had not seen that,' said Hanufer, standing to look closer.

'It was covered by mud and caked blood. It is a delta brand.'

'Does that tell us where he was from or who owned him?'

Both anatomists shook their heads. 'Only that he was a public slave,' Herophilus replied. 'A *demosios*.'

82

'The other thing that we agree on,' added Erasistratus, 'is that while his tunic was bloodstained and the wounds are horrific, something is not right. The goring alone should have produced a cascade of blood, just as the Nile produces torrents at the cataracts. His face is a pulp and the front of the skull is crushed, yet the blood loss from the wounds is not as great as it should be. That is consistent with him being dead before he was put in the bull pen, as you said.'

He signalled to his colleague, and between them they turned the corpse over. With scissors Herophilus started to cut away the hair from the back of the head to expose the puncture wound.

'Erasistratus knows more about the encephalon that anyone,' the dean of the Medical School said, 'so I will leave him to carry out this part of the examination.'

The younger anatomist took up a long metal probe and inserted it into the puncture wound. Withdrawing it after a few moments, he placed it against his hand. 'I agree, it was pushed in as deep as the width of four fingers. To see more, I must look at his whole encephalon. I must extract it from his skull.'

'How will you remove it, sir?' Sabu asked, curiously. 'Our Egyptian embalmers pull it out with a hook through the nose. I have seen it done many times, and surely you will not be able to tell much from that. It comes out like the contents of a broken crocodile egg.'

'That is because they do not preserve the encephalon, but throw it away,' the anatomist replied. 'By doing so, they throw away the most important part of the body. The encephalon is where thoughts and emotions reside.'

'Not in the heart?' Hanufer queried. 'The Egyptian physicians would not agree with you. They would say that the encephalon, as you call it, was merely a jelly through which visions from the eyes enter the body and where messages are sent to make our limbs move.'

Erasistratus gave a sniff of derision. 'We should agree to hold differing opinions with them. You are talking about what they believe to be true. We as anatomists say what we have seen from our dissections and vivisections.'

Picking up a scalpel, he made an elliptical incision across the base of the skull. Then, inserting the handle and his fingers, he peeled back the skin in a flap. Having exposed the bone, he picked up a saw and began to cut through the base of the skull. It took some minutes of careful sawing. When he had cut a large oval of bone, he inserted hooks under the bone edges and gradually pulled it free.

Moments later, skilfully using a variety of instruments and his bare fingers, he pulled the brain out of the skull and placed it in a metal basin on a side table. They could see that the front had been mushed from the facial injuries. Herophilus leaned over and watched as Erasistratus made an incision across the point of entry at the back of the brain. Cutting it in two, he separated the halves.

'The murder weapon was not just shoved into his brain,' Erasistratus said, standing back so that Hanufer and Sabu could see. 'It was shoved in and then viciously rotated. You can see how it created a cone of mushed up encephalon.'

'So, could it have been something like the reed pen that I showed you?' Hanufer asked. 'Could someone like a scribe have done this?'

'Possibly, but not with a reed pen,' Erasistratus returned. 'No, this was done with an item stiffer than a reed. A strange weapon, long and thin, but strong. Something like this copper probe that I used.'

'Or possibly like the long hooks that the embalmers use to remove the brain through the nose?' Sabu suggested.

Erasistratus bit his lip pensively and then nodded. 'Yes, I have seen some of the hooks they use. They are long and tightly curved — so yes, it is possible.'

'There is much for me to consider,' said Hanufer. 'One thing is clear: this person knew exactly how to kill this man. It is also apparent that whoever it was went to inordinate lengths to cover up the murder.'

Erasistratus pointed to the corpse. 'With your permission, we shall make further dissection of the body. We will use it to demonstrate the internal injuries to our students of medicine.'

'Please do,' Hanufer returned. 'But could you make a drawing of the brain injury for me?'

'Indeed I will, and I will have it sent to your office in the *Dikasterion*,' the anatomist replied.

'Oh, and also one of the brand on his shoulder.'

'It shall be done exactly as you ask,' Erasistratus replied. 'Please allow me a day or so, since we are in the middle of a dissection of a body that we are demonstrating to our students at the Medical School. It is a fresh body, and in this heat they quickly begin to putrefy.' With a smile at Sabu, he went on, 'And I shall not throw the brain away, but I shall store it in wine. It will go into one of our cellars to remain cool.'

'I thank you for the thought,' Sabu replied. 'I may not easily get that image out of my head when I next take a cup of wine.'

Hanufer rose from his bench and thanked the two anatomists. He had a feeling that they might never discover who owned the slave, or who he was. More than that, he wondered why whoever had murdered him had considered it so important as to have made his body unrecognisable.

The watcher's stomach was rumbling. It had been several hours since food had passed those parched lips, and yet the feeling of hunger had come as a surprise. Moving the body and arranging everything had been taxing on the nerves, but necessary. So, too, was it imperative that they were not noticed.

The thoughts tumbled one after the other.

*This complication could ruin everything and put more than one life at risk.*

*Pah! It was the fool's own fault. He saw what he should not have seen, and he had already shown that he could be persuaded by the sight of gold.*

*Of course he couldn't be allowed to live.*

*There was too much at stake.*

Further consideration was temporarily banished as the two Egyptian police officials emerged from the Temple of the Muses. They were deep in conversation, one with the wig and his pectoral of office so prominent, and the other with his shaven head and his hand on the pommel of his sword.

*Why was the body taken there?*

*Is this new Overseer going to be as much trouble as the last one?*

*Questions that need answers.*

*Perhaps more deaths will be the answer.*

# CHAPTER 7

Hanufer had barely had any time to spare during his first week in Alexandria. He had been allocated a villa in the Brucheum quarter by order of the pharaoh. It was a two-storeyed building with a flat roof set in a high-walled garden with date palms, fig trees and a lotus pond. A staff of two Greek maids and a middle-aged man from the pharaoh's own staff were also provided.

Delia, one of the young women, was an accomplished cook, while the other, whose name was Ophelia, was so adept at cleaning the villa without being seen that it seemed as if the place was cleaned by magic. Timon, the short and slightly rotund butler with natural laughter lines on his face, explained to Hanufer that he suspected that Harpocrates, the god of silence, had secretly sired both Delia and Ophelia.

'I hope you will not think that all Greeks are as shy as they, my lord. Both have worked in the Royal Palace since they were small girls, but I fear that they have over-learned their lessons to only speak when spoken to.' He had shrugged his shoulders as if at a loss to understand their shyness. 'I try to make them laugh with occasional jokes, but the most I ever get is a smile.'

It was the first indication Timon had given that he actually had a dry sense of humour, and it was his way of seeking his new boss's permission to exhibit it.

'Smiling is good, but the laughter of young women is better,' Hanufer conceded. 'Pray persist with your jokes and amusements, Timon. Just ensure that they are neither sacrilegious nor salacious.'

Timon had looked puzzled. 'I beg your pardon, my lord, but I am a man of limited learning. Could you explain —?'

'Do not make fun of the gods — neither Greek nor Egyptian, and no dirty jokes are permitted.'

With the limits understood, Timon chuckled and scuttled off to his duties and to his self-administered task to make the two young women laugh.

Hanufer broke his fast in the mornings either in a small pavilion by the lotus pond or atop the flat roof garden, where he could enjoy a fine view of the Great Harbour. Timon jovially served him, each time giving him more information about Alexandria and the workings of the Royal Palace, or pointing out different landmarks visible from the rooftop garden.

Sabu had declined Hanufer's offer of a room in the villa, preferring instead to live in the police barracks, a long building that abutted the city wall near the Gate of the Moon.

The murder of the slave bothered him, but preliminary investigations had yielded nothing at all. No missing slaves had been reported.

Apart from organising his office in the city court building, and interviewing and trying to get to know each of the forty-two police *phylakitai* constables under his command, Hanufer had a full list of engagements of one sort or another to attend. Officials from all of the city organisations — business and tradesfolk of the Greek, Egyptian and Jewish communities — had invited him to meet with them individually, view their establishments and hear about their particular areas of expertise or about their problems. In many instances he knew this was to impress upon him how important they were to the city, the pharaoh and, by extension, to Egypt itself.

In addition, each midday or evening he had at least one invitation to a social gathering. Mostly they were dull, formal affairs that he was glad to escape from, except for one that he found particularly interesting and even enjoyed. This was a dinner organised by Thespos, the *Chrematistes*, chief judge, of the *Dikasterion*, the Alexandrian court. Like most of the high officials in Alexandria, he lived in the Brucheum quarter close to the Royal Palace.

Hanufer had quickly discovered that the Greeks had several different ways of entertaining guests. The *symposium* was a banquet and drinking party exclusively for men, where women, usually courtesans or professional singers and dancers, were only permitted to attend in order to entertain the male guests. The *syssitia* was also a men- and youth-only meal, but solely for scholars or the priests of a temple. Curiously, he found that in their own homes men and women did not generally eat together, but the men ate a meal first while the women ate theirs afterwards. Womenfolk of households were of course permitted to attend meals in their own homes or as guests in others.

Judge Thespos had invited Hanufer for dinner one evening after nightfall, when the temperature was cooler. His wife, Lady Ambrosia, was there with her husband to greet him when the servant showed him into their spacious living area, which had a fountain in the middle of the room. Two other guests had been invited — one was a middle-aged priest with a full beard and a headband upon which was a seven-pointed star. Like the judge and Hanufer, he wore a chiton.

'Allow me to introduce Manetho, the high priest of Serapis and a scholar of the Musaeum and the Library,' Judge Thespos said.

The two men bowed their heads at each other.

'And this is Nefrit, high priestess of Isis,' the Lady Ambrosia said.

Hanufer turned his head and found himself looking at one of the most beautiful women he had ever met. She only came up to his shoulder, but she had a voluptuous figure that was barely concealed by a long white sheath dress. Like himself she wore an oiled black wig that matched her kohl-painted eyes. With delightfully high cheekbones and a delicately chiselled nose, her ruby red painted lips made her approach his ideal image of Egyptian beauty. Upon her head she wore a small headdress with the two ivory cow horns containing within them a full silver disc representing the moon.

'I am actually the only priestess,' Nefrit said, demurely bowing her head to the hostess. 'Lady Ambrosia has kindly given me an honour that I do not possess.'

The judge's wife gave a soft laugh. 'Well, my dear, that makes you the high priestess in my view. You do, after all, have two temples of Isis to look after.'

Hanufer and Nefrit smiled at each other and both bowed their heads.

'I thought that you would enjoy the company of fellow Egyptians,' said the judge, more affable than he'd seemed when Hanufer had met him in his official capacity.

'I am honoured to join you in your home this evening, Judge Thespos and Lady Ambrosia,' the new Overseer of Police replied. 'And I am pleased to be able to talk to you, Manetho, about the great god Serapis.' He turned and smiled at Nefrit. 'I do, of course, know more about Isis, one of our most ancient and important Egyptian deities.'

Over a first drink of light wine the guests each introduced themselves, as was the custom.

'I am Manetho of Sebennytos in the Nile Delta,' the high priest of Serapis volunteered. 'Yet I have been in Alexandria since the first Pharaoh Ptolemy Soter invited me to take up a post at the Musaeum and then to become the high priest of Serapis. At Ptolemy Philadelphus's instruction, I am compiling a biography and a listing of all the pharaohs of Egypt and of their families. I am calling it *The Aegyptiaca*. It has already taken me five years of study.'

'A most important work, I am sure,' Hanufer acknowledged. 'I will, if you do not object, call upon you at the Library to seek instruction in this history. As the *Archiphylakites*, I feel that I should know this history as fully as possible.'

The conversation then turned to Hanufer. He told them all about his own background and his career in Crocodilopolis before coming to the attention of Pharaoh Ptolemy Philadelphus. All the while he was conscious of the priestess of Isis sitting close to him. He wanted to look at her, but politeness forbade him from resting his eyes too long upon her.

He listened attentively when she was asked to tell them about her history.

'I am from Philae in Upper Egypt. My father was a scribe and my mother was a priestess at the Temple of Isis there. So, I have worshipped the goddess Isis all of my life.'

Hanufer had noted and admired her deep olive skin and had wondered if she was from the far south.

'I have some skill as a musician and I too was recommended to come to Alexandria. I received a personal invitation from Queen Arsinoe herself.'

Lady Ambrosia gave another of her little chuckles. 'Nefrit is far too modest. She is a highly accomplished musician and singer. You play how many instruments, my dear?'

Nefrit raised her hands. 'Please, Lady Ambrosia, I do not deserve such praise. Like every priestess I am proficient with the sistrum, cymbals and crotals, for we use them in our ceremonies. So too, I have some skill with both the lute and the harp.'

'So good that it was a queen of Egypt who invited her to court,' added Ambrosia.

Hanufer nodded admiringly. 'Perhaps I will have the honour of hearing you play some time?'

Nefrit smiled demurely. 'It would be a pleasure, my lord. You would only have to come to one of the temples when I am there.'

Hanufer beamed back. 'Excellent. I shall do so. I myself have only met Queen Arsinoe when the pharaoh inducted me and gave me my pectoral of office and seal.'

There was an unexpected awkward silence in the room for a few moments, broken by a cough from Judge Thespos. He leaned forward. 'Actually, it was not this Queen Arsinoe, but the pharaoh's first wife, Arsinoe the First, before he repudiated and banished her.'

Nefrit nodded. 'It is as Judge Thespos says; it was the first Queen Arsinoe who invited me and had me installed as the priestess of Isis on the Island of Pharos. When the new Queen Arsinoe came to Alexandria and married the pharaoh, she had a second temple dedicated to Isis built in the Brucheum and I was given the responsibility of being its priestess, too. I am fortunate in having three handmaidens and praise-singers who assist me with both temples.'

Hanufer nodded. 'I have seen both temples from the outside. My — er — assistant,' he began, feeling reluctant to refer to Cario as his slave, 'gave myself and my sergeant a guided tour of the city.'

Nefrit looked down and Hanufer involuntarily followed her gaze, noticing her small feet in leather sandals, each toenail painted ruby red to match her lip shade.

The priestess sighed and looked up at Hanufer, who started as he looked at her, realising that she had noticed him gazing at her feet. 'Only now,' she went on hesitantly, 'Queen Arsinoe is no longer at court, but was banished to the town of Coptos, near Thebes, where she herself is now the high priestess of the Temple of Min and Isis.'

Lady Ambrosia gave another of her little laughs, although this one seemed more of a nervous reaction. 'How strange are the ways of the gods. Nefrit and the first Queen Arsinoe starting at different ends of Egypt and ending up crossing over.'

'The ways of the gods, my lady?' Hanufer repeated.

'Yes, it is unfathomable the way they move our lives around as if we were pieces on a *Petteia* gaming board,' his hostess replied with a chuckle. 'The two queens, both named Arsinoe and one a sister to the pharaoh. You, Hanufer, brought from Crocodilopolis when the last Overseer of Police died suddenly. Nefrit brought to Alexandria because of her gift of music. Surely that is a gift she was given by the gods. These are all matters that the gods decided.'

'Indeed, it is not for us to question the gods,' Manetho agreed. 'Things happen when the gods will it.'

Hanufer shook his head. 'I am not sure that I entirely agree with you. Evil things occur, which cannot be because the gods wish it. As a police officer, I have seen much of it. Murders, rapes, these are evil crimes.'

'Perhaps they are when the god Seth gets his way,' Manetho responded. 'He is the god of disorder, of violence, of trickery. When he comes out of the searing hot desert, he brings evil thoughts into people's hearts.'

Hanufer recalled the examination he had witnessed the two anatomists make. Erasistratus was sure that the brain was the seat of thought and emotions, not the heart as he and Sabu both thought. Yet now he was not so sure, just as he was not so sure about whether all evil deeds were the result of the desires of the red-headed god Seth.

Judge Thespos clapped his hands and two servants suddenly appeared at doors into the room. 'It is time for us to eat.'

Food and more drinks were brought in with great speed, efficiency and deference.

'I know something of the pharaoh's family, of course,' Hanufer went on, once the servants had gone. 'But I should like to know more.'

Manetho nodded. 'Then perhaps this is a matter that I am well placed to discuss with you, Hanufer. Come to the Library when I am there and I can show you some of the illustrious history of Egypt, all the way from the first dynasty of King Khufu to this present day under the reign of Ptolemy Philadelphus and Queen Arsinoe.'

The subject adroitly changed by the priest of Serapis, the party began to eat. And an enjoyable evening they spent eating roast duck, chestnuts, honey cakes and other delicacies, and drinking fine wine from the judge's cellar.

Over their food they talked at a fairly superficial level about the law and how Alexandria operated both the Attic legal system and the Egyptian. As such, Thespos and the other judges had to be adept and well-read in both codes. Then the talk turned to the two cults of Serapis and Isis and how they were related.

'I saw and read the dedication stelae in the pylon gate outside the Temple of Serapis,' Hanufer told Manetho the high priest. 'It is written in both Greek and hieroglyphics.'

'Like his father before him, Pharaoh Ptolemy Philadelphus is always keen to integrate the two cultures,' Judge Thespos remarked. 'Just as we have the two legal systems — the Egyptian and the Greek.'

'I note that Serapis is named as such in Greek, but in hieroglyphics it is as Osiris-Apis,' Hanufer said.

Manetho gave a smile of admission. 'It is simply that we have not as yet devised such a hieroglyph.'

'But does it not show that the god is primarily a Greek deity?' Hanufer asked.

Manetho stopped with a grape halfway to his mouth. He placed the fruit down on the plate before him and devotedly raised a hand to touch his seven-pointed star, the symbol of the god Serapis. Again he gave an indulgent smile. 'The gods have always been there, as I am sure you know, Hanufer. The names are the inventions of we humble people. You should think of Serapis as the great uniter of the Greek and Egyptian peoples, to be worshipped by all as such.'

Hanufer raised his hands apologetically and smiled. 'I mean no disrespect, sir. I merely strive to understand the cultures in Alexandria. I understood that our Egyptian gods Osiris and Apis were seen to be similar to the Grecian gods Hades and Dionysus and so were united into the new cult of Serapis.'

They talked for some time about the cult of Serapis. The god was mainly depicted as a man with a classical Greek beard wearing a cylindrical corn sheaf upon his head, but he was also sometimes depicted as a snake.

'I see how the snake would be associated with the underworld, the realm of Osiris, with whom he is linked,' Hanufer said.

Manetho nodded. 'It is so, but as you also know, all of the gods have different attributes and can come to us in different forms. In Egypt alone there are over two thousand. I know, for I am also compiling a book of all the deities of the known world, including those of the barbarian races. The gods all have different names.'

Nefrit nodded. 'Divine Isis, whom it is my honour to worship, was the wife of Osiris, and she is known as the goddess of a thousand names.'

'Indeed, I am from Crocodilopolis and we have a great temple to Isis, along with one to Sobek.' As Nefrit regarded him, he thought that her eyes were especially beautiful. To divert his mind from such thoughts, he lifted his hands and showed them his two rings, which bore the images of Sobek and of Maat. 'This ring was made from a tooth of the sacred crocodile at Crocodilopolis.'

'But how was this?' Nefrit asked with increased interest. 'Were you once a priest of Sobek?'

'No, but I had solved a crime that was committed within the temple. A particularly unpleasant crime. This ring was made in gratitude on the orders of the high priest.'

The Lady Ambrosia had not spoken much, but at the sight of his other ring she seemed to become animated. 'And the goddess Maat. Surely in her we have the path that we must all follow.'

Nefrit placed her fingertips together and nodded her head. 'You are right, my lady. If we stray from the truth, then we risk losing everything.'

Once again Hanufer's mind was drawn back to images of the murdered slave: first of the pen with the sacred bull and then of the corpse with the brain removed and placed in a basin beside it.

But then these images were quickly shoved from his mind as he glanced at Nefrit.

He determined that this evening would not be the last time that he saw the priestess of Isis.

# CHAPTER 8

Hanufer flicked a camel hair flywhisk at the fat-bodied insects that had landed on the papyrus that he had stretched out on his desk before him. He read the neat Greek writing carefully, assimilating the message that the writer intended to convey beneath the typically florid style that was used.

Sitting at a smaller desk opposite him, Sabu marvelled at the way his own desk had been transformed into a facsimile of that of his boss. He knew that Cario had been at work, following Hanufer's instructions. Although they had only been in Alexandria a little over a week, the clerks and the police constables under his command already knew that Hanufer was going to be a very different Overseer than Gryton of Salamis. The sudden death of the Greek *Archiphylakites* — followed by the retirement of his sergeant assistant, a Thracian called Kraspar, due to illness — had left the Alexandrian police leaderless apart from two or three of the more able constables whom had unofficially assumed command for several weeks. They had also learned that Sabu was going to be a demanding sergeant of police who would brook no insubordination.

Hanufer had instructed Pollio on how he wanted his office and his desk to be arranged. In turn, Pollio had delegated the more mundane aspects of this task to Cario.

All incoming papyri addressed to Hanufer were to be placed in a large basket on the left of his desk directly in front of the figurine of Sobek. This consisted of invitations from officials or businesses, together with petitions to the *Archiphylakites* to investigate professed crimes or complaints against individuals. The basket next to it was for Pollio the office scribe to take and follow the instructions about the papyri in question, which Hanufer would write on an ostracon, one of the little tablets of pottery which were cheaper than papyrus and ideal for making swift notes. Next to this a third basket was for matters that had been dealt with and could be filed in the neighbouring file room by one of the junior clerks under Pollio's command. Finally, in front of a figurine of the goddess Maat a fourth basket was for the documents and ostraca relating to cases under investigation. This was currently about half a cubit high, for Hanufer had instructed Pollio to give him all of the cases which his predecessor Gryton of Salamis had been working on over the past year, together with all of the documents about his death.

Cario had just left, having brought them a jug of beer and a plate of figs as Sabu had ordered.

It was the middle of the day and Sabu was glad to be inside after an energetic morning in the sun. Before he left them Cario had carefully poured a cup of beer for each of them and left a clay straw by each cup.

'There does not seem to be too much sediment in this *heqet*,' Sabu said as he inserted his straw halfway down the beer to avoid sucking up some of the deposit. He took a hefty drink and then placed it on the desk, wiping his brow with the back of his hand. 'The lad is learning. You should try it, sir. Reading cases must be thirsty work.'

Hanufer sat back and took some beer through his straw. He nodded in agreement. 'Cario is intelligent and eager to be useful. Without being disrespectful of my predecessor, he has told me much that explains a lot about obstacles that we may meet, Sabu.'

'Such as, my lord?'

'There is general resentment among native Alexandrians about Egyptians like us being placed in command. The constables, who are mostly Greeks, consider themselves to be more sophisticated and more intelligent than non-Greeks. Not only that, but he has suggested in a subtle manner that there may be some who are open to bribery.'

'I will root them out, my lord!' Sabu said, sitting upright. 'I will —'

'We will not act hastily, Sabu. I want these men to work willingly under my command, through respect, not fear.' He tapped the papyrus in front of him and nodded for Sabu to close the door. The sergeant immediately rose and closed the door before returning to his seat, all attention.

'Besides,' Hanufer went on, 'I am concerned that Gryton, the previous *Archiphylakites*, died suddenly.'

Sabu gave a slight frown. 'What age was he, my lord?'

'Only thirty-five years and seemingly in good health.'

'Perhaps it was the will of the gods, my lord?'

Hanufer recalled the conversations he'd had the night before at Judge Thespos's home and glanced at the figurine of Maat. 'Yes, but his *Hyparchiphylakites* also immediately resigned. From sudden ill health, as I understand from Cario and Pollio. Yet he too had been a fit and healthy man. Cario also told me that he seems to have disappeared completely.'

'So you think there may be a link between Gryton's death and the sergeant feigning an illness and then absconding, perhaps?'

'Such things are possible, as you know. That is why I have been studying these cases that Gryton was investigating. So far, I have seen that he had mainly investigated and dealt with petitions from various people in the city, from the Greek, Egyptian and the Jewish communities, but then things suddenly stopped ahead of his death. Perhaps that is a sign that he was feeling unwell with whatever disease the gods sent him, or…'

'Or what, my lord?'

'That he was working on something else, or preoccupied elsewhere. Pollio the head clerk assures me that he had no other files, so it is perhaps just a case of him being unwell.' Hanufer reached for his cup and, inserting the straw, took some more beer. Then, changing the subject, he asked, 'What is your impression of the constables, Sabu?'

'Well, sir, I can say that having given them a good workout on the parade ground this morning, they are by and large a fit and strong group of men. The two who came with us to the Temple of Poseidon the other day seem particularly solid and trustworthy. They had more or less been in charge lately, because they are the most popular. Pylyp is the more mature, but Filemon has a sharp eye. I was going to wait a bit and then probably suggest to you that we advance them to become corporals, sir. On the other hand, I have also spotted two or three others who seem lazy and who I have seen passing glances between themselves. I think they may be the type who look askance at us.' He gave his boss a meaningful look. 'Shall I question them, my lord?'

Suddenly, from the direction of the Great Harbour came a clamour of drums, trumpets and horns. The noise was continuous and shortly added to by the shouting of a gathering crowd.

Some minutes later there was a knock on the door, and Cario entered at Hanufer's command.

'It is Admiral Patroclus and his fleet, my lord. He returns and they are blowing trumpets. It seems that the fleet have been victorious against the Seleucids in their attacks against their fleet along the coast of Asia Minor.'

News of the fleet's victories spread around Alexandria as if the Greek god Hermes and the Egyptian god Thoth had worked together and whispered in the ears of every man, woman and child. But as well as this news, which was received by the royal family with great celebration, came the announcement that Admiral Patroclus had captured the criminal poet, Sotades the Obscene, locked him in a leaded jar and cast him into the sea.

Pharaoh Ptolemy Philadelphus issued a proclamation that a sacred bull would be sacrificed to Poseidon that evening, when the city would give thanks to the god for giving them victory, for bringing the fleet back safely, and for accepting the miserable poet Sotades into his watery kingdom.

A messenger from the pharaoh's vizier, Admiral Patroclus, whom Hanufer had not yet met, ordered him to arrange for the security of the procession, since the whole city was expected to celebrate it. As Hanufer and Sabu started to make preparations, Hanufer had two thoughts.

Firstly, he looked forward to seeing the priestess Nefrit, if only at a distance. Secondly, he felt he would have to learn more about this poet Sotades and why his drowning should be such a cause for celebration.

Admiral Patroclus was ushered into the lesser throne room in the western wing of the Royal Palace, which Ptolemy Philadelphus reserved for private audiences. The pharaoh sat upon his throne with Queen Arsinoe on her smaller one beside him.

As royal protocol dictated, the vizier entered and walked to the foot of the small dais, his helmet under his arm. He prostrated himself before crawling up the steps to kiss the toes of both pharaoh and queen. That done, further formalities were dropped and he was permitted to stand before them.

'Well, Patroclus, we hear your mission was a great success. The Seleucids have been crushed?'

'Their fleet was no match for us, Your Majesty. But Antiochus Soter will regroup and plot further. As you know, he and Antigonus Gonatas of Macedon are allied and cannot be underestimated.'

'But not for some time, is that correct?'

'Yes, Your Majesty.' The vizier was aware that the balance of power in the area was fragile, but he had to be careful of how he framed that fragility to the pharaoh.

'And did you encounter any trouble from our other neighbours? The Mycenaeans, the Macedonians or even, so help me, my half-brother King Magas of his little kingdom of Cyrene?'

'I saw small numbers of ships, Your Majesty, but they amounted to no more than pirate bands. They would not dare engage with us.'

Ptolemy Philadelphus roared with laughter. 'Pirate bands, I like that. What say you, sister-wife? Do you think our big step-brother King Magas would like to be called a pirate king?'

Arsinoe yawned, as if the audience thus far bored her. 'You know he would hate it, Ptolemy.'

The pharaoh and his vizier talked for some more minutes about the relative strengths and weaknesses of the nations of the Levant and of Egypt's naval supremacy.

Arsinoe suddenly sat forward. 'Enough of this. Tell us what we really need to know. Is that bastard man Sotades dead?'

Both the pharaoh and the vizier were taken aback by the anger in her voice.

'He is no more, Your Majesty. The fish of the deep will have fed on his bloated carcass by now. I had with me the soothsayer and poet Diomedes. He is going to compose a poem and in a few days he will present it to Your Majesties.' He smiled as he thought of the statue that the sculptor Hecataeus was going to bring to court. 'And when he does, there will be another gift for you both. I will, if I may, keep that a secret for now.'

Queen Arsinoe shrugged her shoulders dismissively and rose. 'Another poet!' she said petulantly.

She descended from the dais, forcing the vizier to shuffle backwards so that he stumbled and had to save himself from an undignified tumble onto his back. Without looking further at him, she walked past.

'Sotades was all I needed to know about,' she said as she walked towards the door of the throne room, which was instantly opened at the sound of her approach.

As the door closed behind her, Ptolemy clapped his hands and laughed heartily. 'Despite her manner, my sister-wife is grateful, Patroclus. As am I, so this evening we shall sacrifice a bull in thanks for your safe return and success. And soon, you will be installed as my high priest of the cult of Alexander.'

Admiral Patroclus bowed low. 'You are too kind, Your Majesty.'

# CHAPTER 9

Alexandria seemed aflame after nightfall. The sky overhead was a vault bedecked by the stars, each said to be a pharaoh that had passed into the afterlife.

The great beacon of the lighthouse on the tip of the Island of Pharos cast beams over the city from a great burnished bronze mirror in the chamber beneath the statue of Alexander, just as it sent out powerful rays seawards. Beneath it the great torchlight procession began at the Royal Palace and moved with much trumpeting and drumming south down the Street of the Soma and thence along the Canopic Way, before taking a circuitous route back to the Temple of Poseidon.

Hanufer had stationed his constables along the route and he and Sabu walked ahead of the procession, on opposite sides of the wide streets. A pace or two behind Hanufer walked Cario, ready when asked by his master to give him information about the members of the procession.

All the way along the streets citizens were gathered to cheer the throng as it passed. At the front of the long parade was the sacred bull, its head in a huge gilded yoke and its body covered with garlands, led by Behdet the Keeper of Animals of the Temple of Poseidon. He held a rope that was tied through a ring in the beast's nose. Together they walked with a strange dignity — Behdet with a proud, upright posture, his young, muscular body oiled and glistening in the flickering torchlight. It was only if any looked at his face closely that they would have spied the tears that ran down his cheeks. The bull lumbered a pace behind him, presumably blissfully unaware of the fate in store for it, or of the great bronze, double-headed axe that Kleitos the high priest of Poseidon who walked behind it carried over his shoulder. It would be his task to stun the bull with a blow to its skull at the start of the ceremony, before slitting its throat to let its lifeblood escape. Then he and the other priests who followed would quickly disembowel and dismember its great body before the meat was thrown on the flames. The burning fat and smoke would ascend to the heavens and Poseidon, and then the cooked meat would be distributed in strict hierarchical order, from the pharaoh and his queen downwards.

Also walking on foot behind him came the basket bearer and the urn bearers, who were the highest priestesses from the various temples. The basket bearer had been given the greatest honour, for she carried the long knife that would be used in the ceremony to slit the throat of the beast and drain its blood on the altar in the *temenos*, the circular sacrificial arena reached by passing through the grove close to the Temple of Poseidon. This sacred area with its sacrificial altar was used by several of the temples dedicated to the different gods, both Greek and Egyptian, but did not belong to any. It was a special sanctified place that was used only for this purpose, since no animals were ever to be slaughtered within the sacred space of a temple.

Behind them came the lesser priests, who would not be taking any direct part, but who carried images of their gods to show support for the great sacrifice that was to be given to Poseidon. And after them came the musicians, praise-singers, dancers and temple slaves, many with facemasks of animals or of minor gods, or with their own faces painted in caricatures of the emotions.

Hanufer stopped at the entrance to the Emporium, the great marketplace, as the procession then passed the Musaeum and the Library. He watched Behdet leading the bull, which seemed none the worse for the wounds it had received some days before.

'Look! That is the Lady Bilistiche, my lord,' whispered Cario, as a woman walked by with grace, holding a large basket on her head. Hanufer followed his subtly pointing finger and saw the now famous charioteer, courtesan and basket bearer. Most significantly, she was one of Ptolemy Philadelphus's two mistresses.

'The basket is full of barley, my lord,' the slave explained. 'It conceals the long knife that will be used to slit the beast's throat.'

Hanufer nodded thanks, but then he suddenly spotted Nefrit. She was one of several female urn bearers, carrying water specially blessed for the ceremony. His heart seemed to quicken as he watched her, because she saw him. As their eyes locked, she smiled and nodded her head to acknowledge his presence as she walked on with the others.

A moment later Hanufer felt another tap on the shoulder from Cario. 'And there is the Lady Didyme,' he whispered, pointing equally covertly to another courtesan and priestess, the other mistress of the pharaoh.

When he had taken Sabu and Hanufer on their tour of the city, Cario had told them about the rumours that surrounded the pharaoh's mistresses. The tall, athletic-looking Lady Bilistiche was said to be born either a barbarian princess or was an Argive, from Argos on the Peloponnese, while Didyme was said to be a noblewoman of Nubia. Now Hanufer could see them at relatively close quarters, he could tell that they were both strikingly beautiful women, but totally different. Bilistiche had almost alabaster-pale skin and blonde hair, whereas Didyme was black and sultry-looking.

Behind them came the royal guards and then in a chariot drawn by two white stallions came Admiral Patroclus, the hero who was being honoured by a sacrifice to Poseidon, and whom a royal proclamation had confirmed was to be given the title of high priest of the cult of Alexander at a later procession. This, in addition to being the pharaoh's vizier, would make him the second most powerful man in all of Egypt. And he looked powerful, too. Tall, muscular, with a well-groomed black beard.

'He bears a fitting name for a hero, does he not, my lord?' Cario whispered as the chariot rumbled past them. 'You could imagine him as a friend to the mighty Achilles.'

Hanufer nodded. 'Yet in *The Iliad*, the great work by Homer, he has a tragic fate. It is my task and that of the police to ensure that no harm befalls him. And more importantly, those who are following him.'

He nodded in the direction of the great war chariot that followed Patroclus. This was drawn by four white stallions and was driven by Pharaoh Ptolemy Philadelphus himself. Standing beside him in it was Queen Arsinoe the Second.

Hanufer nodded to Cario and they walked on, keeping pace with the chariot as they moved past the crowds who were cheering, then bowing as the two chariots passed by them. Behind the chariots came more guards.

Eventually, the procession turned into the grove, towards the *temenos*, where the crowd was only permitted to filter around the perimeter in order to watch the ceremony. Behdet entered and then stopped with the bull. He stood leaning his head against the great bull's head as he whispered soothing words in its ear.

Kleitos laid his great axe on the ground and raised his arms. Almost immediately, the music and drumming stopped. He pointed towards the altar, which had been specially whitewashed for the occasion. It was a large, circular wall which contained a pyre with a grid on top of it. In front of it could be seen a large pile of extra wood to fuel the pyre.

'Urn bearers, go and anoint the altar,' he ordered. 'Torch bearers go too, and light the pyre.'

Then, turning, he signalled for those following him to move apart so that the two chariots could advance into the *temenos*.

Hanufer watched intently, for one of the urn bearers was Nefrit.

'Behdet, bring the sacrificial beast closer,' Kleitos commanded.

The Keeper of Animals whispered to the bull, gently tugged the rope and then advanced.

Cario leaned close to Hanufer. 'They will light the fire, so it will be blazing by the time the bull is killed and butchered. The priest will probably take out its liver and its organs to see if the gods have sent any message. The first urn bearers will anoint the altar, and then one will pour a libation over the bull's head. That will almost certainly be the Lady Didyme, the pharaoh's mistress. That libation will make it nod its head, always a sure sign that the beast is ready to be sacrificed to the gods. Then the priest will stun the bull with his axe and then use the knife that the basket bearer, the Lady Bilistiche, is carrying in her basket disguised as an offering. He will slit its throat and then he and other priests will butcher it while its heart still beats. Once they have —'

Suddenly, as the urn bearers reached the altar, they turned and screamed out. Kleitos spun round and saw them gesticulating for him as the torch bearers held their lights aloft on either side of the altar. He walked quickly towards them.

'What is the meaning of this?' he demanded of one of the urn bearers who had reached the altar ahead of Nefrit. She was a young Greek woman who was pointing to a large metal jar on the ground in front of the altar, which had not been visible because of the pile of wood placed there to fuel the pyre.

Kleitos looked into the great jar and made a strange spluttering sound, and then turned and ran towards the chariots of Patroclus and the royal couple.

'There has been sacrilege, Your Majesty. We ... we cannot make a sacrifice. Someone has left ... *eels*.'

Hanufer detached himself from the crowd and came forward. 'Show me what is the problem, Kleitos,' he ordered.

The priest looked hesitantly at Hanufer and then at the vizier in his chariot over the heads of his stallions.

Patroclus immediately jumped down from his chariot, barely able to conceal his anger. He strode towards the altar, Hanufer and Kleitos walking quickly after him.

The pharaoh also dismounted from his chariot and followed them, protectively surrounded by his guards.

'There, my ... my lord,' stammered Kleitos, pointing to the large metal jar. 'It ... it is full of eels. Dead eels, my lord.'

Hanufer knelt down by the jar. The jar was a cubit tall and full of dead eels, as the priest had said. But they were not just dead; their tails had been shoved into their mouths, so they formed macabre circles.

'The altar and the *temenos* have been desecrated. We cannot make a sacrifice,' cried out the flustered Kleitos.

But Hanufer was not looking at the eels any longer. He was examining the whitewashed wall of the altar. Upon it in what seemed to be blood or some sort of red dye were three hieroglyphs, and below that a couple of lines in Greek.

'There is writing here, my Lord Patroclus,' he said, straightening up and pointing to it.

Ptolemy Philadelphus had reached them, and he and Patroclus bent to look at the hieroglyphs and the writing on the altar.

*In the land of the Nile where dogs are gods,*
*A king stuck his prick in an unholy hole.*
*In that unholy hole a king's prick stuck,*
*Where gods are dogs to the vile of the land.*

Ptolemy and Patroclus stared at the writing and then at each other.

'Sotades the Obscene!' Ptolemy Philadelphus said through gritted teeth. 'You said you dealt with him.'

'Your Majesty, I ... I did,' the admiral protested.

But the pharaoh had turned and stomped purposefully off to his chariot and his anxiously waiting queen. A few moments later she yelled in rage. The pharaoh urged their horses onwards and the chariot did a rapid circle of the *temenos*, going right around the altar, causing all in their way to scurry for safety. The guards started to run in disciplined unison after the royal chariot.

Patroclus himself was seething with rage. He turned on Kleitos with eyes blazing. Without warning, he dealt the priest a backhanded blow across the face.

Then, turning to Hanufer, he glared. 'You must be the new Overseer of Police?'

Hanufer bowed. 'I am, my lord.' He braced himself in anticipation of receiving a similar blow.

But it did not come. Instead, Admiral Patroclus growled, 'Come to the vizier's office in the Royal Palace at the first hour after daybreak. Tell the guards you come to see Admiral

Patroclus.' He turned and walked away, looking over his shoulder to add, 'The pharaoh and I will have words with you.'

As the abandoned procession retraced its steps, Hanufer looked again at the writing on the altar, but he could not see it clearly enough. He ordered Sabu to get Pylyp and Filemon, the two constables whom Sabu considered the most trustworthy, to stand guard by the altar and let no one close to it until he returned the next morning. Then he instructed Cario to take the jar of eels to his office and also stand guard over it until he could view first the altar and then the jar by daylight.

'Also, Cario, see to it that both Pylyp and Filemon receive food and drink before daylight,' he commanded.

The procession had dispersed by the time that Hanufer looked around for Nefrit, and he was disappointed to see that she too had melted away with the crowd.

Behdet the Keeper of Animals had remained at the entrance to the *temenos* with the sacrificial bull as Kleitos had instructed him, until he was told that Hanufer had no further need for him. Kleitos had said to tell Hanufer that he had gone, because he thought his nose had been broken. One of the other priests had also been told to remain and held a torch overhead.

Behdet was stroking the head of the sacred bull and whispering in its ear.

'Can you keep him subdued and occupied enough for me to look at his wounds?' the Overseer of Police asked.

'Apis will not move if I talk to him, my lord. Just please do not actually touch him. He may kick out otherwise, and a kick from him could kill a man.'

Hanufer was in no doubt about the bull's power, having seen the trampled, broken body of the unknown slave. He gingerly approached the bull's buttocks while Sabu took the torch from the priest and held it at the best angle for his boss to see.

It took but a few moments for Hanufer to see that the seven small wounds, puncture marks all covered in Behdet's salve, had almost healed.

'Return to the temple and let Apis enjoy his pen,' he told the Keeper of Animals.

Behdet sighed with relief and bowed, his face creased by a beaming smile upon learning that the bull had been reprieved, if only temporarily.

As he led the bull away, walking with the priest who had been given his torch back, Hanufer nudged Sabu and pointed to the strange shadow created by the flickering flames. For a few moments, part of the shadow looked like a man with the head of a bull.

'My lord, it … it looks like the god Apis!' Sabu exclaimed with awe. 'Is it a sign from our gods?'

'Maybe, sir,' whispered Cario. 'But perhaps not Egyptian gods. That shadow is more like our legendary Minotaur of Crete.'

'Who was this Minotaur, Cario?' Sabu asked.

'He was a creature, a son of Queen Pasiphae, the wife of King Minos. He had been sired by a white bull that the Greek god Poseidon sent Minos to be sacrificed in his name, but the king kept it as part of his own herd, then sent another bull to be sacrificed. Poseidon was furious about being tricked and punished King Minos by making his wife fall in love with the bull. The child of that union was a monster, the Minotaur who was born with the head of a bull.'

Hanufer nodded. 'I have read of this Minotaur. He was forced to live in a labyrinth on Crete.'

'And what is a labyrinth, my lord?' Sabu asked.

'A maze. A sort of puzzle,' Hanufer replied. 'King Minos had it made and fourteen young men and women were sent as sacrifices to the Minotaur each year.'

Cario nodded. 'You have studied our legends well, my lord. Do you think that perhaps the gods, both Egyptian and Greek, are playing with us, sir?'

'Or someone is,' replied Hanufer as the coalesced shadow broke up into that of a man leading a bull. 'But I fear this is not a game.'

Later, in a hall in one of the great villas in the Brucheum, three people sat drinking wine by the flickering light of several oil lamps.

'You are sure that none saw you come here?' one demanded of the others.

'None saw us, Magnificence. We are used to being discreet.'

'But less used to being careful, it seems!'

The man shrugged. 'He was a liability. He would have had to be eliminated at some stage.'

'It is true,' agreed the third person. 'After the other one, we took the necessary steps and we covered the killing.'

'What of this new *Archiphylakites* and his *Hyparchiphylakites* that you told me about?'

'There will be no problem. They are just Egyptians.'

The cup of wine was halfway to the questioner's lips. 'Careful! And never show disrespect like that again. You could reveal yourself.'

'I meant all was taken care of, just as it was this evening. Everything was done as you wanted. And it worked just as you said. The pharaoh and his whore and their lapdog sailor went off like dogs with their tails between their legs.'

'They all have blood on their hands and they will pay for what was done to me.'

'Will it all still work, now that the Trojan Horse is —'

'If you do as I say, everything will come to pass. First we have to make them fear me.'

'Which makes it imperative that they don't find you.'

'So there will be no mistakes. None of us or any of our powerful friends can afford that.'

The cup of wine was raised again, this time as a toast. 'To the next stage and to success.'

They laughed and then they all drank.

# CHAPTER 10

Hanufer had little appetite to break his fast the following morning, having slept poorly. The upcoming meeting with the vizier, Admiral Patroclus, filled him with some trepidation, since the abandonment of the sacrifice had been a disaster and a humiliation. Pharaoh Ptolemy Philadelphus and Queen Arsinoe had both been as furious as the vizier, so he anticipated recriminations, and some form of punishment was not out of the question.

Sabu was waiting for him in the garden at daybreak as they had arranged the night before.

'I still cannot understand why that jar of fish should have caused such outrage, my lord,' Sabu said as they walked to the Royal Palace.

'They were eels, not fish. I had not realised, but Cario explained to me that in the religion of the Greeks eels are considered an insult to the gods. It is a strange thing that although they consider eels good enough to eat, and indeed good enough to leave as an offering to the gods — just as we Egyptians leave offerings every morning to our gods — as a sacrifice eels are thought to be an insult.'

'And the writing, my lord? Some sort of insult, you told me.'

'Not just an insult, Sabu, but seemingly a message. I do not fully understand it, but the pharaoh himself said the name Sotades.'

'The poet they were all talking about yesterday? The one the whole city seemed to be pleased that the admiral had executed?'

'It seems so. I am sure that I will discover more when I see the vizier this morning. But one thing is clear, Sabu.'

'My lord?'

'Not everyone was happy about the death of the poet. One person at least was sending a message.'

As they reached the gates to the Royal Palace complex, where two heavily armed guards were standing either side, Sabu pointed to the shade of a nearby palm tree.

'Shall I wait here for you, sir?'

Hanufer thought for a moment and then shook his head. 'No, I want you to start making investigations. I want to know more about the pharaoh's mistresses, the Lady Bilistiche and the Lady Didyme. I want you to find out where they live, how they live, and what their servants are willing to tell you about them.'

'And I am to do this discreetly, my lord?' Sabu asked with a wink.

Hanufer reached into his chiton and took out a purse. He tossed it to his sergeant.

'Discreetly, as an interested traveller with money rather than as a sergeant of the *phylakitai*. Meet me outside the *temenos* in about two hours from now. I imagine that I may have a lengthy meeting with the Admiral Patroclus.'

Hanufer barely had time to look around the sumptuous office of the vizier with its huge ebony desk and chair, where he had been shown by a clerk, before a bead curtain was roughly parted and Admiral Patroclus strode in with an armful of scrolls. He was dressed in a blue chiton with a white chlamys over it. With a nondescript grunt at Hanufer, he tossed the scrolls onto the desk.

*Now I am to be castigated for my failure*, Hanufer thought.

But instead, the vizier merely stared at him for a moment and then gave a resigned smile. 'We did not meet under the best of circumstances, Hanufer. I should have welcomed you as the new *Archiphylakites*. But I was distracted by the sacrilege to say the least.'

Hanufer felt a slight relief at the words and bowed respectfully. 'It was totally understandable, my lord. I saw that —'

'We will talk about what you saw in a few moments, to Pharaoh Ptolemy and Queen Arsinoe themselves. It is the time for my morning audience with the pharaoh, and today Ptolemy and Queen Arsinoe want to see us both. You will understand they are angry — and deeply concerned over this outrage!'

Hanufer swallowed hard. He had expected that his meeting with the vizier might be challenging, but he had not expected to have an audience with the royal couple so soon after his appointment — especially when they were angry.

He followed the vizier along the wide, colonnaded marble corridors, passing through several doors attended by armed guards. Within them he saw scribes and clerks busily working away, presumably organising the working of not only the city of Alexandria, but the whole of Egypt. From these offices, the edicts from the pharaoh and of the vizier were sent to the nomarchs of the country by messengers travelling on horse, camel and down the Nile by boat.

Finally, they entered the lesser throne room where the pharaoh and his queen were sitting enthroned on a dais with seven steps. They were both dressed in white and silver; the pharaoh with his *hedjet*, the conical white crown of Upper Egypt, but without the long ceremonial *postiche*, the false beard that he'd worn at Hanufer's installation as *Archiphylakites*. In its place was a small actual beard that protruded a thumb's length from the tip of his chin. The queen had her hair in a silver hairnet, with a simple silver band over her forehead. Three more guards with swords and spears stood motionless on each side of the throne room.

Hanufer followed the admiral's lead and prostrated himself on the floor at the foot of the steps in front of the royal couple. As Patroclus was about to crawl up the steps, the pharaoh clapped his hands.

'Stand and be at your ease, Admiral Patroclus and Overseer Hanufer,' he said. 'We seek answers for this outrage.'

Both men stood. 'Your Majesty, I beg that —' Hanufer began, only to be cut short as the pharaoh raised his hand.

'One moment, Overseer Hanufer. It is our friend Patroclus that we wish to hear from.' Ptolemy turned to his vizier. 'You assured us that you had executed the poet, Sotades the Obscene?'

Patroclus bowed his head. 'I did, Your Majesty. I sealed him in a large pithos jar, which was filled with lead ingots. He was manacled at his feet and tossed into the waves after he continued to hurl insults at myself and at Diomedes. Diomedes had accompanied the fleet as a soothsayer, but also with the intention of recording our victories in poetic form for Your Majesty.' He glanced hesitantly at Queen Arsinoe, then added, 'And Sotades was again insulting about both of Your Majesties, and about the gods. More than that, he bragged that he had said the same to Lysimachus of Thrace when he was still alive, and Demetrius in Macedon, and to Seleucus Nicator, when he was court poet in all of their realms.'

Queen Arsinoe leaned forward. 'I had heard his despicable rantings when I was married to Lysimachus. So tell me, what did he say of me? Was it the same sort of insults as before?'

The admiral nodded. 'He repeated the obscenity, and seemed proud to do so, Your Majesty.'

'You saw him drown?' she asked, her beautiful face showing some anxiety.

'I did. I watched the bubbles with Diomedes. He had bragged that he could swim like an Olympian, but I assure you Poseidon himself would have been hard put to struggle free and swim with such weight dragging him quickly to the bottom of the sea.'

Ptolemy reached out a hand to his queen, who grasped it as they smiled lovingly at each other.

'Do you know how I came by my name, Hanufer of Crocodilopolis?' the pharaoh asked with a rapid change of subject.

'I do, Your Majesty. It is because you and Her Majesty were born of the same parents. Philadelphus means "friend of his siblings." I understand that your subjects started to use this name and —'

'And we liked it, so I kept it as my official name,' Ptolemy anticipated, again squeezing the queen's hand and smiling at her. 'To marry one's brother or sister is not the Greek way, but since my father became pharaoh of Egypt our family has adopted Egyptian ways, even though you will perceive that we also retain some of the Greek way of life. Both I and my sister-wife were brought up in this palace and I have lived virtually all of my life in Alexandria. We are thus the embodiment of Egypt and are proud of our marriage in the Egyptian tradition.'

Hanufer bowed. 'Indeed, and I am sure that the whole of Egypt is proud that you have adopted the ways of our great land. Many of our gods have had such marriages and it is upon them that we model our lives. Shu and Tefnut, Geb and Nut,

Osiris and Isis, and even Seth and Nephthys, they all wed as brother and sister.'

His mind immediately took him back to the conversation he'd had with Manetho at Judge Thespos's home about the god Seth, the trickster, the spreader of disorder and violence.

And again in his mind's eye he saw the lovely Nefrit, the priestess of Isis looking demurely at him during that discussion.

'But Seth is not a god to revere,' Queen Arsinoe said, instantly bringing Hanufer's mind back to the present.

Hanufer immediately bowed his head. 'Your Majesties, I meant no offence by mentioning the god Seth.'

'Seth is to be placated, sister-wife,' Ptolemy said, patting Arsinoe's hand. 'We must be aware of his power and his temperamental nature. We must still venerate him in order to curb his temper and stop his ravages. After all, it was Seth who murdered his brother Osiris.'

'And Isis bandaged his body and restored him to life with her magic,' Hanufer volunteered. Once again, his mind conjured up an image of Nefrit.

*Stop thinking of the priestess of Isis*, he chided himself. *I must concentrate on what the royal couple are saying.*

Queen Arsinoe stared intently at him for a moment, and Hanufer wondered whether she had somehow detected that his mind had wandered. Then she spoke.

'As our Overseer of Police, your work must be to protect our people from evil Seth. It is not beyond him to try to attack or kill Isis herself.'

*Great Sobek preserve us, the queen must indeed be able to read what is in my mind*, Hanufer thought, striving hard to imagine the crocodile-headed god in order to stop thinking of the priestess of Isis.

'You must find whoever committed this crime,' Arsinoe continued, still staring hard at him, her voice rising in volume as she spoke through slightly gritted teeth. 'I need to know that Sotades, Seth's creature, is truly dead.'

Ptolemy placed both his hands on the queen's. 'Hush, my love. Sotades can do no more harm. We will see that the perpetrator of this outrage is found and punished. You are getting overwrought by it, so I think it would be a good thing to have the protection of Isis. I will arrange for the priestess to come to the Temple of Isis in the Brucheum to say prayers with you.' Turning to Hanufer, the pharaoh asked, 'Do you know how the poet Sotades insulted our royal persons?'

Hanufer nodded. 'I do, Your Majesty. I have been told that he wrote an obscene and traitorous poem about your persons.'

'Sotades was the very image of Seth,' Queen Arsinoe went on, her voice now lowered, the expression of revulsion on her beautiful face emphasising how upset she still was. 'He had red hair like Seth and he spewed obscenities everywhere. His poem insulted both my brother-husband and myself. He also insulted Egypt.'

The queen suddenly seemed full of spite. Hanufer had heard that she had been married to King Lysimachus and he had heard rumours that she could be ruthless. He made a mental note to discover more about this.

Yet the pharaoh, the most powerful of men, in his attempt to mollify her gave the impression that he was a totally devoted husband. It made Hanufer wonder how true that was, since two of his mistresses had been very prominent in the procession the night before. He wondered how Queen Arsinoe regarded the two women who had a part to play in her brother-husband's life and who obviously shared a bed with him on occasions.

Patroclus gave a slight cough, drawing attention to himself. 'I assure you Sotades is no more, Your Majesty.'

'Then what happened last evening?' Queen Arsinoe asked coldly, sitting back in her throne. 'My brother-husband tells me that there were dead eels in a metal jar and the poem was written in red ink or dye on the altar, along with Egyptian hieroglyphs. Was it the same poem?'

Patroclus nodded. 'From the cursory reading I gave it, it appears so, Your Majesty.'

'Then someone committed this outrage and insulted both my queen and I,' agreed the pharaoh. 'Hanufer of Crocodilopolis, I task you to find out all that happened and uncover whoever committed this sacrilege. I want to be kept informed of your progress.'

'I will begin my investigations straight away, Your Majesty,' Hanufer replied.

Turning again to his vizier, the pharaoh asked, 'And you are in no doubt that the dog Sotades is dead?'

'Poseidon himself will have taken his soul and the fish of the deep will have fed on his flesh, Your Majesty.'

Queen Arsinoe stared at the vizier for a moment and then tapped her brother-husband's wrist. 'In which case there is no need for a further sacrifice, is there, My Pharaoh?'

'I shall consider this, my sister-wife. Yet there is still a need to officially install Patroclus as the high priest of the cult of Alexander at the opening of the new Temple.'

The vizier bowed. 'Your Majesty is too kind to bestow this honour upon me.'

Ptolemy gave the merest of nods and suddenly rose from his throne, holding his hand out to his sister-wife. 'Come, sister-wife. I will take you to our royal apartment, and there you will drink and wash the bitter taste of Sotades and this outrage from your mouth. I will send for the priestess of Isis, and when she arrives you will say prayers with her.'

Again turning to Patroclus and Hanufer, he said, 'I would like you two to walk with me and see my zoo. Meet me there when the shadow on the obelisk reaches the next mark.'

Both men bowed and, keeping their heads down, backed away as the royal couple descended from their dais hand in hand.

It seemed that the pharaoh wanted to talk privately with them.

# CHAPTER 11

Judge Thespos had told Hanufer that Ptolemy Philadelphus was exceptionally proud of his zoo, which occupied a vast area within the Royal Palace enclosure. The citizens of Alexandria were not permitted to enter, of course, but many of the animals and birds were seen whenever there was a major procession to celebrate one or other of the festivals. The old pharaoh, Ptolemy Soter, had been against the extravagance of such processions. Ptolemy Philadelphus, however, avowed that such displays to the gods and to the citizens were great symbols of the throne's dedication to Egypt, as well as serving to show the world their power and wealth.

'Poets write of these processions, my lord,' Cario had told him and Sabu when he had guided them around the city. 'And poets travel around the world reciting these poems. Truly, poets are the mouthpieces of the gods.'

Sabu had sneered at that, just as he generally took a much more down-to-earth view of life, but Hanufer thought that Cario was a young man of considerable intelligence and talent. It seemed unkind that the gods should have willed for him to be a slave.

Hanufer had heard the noises from the zoo from his villa, but he was intrigued and more than a little excited to walk with the pharaoh and see the royal zoo for himself. While they awaited the pharaoh's arrival, Patroclus explained that Ptolemy had many intellectual interests, which was why the Musaeum, the Library, Medical School and the zoo all had his patronage. Expeditions were sent out to all corners of the world, to Kush, to Punt, the deserts to the east and to the south, in search of the most unusual and the wildest of creatures. The small army of animal handlers who fed, exercised and looked after them were all experts in the creatures under their care.

'Each of my beauties is treated like a king or a queen,' Ptolemy explained as he led Patroclus and Hanufer around the great zoo, followed at several paces by two armed guards. 'I wanted to talk without Queen Arsinoe being present. The poet Sotades was a mongrel and he insulted us both. He called me a prick, a cock.'

The pharaoh's use of these terms in such a matter-of-fact manner surprised Hanufer, but he knew it was prudent to make no reaction unless Patroclus led the way.

'Worse, he called the queen a whore. He said I, the royal prick, got stuck in her unholy hole. I sentenced him to death for that, but I had wanted him to fester in jail for some years first. So when he escaped it angered me, and had Patroclus brought him back alive I was contemplating having him impaled on a stake, in his own unholy hole.'

Patroclus coughed apologetically. 'I thought the moment right when he started bragging about his ability to swim, Your Majesty.'

Ptolemy shrugged. 'He has gone, that is all that matters. Yet after last night, are you sure that he hasn't actually survived? Could he have somehow freed himself and swum here?'

Patroclus snorted with mirth, then immediately apologised for his presumption. 'He would have had to have swum as fast as a trireme, Your Majesty. No, he is no more.'

'Good, in that case you should know I am going to have another great procession, to mark the birth of Divine Alexander. That is when you, Patroclus, will be installed as the high priest of the new cult of Alexander, and that is when we shall make another sacrifice. An appropriate sacrifice. A horse, yes, let it be a horse for Alexander.'

Patroclus bowed. 'I am most grateful, Your Majesty. But such an honour —'

'Such an honour is what you deserve. I shall tell my sister-wife.' He walked on, beckoning them to follow. 'This is partly why I wanted you both here. We shall be having a far grander procession than last night, and I want to show all of my beauties.'

Patroclus looked hesitantly at the pharaoh. 'When do you plan this, Your Majesty? A major procession will take much time to organise —'

Ptolemy Philadelphus shook a hand. 'There is always time if I say so, and you can get your minions to arrange it. Now come, let me show you.'

Hanufer glanced at Patroclus and saw his jaw muscles tighten, a sign of exasperation or irritation, or both. They followed the pharaoh.

The zoo had been beautifully planned, meandering through sycamores and various types of palms and all sorts of lush groves that showed that it was not merely creatures that Ptolemy had sent expeditions out to procure, but also plants from all corners of his empire.

He showed them lions, hippopotami, zebras and giraffes in their enclosures. Monkeys and baboons in huge roped cages, birds of many types from the ibis to the flamingo and all of the many hawks of Egypt, as well as pools in which crocodiles and other aquatic and mud-living creatures dwelt.

'Observe also that at each there is a shrine to the god that looks after them and whose image he or she sometimes takes on.'

As they walked through the groves, he pointed to various shrines with small anthropomorphic figures by each enclosure or cage. 'See, there is Sekhmet the lion, Ipy the hippopotamus, Thoth who is sometimes a baboon and sometimes the sacred ibis, and Horus the hawk. There, Hathor, the cow goddess and here,' he said, stopping and pointing to a large empty paddock, 'here there should be Minos, the bull.'

'You named him after the King of Crete, Your Majesty?' Hanufer asked.

'I did. If you know the legends of the Greeks, you will know about the Minotaur.'

Hanufer suppressed a smile as he recalled his conversation with Cario after the procession. He nodded. 'Indeed, Your Majesty. The Minotaur was the son of the Cretan Bull sent to Minos by Poseidon.'

Ptolemy laughed. 'My old tutor liked to tell me all of these old tales. I thought it a fine jest to name the bull after the bull-cuckolded king.'

'But the enclosure is bare, Your Majesty,' said Patroclus, pointing to the empty enclosure behind the Apis shrine.

'Sadly, the bull died last week,' the pharaoh replied.

'Might I make a suggestion, Your Majesty?' Hanufer ventured.

'Speak, Hanufer.'

'The bull that was to be sacrificed last night, Your Majesty. Queen Arsinoe said that perhaps a sacrifice would not be necessary.'

Almost as soon as he had said it Hanufer wished he had held his counsel, for he caught the angry flash in Patroclus's eyes.

The pharaoh stroked his small beard. 'And you suggest that the beast should replace the dead bull? It is an excellent idea,

Overseer Hanufer.' He turned to his vizier and nodded. 'See to it Patroclus.'

Risking further recriminations from the vizier, Hanufer continued, 'The bull has a keeper called Behdet, Your Majesty. He is attached to the Temple of Poseidon, but he has looked after that bull and he seems to have a special relationship with it.'

He wondered if he should mention the case of the slave that the bull had been urged to trample and disfigure, but decided to say nothing at this point. Keeping the animal alive and safe in the zoo might be useful if he felt the need to examine it further.

'Then Patroclus will also have him reassigned,' the pharaoh replied. 'The previous bull keeper did not look after Minos as well as he should, so he has already been dismissed and sent to the delta.'

Hanufer wondered if being sent to the delta was a pharaonic way of meaning something else. He did not yet know enough about Ptolemy Philadelphus to make any such judgement.

Suddenly the pharaoh laughed again, pointing out a shrine containing a figurine of a crocodile-headed man. 'And look, there is Sobek, especially for you, Overseer Hanufer.'

Both Patroclus and Hanufer dutifully laughed. Hanufer brushed a thumb over the ring bearing the image of his god and mentally acknowledged his own devotion, asking for help in his future investigations.

'Ha! He must know that you are a devotee, Hanufer,' the pharaoh said, pointing at the great creature in the pool that slowly turned its head in the water to stare at them, before equally slowly submerging for a moment, then resurfacing.

Hanufer bowed in the creature's direction, taking it as a sign that the god had heard his mental plea.

Ahead of them they saw several scholars in white himations sitting or leaning against enclosures, some making notes on ostraca, others making sketches or painting portraits of the animals and birds. As the pharaonic party approached, they all stood and made ready to bow low.

'These are my natural philosophers,' Ptolemy remarked, pointing to them as if they too were exotic animals in his zoo. 'They are permitted to study my beauties. They make discoveries all the time. Some even taught me when I was a boy.'

Passing through the academics, some of whom Hanufer had met at a Musaeum *syssitia* some days before, the pharaoh pointed to a grove of fig trees which surrounded a large, limestone, four-tiered building constructed like a stepped pyramid. When they reached it they saw a shrine on each side of the wide doorway. One figurine depicted an enthroned goddess with the head of a cobra. The other showed a great snake with compressed coils, poised as if about to strike out if anyone stood too close to the shrine.

'Renenutet, goddess of agriculture, fertility and protection,' mused Hanufer. 'And Apophis, the god of darkness and chaos. He who each night tries to subdue Ra, the sun god. Two interesting and very different deities, Your Majesty.'

The pharaoh smiled. 'Two opposites to venerate whatever is inside. Come, see the many wondrous creatures that I am proud to possess. You recognise the design of the building, I presume, Overseer Hanufer?'

'It is a smaller version of the ancient step pyramid of King Djoser, Your Majesty.'

Patroclus and Hanufer followed the pharaoh into the building, which was mainly in shadow, the light coming through the open doorway and from a central square opening in the roof.

An almost overpowering odour of musk greeted them as they entered. From behind, Hanufer heard the muttered complaints from the two armed guards as they stepped inside after them. It was evident that they did not relish being in the presence of whatever was inside the building.

As their eyes became accustomed to the shadowy interior they saw many cages, both large and small, around each wall, the gaps of which were very narrow, being formed from a latticework of woven wood or rope slats. Inside the cages on rocks or on tree branches they saw a beautiful array of different coloured snakes.

'In each of the layers of this step pyramid, which I call my King Djoser House, the surroundings have been adapted to the different types of land whence these snakes were brought. Desert, forest, mountains and swamp, my Keeper of Snakes looks after each of my beauties in comfort. And each is given the food that it would eat where it lived.'

Ptolemy led the way up steps to the next floor, where more reptiles could be seen, their cages and the contents reflecting the environments from which they had been captured. Then on the next level a deferential voice came out of the shadows. 'Your Majesty, welcome.' A moment later a man stepped towards them. In one hand he held a basket full of dead rats and in the other a snake stick.

'Weneg, I have brought my Vizier and my Overseer of Police to see your charges,' Ptolemy said to the man who had dropped to his knees before his pharaoh. As he did so he deftly held the basket and the stick to his sides, careful not to drop them or spill rat corpses.

Ignoring him, the pharaoh pointed around at the cages. 'You will have seen that as we have gone higher up my King Djoser House, the snakes have become larger. First we had asps and vipers and now cobras.'

Hanufer instinctively kept his hands at his sides and looked round at the various specimens. Magnificent though they undoubtedly were, with varying colours, different patterns of speckles, hooded or not, he was not over enthusiastic about getting close.

The sound of hissing from some of the cages made him yet more wary. 'Is ... is there not a danger of their bites, Your Majesty?'

The pharaoh pointed at Weneg. 'My Keeper of Snakes keeps them happy and our gods at the entrance keep them safe, is that not so, Weneg?'

The man had stood up, yet still appeared to be bent. He was shaven headed and naked except for a loincloth. It was obvious now that he had some malformation of his spine, which gave him a strangely appropriate stooping posture that was in itself quite serpent-like.

He bowed his head and gave a toothless grin. 'His Majesty is right. I look after them and I pray to the gods to keep them calm. A calm snake that does not feel under attack will not harm anyone.' He held up his stick. 'They know that Weneg will never harm them or let anyone hurt them.'

Ptolemy laughed and pointed to the steps leading up to the top level. 'Is Apophis well?'

'He is not very active, Your Majesty. He is approaching the time.'

The pharaoh nodded sagely. 'Then go first, Weneg, and let us show Vizier Patroclus and Overseer Hanufer my most precious pet, Apophis.'

Weneg deferentially sidled across the room to the steps and scuttled up them, still holding both his bucket of dead rats and his snake stick.

Ptolemy followed up the now narrow steps, with Patroclus and Hanufer coming after. Reaching the top level, Hanufer gasped and took a step backwards at the sight that greeted them. A gigantic rock python with distinctive olive, green and yellow blotches that joined up into irregular wide stripes, with a body the width of a tree trunk and a length that must have been four or five times as long as any snake he had ever seen before, was lying at the bottom of the cage, which contained large boulders and a pool of water.

Ptolemy laughed. 'Did my Apophis alarm you, Overseer Hanufer? Is he not incredible? He is the largest python that has ever been found. He is fully twenty cubits long.'

He waited while Hanufer made suitably impressed noises.

'He is a suitable pet for a great pharaoh,' said Patroclus.

Ptolemy favoured his vizier with a thin smile. 'I sent an expedition to distant Aethiopia, and two men lost their lives in attempting to capture him on a first occasion. Weneg was there, so tell them how you snared him.'

Weneg grinned and recounted the capture, for which they'd used rushes woven into a circular net like a fisherman's creel of the type used on the Nile by fishermen for centuries. There were archers, men with slingshots and even men on horseback. Over several weeks they had staked out the creature's lair and determined its feeding times, when it came out to hunt. Also, they marked the different holes through which it made its entrances and exits. When the time came, and they knew the creature was in its lair, they plugged its other entrance with boulders and dug a hole near the exit where they hid the creel trap. When it came out to feed, they let it pass and then blocked its hole. Then the archers and others diverted it, trumpeters and drummers made a din and it slithered back, but fell into the trap.

'On the journey back, which took many weeks, I soothed it and fed and nurtured it until it lost all wildness,' Weneg explained with glee. 'Now only I and the scholar can get close to it.'

'Is he approaching the time of shedding, Weneg?' Ptolemy asked.

'I think so, Your Majesty. He is a little more sluggish today and his skin started to change colour four days ago. That is a sure sign when they are getting ready to shed. If he would rise or turn a little, you would see that his belly has turned pink.' He pointed to the cage door. 'Shall I enter and show you, Your Majesty?'

Ptolemy shook his head. 'Let him rest. Has Philitas of Cos been here this morning?'

'He has, Your Majesty. He came early and spent an hour watching and whispering to Apophis. He is very keen to be here when the shedding begins.'

'Philitas of Cos is a most interesting and learned man,' Ptolemy said, turning to Hanufer. 'He was brought to Alexandria by my father and employed as my tutor. He taught me and Queen Arsinoe my sister-wife much of what we know, and he gave me a love of philosophy and all forms of learning. He is a poet, scholar and the man who knows more about natural philosophy than any man ever did, since the great Pythagoras himself. He has free access to my zoo and makes frequent study of every creature, from the smallest to the greatest.'

'I explained this to Hanufer, Your Majesty,' Patroclus said.

'Indeed, Your Majesty,' Hanufer agreed, although the vizier had made no such mention of Philitas of Cos.

'Philitas believes it should be possible to teach creatures to understand language,' Ptolemy explained. 'You should meet him. In fact, I had hoped that he would be here now.'

'To tell me about speaking with Apophis, Your Majesty?' Hanufer queried, feeling rather puzzled.

'No, to tell you of Sotades the Obscene. Among other things, Philitas of Cos is one of our finest poets and a great critic. He is the greatest grammarian there has ever been. He can tell you much about Sotades and his poetry, is that not so, Patroclus?'

'Indeed, Your Majesty,' the vizier replied after a moment's hesitation.

Once again, Hanufer noticed a look of exasperation that the vizier had been swift to hide. He had also formed the impression that the pharaoh was giving him a subtle message rather than a command.

# CHAPTER 12

Shortly afterwards, Hanufer sat in the chair opposite the vizier's grand ebony desk and waited while Patroclus poured two cups of palm wine.

'So, His Majesty's wishes are quite clear, Hanufer of Crocodilopolis. You must find who committed this crime against the royal couple and defiled the altar in the *temenos*.'

Hanufer inclined his head. 'Indeed, my lord. As I said to His Majesty, I shall begin my investigations straight away.' He reached forward and accepted the cup of palm wine. 'In fact, if you will permit it, I will begin by asking you some questions.'

Patroclus raised his cup and made a toast. 'May the gods help you in your quest. Ask what you will.'

'May the goddess Maat show me the truth,' Hanufer replied, raising his cup. He took a sip and then laid his drink on the edge of the desk. Reaching inside his chiton, he withdrew a piece of papyrus and his writing set. 'I will make some notes, if I may?'

Patroclus raised his cup again and nodded. Hanufer dipped a finger in his wine and dropped moisture onto the small ink cake on the thin sandalwood writing palette. Then he selected a reed pen and pensively applied ink to its point.

'I have only the sketchiest of information about the poet Sotades, but I shall remedy that as soon as possible. Pharaoh Ptolemy and Queen Arsinoe were obviously deeply insulted and wounded by his poem. You told His Majesty that the poem written on the altar seemed to be the one that Sotades had composed.'

Patroclus grunted assent. 'As far as I can remember. Virtually everyone in Alexandria knew of it. As you are undoubtedly aware, poems get recited and passed by word of mouth.'

'So, by that token, almost anyone in the city could have written that version upon the altar in the *temenos*?'

'If they could write, yes,' Patroclus agreed.

'When did Sotades write this poem, sir?'

'Several months ago, before you came to Alexandria. When Gryton the previous *Archiphylakites* was in charge.'

'Ah yes. The poor man died suddenly, while still relatively young?'

The vizier shrugged. 'The gods must have willed it.'

'Did he arrest Sotades?'

'He did. His Majesty had ordered that the dog should be thrown into prison. He should have been there even now, until His Majesty finally decided when to execute him. As you heard Pharaoh Ptolemy say, he had wanted him to suffer by festering in prison. Somehow the dog escaped.'

'Still, one cannot blame him for wanting to escape.'

Patroclus harrumphed. 'It was inconvenient of him to do so.'

Hanufer made notes in demotic, the written form of Egyptian that came naturally to him. He would transcribe it in Greek later on. 'Which prison was that, my lord?'

'The Necropolis prison, outside the city walls close to the City of the Dead. He escaped and somehow made his way to sea. Captain Nestor, the one who notified me, had not known that he had a stowaway onboard his ship. When he did discover him in his cargo of leopard skins, wine and timber, he diverted his journey from Crete to the Island of Caunus where a friend, a sculptor called Hecataeus, had a villa. They agreed that Hecataeus would hold Sotades prisoner until Nestor was able to direct authorities to the island to take him into custody again, or he would pick him up himself and take him back to Alexandria.'

The vizier sipped more wine while Hanufer wrote notes.

'I had Diomedes, a poet and soothsayer, on board my ship,' the vizier went on. 'As you heard me saying to Their Majesties, I had him accompany the fleet for his soothsaying skills and also with the intention that he would record our victories in poetic form for Pharaoh Ptolemy.'

'And was his soothsaying useful?'

'Obviously it was,' Patroclus replied curtly. 'After our great victorious assault on the coast of Syria, Diomedes received a message from the gods to go to Crete. We did and took the fleet to the naval base I had already built there two years hence. When the fleet laid anchors and we arranged supplies, this Captain Nestor came and told me about Sotades being on Caunus. Diomedes was right.'

'Can you recall exactly what the prophesy was, my lord? Did he say that Sotades would be in Crete?'

The vizier frowned. 'I cannot remember exactly. He said it was desirable that we should go to Crete.'

Hanufer made a note to interview this Diomedes fairly soon. He had never actually come across a soothsayer who gave precise, defined prophesies. It did not sound as though he had been given a direct message about Sotades. It may have been no more than a happy chance.

The vizier resumed his tale. 'So, I made for Caunus in my ship, having ordered the fleet to make their way slowly to Alexandria, but not to arrive before I re-joined them.'

'And as I understand it, you had Sotades tossed into the sea in a pithos jar weighed down with lead ingots?'

'That is so.'

'Was it Pharaoh Ptolemy's wish that you should drown him?'

Patroclus shrugged his shoulders. 'After Sotades escaped from Alexandria, His Majesty told me that if he was found I could use my discretion. He had been condemned to death already.'

'But did you do that? Use your discretion, I mean?'

'I did. He showed no contrition, no remorse, and no shame for having insulted the royal couple, Egypt or myself.'

'Yourself? He had insulted you, my lord?'

Patroclus stared at him with beetled brows. 'Had you not heard? The dog had written his own perverse version of *The Iliad*. By doing that he insulted Homer, and he certainly insulted me with his doggerel.'

'I had not known this, my lord. But as I said, I shall study this poet Sotades's history.' Hanufer picked up the papyrus he had been writing on and blew it to dry the ink. 'One final question, then. How did Sotades escape from prison?'

'I don't know. That is one of the things Overseer Gryton was dealing with.'

'Do you know how Overseer Gryton died?'

'It will be in the records.'

'I will study them, my lord. And his sergeant, I understand that he also became ill and has retired from the police.'

'I know nothing of his sergeant. I know only that the position of Overseer fell vacant, and Pharaoh Ptolemy had heard good things about you as a thief-taker and a suppressor of riots in Crocodilopolis. It was entirely his decision to appoint you.'

Hanufer interpreted this to mean that Patroclus was not in favour of his appointment. He wondered whether it was because he was Egyptian.

'Can you describe Sotades for me?'

'I don't see why it would matter, since you'll never see him. He's been drowned, remember.' He frowned. 'He was in his middle or late thirties, I suppose. Quite muscular — he bragged about his swimming and his former skill with a javelin. Ginger beard and hair, blue eyes and what some people would call an engaging smile. It was in truth a perpetual sneer.'

Hanufer nodded. 'Could you tell me where the poet and soothsayer Diomedes lives, my lord? I would like to pose some questions to him to get as full a picture as possible.'

'You can ask him yourself this evening. A friend of mine, Obelius of Pella, is hosting a symposium at his villa near the obelisk of Ramesses the Great. He is our most important merchant and banker in Alexandria. You will not miss his villa, for it has a shrine to the god Harpocrates above the door. Diomedes is also attending, and undoubtedly he will be giving a first reading of his poem about the dog poet Sotades the Obscene. You will come at my invitation. Obelius and his wife Eupheme will be happy to receive you.'

'I have seen the villa and will attend, of course. I thank you for the invitation. Will you be going, my lord?'

'Possibly, I haven't decided yet. I have had enough of Sotades. Even his name leaves a foul taste in my mouth.' The vizier picked up a scroll and began to unroll it. 'Just one more thing, Hanufer. His Majesty wants to be informed about everything, but make sure that you inform me first.'

Hanufer understood that the interview was at an end.


As he was about to leave the cool of the marble palace and step back into the oppressive heat, Hanufer paused as he heard men marching along the path. He waited until two guards went past followed by a litter carried by two men at each end, and then by another two guards, all marching with military precision. Upon the litter sat Queen Arsinoe. She was leaning back in a high chair, her eyes closed against the sun. He noticed that her beautiful face no longer looked stressed or angered.

*She must have visited the Temple of Isis in the Brucheum, as the pharaoh said he was going to arrange,* Hanufer thought.

Smiling to himself he made his way to the Temple of Isis, which was built on a raised platform between the Small Harbour and the Royal Harbour, both within the Great Harbour. The small bow-shaped island of Antirhodos, some little distance from it within the harbour, created the illusion that a gigantic, god-like hand guarded the temple. Steps led up to a white marble building with a vaulted roof. Twin statues of Isis stood either side of the great door through which Hanufer walked to find himself in a colonnaded court. A small stream ran through it. This he knew to be the *purgatorium*, the space with water from the River Nile that was used in sacred ceremonies in temples throughout Egypt. This purifying water was diverted from the Canopic Canal that ran from the town of Canopus on the west of the delta, some five leagues from Alexandria.

The sound of a lute drifted from the temple.

Two maids came out of the *naos*, the main building opposite wherein he knew would be the statue of Isis.

'I have come to see Nefrit, priestess of Isis,' he informed them.

Without speaking a word, they led him up yet more steps and showed him into the sacred space, dominated by the brightly coloured image of the goddess. Kneeling in front of it he saw Nefrit, playing an Egyptian long-necked lute. At the sound of his entry she stopped and turned with a smile. And then, swiftly turning back to the statue she stood, bowed and touched her forehead.

'My Lord Hanufer,' she said, placing the instrument on the floor and coming to meet him. She pointed to a door at the side, which led through a corridor to a chamber where there were various ceremonial articles and a number of musical instruments. From there she led him out into a small garden with fruit trees.

'Your pardon, my lord,' she said, gesturing to a bench. 'I have just been saying prayers to Isis with Queen Arsinoe, and I have been purifying the temple once more and playing to thank our goddess.'

'I was sorry to miss you last night,' Hanufer said, waiting for her to sit before he did too.

She cast her eyes downwards. 'I ... I did not want to stay after the sacrilege. I felt ... bad about not seeing you.'

'But at least now I have heard you play. Lady Ambrosia was quite right, you have a remarkable talent. I hope that I will hear you play more, perhaps somewhere other than here?'

Little pinpoints of colour formed on the priestess's cheeks and she looked up into his eyes. 'I ... I think I would like that, my lord.'

'Hanufer. Simply call me Hanufer.'

She smiled. 'And you know that I am just Nefrit. I am pleased to see you today. Her Majesty was upset and we asked Isis to wrap her protective wings about her, just as she fanned life back into Osiris and then protected him until he was revived and recovered.'

'Does the queen need protection, Nefrit?'

'She is upset that the dreadful poem by Sotades the Obscene has again been used to insult her and her brother-husband.'

'But Sotades is dead; he is no threat.'

'Only his body is dead, Hanufer. The words he used to besmear both the pharaoh and the queen still live.'

Hanufer nodded. As an Egyptian, he was only too aware that as long as his words lived, then so did he. It would only be when his name was forgotten that he would be cast into the void and the many parts of his soul be eaten up by Ammit, the devourer of the dead. It was she that all Egyptians hoped to avoid when it was time for their journey through the Hall of Two Truths after they died, when Anubis would weigh their hearts against the feather of Maat. Unconsciously, his thumbs stroked both of his rings with the images of Sobek and Maat.

Hanufer and Nefrit's eyes found each other again, and for a moment they said nothing. Hanufer wondered if the priestess was thinking the same things as he, feeling the same attraction.

'What were your thoughts when you arrived at the altar in the *temenos* and saw the jar of eels and the writing?'

'Horror, Hanufer. I read the writing and knew that it was intended to halt the sacrifice.'

'And did you notice how the others who had also reached the altar reacted?'

Nefrit's kohl-painted eyes suddenly widened and she took a rapid breath. 'Everyone was amazed and repulsed, Hanufer. It … it happened so quickly.'

'Then try to imagine it slowly, Nefrit. I need to understand everything exactly as it happened. Who was the first to reach it?'

The priestess stared at him uncertainly for a moment and then closed her eyes and concentrated.

'The Ladies Bilistiche and Didyme were both close to the altar. I and the other four urn bearers were to pour libations upon the altar and then we were to wait for the bull to be brought forward. Didyme, the chief urn bearer, was to pour water over its head to see if it nodded and agreed to be sacrificed. Then Bilistiche would lower her basket so that Kleitos the high priest of Poseidon could make the sacrifice. But none of that happened, because then … then we saw —'

'You all saw the jar and the writing. Were you all equally shocked?'

Nefrit bit her lower lip and shook her head curtly. 'No! Both Bilistiche and Didyme reacted the same way. Hanufer, I saw they were both smiling.'

# CHAPTER 13

Hanufer found Sabu waiting for him at the entrance to the *temenos*, as he had instructed. He was not surprised that his sergeant smelled of wine.

'Were you successful, Sabu?'

Sabu grinned and nodded. 'I was in some part successful, my lord. I invested in a goatskin of wine and played the part of a well-off horse trader from Memphis. First I found the Lady Bilistiche's mansion. She has stables where she keeps half a dozen fine chariot horses. It was not difficult to find her stable manager and engage him in conversation. He was ready to share my wine.'

'And what did you discover?'

'That all of her servants adore her. There is no disguising that she is a courtesan, but to the Greeks that is perfectly acceptable. They think of courtesans, or *hetairai*, as high class, witty, accomplished women who are available as mistresses, as opposed to what they call *pornai*, or common whores. Leon, that was his name, had all sorts of names for *pornai*, things like ground-beater, two-obol woman, flute-girl. But when he talked of the Lady Bilistiche, it was as if he was talking of a goddess.'

'And he confirmed that she is the pharaoh's mistress?'

'Indeed, my lord. It is all done discreetly, as you would imagine.'

Hanufer nodded. 'And what of the Lady Didyme?'

'Ah, that is where I was less successful. She lives in a villa in Rhakotis, where many of the wealthier Egyptians and Nubians live.'

'Did he have any knowledge of her?'

'Only that she is also a *hetaira*, but no horsewoman or charioteer, which seemed to be his measure of the worth of a woman. He said she was a musician and a poet.'

'A poet,' Hanufer mused. 'Well, we can do some further digging in Rhakotis later. In the meantime, let us go and look at the poetry that caused the procession and sacrifice to be abandoned last night.'

They walked up the path into the *temenos* and found Constables Pylyp and Filemon dutifully standing guard over the altar. Their red-rimmed eyes were testament to their lack of sleep.

'No one has been here all night, sir, except for the slave that Cario sent with refreshments, as you ordered,' Pylyp replied in answer to Hanufer's question. He shivered and then added, 'We kept the torches burning all night, but no one dared to come when they saw that we were on guard. Neither of us slept just in case.'

'In case of what, Constable Pylyp?' Sabu demanded.

'In case spirits were hovering, after the sacrilege with those eels,' the older of the two constables replied.

Constable Filemon leaned forward and offered his explanation. 'Also, we wanted to be alert if he came back, sir.'

'Meaning who?' Hanufer asked, less brusquely than his sergeant.

'Him, my lord! The poet Sotades,' Filemon replied, pointing at the writing and the hieroglyphics on the altar wall.

'Do you think that he could have been here himself?' Hanufer persisted, curious to know what the constables thought. 'The whole city has heard that he was executed, drowned in a jar by Admiral Patroclus, somewhere in deep water near the Island of Caunus.'

Filemon looked at his comrade, who shrugged his shoulders and nodded for him to continue. The young constable again pointed to the poem. 'Well, that is his poem, isn't it, sir? Neither Pylyp nor I are scholars, but we can both read well enough to know that is his poem. We didn't want him or his ghost to sneak up on us, so we talked and played knucklebone to stay awake, sir.'

'As you are expected to do when you were given a guard duty,' snapped Sabu. Then more sympathetically, 'But you were right to be vigilant. Whoever wrote that could have come back in the night to add to it or to remove it.'

Hanufer had knelt down by the altar to inspect the writing again. 'What do you make of it, Sabu?' he asked over his shoulder.

'Not a lot, my lord. It is surely just the sort of rubbish that young boys scratch on walls. It's just crude.'

'So you do not think it is proper poetry?' Hanufer queried as he took out his writing set and a fresh piece of papyrus. 'Well, perhaps it is and perhaps it is not, but I shall make an exact copy.'

He pointed to the flask of weak beer and the remains of the food that Cario had obviously delivered to the constables before daybreak. Sabu understood and passed it to him so that he could moisten the ink block in his writing set.

The others watched and kept silent while he reproduced the hieroglyphs and the writing. Once he had finished to his satisfaction, he picked up a pinch of sand and scattered it on the papyrus shard before blowing it and shaking the papyrus to dry the ink. Finally, he rolled up the papyrus and replaced it and the writing set inside his chiton. He stood up.

'We are going back to the police headquarters in the *Dikasterion*. You have done well, Constables Pylyp and Filemon. You can both go home and sleep now.'

'Shall we have this washed away, my lord?' Pylyp asked.

'No, leave it. Anyone who wants to may enter the *temenos* now.'

As the dismissed constables left, Hanufer spent several more minutes going round the altar, looking for any signs that could help him. There were plenty of footprints in the dust, of various sizes, but none that stood out in any way to his mind. He shook his head with a resigned shrug.

'Come, Sabu, let us now look at that jar of eels.'

They had walked no more than fifty cubits when Hanufer turned and nudged Sabu's arm.

'See, already a crowd of curious citizens want to see what all the consternation was about. Soon the whole city will be humming with what they see there.'


Pollio was reading through and arranging several papyri when Hanufer and Sabu arrived at the office.

'There are two new petitions, my lord,' he said. 'I was going to put them in your basket and see if there were others that you had dealt with, but I saw that Cario was sleeping in your office. I concluded that he must have been sent by you, otherwise he would not have had the audacity to enter your office so early. I left him asleep.'

'That was kind of you and quite the correct thing to do, Pollio,' Hanufer replied. 'Give me the petitions and I will put them in my basket now, and I will consider them later.'

Cario was not sleeping, but was standing at attention when they entered the office. He had placed the large metal jar of dead eels by the shuttered window and covered it with an old goatskin so that the smell would not be too overpowering.

'You look fresh, Cario,' Hanufer remarked. 'Have you slept?'

The young slave nodded. 'I have, sir, but only for moments. My body is used to doing with only fragments of sleep and even then, like a guard dog, I am instantly awake if required for any duty or task.'

Hanufer knew that the life of a slave was never easy. Many owners, both Egyptian and Greek, regularly flogged their slaves for the merest of reasons, as the law entitled them to do. It was not a situation that he approved of and he himself had vowed that he would never own a slave. To find himself given a public slave in the form of Cario had already caused him considerable personal disquiet.

When he was a captain of the Medjay police in Crocodilopolis, he had arrested a wealthy merchant for the murder of a female slave. People had wondered at his audacity for doing so, but to him a life was a life and murder was murder. The poor young woman had died because the man had gone too far with his particular sexual depravity, and Hanufer had been sickened by his casual indifference to her death. When his case was quashed by the local judge, he was silently angry. A week later, when the said merchant was found unconscious in the garden of his own house, stripped naked and with his genitals covered in honey, which had attracted an army of ants, he was quietly jubilant and took great pleasure in making only the most cursory of investigations. The culprit or culprits went undiscovered.

'While you work under my order, you will sleep when you are off duty,' Hanufer now told Cario. 'I need men whose minds have had the succour of rest, so that their thinking is not impaired.'

149

Cario looked bemused and slightly anxious. 'I hope that my thinking is sharp enough and does not displease you, my lord? Has ... has Pollio said that I am lazy?'

'Have no fear — when I first came, Pollio told me that you are the most hardworking *demosios* in Alexandria and that you can be trusted with any errand. So far I agree with him and in answer to your other question, your thinking pleases me greatly, Cario. This is why I want you to be fully fit and properly rested, for in the future I may have other tasks for you than just maintaining my desk.'

The young slave beamed and bowed deeply. 'May I bring you beer and figs, my lord. Or nuts, perhaps?'

Sabu grinned and held up the flask of wine he had purchased and used to 'moisten the tongue' of the Lady Bilistiche's stable manager. He shook it to show that it was empty. 'I have had enough to drink until at least late afternoon.'

Hanufer also refused. 'First, throw open wide the shutters and then bring me that skin and the jar of eels. Then bring a stool and join us.'

A few moments later, with the goatskin on the floor Sabu poured the contents of the jar onto it.

'The eels are dead. So why would someone shove the tails down their throats so that each one forms a ring?'Hanufer mused.

'It is surely a sign, my lord,' said Sabu.

'An elaborate sign,' agreed Hanufer. 'But of what? And could there be a significance in the number of them?'

'Seven, my lord?' Sabu said with a frown. 'I cannot see anything in it.'

'Nor I, sir,' added Cario.

Hanufer nodded. 'Perhaps the number has no significance. Well then, let us turn our attention to the writing that we found on the altar.'

The Overseer of Police took out his writing set, the scrolls of papyrus that he had used to make notes of his interview with Patroclus, and the copy he had made of the markings on the altar. He flattened the papyrus on his desk and signalled for them to come closer.

'What do we make of the hieroglyphics first?' He pointed to them.

'It means nothing, my lord,' replied Sabu. 'It doesn't make a word. It reads *mw-ib-mw*. Which is meaningless.'

'I agree, Sabu,' Hanufer replied. Then turning to Cario, he explained, 'In Egypt we have several thousand different hieroglyphs, Cario. You may think they are a sort of picture writing, but they are far more complicated than that. Each is an image and a sound. The sounds those hieroglyphs make is nonsense.'

Cario looked puzzled. 'To me as a simple Cretan slave, they also mean nothing, except that it looks like wavy lines with a pot or a jar in water.'

'Which is precisely what I think it is meant to make you think,' Hanufer returned. 'The person who drew these wants you to think that a jar is in the water. Since everyone knows that Admiral Patroclus had just returned to Alexandria having tossed the poet Sotades into the sea, it suggests what, do you think?'

'Sotades!' Sabu and Cario chorused.

'Of course. Especially with the eels in the jar. And even though only a few people saw those hieroglyphics, they are simple enough to either reproduce or tell others about. And that is precisely why I said to Pylyp and Filemon that the writing should not be washed off. It will soon be all round the city.'

'But sir, that is not the hieroglyph for a jar, is it?' Sabu queried.

Hanufer smiled. 'No indeed, it is the hieroglyph for the heart, the *ib*. I think a Greek would think it a jar, but an Egyptian with a knowledge of hieroglyphics would know it for a heart. Which makes it look likely that a Greek wrote it, but he was trying to make it seem as though an Egyptian had done so by adding hieroglyphs.' He stroked his rings thoughtfully. 'But that makes it even more nonsensical. Unless it was an Egyptian trying to make it look as if a Greek had done it.'

Sabu shook his head in puzzlement. 'But is it a good thing to let it be widely seen, my lord? Will not Pharaoh Ptolemy and Queen Arsinoe be angered?'

'They might, but on the other hand if I suppress it, then whoever put it there will not see that the whole city has heard about it. This way at least the perpetrator, whoever that may be, might give him or herself away to someone and we may be led to them.' He looked at Cario. 'This is all totally confidential, so you must say nothing to anyone of this discussion.'

'My lips are sealed, my lord,' the young slave replied.

Hanufer pointed to the poem. 'I talked with Admiral Patroclus. To the best of his knowledge, this poem is the one composed by Sotades the Obscene.'

Sabu clicked his tongue. 'Perhaps we should consult with someone who is more familiar with Sotades and his poetry, my lord?'

Hanufer nodded. 'That is my intention.' He rolled the papyrus up and placed it in his chiton, then took a pristine piece from a basket and taking out his writing set, he composed a message. Finishing it, he pressed his seal of office on his pectoral upon the writing set ink block and applied it to the papyrus.

'Take this to the Musaeum and put it in the hand of Philitas of Cos,' he instructed Cario. 'I will call on him presently. His Majesty said that he was the man that I should consult about Sotades. On your way, tell Pollio that you are going on an errand for me.'

Cario took the message and left with a bow.

'Shall I accompany you, my lord?' Sabu asked.

'No, I want you to continue with your review of the constables. You said that two or three of them seemed lazy. Also, discover what you can about Overseer Gryton and find out where his sergeant, Kraspar, lives. Pay him a visit to see how he fares and find out if he knows what Gryton was investigating. Also, make it known that Pylyp and Filemon are to be promoted to corporals straight away.'

Sabu grinned. 'That might stir up the bees, sir. But I will take care that if there is any stinging to do, it is done by me.'

'Well, report back to me at my villa before I go to this symposium tonight.'

Hanufer instructed Pollio to remove the dead eels and the jar, then sat down to study the piles of papyri and ostraca in his baskets. He took out the latest two petitions that he had been given by Pollio before they had looked at the jar of dead eels.

A petition to the police was the well-established method for any Egyptian citizen, other than a slave, to seek justice for a crime or a wrong done against them. Educated persons could write directly and have the petition delivered to the police office. Those unable to write could seek a scribe who would write on their behalf for a fee or for an agreed portion of a sum of recompense should the case proceed to the courts for judgement. Once a petition was received in the police office, it was catalogued or copied if it was deemed necessary to forward it to a higher authority. In Alexandria, the only higher authorities above the *Archiphylakites* were the vizier and the pharaoh himself.

When he first talked with Pollio about the way the office was organised, Pollio told him that all petitions came through him and that he did the cataloguing and arranged for any that required copying to be sent to one of the copyist publishing houses that the station usually employed. The main one was Saul Sofer's establishment in the Emporium.

Reading the first petition, Hanufer was pleased to see that it had been dated by the writer, probably a professional scribe by the look of it. Pollio had stamped it with the official police seal, indicating that it had been accepted by the department. As with all petitions that reached the Alexandria police department, it was written in Greek. Even those that had come from the Nile Delta and which were sent on from a rural *phylakeion* had been translated into Greek from Egyptian demotic either by a temple or an official scribe.

The petition was a request to investigate an unlicensed drinking house that was causing trouble due to noise. Hanufer made a note on a piece of ostraca to send a constable to look into it and went over to Sabu's desk, where he left it in his basket.

Taking the second petition, he smoothed it out on his desk and again nodded with approval to find that it had also been dated and that Pollio had stamped this, too. He read it, noting that it bore the usual platitudes and florid openings used by professional scribes. This one was penned by a different scribe with a firmer hand.

*To the Archiphylakites, Hanufer of Crocodilopolis, right hand of Maat, successor to Gryton of Salamis, Hashem yikom damo, greetings from Zachriel Cohen, scholar and scribe of the Tribe of Simeon, dwelling in the Mansion of the Clerics upon the Island of Pharos.*

*I write this petition with a heavy heart, for we the scribes of the twelve tribes live and work in luxury thanks to the benevolence of Pharaoh Ptolemy Philadelphus and of Queen Arsinoe, yet I have been the victim of a grievous crime committed upon my person. On the last day of Sivan, I and my fellow scribes were permitted an afternoon freedom from our great labour. I, being of a curious nature, decided to visit the city of Alexandria and seek out the holy house that is used by the citizens of my own faith. I had upon my person some obols and was set upon by thieves. First they befriended me, made me drink and sup with them, pretending to be of my faith. Afterwards, they took me to a dark place and forced me to drink from an unclean vessel and eat forbidden food. And then they beat me and stole my purse. I beseech you, Hanufer of Crocodilopolis, to hear me. To come and see the state that I am in and to listen to me in private. If you are a good and wise Archiphylakites, then you will understand this petition and come to me so I may tell you what these criminals look like, so you will see justice is done to our house.*

Hanufer frowned and read the petition over again. Then with a sigh he rolled it up and put it inside his chiton. If he had time after seeing Philitas of Cos, he would walk over the *Heptastadion* to Pharos and visit the petitioner. It would give him an opportunity to see how the famous seventy-two Hebrew scribes worked.

# CHAPTER 14

Cario was waiting for Hanufer at the entrance to the Musaeum.

'I delivered your message to the scholar Philitas of Cos, my lord. He seems to be a most genial and welcoming man, if you don't mind me saying. He smiled and asked me to stay while he read the message in case he needed to send a reply. In fact, he reminded me a lot of my own old master, Apollinarus.' He grinned and added, 'Except my old master was over fond of symposia, with all of the wining and dining. You will see what I mean, sir.'

A young servant of about sixteen who introduced himself as Icarion showed Hanufer into the study of Philitas of Cos while Cario waited outside. Ptolemy Philadelphus had told him that Philitas was a poet and had been tutor to the pharaoh and his sister-wife, Queen Arsinoe, when they were both children.

The room was crammed on one side with tables upon which were all manner of devices, instruments and flasks. A cabinet was full of large glass jars containing the bodies, or parts of bodies, of fish, birds and other animals. Another cabinet was entirely taken up with row upon row of tools and instruments. The other side of the room held racks of scrolls and books. The room and its furnishings seemed more like a workroom where things were taken apart, built from scratch, or devised wholly from the mind of a natural philosopher.

At the far end, by a window, Philitas of Cos was sitting at a desk, with his back to the room. The servant coughed and announced Hanufer, but the philosopher continued to work at his desk.

'My master does not always hear things,' Icarion explained, as he announced Hanufer again in a louder voice.

The chair creaked as the philosopher turned round, grunted an acknowledgement and stood up.

'Can I bring you some food, master? Some refreshment for your guest?'

'Nothing for me, thank you,' said Hanufer, holding up his hand.

'Some fresh fruit then, master?'

'Thank you, Icarion,' Philitas said, flicking his hand good-naturedly as if to shoo the young man away. With a bow to them both, Icarion left.

The Overseer of Police was surprised to see how thin and frail the scholar seemed. He was not as tall as Hanufer and looked as though he barely ate. Unlike most of the scholars in the Musaeum, he was clean-shaven, which revealed his venerable and wrinkled visage. As he advanced down the room to exchange greetings, there was a clinking noise from his feet. Looking down, Hanufer saw that he had thick iron rings like unchained shackles about each ankle.

'Ha! You have noticed my irons,' the philosopher said, his wrinkled face creasing up with laughter lines. He raised his hands to exhibit similar iron bands around his wrists. 'When the pharaoh and his brothers and sisters were young, I used to tell them that I wore these iron bands to stop the wind from blowing me away.'

'If you have worn them for a long time, then I am sure they will have made you strong,' Hanufer replied with a smile.

As they then formally greeted one another according to the accepted etiquette, Hanufer noted how the scholar spent time appraising him, his wig, his features and his overall build, as he imagined he did every living creature. There was none of the animosity or suspicion with which other officials and scholars greeted him, just curiosity.

'The truth is that I wear them as a symbol,' Philitas went on. 'I am a free man, a free thinker, yet as with every person I am chained to this life. I am a slave to learning.' He gave a cheerful laugh. 'I do not myself approve of slavery, but how could I want for more as a slave to learning, when I live in such a place as the Musaeum at Alexandria, with access to the Great Library?'

'And to the Royal Zoo. His Majesty told me that you had been there this morning to see his python.'

Once more the scholar's face creased into a smile. 'Ah, Apophis. I am sure that there is great reasoning in the mind of that great creature. I am trying to communicate with it and see if I can detect some form of language, whether by sound, the way it uses its tongue or movements of the body.'

'I understand from what His Majesty and Weneg the Keeper of Snakes told me that you are awaiting its shedding?'

The scholar's eyes seemed to glow with enthusiasm, and he pointed to a chair beside his desk for Hanufer to sit down.

'Indeed I am. You can tell the signs. Over the last week, his skin has become darker and his belly has turned pink. His eyes have begun to turn slightly milky with a tinge of blue. Any day now he will shed his skin, all of it, even the covering of his eyeballs. I want to see that, for it will make the most incredible object of study.' He gave a short, giggling laugh. 'It will be as if a snake god has shed its skin.'

'He looks a most formidable snake. Pharaoh Ptolemy told me that two men died during the expedition to capture him. Weneg described how they did it and how dangerous it was. He also said that the snake will only be calm when he is near.'

'It is true. While these great snakes are about to shed their skin, they will not take food until the splitting begins. Then they will make up for it and gorge themselves and find somewhere to sleep and digest.' Suddenly the philosopher pointed to a bowl with several pieces of fruit that had all dried up and almost desiccated. 'Not like me! My servant Icarion worries that I do not eat. He keeps bringing me fruit and I forget it. That is not to say that the fruit is not useful. I study them all as they shrivel up. There is a lot you can learn when something dies.'

Hanufer smiled. 'In Egypt we have developed the fine art of preserving bodies after death.'

'Ah yes, mummification, of course. I think Icarion worries that I am becoming a walking mummy.'

'He seemed very solicitous of you.'

'He is a good lad. He was a family slave until I decided to affranchise him before I die, just in case I forgot to do so and he became a *demosios*. Now he fusses over my diet as if he was a mother hen.'

Hanufer smiled, thinking how fortunate Icarion was. The lad was only a few years younger than Cario, who faced a lifetime of enforced slavery.

'But you were saying about the pharaoh's python,' he said, bringing the philosopher back to the subject.

'Ah yes, Weneg is the only person Apophis will permit close. These Keepers of Animals seem to be able to form bonds with creatures that others, myself included, cannot. Weneg says he can talk to it, yet he uses either Greek or Egyptian, not some strange snake tongue. I am trying to discover how his communication works, for only we humans seem to have the ability to speak. It is a mystery.'

Hanufer brushed the images on his rings with his thumbs. 'I do not doubt it, Master Philitas. The gods of Egypt, after all, at times take on the images of all manner of creatures, and surely none would doubt that they can all communicate.'

'Ah yes, the Egyptian gods — there are so many of them, while we Greeks have relatively few. And they are all so very different from our own deities, all of whom have the bodies of men or women, excepting of course if they choose to take the form of a creature on some quest or adventure.'

'I am a devotee of Maat, the goddess of truth,' Hanufer said, raising his hand and showing his ring with her image upon it. 'She is an exception and has a womanly form and wears the feather of truth in her headdress.'

Philitas smiled and nodded his head. 'A beautiful ring and a most appropriate goddess for an *Archiphylakites*, Overseer Hanufer. Indeed, she has a queenly form, not unlike Queen Arsinoe.' He suddenly frowned. 'Like the first Queen Arsinoe, I meant. She was a beautiful woman, and I regret the way —'

He unconsciously began to rotate one of the iron bands upon his wrist. As he did so, Hanufer noticed how chafed the flesh was underneath. A quick glance at Philitas's feet confirmed that the skin around the ankle rings was similarly thickened and chafed, consistent with perpetual wearing.

Philitas suddenly clapped his hands and sat forward, as if conscious that he was drifting off into some reverie. He smiled. 'But we have an equally beautiful and gracious queen now. And just as Maat is a goddess that I as a Greek philosopher much admire, we Greeks and Egyptians both also have Serapis, who looks like the finest Greek warrior with his great beard and the corn sheaf modius upon his head.'

'Unless he chooses to take on the form of a great snake,' Hanufer said. 'This is said to show his connection with the underworld.'

Philitas gave his curious little giggle. 'Like Apophis. And so, we come back to the subject of snakes.'

He pointed to the papyrus on his desk, which bore the message that Hanufer had sent Cario with. He reached for it, and suddenly a black polished rock the size of a duck egg that was hanging from a chain on the ledge of the window started to swing of its own accord.

Hanufer sat back in amazement as the rock pulled at the chain, as if it wanted to fly towards the philosopher's hand.

Philitas giggled again and reached slightly nearer it, causing the rock to hover in the air, restrained only by the chain. 'Do not be alarmed, Overseer Hanufer, it is simply a polished lodestone. When it is near anything fashioned from iron, like my bands, it will try to fly to them as they will fly to it. No other metal will be so influenced.'

'How is this possible, Master Philitas?'

'Thales of Miletus, our first natural philosopher, described them over three centuries ago. It was his belief that they and all things iron have life within them and that they yearn to be together whenever they sense the other's presence. I am not entirely sure about that, hence my interest in studying them.'

Philitas leaned even nearer, and the ring on his wrist suddenly pulled his hand until it connected with the lodestone with a clunking noise. With a broad smile, he pulled them apart and the lodestone fell away, to swing back and forth until it stopped.

He tapped the papyrus message with a forefinger. 'Yet I trust that is not the real reason why you have come to see me, Overseer Hanufer. You said that His Majesty suggested that you visit me, but I wonder if it was for more than to talk about natural philosophy, interesting as that always is to me. Was there something you particularly wanted to discuss?'

Looking warily at the lodestone, Hanufer nodded. 'Indeed. You have heard about the sacrifice to Poseidon that was to be made upon the return of Admiral Patroclus?'

Philitas nodded. 'Of course. The whole city knows about it. It was abandoned because of a sacrilege.'

'A large jar of dead eels was left by the altar in the *temenos*. A message was left there, seemingly a poem by the poet Sotades.'

Philitas chuckled and then immediately stroked his cheeks as if to wipe away a grin. 'Forgive me. I do not laugh at the sacrilege, but because that is precisely the sort of thing that Sotades the Obscene would do. The fool escaped from the pharaoh's prison and now, if he still lives, for this desecration he will face certain death.'

'Had you heard that he was still alive? Admiral Patroclus was adamant that he had put him in a pithos jar loaded with lead and tossed him in the sea near an island called Caunus. He said he watched him drown.'

'And yet the rumour is that he is alive. It is all that the scholars and the staff here at the Musaeum and the Library are talking about today, and I heard several of the Keepers of Animals mumbling about it when I was at the Royal Zoo this morning.'

'What do you think?'

'Sotades boasted about his swimming skill, just as he boasted about everything. If he was tossed into the sea at Caunus, it would be a long way to swim — but it is possible, I suppose, that a boat, perhaps a fisherman, picked him up and saved him.'

'If he could free himself from the jar? I understand he was also shackled at the ankles.'

Philitas shrugged his shoulders. 'It seems unlikely, but it is still possible. I spend my life looking at possibilities. There is always possibility in a rumour, even though the likelihood is that it is merely based on belief. Belief and truth are often far apart.'

Hanufer nodded and suppressed an urge to smile. He had anticipated that a rumour would spread by leaving the writing on the altar to be seen. Yet it was not a ploy that he was about to talk about with Philitas. Instead, he shook his head and said, 'I think that is a rumour that will not please Pharaoh Ptolemy Philadelphus, and far less Queen Arsinoe. But it is to learn more about Sotades that he sent me. He told me that as a poet yourself, you probably know more about him and his poetry than anyone.'

Again the scholar smiled. He spread his hands towards the door. 'Out there in the Musaeum, you will find scores of poets. I am perhaps the oldest of them, and indeed I taught many of them.' He gave a short guffaw. 'Every one of them thinks they are the best, and all of them consider me a pedant, because I am the best grammarian among them.'

Hanufer noted that the smile had been replaced by a look of utter seriousness.

'Zenodotus, Theocritus, Callimachus and Hermesianax were all pupils of mine,' Philitas went on. 'I taught them all to be critics. Now Zenodotus of Ephesus is the head librarian, and Callimachus of Cyrene is considered a master of every type of poetry, but especially of the elegy, although nowadays he seems to favour the epigram, the shorter poem. Theocritus of Syracuse is a genius of the pastoral form and bucolic poetry, while young Hermesianax of Colophon is much given to writing about love.'

'And what sort of poetry did Sotades write? I hear him called the Obscene.'

'A well-deserved and well-earned epithet, Overseer Hanufer. Sotades wrote obscenities, disguised as satire. His greatest influence, I think, was Hipponax of Ephesus. He has been dead over three centuries now, but he was famous for his deliberate vulgarity. They say he was incredibly ugly, but despite that had many lovers and caused many of his opponents in venery to take their own lives, just by virtue of his poems. He ridiculed one, a sculptor called Bupalus, who had refused to allow Hipponax to wed his daughter. He therefore wrote a poem and called Bupalus a *metrokoites*.'

'That is not a Greek word I know.'

'It means a man who sleeps with his mother. Bupalus committed suicide as a result. Sotades strove to emulate him, I believe.'

'Do you and the other poets of Alexandria consider his poetry to be good?'

Philitas chuckled. 'Ah, now that is a difficult question. He and I quite frankly did not like one another, yet as a scholar and a critic I have to admit that he is a paradox. He has lived well, being able to inveigle himself into the courts of all the rulers of the Levant over the years. He has insulted every one, while praising whichever one's patronage he was enjoying at the time. Many in the Musaeum are disparaging about him, but I think he should merit more attention than he does. Or rather, more than he did before he ruined his own reputation by insulting the royal couple.'

Hanufer nodded. 'Was he a court poet to Ptolemy?'

'Once he enjoyed favour, but not after the pharaoh repudiated his first queen and married his sister.'

'This was not popular among the Greeks, I have heard.'

'It was not popular among many Greeks, or at least those who still consider themselves to be Greek rather than Egyptian. The royal couple, like their father, have adopted Egyptian customs, but still retain Greek identity — that is how I see it.'

'Tell me more of Sotades's poetry.'

Philitas fiddled with one of his iron wristbands and sighed. 'He wrote a satire of the great Homer's *Iliad* and of *The Odyssey*, using the style and form that he has made his own. He calls it palindromic poetry, meaning that he writes poetry with lines that read back and forth, but in such a way that the meanings can be quite different. That is clever and he was certainly an innovator, if not actually the genius that he thought himself.'

'Did you think him a genius?'

Philitas clicked his tongue. 'I do not know what that means, Hanufer. There are many scholars here in Alexandria who consider themselves to be in that rarefied group, who have been given gifts from the gods, yet I do not feel that I personally have enough judgement to say whether any one person is a genius or not. What I will say is that people listened to his poetry. He had the ability to sway men's minds, to persuade them about things. While he was no diplomat, politician, nor even a philosopher, he was an influencer!'

'Who did he influence, if not his fellow poets?'

Philitas chuckled. 'He could influence the ordinary people, and more importantly he could influence those in power. I mean the kings, the nomarchs, the emperors and the dictators. Using his poetry he gave them intelligence about their neighbours, be they enemies or allies. No other poets had such influence, and therefore I think that many in Alexandria were jealous of him. Therein lies the reason they are all so critical of him as a poet.'

'Do you include yourself?'

Again the throaty chuckle. 'No, I am close to the end of my life, when such things do not matter. As I said, I am a slave only to knowledge. I am a teacher and a quester for the truth, that is all.'

Hanufer unconsciously touched his rings. 'The truth is also my goal, Philitas. If you cannot say whether he was a genius, do you think he was good?'

'Some of his poetry is very witty, certainly. That perhaps is as far as anyone can truly go, because it is dangerous to praise him in these days, after he so insulted the pharaoh and his queen. That was what got him thrown into prison with the threat of execution hanging over him. And now, perhaps he is dead, drowned at the hands of Admiral Patroclus.' He smiled, then added, 'If he did indeed drown!'

Hanufer reached into his chiton and drew out the papyrus upon which he had copied the hieroglyphics and the poem found on the altar in the *temenos*. He unrolled it on the desk, and Philitas looked over and read.

'That is the poem that got him into trouble,' the philosopher said, nodding.

Hanufer looked at him for a moment. 'Did you recognise the handwriting on the original?'

Philitas shook his head. 'No, but I do not remember what Sotades's handwriting looked like. I just remember the words, and those are the words he used.'

'For this to be written on the altar in the *temenos* was certainly a desecration, a crime that cannot be treated lightly.'

The scholar nodded. 'Indeed, especially since the pharaoh and the queen had previously been so outraged by it. What you have to understand is the strength of feeling that was aroused by the pharaoh's incestuous marriage. It divided the Greeks in the city. Theocritus of Syracuse was one who praised them and wrote a poem that compared their union to that of Zeus and Hera. In contrast, Sotades was probably the most vocal of all the critics, and he somehow naively thought that he could get away with this because he was voicing what many people thought. Maybe he did not think it would get to the ears of the royal couple. You can see how insulting it is to them, but also to —'

'To Egyptians,' Hanufer agreed. 'He insults our religion, our gods. But can I ask what your own view is of the royal marriage?'

Philitas of Cos laughed and clapped his hands so that the metal rings clinked together. 'A most interesting question, Overseer Hanufer. Before I answer it, let me ask you if you are familiar with Eubulides of Miletus?'

Hanufer shook his head.

'He was the philosopher of the Megarian School, and he invented several important paradoxes in logic. One which I have struggled with for a long time is the liar paradox. Essentially, if someone says I am lying, you have to ask is he telling a lie or telling the truth?'

The overseer thought for a moment, then smiled. 'So, if he was telling the truth he was lying, but if he was lying he must have been telling the truth.'

Philitas chuckled. 'So, I am merely going to tell you that I accept that they have married and that they are the royal couple. I like them both and have known them since they were children. I still like them.' He smiled and pointed to the hieroglyphs that Hanufer had copied from the altar. 'I presume that these hieroglyphics mean that the jar is in the water. Could that be Sotades announcing his return to plague Pharaoh Ptolemy and Queen Arsinoe?'

'Possibly,' Hanufer replied, rolling up the scroll and replacing it in his chiton. He noted but did not correct Philitas's assumption that the middle hieroglyph depicted a jar and not a heart.

'Does the librarian Zenodotus have copies of the poems of Sotades? I should like to study them further. I understand that he also insulted the Lady Bilistiche?'

'He did insult her, but you will not find copies of his poems. Ptolemy ordered them all destroyed, which they were. Burned and then the ashes were scattered to the wind and sea.' He chuckled. 'But Sotades wouldn't have worried about that. He intended that his poetry should strike notes in the minds of men and women and be spread by word of mouth, so that it would be remembered long after ink had faded and papyrus had crumbled to dust.'

'His poems scattered as ash to the sea,' Hanufer repeated. 'We come back to water once again.' He stood up and rubbed his chin. 'One last question. Why do you think dead eels were left at the altar?'

'It is an insult to the gods. Poseidon would have been angered to have the sacrifice tainted by this.'

'Pharaoh Ptolemy has decided to abandon it altogether.'

'A good thing, in my opinion.'

'None know this, but the dead eels had their tails stuffed into their mouths, so they were like rings.'

'Like palindromes!' Philitas said with a smile.

# CHAPTER 15

After leaving the Musaeum, Hanufer sent Cario back to the police office to help Pollio. He wanted to be on his own without the distraction of the young slave's constant desire to talk and to please him with whatever task he was set.

The *Heptastadion* was busy as Hanufer walked across, and he found himself accosted several times by market traders in the little town of Pharos. For a small coin a young boy led him through the backstreets to the bottom of a hill, on top of which was the Mansion of the Clerics. As he climbed the slight incline, he saw that Pharaoh Ptolemy had generously built them an impressive limestone building that was both a dwelling and a place of scholarship, like the Musaeum in miniature. Unlike the Musaeum, however, there was no temple dedicated to the Muses through which the visitor passed. Instead, a large gateway led to a shaded garden heavy with the scent of olives and thence into a hall.

Two guards wearing cuirasses and light helmets were sitting in the cool interior by another door, playing some game that involved money and knucklebones. At the sound of Hanufer's entry, they both shot to their feet, simultaneously hiding evidence of their game and clutching their spears.

'Halt!' one snapped aggressively. 'No Egyptians are —'

But the other, seeing Hanufer's pectoral, nudged him before stepping to the other side of the door to stand at attention. The first followed his example.

'I am *Archiphylakites* Hanufer of Crocodilopolis. I have come to see one of the Jewish scholars.'

'Of course, sir. We have been told about you,' said the guard who seemed the more astute of the two. He turned and opened the door, then stood aside. 'We are ordered to stand guard, but not to interfere with the scribes, sir.'

Footsteps sounded on the marble floor within and a distinguished-looking middle-aged man with a long grey beard appeared. He was dressed in a grey full-length robe with a sudarium, a white linen head-covering wrapped around his head with the ends falling down on his shoulders.

He greeted Hanufer and bowed. 'I heard your name, *Archiphylakites* Hanufer of Crocodilopolis. You will excuse me if I do not use the term "overseer," for it has connotations of slavery for our people. I am Zachriel Cohen, scholar and scribe of the Tribe of Simeon, one of the elders who is pleased to be employed by Pharaoh Ptolemy Philadelphus on this great project to translate our holy books into Greek.'

Hanufer nodded without displaying any emotion. It interested him that it was the second time that afternoon that he had found himself talking to someone with an antipathy towards slavery. 'Let us dispense, then, with titles,' he said. 'Suffice it to say that I come to see the great work that you talk of, having been told of it by Pharaoh Ptolemy Philadelphus himself when he was describing the Library of Alexandria. As the official in charge of the pharaoh's law, I felt that I should introduce myself so that I can see exactly how I can ensure the safety of such an important endeavour.'

The elder bowed his head and stood aside to let Hanufer pass. 'Allow me to guide you.'

He led the way in silence along marble corridors and showed him through several large rooms, in each of which six scholars, all of similar or older age than Zachriel Cohen, were sat at desks, their holy words on scrolls set on rests in front of them.

Few looked up as Zachriel and Hanufer passed by them, and only two graced the Egyptian with the slightest of smiles. Some assiduously wrote, others were more methodical and penned slowly, and yet a few mumbled to themselves as they worked. Not having a knowledge of the Hebrew language, Hanufer was unable to discern whether they prayed, sang or were in the process of translation.

'There are seventy-two of us altogether, six from each of our twelve tribes,' the scholar explained. 'Each room belongs to a single tribe. Thus we have passed through the rooms of Reuben, Judah, Issachar, Zebulun, Dan, Naphtali, Gad, Asher, Benjamin, Ephraim and Manasseh.' He parted a curtain to another room, where five scribes were working. 'And finally, this is my Tribe of Simeon. And as you have seen, we are translating the holy books into Greek.'

'And how exactly is it done? Does each elder translate a section? If so, who is responsible for collecting them into one work?'

The elder of the Tribe of Simeon shook his head. 'These are the words of God. They must be written exactly with no mistakes. Each scholar is working on making their own translation into the Greek. When we have finished, there will be seventy-two copies and we shall read through each to ensure that they are all faultless translations. Such is the way that the word of God must be transmitted.'

'I am in awe of such scholarship and dedication,' Hanufer replied sincerely.

Zachriel Cohen pointed to the empty desk similarly laden with scrolls and the paraphernalia of writing. 'We all work at different speeds. My good friend over there is very methodical and is on the second book that in Hebrew we call *Shemot*. That means Departure from Egypt or *the Exodus*. At the back of the room, his cousin is at work on the third book that we call *Vayikra*, but in Greek will be *Leviticus*. I myself am a fast translator and am on the fourth book, which is called in Hebrew *Bemidbar*, or *In the Desert*. In Greek, it will be called the book of *Numbers*. I find it helps me to have a break every now and then and go back and check what I have written.' He pointed to the neat and precise papyrus scroll that was laid lengthways across his desk, with the Hebrew text on a rest for him to read from. 'Are you familiar with the Torah, our holy book?'

Hanufer nodded. 'I understand that there is much about the history of both your and my people.'

'Indeed, this one is about the way our leader Moses led the people from Egypt after the seven plagues that swept across the country.' He reverentially touched the papyrus scroll with a finger and then sighed. 'It is indeed strange for us to be here in the capital of Egypt at the request of another pharaoh to write the holy words in a totally different language.' His eyes narrowed as he looked at Hanufer. 'Imagine, we are writing about our escape from Egypt, our wanderings in the deserts to reach the lands promised to us by God, and of the laws about purity, idolatry and how sacrifices should be prepared and made. It is all so different from the religions and ways of worship of both the Greeks and the Egyptians.' Then he smiled. 'It is both a poignant task and a strange honour that has been bestowed upon us.'

Hanufer nodded. 'It must indeed seem strange. And what will happen to all of these translated works once you have finished? Will they be stored in the Library here in Alexandria?'

'Much will depend upon Pharaoh Ptolemy Philadelphus, but he has told us that we will have several copies to distribute to our twelve tribes.'

'And will you use local publishers and copyists to make yet more copies?'

A look of alarm crossed the elder's face, which was almost immediately followed by one of suspicion. He shook his head. 'No, these are translations written by the seventy-two scholars. They will be the true translations.'

'And yet I understand that there are many publishing houses in the Jewish sectors of the city. They do much work in Greek for the law courts and are used to copy any books that are brought into Alexandria.'

'I do not know any of these publishers. Neither I nor my fellow elders have visited the city apart from the Musaeum, the Library and the Royal Palace. Even then, only with guards.'

'Really? That surprises me, for I have received this petition, purportedly written by you yourself.'

Hanufer took out the petition scroll from his inner chiton pocket and unrolled it for Zachriel Cohen to see. He watched as the Jewish elder read it with increasing puzzlement.

'I did not write this, and I can say that none of my fellow elders would have done so either. I do not know this city, other than in the way I just told you.'

It was not the response that Hanufer had expected. He could not imagine that such an apparently devout man should tell him a lie, and a mere glance at the text on the papyrus that Zachriel Cohen had been working on confirmed that the petition had been written by a different hand.

For some reason that he could not account for, he felt a shiver run up his spine.

Sabu arrived at the villa before Hanufer and was shown into the garden to await the Overseer of Police, because he smelled strongly of smoke. The two housemaids Delia and Ophelia served him beer and honey cakes and giggled as he flirted with them, much to the consternation of the butler Timon, who had rarely managed to make them smile.

Hanufer joined him upon his return, having asked for and been served a small beer.

'You need to have a bath, Sabu. You reek of smoke.'

His sergeant grinned. 'It is the smell of honest toil, as I will tell you, sir. But it will not please you, I think. It is not just me that stinks!'

'You have intrigued me,' Hanufer said as he picked up his beer and nodded for him to proceed.

'I learned some very interesting things, my lord. And yet other things that puzzled me. Firstly, I found that Overseer Gryton was both liked by some of his men and yet despised by others. Also, Sergeant Kraspar may not have maintained as much discipline as he should.'

'Did you find out what cases Gryton had been working on latterly?'

Sabu shook his head. 'Apparently nothing outside of the ordinary, but he had not been there as often as usual. Nor was Kraspar. Some of the more disgruntled constables, two in particular named Sidvain and Rhoglos, both Thracians like Sergeant Kraspar, told me that they thought he was just getting lazy. They were the two that I had mentioned to you earlier, sir. Others thought it was because he wasn't well.'

Hanufer sipped his beer. 'So it is possible that he was working on something on his own. Or with Kraspar?'

'That is what I wondered, my lord. So I went to Gryton's home, which was down near the Lake Mareotis harbour. That is why I smell of smoke, sir. There was a fire there yesterday and the place was burned to the ground. I had a look through the ruins, but I found nothing except this.'

He reached into his chiton and took out a small metal box. He shook it and it rattled. Opening it, he poured a number of coins onto the small table.

'From what I can make out there are coins from Thrace, Cyrene and the Seleucids. Some gold, silver and bronze. I found this hidden under a tile in the floor. There is more, but I thought I would just bring this sample to show you. All the furniture had been burned, so there is no way of telling for sure, but I suspect someone had gone through things before putting it to the flame.'

Hanufer picked up several coins and examined them. 'But look at these; I believe they are Judean.' He dropped them with the others and stroked his chin with a finger. 'Interesting. I think you had better take two men and go back and collect the rest of the money. But were there any papyri, or ostraca?'

'None that I could see, sir.'

'Did you tell the men about the promotion of Pylyp and Filemon?'

'I did, my lord. Sidvain and Rhoglos and their comrades were not happy, not that they dared say so to me, but I could tell. The rest were pleased, as were Pylyp and Filemon themselves. I dropped into the barracks to tell them.' He grinned. 'Good men, both of them, sir. I did not even have to wake them, as they were already prepared to return to duty.'

'Did you find out about Kraspar?'

'Yes, my lord. He had been a soldier and had fought under King Lysimachus in Macedonia, but received a spear through his thigh, which caused him to be invalided out of the Thracian army. He made his way to Alexandria and was recruited into the police, even though he'd had a limp ever since his wounding. He had lived at the barracks, but after Gryton died and was cremated he complained of feeling ill and retired. That was the last anyone saw of him. I was told of the place that he went to rent a room in Rhakotis, but when I went, it appeared he had never been there. He has totally disappeared, my lord.'

At about the same time, a meeting between two people was arranged as a matter of urgency.

'I have to be swift, or else it may be noticed.'

'Do you think that he suspects something?'

'I am sure of it. Why else did he pay these visits? And why not with constables?'

'You are right. It is suspicious.'

'Added to that suspicion is the danger if he talks to the poet, and that seems inevitable.'

'Then you will have to be vigilant. You know what you may have to do.'

'We know.'

'And you know that any message must be left so that everyone in the city will know of them.'

'It shall be done as if the words had just been spoken.'

# CHAPTER 16

It was a balmy evening and a slight breeze coming off the sea was welcome after the oppressive heat of the day. Darkness was starting to fall, and the fires in the great Pharos lighthouse had been lit and were already sending out beams of light over the Great Harbour, the Royal Palace and much of the surrounding city. Already Alexandria was transforming itself from a city of business and trade into one of entertainment and revelry.

Hanufer was much preoccupied with thoughts about the death of his predecessor *Archiphylakites* Gryton and the disappearance of his sergeant, Kraspar. However, as he made his way to the villa of Obelius of Pella near the obelisk of Ramesses the Great, he could smell the aroma of cooking goose, and it made his stomach rumble. The villa was set back from the boulevard and he saw, as Patroclus had told him, the terracotta shrine to the god Harpocrates built into the wall above the door. A burning torch on each side of the great doors illuminated the shrine and the whole frontage of the villa.

Hanufer brushed his rings as he stood for a moment, looking up at the shrine. The god Harpocrates was not one of his favourite deities. Like Serapis, he was a god that had been adapted by the Greeks from one of the most important of the Egyptian deities. He was said to be the embodiment of the child-god Horus, the son of Osiris and Isis, who represented the newborn sun. In the Egyptian he was called *Har-pa-khered*, which the Greeks had Hellenised to become Harpocrates. But whereas Horus in the old religion was represented as the hawk, or as a man with the head of a hawk, the new god Harpocrates was shown as a child pharaoh with a finger raised to his lips, fitting for the god of silence and secrets.

There had been a temple dedicated to Harpocrates in Crocodilopolis, whose high priest Sennedjem had indeed been a man of many secrets. After a young prostitute had been found strangled with her own hair, Hanufer had followed a trail that led to the priest, and to his depraved secrets that he had been prepared to kill for. His investigations also revealed that he had been extorting money from temple worshippers in exchange for his silence about made-up peccadillos.

Things had escalated rapidly from that point. The priest had been working with a gang of criminals that had spun a malignant web across the city. The priest's exposure caused individual strands of the web to shake, and many people grew nervous.

Hanufer had used the Medjay police force under his command to strategically outmanoeuvre the criminal factions, while arresting those involved in murders and corruption. It was for this that the Greek nomarch in charge of the city of Crocodilopolis had written a letter to King Ptolemy Philadelphus himself, extolling his virtues and skills as a policeman and a solver of crimes. It also happened that the murdered family were related to one of Queen Arsinoe the Second's handmaidens.

From that day Hanufer had been suspicious of the god Harpocrates, but he remained respectful in case it had actually been the god that had revealed the secrets of the high priest Sennedjem to him. Yet it was also for this reason that he venerated Maat, the goddess of truth, above all others. He far preferred truth to secrets.

A man in a short chiton greeted him at the door of the villa.

'You are most welcome, *Archiphylakites* Hanufer. My master and mistress are expecting you. I am Erasmos, their head slave. If you will follow me, please.'

He led the way through a large atrium lit by torches in brackets upon the walls, which were decorated with murals of Greek gods. They seemed so lifelike in the flickering lights it was as if they danced around a central fountain. From there they walked along corridors with marble tiled floors and several doors until Erasmos showed Hanufer into a beautifully furnished hall that positively glowed with strategically placed oil lamps. To his surprise, it was filled with women dressed in silks, some reclining on couches, others in groups chatting and drinking wine from silver goblets.

Erasmos coughed and announced Hanufer.

'Ah, it is our honour to welcome you to our home this evening, *Archiphylakites* Hanufer,' said an attractive woman dressed in a blue peplos with silver buckles at the shoulders. Her auburn hair was tied up in a large bun at the back of her head with a fashionable Greek silver hairpin, on the end of which was a gem of lapis lazuli. She had a matching lapis lazuli ring on the hand that held a goblet, and Hanufer was struck by how closely the gems matched the colour of her eyes. 'I am Eupheme, the wife of Obelius of Pella.'

Hanufer bowed. 'The honour is mine, my lady. You will forgive me, but I had been told by Admiral Patroclus that this was to be a symposium and I would —'

'That you would be solely in the company of men,' she returned. 'And so you will, but I have taken the opportunity to host a party for some of my lady friends this evening as well.' She hooked his arm and led him into the gathering. 'There are at least two ladies that I know you have met.' As they moved through the hall, groups parted to let them pass.

'Good evening, Hanufer,' said the Lady Ambrosia. 'I heard and now I see that you are becoming acquainted with Alexandrian society.' She graced him with a smile before turning and waving to someone over the heads of a trio of elegant ladies. 'Nefrit, come and see who is here,' she called.

The ladies between them obligingly parted and Hanufer saw the priestess of Isis sitting on her own in a corner, arranging several musical instruments. She had looked up on hearing the Lady Ambrosia call her name.

When she saw Hanufer, she smiled, showing ivory white teeth. Standing quickly she came over to join them, still holding a long-necked lute. As usual she wore the headdress of Isis, the two ivory cow horns containing within them a silver moon disc. Her white sheath dress was complemented this evening by a strophion, a high belted band which emphasised her bosom.

The Overseer of Police had not expected to see her this evening and was delightfully surprised to do so. They greeted each other cordially, although Hanufer regretted that he could not have a few moments of her company on his own.

'Nefrit is going to play for us this evening,' said Eupheme.

Before Hanufer could say anything further, a hand was placed on the hostess's shoulder and she turned to meet two beautiful women, whom Hanufer recognised immediately.

'Ah, my ladies Bilistiche and Didyme,' said Eupheme. 'Allow me to introduce *Archiphylakites* Hanufer.'

The hostess formally completed the introductions and Hanufer bowed to each of the courtesans.

Didyme flashed a smile at Hanufer. 'I have heard that Crocodilopolis is a fabulous city,' she remarked. Then, with a shiver, 'Except I do not like the idea of all those crocodiles.'

Hanufer laughed. 'The whole Nile is home to the creature, my lady, just as it is to the hippopotamus and the ibis. Our gods, Sobek, Taweret and Thoth protect us.'

Bilistiche smiled at Didyme without conveying any warmth. 'Some of us need more protection than others, though — don't you think so, Lady Didyme?'

The look that was returned told Hanufer that there was little love lost between the two women.

'Tell us, Overseer Hanufer,' said Bilistiche, 'have you been investigating the sacrilege from the other night? I and the Lady Didyme and the other basket and urn carriers were so shocked by the insult.'

Didyme nodded in agreement, seemingly as if any animosity between them did not exist, but her beautiful brow creased with distaste. 'It was a horrible insult to His Majesty, which grieved me to witness.' She shook her head in obvious displeasure.

'And to her,' Bilistiche added.

'Indeed,' Didyme agreed, any vestige of a smile disappearing.

Hanufer was on alert, conscious that he was facing two women who both shared a bed with the mighty pharaoh. Two women who could not have been more unlike one another. Their choice of words had not gone unnoticed by him, either. He realised that the 'her' to whom they were referring had to be Queen Arsinoe.

He glanced at the priestess of Isis and noted that her kohl-painted eyes were fixed on him. He fancied that her ruby lips quivered to give the slightest impression of a knowing smile, and he took it as confirmation of his impression about the relationship between the two women and their attitude towards the pharaoh's wife.

'I have been looking into it, ladies,' he replied. 'But as yet —'

'Was it that nauseating man, Sotades?' Bilistiche asked. 'He insulted me, too, you know.'

'A brave man to do so,' Didyme interjected. 'Everyone knows how hard you can be on stallions.'

The little group had gathered a cluster of the other guests, intrigued by the attention the famous royal courtesans were giving to the Overseer of Police. A murmur of amusement was apparent.

Bilistiche looked sharply at Didyme and raised an eyebrow in unsmiling displeasure.

Ambrosia was quick to smooth any ruffled feathers. 'But I heard that Sotades the Obscene had been drowned?'

'Executed by the Admiral Patroclus,' someone at the back of the gathering ventured.

'What did you make of the writing? Of the hieroglyphics?' Bilistiche questioned Hanufer.

'Oh, I saw the Egyptian picture writing,' another voice piped up.

'As did I. Everyone is talking about it,' someone else said.

'He is back. It was Sotades.'

'Ladies, please,' said Eupheme. 'The *Archiphylakites* is not here to join us, merely to —'

'No, he is here to join *us*!' a gruff male voice intruded.

The female gathering fell back to reveal three men. The speaker was a large, red-cheeked man with thinning hair and a full beard that had been carefully groomed.

'Overseer Hanufer of Crocodilopolis, I see that my good wife has greeted you and introduced you to the good women of Alexandria. I am Obelius of Pella. Welcome to my humble home.' He stepped forward and clapped a brawny hand upon Hanufer's shoulder. 'Come, let me lead you to the safer company of men for some food, wine and intellectual discourse.'

Admiral Patroclus, the pharaoh's vizier, stood a pace behind him. 'I hear nonsense being talked here about the oaf, Sotades,' he said, his voice booming even louder than that of Obelius. 'Let none here be in any doubt: Sotades the Obscene is dead and gone. And if you still have any doubts about it, friend Diomedes here will dispel them for you.'

He pointed to the third man, a good-looking fellow who was flamboyantly dressed in an orange chlamys, which was fastened at his right shoulder. He wrapped it over a forearm in an affected way.

'*Archiphylakites* Hanufer, this is Diomedes, the poet and soothsayer,' Obelius said.

Merely nodding at Hanufer, Diomedes immediately took the opportunity to address the audience before him.

'It is true, ladies, for this humble poet and soothsayer of modest ability that I am, first saw the dog Sotades in a vision as was revealed to me by Harpocrates, the god of secrets. Then when the admiral so graciously followed my directions and apprehended the scullion, these mortal eyes of mine watched him being stowed in a pithos jar laden with lead ingots and hurled into the sea. The Obscene Sotades is no more, fish fodder only.'

'Tell us more!' a voice called out. It was followed by laughter and enthusiastic chatter.

Obelius stood with his hands on his hips and shook his head. 'Eupheme, see what you have done with your party of ladies? You have waylaid first my esteemed guest the Overseer of Police and now the silver-tongued Diomedes.'

Eupheme smiled at her husband. 'Behave yourself, my husband. I have had the *andron* prepared for you, have I not?

Just let us keep Diomedes for a little while, so that he can regale us with his latest adventure.'

'And perhaps a foretaste of the poem I am composing for His Majesty Pharaoh Ptolemy Philadelphus and the lovely Queen Arsinoe,' Diomedes put in. He turned to Obelius in a mock beseeching manner. 'I pray that you will permit me a few minutes to tell the ladies of our exploit, and then I will come straight to you.'

Obelius rolled his eyes. 'Pah! Very well, but my other guests are already at the symposium and will be eager to dine and sup.'

Patroclus reached out and gave Diomedes a friendly tap on the head. 'Be not long, we men have need of your words, too.'

Eupheme touched Ambrosia's hand. 'Have no fear for your husband, Judge Thespos.' She pointed to a far door where the head slave was standing at attention, looking straight into the room, but so unobtrusively that he could almost have been a statue. 'I have told Erasmos to ensure that the wine is well watered.'

Ambrosia clinked her goblet against Eupheme's. 'Just as long as mine is untainted, my dear. You know how I dislike water.'

Bilistiche reached for Diomedes's arm and began to guide him towards a vacant couch. 'If you dislike water, my lady, then perhaps this tale about Sotades will not be for your ears.'

Didyme, not to be outdone, hooked her arm through Diomedes's other arm. 'But perhaps you had also better take care, Bilistiche. Our fair Diomedes may also have looked into the future and written about you and your stallions in this poem of his.' She looked at the soothsayer and wrinkled her nose coquettishly. 'So come, my Diomedes, you can tell my fortune if you dare.'

Obelius guffawed as the poet was bustled away with a courtesan on each arm. 'As Admiral Patroclus ordered, come soon, Diomedes. If you are telling these ladies' fortunes, make them short.'

The banker turned to his male guests and held out a hand to invite them to head towards the far door, where Erasmos awaited them. After they had bowed to the ladies, Hanufer left with Patroclus. Going to a symposium was now the last thing he wished to do; all he really wanted was to stay and listen to Nefrit play her lute and sing.

Erasmos held the door open for the three men and once they had passed through, he fell into step behind them.

'I am pleased to see that you decided to come this evening, my lord,' Hanufer said to Patroclus.

Obelius immediately looked at the admiral. 'You were thinking of staying away, Patroclus?' he queried.

The pharaoh's vizier cast a sour glance at Hanufer, then shook his head emphatically. 'Not at all, Obelius. I would not miss one of your symposia for the world. I think our Overseer of Police misunderstood me. Let us hope he does not make such mistakes in his investigations.'

Hanufer muttered an apology and walked along as Patroclus and Obelius talked between themselves as if he was not there. They ambled through a series of corridors in the great villa, followed at a discreet distance by Erasmos.

They stopped in front of a pair of huge, heavy doors. The large banker turned and signalled to his head slave.

'Erasmos is my *symposiarch* this evening,' he explained to Hanufer. 'That means he has prepared the wine and the little delicacies we shall enjoy tonight. We always water our wine down in Greece, as a matter of good taste.'

Patroclus snorted disdainfully. 'We heard your good wife telling Judge Thespos's wife Ambrosia that nonsense. You know me, Obelius. I like a good wine and if it is over-watered, I'll know it is because you are being mean and are watching the obols rather than showing good taste.'

Obelius clapped the vizier on the shoulder and snapped his fingers at Erasmos, who stepped smartly ahead and opened the doors.

'Patroclus, my old friend, go in,' Obelius said. 'My son Stratonicus is already there with Judge Thespos and the others. He will look after you. I just want a word with Hanufer.'

Patroclus grunted and entered.

Obelius turned to Erasmos. 'Have the wine pitchers been drawn from the *krater*?'

Erasmos bowed. 'They have, my lord. My mistress instructed me herself. Three pitchers by every couch and the *krater* has been filled again with the very best red Shedeh wine, should you require replenishments. I will be outside the door all evening awaiting your further instructions, sir.'

Obelius nodded with satisfaction. 'This is an important symposium, Erasmos. I want our Overseer of Police to see how Alexandrian society works in miniature. Now go back and tell my wife not to let her friends keep Diomedes overlong. He enjoys flirting — with both sexes.'

Once the head slave had retraced his steps along the corridor, Obelius pursed his lips. 'Admiral Patroclus is the vizier, and as you will already have gathered he is a man used to being both obeyed and fawned over. I am just a simple merchant at heart, but I have gradually accumulated wealth and with it a modicum of influence. From being a simple market trader in the Emporium when I was a youth, I have built my business interests so that I now have a fleet of ships that I use to trade around the Levant. Precious metals, grains, silks, spices, wine, ivory and ebony; you name it and I will find it for you and trade whatever commodity you want. People like me are useful to Admiral Patroclus and to his boss, Ptolemy Philadelphus. I also know that it is because I am rich that people trust me to be the banker they come to as a source of money for their enterprises and plans.' He grinned and squeezed Hanufer's shoulder. 'You will see that tonight, for all of my guests and virtually all of my wife's guests also have need of me, my wealth and my connections. Arrogant, useless wasters they are, yet it amuses me to see the way they buzz around me like wasps around a honey pot.'

'I appreciate your candour, Obelius. But why are you telling me this?'

'Because things in Alexandria are perhaps not as smooth as they should be, and have not been for quite some time. There are undercurrents at work that are affecting business, trade and relationships among the different groups of our society. As a banker I see it all at first hand. If you ask me, it has much to do with Sotades the Obscene.'

'How, exactly?'

Obelius smirked. 'You will see. As soon as the name is dropped into the conversation, it will be like feeding the fishes.'

Hanufer was about to ask another question when Obelius smiled and grasped the handle of the door, pulling it open. The banker winked. 'Let us feed the fish.'

The *andron* where the symposium was to be held was a large room with a number of long windows just below the high ceiling. The walls were painted with scenes of the Olympian gods, but the most detailed was an erotic scene depicting Dionysus surrounded by nymphs and revellers. As in the other hall, light was thrown out from a profusion of oil lamps and round the walls there were urns with ostrich feathers and potted palm trees, bougainvillea burgeoning with vines on tall trellises. Several couches were set in a circle around a large glazed jar, which Hanufer knew from previous symposia he had attended was the *krater* that Obelius and Erasmos had referred to. Pitchers of wine with drinking bowls were placed in readiness by each couch, along with low tables laden with plates of cooked meats and delicacies, and large bowls of assorted fruits, figs and dates. At the far end was a doorway with a curtain, which Obelius informed him was a cubicle where they could relieve themselves throughout the evening.

Hanufer noted that Admiral Patroclus had already lain down on a couch between one occupied by Judge Thespos and another by a man who looked to be a younger and slimmer version of Obelius. They were chatting animatedly.

'My friends,' Obelius announced to them and to three other men, who were also lounging on couches and were deep in conversation. They all stopped talking and looked round. 'Allow me to introduce you to those who have not already met him, Hanufer of Crocodilopolis, our new Overseer of Police. We will be joined soon by Diomedes, if the good ladies will allow him to escape their clutches.'

The younger man next to Patroclus jumped up and bowed.

'This is my son, Stratonicus,' said Obelius. 'He is my right hand as well as an artist of some skill.' He spread his arms out towards the wall murals. 'He brings the gods to life like no one I know.'

'Incredible skill, Master Stratonicus,' Hanufer said admiringly.

'I would like to do the same with some of the Egyptian gods and goddesses,' Stratonicus replied with a self-deprecating smile. 'Yet I would not wish to offend Egyptian sensitivities.'

'Why would anyone be offended when you can paint like this?' Hanufer protested.

'Because from all that I have seen of Egyptian art when I have been on my travels, it conveys less movement than I like to impart to my subjects.'

'I agree, Hanufer,' said a familiar-sounding voice, as one of the other men rose from his couch, a drinking bowl in hand. 'My apologies for not having sent that thing you wanted to your office. I and my colleague Herophilus have been busy with the other issue I told you about. In this heat, we have to work quickly.'

Hanufer nodded to the physician and anatomist Erasistratus. 'I understand. I would still welcome it as soon as you can manage it.'

'So you know our good physician, I see,' said Obelius. 'And perhaps also our high priest of Serapis.'

'My Lord Manetho,' said Hanufer as the priest rose and they exchanged bows. 'I did not see you at the sacrifice that was abandoned. I am sure that you heard about it, though.'

'I did hear, Hanufer. I had chosen not to be present, since I only wish to see bulls that are to be sacrificed to Serapis, not to other gods. It did not seem appropriate for me to attend, yet I am sad that such a travesty occurred at all.'

Admiral Patroclus swung his legs off the couch and sat forward belligerently. 'That bull was being sacrificed to thank Poseidon for my fleet's safe return. And to honour me.'

The priest of Serapis raised his hands apologetically. 'I meant no offense, Admiral Patroclus. I merely meant that since bulls are the creatures of the great Serapis, it would have been more fitting to have sacrificed some other animal.'

Judge Thespos was still lying on his couch. 'It is the poor bull I feel sorry for. It had been sentenced to death and now it will have the agony of having to wait before it meets its fate. I am not so cruel to those I sentence in my court.'

'It is good to meet you again, Judge Thespos,' Hanufer interjected. He had been slighted mere minutes before by the poet Diomedes and was not prepared to be snubbed again by the judge whom he had met so recently. 'You may be pleased to hear that the bull has been spared, by authority of the pharaoh.'

'Indeed?' the judge exclaimed. 'I had not heard that.'

Patroclus looked sideways at him. 'I thought that I had told you, Thespos. But it is of no great matter. His Majesty has other plans, I understand.'

Obelius nodded to the other man, who jumped up. 'Finally, Hanufer, this is Hilarian, one of our greatest horsemen and charioteers. Not only that, but he is a playwright to look out for.'

Hanufer smiled at the tall, broad-shouldered, athletic young man who looked exactly as Homer had described Achilles, the great hero of *The Iliad*.

'It is my honour, Hanufer. I have heard much of you.'

'You have me at a disadvantage, I am afraid,' Hanufer replied.

Hilarian grinned, showing perfect white teeth. 'I have kinsmen living in Crocodilopolis. They told me that the city's loss is Alexandria's gain. And that you solved a crime for which our queen is grateful. For this, Pharaoh Ptolemy has decreed that the city will be honoured by being renamed after our Queen Arsinoe.'

Obelius clapped his hands. 'A great honour, all down to our friend Hanufer. Now, noble guests, our food is getting cold and I am getting thirsty. I will serve your first drink myself. Please, sit and let us have some pleasurable discourse.'

Hanufer took one of the three vacant couches while Obelius picked up a pitcher and began to circulate, pouring wine into those drinking bowls that were empty. He observed that all of the men seemed to be fond of the good Shedeh wine.

'It looks as if the ladies greatly outnumber the men this evening,' Hanufer remarked as he took his drinking bowl.

'It is always thus,' Obelius replied. 'My wife takes any symposium I hold as an opportunity to invite half the womenfolk of Alexandria. But let us forget them for a while and indulge ourselves.'

And so the symposium began.

One by one the guests, including Hanufer, introduced themselves more formally, as was the custom. Obelius interjected frequently, adding little witty anecdotes about each person. His guests all dutifully laughed at each one, suggesting to Hanufer that Obelius's earlier remarks about them all being dependent or beholden to him in some way was true. He was also sure that it was Obelius's subtle way of deliberately letting him know about those links.

Stratonicus, as his son, clearly owed his whole livelihood to his father and his business interests. Judge Thespos enjoyed wine and luxuries from lands throughout the Levant, as had been apparent when Hanufer had dined at his home. Manetho, as high priest of Serapis, would undoubtedly receive some of the considerable donations made to his temple, and Obelius did not hesitate to add that he was the principal supplier of papyrus to the Library of Alexandria. Hilarian's plays were performed and published thanks to the patronage of Obelius, who owned his own publishing house, and his horses were part-owned by him through his bank.

Hanufer watched the physician Erasistratus squirm when Obelius implied that it was thanks to him that he'd obtained some of the necessary supplies for the Medical School.

Even Patroclus somehow owed money to the banker for some transactions he was making on his behalf.

Niceties over, they helped themselves to food, drank a few toasts to Ptolemy Philadelphus and Queen Arsinoe and praised the gods, both Greek and Egyptian.

They talked superficially about the chariot races and the pharaoh's continuous building programme. They also spoke of the political situation throughout the Levant and the hostilities with the Seleucid empire along the coast of Asia Minor.

It was then that the doors were opened and Erasmos introduced Diomedes. The poet entered flamboyantly, his face flushed and his breathing slightly heavy. There was evidence of female make-up on his neck and on his chlamys.

# CHAPTER 17

'My noble host and friends,' Diomedes said, striding to the empty couch next to Hanufer and dropping down upon it. 'These ladies, they would have been the death of me.' He accepted a plate of food, swiftly served by the head slave, and pointed to the table for him to lay his drinking bowl upon. He smirked. 'Indeed, two or three almost were.'

'Diomedes, you are a rogue,' said Obelius with a booming laugh. 'I don't care who you were molested by or fornicated with, as long as it was not my wife.'

Judge Thespos had enjoyed several bowls of wine already. 'It was not my Ambrosia, or you would not be here even yet.'

Hanufer looked at the judge and mused that the mood of the all-male symposium revealed a different side to the man. Rather than the stiff, very correct host who had entertained him when he first met Nefrit, he was showing that he had a decidedly lude side.

Stratonicus noticed that the judge's pitcher was almost empty so picked it up and went over to the *krater* to refill it. 'Good old Diomedes,' he said with a laugh. 'Surely there are few ladies — or men — who can resist his charms.'

Diomedes graced him with a smile. 'You are a man after my own heart, Stratonicus.' After a pause, he raised his voice in mock suspicion. 'Are you after my heart, sweet boy?' He pointed to the images of the gods dancing around the periphery of the room and added, 'Or do you just want the premier poet in Alexandria's endorsement of your daubs?'

Stratonicus laughed. 'Oh, what would we do without your wit, Diomedes?'

'You would miss it, for none have the like.'

'You really should not pretend to be more of a man than you are, Diomedes,' said Hilarian unsmilingly. 'You can besmirch your own self, but there is no need to impugn the reputation of any lady.'

Diomedes smirked. 'Ah ha! So has bold Hilarian cast his eyes on one of the fair ladies here tonight, or even one not so fair? Is it an actress, a poet, or one who likes to play rough with horses as he does?'

Hanufer noticed how Hilarian opened his mouth to reply, but seeing Diomedes's haughty look as if awaiting a response upon which he would pounce, he thought otherwise and reached for his wine instead.

Erasistratus did not choose to let the matter close. 'You worry too much, Hilarian. I think Diomedes merely wishes he could dally with any of these fine ladies, when the truth is that the skills of which he boasts are all unseen, just as his conquests always occur when no one can confirm them. I would not be surprised if the kohl and lip make-up that he is smeared with are not just his own.'

The soothsayer-poet tossed his head back and laughed. 'Why, the man who cuts up live criminals and defiles their bodies also has his eyes on some lady. I think there is envy in his blood. Now, which lady could it be? Is it —?'

'Diomedes, stop playing the fool!' Admiral Patroclus snapped.

Hanufer wondered if the irritation the vizier was showing had a jealous edge to it. And then he was aware of some irritation himself, lest one of those the poet had dallied with in some discreet corner had been Nefrit.

He quickly chided himself, for as an investigator he knew that he should never allow his mind to get distracted by personal matters. Thus calmed, he realised that there was much tension within the room already, and it had been triggered by the mere presence of the poet.

'We know your game, Diomedes,' Patroclus went on. 'You like to play the fool and whip people up one by one to create an argument that you always think you will win.'

Diomedes sat up straight away and pouted, but there was a look of triumph already in his eye. 'My lord, a fool I am not, as the good ladies will attest. I am a poet as well as the ear and mouthpiece of the god Harpocrates. Did I not listen to the god's message and tell you to go to Crete after that god had already correctly told you that you would be victorious over the Seleucids? And did we not then find the ship's captain, who told us where to find the dog Sotades?'

Patroclus sipped some wine. 'You did.'

'And did I not have discourse with the sculptor Hecataeus on the Island of Caunus?'

Patroclus sighed. 'Yes, Diomedes, you did.'

'And we watched Sotades disappear beneath the waters in the pithos jar, just as I predicted he would after divine Harpocrates had given me his message.'

'Your point being what, exactly?'

Suddenly the poet beamed. 'Why, just that I deserve a little respect. You, Admiral Patroclus, gained the honours from our wonderful Pharaoh Ptolemy Philadelphus and Queen Arsinoe, but it was due to me that Sotades was caught in the first place.'

'I did not receive an honour, Diomedes. The sacrifice was not made, thanks to whoever committed that sacrilege.' He suddenly shot a glance at Hanufer and demanded, 'Have you discovered anything yet, Overseer Hanufer?'

'I am investigating, my lord,' Hanufer replied calmly. 'In fact, as you yourself said when I was invited here, it gives me the opportunity to talk to Diomedes.' He turned to the poet and with a polite smile said, 'We have not been properly introduced, but now that we are both here, can you tell me more about Sotades and his capture and his — execution?'

Diomedes slurped some wine from his bowl and then reached across to his low table and picked up a handful of peeled quails' eggs.

'My apologies to you, *Archiphylakites*, if I did not wave harder when we met. So what exactly do you want to know?'

'I know something about Sotades, yet I have not been able see any of his poetry. Philitas of Cos told me that Pharaoh Ptolemy Philadelphus ordered that all of his poetry should be burned and scattered to the wind and sea.'

'Where it belonged,' said Diomedes.

'Not all of it deserved that fate, Diomedes,' interjected Obelius. 'You have to admit some of it made one smile. Laugh, even.' He grinned and then added, 'Not the insults to the pharaoh and his queen, of course.'

Patroclus shook his head. 'It did none of these things, Obelius. The man was an abomination in all things. He wrote about his relationships and he insulted people of all stations.'

'I agree,' Hilarian said, selecting a fig. 'Although I defend his right to express an opinion, he could never stop himself from going that extra league. He made an art out of insulting people. He insulted my plays and he insulted my horsemanship and some of my friends.'

'Ah yes, your friends,' said Diomedes. 'Or your friend! You should be careful, though, good Hilarian — some friends are other people's special friends, and that can be dangerous.'

Hilarian scowled but said no more.

'Were you not one of his patrons, Obelius?' Erasistratus asked.

'I was. I was publishing his work,' the banker admitted.

'But why were you publishing him, when seemingly no one thought very highly of his poetry?' Erasistratus queried.

'That is what I would like to know, too,' Hanufer interjected. 'I understand that he had been a court poet all over the Levant. Earlier today I talked to Philitas of Cos, and he told me that Sotades had written versions of *The Iliad* and *The Odyssey*. Philitas gave me the impression that he did not like his work himself, but he suggested that he was underrated as a poet. He had actually invented a new type of verse that he called palindromic poetry. It could be read back and forth, yet had different meanings in each direction.'

'Philitas of Cos is a great scholar,' said Erasistratus, helping himself to more wine from the pitcher by his couch. 'He taught Callimachus, Theocritus, Zenodotus and others and is a poet himself — and possibly the greatest poetry critic and the finest natural philosopher in the Musaeum. He also taught the pharaoh and queen, do not forget.'

'Pharaoh Ptolemy himself told Hanufer that Philitas of Cos knows more about Sotades than anyone else,' Patroclus added.

'That was certainly the impression I received,' Hanufer returned. 'In particular, he confirmed for me that the poem that was written on the altar of the *temenos* was exactly the poem that Sotades had written.'

'Which I also told you,' Patroclus said with a trace of impatience.

'And now there is none left,' said Stratonicus. 'We burned every last piece of papyrus with any of Sotades's poems.'

Diomedes snorted derisively and shook his head as he continued to shell quails' eggs.

'The people of Alexandria liked his poems,' Obelius pointed out. 'There are many people who wanted to own copies of his works.'

'So you can see, it was a good commercial arrangement for our publishing house,' Stratonicus added. 'It would have made us a lot of money.' Then, with a shrug of the shoulders, he added, 'But His Majesty had to be obeyed, and when Sotades was thrown in prison we had to drop the plans.'

'Did you try him in court, Judge Thespos?' Hanufer asked.

'No! His crime was against the pharaoh and the queen, so there was no trial. Patroclus, as the pharaoh's vizier, deals with such matters for Ptolemy Philadelphus.'

The admiral nodded. 'That is correct. I issued the order and Sotades was arrested and thrown in prison.'

'Was he arrested by *Archiphylakites* Gryton?'

The judge shrugged. 'Of course. And imprisoned by him in the Necropolis prison, which is just on the outskirts of the city by the City of the Dead.'

'Do you know how he escaped, Judge Thespos?'

'No one knows for sure. Gryton may have discovered something, but if he did that knowledge died with him. I suspect that he bribed one of his jailors. I do not have the details, other than that the jailor absconded. As a *demosios*, the jailor will be sentenced to death if you or your constables find him.'

Hanufer had not realised that the prison guards were public slaves. He was about to ask another question when Diomedes, having finished his quails' eggs and washed them down with more wine, sat up and cleared his throat.

'All of this is in my poem, as I told Admiral Patroclus it would be. I gave the ladies a small rendition, but since it is not yet completed I am not in a position to give anything more than a fragment.'

'Remember, I am paying to have it published, Diomedes,' said Obelius abruptly. 'That being the case, I forbid you to reveal too much.' He beamed at the rest of the gathering. 'Since Sotades caused the royal couple so much distress, we are going to present it to them.'

Diomedes noisily slurped more wine. 'Yes, yes, Obelius. But as I say, it is not yet complete. For one thing, I have yet to finish a small verse about this pathetic desecration at the sacrifice. I couldn't be there myself, as I had an unsettled stomach after our return to port. Though,' he said, beginning to giggle, 'that thing with the eels made me laugh. Eels, of all things!' And he went into a paroxysm of mirth.

'Why is that so amusing?' Hanufer asked, and the poet's laughter halted abruptly. 'I understand that eels are regarded as an insult to the Greek gods. What is amusing about them?'

Patroclus drained his drinking bowl and then belched loudly. 'Diomedes has peculiar pastimes. He has many fishponds in his villa garden, all of which are connected by conduits from the Canopic Canal. He has a passion for all sorts of fish and sea creatures, including eels.' He tossed a grape at the poet, who casually caught it in his mouth. 'Tell the *Archiphylakites* how many you have.'

'I have a dozen ponds, each stocked with different types of fish. They are my darlings. Some people keep birds, others have dogs, but I adore fish and eels. The god Harpocrates uses them to send me messages. I can tell much by the way they come to feed, or the way that they swim. The eels especially.'

'But I hear these were dead eels that were left at the *temenos*?' Hilarian asked Hanufer, his voice slightly slurred.

'There was a smallish pithos jar full of them, but again, I don't understand why Diomedes considers eels so amusing,' Hanufer replied. So far, no one other than he, Sabu and Cario knew that they had had their tails stuffed into their throats, so if anyone mentioned it he would want to know how they knew.

'Go on, Diomedes, tell the overseer the whole story,' Patroclus urged.

'Very well. I don't know if you are aware, Hanufer, but there are many types of eels. In my pond I have the *muraina* eels, each as long as a man and many as thick as a man's thigh. My eels are famous in the city and many wonder at them when I hold parties. Philitas of Cos used to come to watch them feed. Inevitably he said he wanted to do an experiment, to see how they would behave if I didn't feed them for a while.'

'This was Philitas's idea?' Hanufer queried.

'Yes, and it was with glee that he was there on the morning when the largest of them started to eat the smallest. It ate six of them, in fact.' He gulped wine. 'It was quite amusing really.'

*So eels turn into cannibals when they are hungry. Does that mean that if there were no others and the eel was starving, it would eat its own tail?* thought Hanufer. *But it surprises me that Philitas the philosopher would enjoy observing starving creatures. He seemed a more gentle man than that.*

'Tell the rest of the tale, Diomedes!' Patroclus said, pouring more wine. 'What happened then?'

'The great beast died. Philitas took the body away, or rather he brought a young servant to help him carry it, as he can barely walk himself with all that ridiculous iron jewellery he wears. Anyway, back in the Musaeum he cut it open and took out the half-digested eels and the juices from its stomach. He put the juices in the water of rats he was studying, and they too died. The reason, he said, was that the slime the eels cover themselves in is poisonous. The great eel poisoned itself when it ate the others.' He folded his arms and pouted. 'There, that's the story.'

'Not all of it,' the admiral said. 'Who heard about it?'

Diomedes glared at the vizier. 'The buffoon Sotades.'

Hilarian snapped his fingers. 'That's right. I had forgotten. And he made up a poem about the eels. How did it go —?'

Erasistratus laughed. 'I don't remember exactly, but it was something about a soothsaying eel having an ear to the god of silence and secrets, but the secret and silent god had no tongue, so he couldn't tell the soothsaying eel he was covered in poison.'

Judge Thespos had been drinking his wine, but suddenly laughed, spraying a mouthful all over the floor.

'Was Philitas of Cos mentioned in this poem?' Hanufer asked, his interest piqued. He thought that Philitas would surely be a suitable subject for mirth, with his strange interests and the iron bracelets and anklets that he wore. If he'd correctly interpreted what the philosopher had said, then the irons were a symbol of freedom. He disapproved of slavery, when it was all around him.

Erasistratus was swift to reply. 'Sotades would not have dared to challenge the intellect of Philitas.'

'And yet he was derogatory about other rulers in the Levant and even had the temerity to criticise the pharaoh and his queen,' remarked Hanufer. 'Most curious.'

'Ha!' exclaimed Hilarian. 'We can see that you are an Egyptian and think as an Egyptian does, Hanufer of Crocodilopolis. Sotades is a Greek and has the Greek prejudices. He disapproved of their incestuous marriage, as so many still do.'

Patroclus glared at him. 'Have a care, playwright. Pharaoh Ptolemy and Queen Arsinoe now view themselves — and all of us — as Egyptians. And just so you don't forget, Sotades is dead. He was a Greek, but a miserable one that the world is better off without.'

His voice had a distinct slur to it, making Hanufer even more conscious of the strength of the wine from the *krater*. He determined to drink even slower.

Hilarian did not seem ready to quit now that he had the group's attention. 'I think we all know Sotades is — or was — a dolt. I have no cause to love him, but I worry for our art, all the literary arts — poetry, prose and the most meaningful of all, plays. What happens when we are forbidden to write about certain things because we might offend?'

'Do your plays offend anyone, Hilarian?' Hanufer asked.

The young playwright grinned. 'Not yet!'

Obelius chortled. 'And you may find yourself without a patron if you choose to cross that line. Remember, Hilarian, some lines are not for crossing.'

Patroclus grunted. 'Good advice that you should listen to yourself, old friend.'

Hanufer thought he saw Obelius flash the vizier an angry glance, but it disappeared almost instantly. Nevertheless, an awkward silence fell over the group, broken by Diomedes.

'Well, apart from that,' Diomedes went on, with a contemptuous wave of his hand, 'we were talking about my poem. Proper poetry, not Sotades's doggerel! I have to consult Hecataeus the sculptor about some of the things that happened on the Island of Caunus.' He grinned suggestively. 'I suspect that he and Sotades were lovers while he was there. It would not surprise anyone, for as you will see when he comes to Alexandria, the sculptor is himself well sculpted.'

'Diomedes!' Patroclus exclaimed sternly.

'Nothing wrong in that, is there?' the poet replied petulantly. 'Anyway, he has certain embellishments that I need to be clear about, as it will make the poem a classic.'

'When does he arrive in Alexandria?' Patroclus queried. 'I gave him a pass to come to see me when he comes to the Royal Palace.'

'He plans to come the day after tomorrow and bring the statue of the goddess Tyche that he has been working on as a gift to Ptolemy and Arsinoe. I will see him first, so that I can complete my poem.'

He filled his drinking bowl with wine and drank it all off in one go. It was the sixth time he had done so since coming into the *andron*. He peered into the empty pitcher and smacked his lips noisily.

Stratonicus pushed himself off his couch with a laugh. 'Why, Father, we are not being as solicitous to our guests as we should. The pitchers need replenishing, and I think we may need Erasmos to recharge the *krater*.'

As he went round collecting, then filling and dispensing the wine pitchers, Diomedes stood up unsteadily.

'I will give you fine friends a taster of my poem about the life and death of Sotades the Obscene.'

Hanufer realised that only he and Obelius had barely drunk any of their wine. In his case it was because he wanted to gather information, and when others loosened their tongues with wine it was too important an opportunity to miss. He wondered whether Obelius just had a good head for his wine, or whether he had in fact only pretended to drink as freely as his guests. Perhaps as a businessman he too wanted to gather information that could be useful to him. Either that or he was being faithful to the god Harpocrates, whose shrine above his entrance door proclaimed that he was a devotee of secrecy.

He pondered this as he half listened to the rambling verse of the drunken poet. Was Obelius more than just a businessman and banker? Was his veneration of the god of silence and secrets an indication that he was a spy? If so, for whom?

Then Obelius winked at him and with a hand made a back and forth movement like a swimming fish.

It was the middle of the night by the time they had reached safety and washed away all traces and smells of their deeds. Then, slowly, they anointed each other's body to take away all impurities before they fell onto the bed and made passionate love.

'The Magnificence will be pleased this time.'

'But not until the other matter is taken care of.'

'It will be as we planned, when the day has dawned.'

'Soon, revenge will be complete.'

'And it will all begin.'

They made love twice more before dawn, when they had to part to attend to the other matter.

# CHAPTER 18

The following morning, as soon as Hanufer and Sabu sat down at their desks, Cario appeared. He had a black eye and a split lip.

'How did you get those?' Hanufer asked.

Cario winced as he smiled and pressed the back of his hand to his lip. 'From asking questions at the fish market, my lord. I thought that if I could find out who had sold a large quantity of eels, then I could find out who had purchased them.'

'And did you?'

'My questioning was not popular, sir. There are many fishermen and fish merchants who sell their goods in the markets, but I think they were all frightened of being found to have sold the eels that were used to desecrate the *temenos*. I was struck to the ground by one seller and again by another at the other end of the market.'

'Is that where you went after we left the Musaeum?'

Cario looked abashed. 'I did, sir. It was not far out of my way, and I came straight back afterwards to help Pollio.'

Sabu frowned. 'You should not have gone by yourself, Cario. If you had a constable with you, there would not have been any violence towards you. And those ruffians who cuffed you would have cooperated.' He looked over at his boss. 'Shall I follow this up, sir? I could go myself or take Cario so he can identify these fellows.'

Hanufer shook his head. 'No, I want you to come with me to Rhakotis, but tell either Pylyp or Filemon to go with Cario. They are to impress on the fish merchants that the law does not take kindly to having our *demosios* abused like that.

Meanwhile, where did you put the money you collected from Overseer Gryton's house?'

'I have it secured in my chest, my lord.' He rose and went to a large chest that he had brought with him from Crocodilopolis and unlocked it with the wooden key he always kept with him. He took out a heavy sack of money and laid it on Hanufer's desk.

As Sabu went off with Cario to pass on these instructions, Hanufer called Pollio through.

'I want to see the papyri concerning the appointments of both *Archiphylakites* Gryton and Sergeant Kraspar. Anything you have about them personally.'

Pollio looked puzzled. 'There will not much, my lord.'

While the scribe scuttled off to look, Hanufer turned his attention to the sack of money. As he went through it, he saw that there was a considerable amount from outside of Alexandria. Gold, silver and bronze, just like the samples Sabu had shown him the evening before.

*So where has all this come from? Money from different lands, but why? What was Gryton up to? Were these bribes of some sort? And why is there so much Judean coinage?*

Replacing the coins in the sack, Hanufer went over and laid it in his own chest. It also had a good Egyptian lock, which he considered far superior to the crude Greek locks. Securing it, he sat back down and proceeded to check through the cases that Gryton had been working on. It was clear that there were a few outstanding petitions that he would have to deal with.

But the documents did not explain what Gryton had been spending his time on until his death.

The Cibotas Canal ran through the middle of the old town of Rhakotis. It was spanned by two bridges: an old wooden Egyptian one and the other newly built by Greek engineers during the reign of Pharaoh Ptolemy Soter. Hanufer and Sabu crossed it on their way to the outer city wall where the Necropolis prison was to be found.

It was an old, sandstone, one-storeyed building with a flat roof, slit windows covered in iron bars, and a heavily bolted door. Sabu thumped on the door with the pommel of his sword and a grille slid open. When Hanufer showed his pectoral of office, they were admitted by a surly-looking fellow wearing a short, grimy chiton with a thick leather belt round his waist, from which dangled a prodigious bunch of metal keys. He wore thick cothurnus boots and tucked into the top of one was the handle of a dagger.

Sabu quickly assumed his authoritative manner and barked questions at the man. His name was Taras, and he was a *demosios*, like Cario.

'It is not often that we get visitors here,' he said as he led them into the building, which was swelteringly hot, due to its lack of windows. 'Indeed, you are the first officials since Sotades escaped and the police stopped coming. Before that, of course, we occasionally had the pharaoh himself.'

'Pharaoh Ptolemy?' Hanufer asked in surprise.

'Himself and his vizier and their bodyguards,' Taras replied, showing them into a large, sparsely furnished room containing only a table and a few stools, a rack with lashes, and another table with piles of mugs and food bowls. It was clearly the jailors' room, for bolted doors on three other walls led from it. 'We guards were not allowed to stay in the pharaoh's presence, of course. He used to come every now and then to talk to the poet.'

'How many prisoners are there here?'

'Only two dozen. There are many more in the main prison by the Mareotis city wall. All who came here were under sentence of death, so they knew that their next stop would be the City of the Dead, if they were permitted burial or cremation after the sentence was carried out. The City of the Dead caters for all — embalming and entombment for the Egyptians and those so minded, or cremation for the Greeks.'

'Where is the death sentence carried out?' Hanufer asked.

'That depends on the sentence given by the judge. It could be drowning, impalement, decapitation or burying alive in the sand. All of that would be outside the city walls.' He took a rapid breath. 'Or pulled limb from limb by driven horses. That would be either in the stadium just south of here or the hippodrome by the Canopic Gate.'

'And if they were not permitted burial or cremation?' Sabu asked, suspiciously.

'Then they would be transported to the Musaeum, to the flesh cutters in the Medical School.' He looked sideways as if he meant to spit, but restrained himself in the presence of the two police officials. 'We sometimes never know what happens to their bodies. It is not for the likes of us to question, is it, sir?'

*It is just as Erasistratus said,* Hanufer thought. *Ptolemy Philadelphus permits vivisection, the dissection of live criminals.*

'How many jailors are there at a time?'

'Two of us, always.'

'Then how did Sotades escape?'

Taras looked nervously at his interlocutors. 'I had no part in that, my lord. It was Zalmoxis and Damon. Damon was ill and wasn't here, and Zalmoxis let him free. Then he ran off and we never saw him again.'

'Zalmoxis, that sounds to be a Dacian name?' Sabu queried.

'He was, sir.'

'Did *Archiphylakites* Gryton and his sergeant investigate?' Hanufer asked.

'They did, but what was there to find? Nothing. Zalmoxis had gone, paid off by Sotades's rich friends.'

Hanufer grimaced. 'Show me his cell.'

Taras called out to his fellow jailor and unlocked the middle door. Hanufer and Sabu followed him, passing along the lamplit corridor with dingy cells on either side. The occupants all showed complete disinterest as they moved along.

'Here, sir, the best cell was given to him. As you see, it has a grille window in the ceiling so he had real sunlight in the day, with shade enough, and at night he could see the stars.'

'Was he allowed to read?'

'No, my lord, nor to write. Though that didn't stop him making up his poems. He used to amuse us with them, sir. Ruder than any drunkard he was, and he could describe any kind of fornicating. You only had to ask. While he was here he would shout out his poems and give these doomed fellows some cheer. Now they have none. They are just waiting to die.'

'Yet the pharaoh didn't give a time when Sotades was to die?'

'No, my lord. If he hadn't escaped, he'd probably still be living and breathing here in this cell.'

'But now he's dead,' said Sabu. 'Drowned in a jar.'

Taras shrugged his shoulders. 'Yes, sir. If you believe that he's dead, but that isn't what they are all saying. The word is that he lives and he showed that when the bull was to be sacrificed at the Temple of Poseidon.'

Hanufer and Sabu had just crossed back over the canal and were walking along one of the more affluent streets with large villas behind high walls when they saw a litter carried by two swarthy servants. It was passing through the gates leading to a whitewashed villa surrounded by palm trees and acacias. The lady being carried under the canopy was the unmistakeably beautiful Lady Didyme. They watched as guards closed the gates behind her.

'So now we know where Pharaoh Ptolemy's other mistress lives,' Hanufer remarked. 'After the revelries last night, I am surprised that she is abroad so early.'

'I thought it was a symposium, my lord. That means men only apart from entertainers, doesn't it? I know that she is a musician and a poet, as the Lady Bilistiche's stable manager told me, but was she entertaining you?'

Hanufer explained about Eupheme, Obelius's wife's party. 'If their party was anything like the symposium, then she may have had much wine to drink. Certainly, my fellow symposium guests had eaten and drunk far more than was good for them. At least three of them required servants to assist them. Diomedes the poet grew quite passionate telling us about a poem he is writing about Sotades. He said he was not done partying and had it in mind to end the evening in debauchery and that he knew a woman who would succumb to his charm. What he meant, I don't know. I think his brain was addled with wine by that time.'

Sabu nodded his head sagely. 'People often start thinking about such things when wine or beer takes away their usual sense of civility, my lord.'

For his own part, Hanufer regretted that he had not seen Nefrit again the previous evening, as the ladies had all departed before the symposium ended. There were many things he had wanted to ask her.

Sabu tapped his head. 'I understand, my lord. I wish that I had supped a little less beer last night. I take it that you used your hand as often as you usually do?'

Hanufer smiled. His sergeant knew him well enough to know that he never allowed a drinking bowl or goblet to be filled more than twice.

'You are quite right, Sabu. There were things that —'

They heard the sound of a horn being blown from quite near and then the sound of horses galloping. Moments later, they saw people stepping quickly aside to clear a path as Pylyp rode towards them, leading a second horse by its reins.

The corporal drew to a halt before them and dismounted swiftly by flicking a leg over his mount's neck and landing adroitly on the balls of his feet.

'My lord, you are needed urgently. There has been a death in the Brucheum. Pollio told me you were coming here with Sergeant Sabu, so I brought these two horses.'

'Who has died, Pylyp?' Hanufer demanded.

'The poet Diomedes, my lord. His house slaves found his body this morning at his villa, when they were tending to the fish. He had drowned.'

A crowd had gathered outside the villa of the poet Diomedes. The gates were closed, but as Hanufer and Sabu rode up the two servants on guard duty opened them.

'Look, my lord,' Sabu said, pointing to the wall beside the gate. 'There is writing upon the wall.'

Looking down from his mount, Hanufer saw that someone had drawn a few hieroglyphs and underneath them had written something in Greek.

'No one is to touch what is written there!' Hanufer ordered the servants as he rode his horse through the gates. 'I will return to inspect it.'

They dismounted in the villa courtyard where one young slave took their reins while another older man with tear-stained cheeks anxiously led them along a meandering path through a landscaped garden full of palm trees, acacias and several ornamental ponds full of different types of fish.

Two more house slaves were kneeling, wailing beside the body of the poet, which was lying on its front on the marble tiles beside a large pond. Diomedes's chlamys was soaked and clung to his body, and his bared arms and legs were covered in gaping wounds, where small chunks of flesh had been torn away. Blood had oozed from his wounds and coalesced into a pool around his head. Lying on the edge of the pool was an overturned flask of wine.

'He … he was floating face down in the pond and they … they were feeding on him,' one of the slaves sobbed as the older one who had led Hanufer and Sabu ordered them to stand up.

Sabu knelt down and felt the poet's neck, and after a moment he looked up at Hanufer and shook his head. 'There is no doubt. He is dead, my lord. Shall I turn him over?'

'It is horrible —' began the youngest of the weeping servants. 'That's why we —' His voice trailed off and he covered his mouth as Sabu turned the body over.

The face had virtually been eaten away. The eye sockets were both gory holes and the nose, earlobes and lips had been torn off. Worse, within the mangled mouth only a stub of the tongue remained.

Blood had soaked his chlamys where it hung over his groin.

Hanufer knelt down and grimaced as he looked under the chlamys and saw the horrific injuries that had been done to the soft flesh beneath. Then he turned his attention upwards and looked closely at the mutilated visage.

'I can smell wine, but also something else,' he said to Sabu. He leaned even closer and sniffed. 'Vinegar! His hair smells of vinegar.'

He stood and looked at the pond. Among the lotus plants on its surface were great snake-like bodies with long ribbon fins running down the lengths of their backs, weaving in and out. They were of different colours, some yellow and black, others black or green. Some were freckled, others striped.

'Fetch me some vinegar and some meat,' he ordered the older man, who appeared to be the head house slave. 'You others go inside the villa.'

Once on their own, Hanufer turned to Sabu. 'Diomedes was very drunk last night, as I told you. He said he wanted to find a woman as debauched as he.'

'It looks as if he drank even more when he returned here, my lord. Perhaps he did meet the woman he lusted after and came home to celebrate, or to drown his sorrows if he was unsuccessful. Perhaps he just fell into the pond.'

'And was mauled by his eels? I am not convinced, Sabu.'

The head slave returned with a small flask of vinegar and some pieces of cold roasted chicken. Hanufer took them and tossed a piece of chicken into the pond close to three large eels. They languidly glided towards it, and one snatched it. A moment later he poured vinegar over several other pieces of meat and then tossed them further into the pond. A few moments elapsed, and then the surface of the water seethed as several eels congregated on the chicken pieces and a feeding frenzy erupted.

'It is true, it seems,' Hanufer said. 'Vinegar sends them mad.' He turned and pointed to the body. 'Why does Diomedes reek of vinegar unless someone poured it over him and perhaps pushed him in the water and held him so that the eels could feed on him?'

He turned to the head slave and ordered him to get a blanket to cover the dead poet.

'What shall we do with the body, my lord?' Sabu asked.

But Hanufer put a finger to his lips and knelt again by the body. 'Help me turn him over again.'

Mystified, Sabu did as bidden and watched while his boss felt under the matted hair, running his hands up the back of the neck. A moment later, Hanufer nodded.

'I had a feeling that there might be a puncture wound here. This was no drunken accident. I am almost certain that Diomedes was murdered in the same way as the slave that we found in the bull pen at the Temple of Poseidon. He was dead before he was dumped in this pool.'

Corporal Pylyp had commandeered a horse from the mansion of Didyme, as Hanufer had instructed him to, and followed as quickly as he could, calling at the station on the way to bring two or three more constables with him. While they waited, Hanufer took out his writing set and wrote a message. He ordered one of the constables to return to the station and bring a cart to transport the body to the Medical School, where it was to be delivered to the anatomists Herophilus and Erasistratus.

The two other constables he ordered to stand by the gates and let no one else in or out of the villa until they were relieved.

Sabu led the horses as they walked through the gates to view the hieroglyphs and writing on the outer wall. He leaned close and under his breath informed Hanufer that the two constables were Sidvain and Rhoglos, the two Thracians that he was less than happy about.

'Then perhaps they can redeem themselves in your eyes,' Hanufer returned.

If anything, the crowd around the gates of the villa had increased in size and people were noisily talking about the writing on the wall. Sabu ordered them back so that Hanufer could examine it. They saw a single line of hieroglyphics and some writing in Greek beneath it.

*The gods grew angry at his poisoned visions,*
*And even the eels spat out his vicious poisons.*
*Treacherous dogs beware for revenge is sweet,*
*Soon the poisonous toad will lie at Hector's feet.*

'It is another message like the one at the *temenos*, my lord. But what does it mean?'

'I think it may be another of the poems of Sotades. Last night at the symposium I heard that Sotades composed a poem about Diomedes's eels. The anatomist Erasistratus did not remember it clearly, but said it was about a soothsaying eel having an ear to the god of silence and secrets. But the secret and silent god had no tongue, so he couldn't tell the soothsaying eel that he was covered in poison. This is not that poem, but it does refer to eels and the poison that they are covered in.'

'Does that tell us anything, my lord?'

'I am not sure. Apparently, Sotades wrote it because Philitas of Cos had performed an experiment on Diomedes's eels to see what happened if they were not fed. They turned cannibalistic and one ate several others. Diomedes took exception to the poem, but it seems to have been very popular and caused much amusement in the city.'

Sabu pointed to the writing and then indicated the crowd with his chin. 'Shall I have it washed away, and the crowd dispersed, my lord?'

Hanufer shook his head. Drawing Sabu close so they would not be overheard, he said, 'Not yet. As with the one at the Temple of Poseidon, I think it is important that people see it. Particularly with this one, we can't be seen to be hiding something. Diomedes was a famous poet and he is dead. It will soon circulate that he died in his pool and was savaged by his eels. That is what the killer wants to be known, that there have been two messages and that the second one is linked with the sudden unexpected death of Diomedes. But as yet the murderer doesn't know that we know that the slave found in the bull pen was murdered and that we have found that there is a link between that murder and Diomedes's death. More, we know that Diomedes was murdered in the same way, which indicates that the murderer of both is the same person. That is why I want the anatomists to examine the body to see if I am correct.'

'But will people realise that whoever put this message up caused the death of the poet? If that poem you heard about last night was widely known, then surely they will think that Sotades was here. That his presence, man or ghost, caused the death.'

Hanufer had taken his writing set out and had knelt down on the ground to prepare it, before making a copy of the text. 'That seems to be part of the reason for the message. But there is more to it than that, Sabu,' he said as he worked. 'There is a warning here. But we shall consider it later, after we have seen the anatomists.'

He stood up and looked round at the crowd of onlookers, all craning to see the message. He took the reins of his horse from his sergeant.

'Let us give people some time to see this strange message, and we shall see what rumours circulate about the city. When the guards are relieved later this day, you can arrange to have this message and the one in the *temenos* removed. Now, you ride ahead to the Medical School and I will follow soon.'

He mounted his horse and looked down at Sabu. 'I shall go and inform Admiral Patroclus of this sad occurrence. He is sure to be upset, and Pharaoh Ptolemy must also be informed.'

Admiral Patroclus had already heard the news when Hanufer was shown into his sumptuous office. His eyes were red, and it looked as if he had wiped tears away. He pointed at the chair on the other side of his desk and Hanufer sat down.

'I was about to send for you, Hanufer,' he snapped. 'It is almost time for me to go to my morning audience with His Majesty, and I need to know more about this atrocity. Mighty Zeus, but it is unbelievable, my good friend ate and supped with us at Obelius's symposium last night. What happened? I heard that he drowned in one of his pools.'

'It was more than drowning, my lord. His body was mauled by his eels.' Hanufer had decided not to mention his suspicions of murder until he saw how the pharaoh's vizier reacted. Since he had not told him of the death of the slave in the bull pen,

217

he saw no reason to inform him yet that the two deaths seemed to be linked.

'Eels!' Patroclus gasped. 'We ... we were talking of those last night.'

'And there was another message written on the walls outside his villa. Hieroglyphs and a few lines.'

Hanufer drew out the scrap of papyrus on which he had copied the message and the hieroglyphs. He handed it across the desk to the vizier and watched as he read it with a puzzled expression and then with a slight look of horror.

'Do you know what this means?'

'Not yet, my lord, but I am going to study it.'

'This was on the walls outside the villa, you say?'

'I have men guarding it and I have arranged for it to be removed later today.'

Patroclus sat back and chewed his beard for a moment, then he pushed the papyrus back across the desk. 'I am distraught to lose Diomedes. He was a good soothsayer and a great poet, and — my friend.'

Hanufer nodded empathetically. 'My condolences, sir.'

'And Obelius was going to publish his poem about the death of Sotades.'

Hanufer nodded. 'So I understood from the symposium, my lord. I am sorry about his death. I am sure that all who attended the symposium will be, too.'

Patroclus nodded absently, as he continued to chew his beard, seemingly in deep thought. Then, suddenly, he stood up and waved a hand dismissively. 'Come, we must go to the audience and tell Their Majesties of this tragedy. Bring that papyrus and the doggerel on it. It will be as well that they know about it straight away.'

Hanufer stood, rolled the papyrus up and stowed it in his sleeve.

'Do you think it has anything to do with the poet Sotades, my lord?'

'Of course not! Sotades is dead! This is just someone making mischief! One thing is certain, though; the pharaoh and his queen will be mightily distressed by the death and angered by this message. It will be your job to find out who is behind it as quickly as possible.'

Hanufer bowed. He did not relish the prospect of an audience with the pharaoh and his queen, but at the same time he wanted to see how they would react.

# CHAPTER 19

A young student physician led Hanufer and Sabu into the anatomy amphitheatre, where Herophilus was busily demonstrating on a corpse. Most of the benches on the tiers were occupied by other young men who were watching intently as the anatomist deftly dissected muscles away from the thigh of the cadaver. The individual muscles were peeled back from the top of the leg and spread outwards like the petals of a flower. A leather hide was spread over the rest of the body so that only the leg that Herophilus was working on was visible.

Seeing the Overseer of Police and his sergeant, Herophilus paused with scalpel and forceps in hand. 'Welcome, *Archiphylakites* Hanufer and Sergeant Sabu. If you will sit for a few minutes while I finish this demonstration, then I shall be with you.'

He pointed the scalpel at the young students sitting on the nearest bench and gestured for them to move further along.

The two police officials sat and watched as Herophilus continued to dissect and lecture. An all-pervading smell of blood, natron and vinegar was almost overpowering and caused both Hanufer and Sabu to cover their mouths and noses as they watched.

*It looks as if one gets used to the stench of death*, thought Hanufer. *These young men hardly seem to notice the odour, and old Herophilus notices it not at all.*

'I have now detached all of the muscles from the pelvis and from their uppermost insertions in the thigh bone. Can you all see this middle part of the bone?'

The student physicians all nodded and answered in the affirmative.

'Look at the skeleton hanging from the wall and tell me what you see.'

'It looks as if there is bone growth around it, master. He had a broken and healed leg, perhaps,' called out a student next to Hanufer.

'That is correct. He was fortunate, as such injuries are often fatal. He would have walked with a limp ever after, as you can see from these muscles, which had been badly scarred.'

He put down his instruments and, reaching under the splayed-out muscles, lifted a great roll of flesh from underneath them, which was now clearly the cadaver's skin. He raised it so that they could see it as he pointed to the large, ugly scar.

'This was no ordinary break from an accident, but from a wound. He was doubly fortunate, therefore, as such injuries usually produce much pus. A surgeon probably wanted to amputate it, but had that been done I doubt that he would have lived as long as he did. He would have died long since, and you would not have the privilege of learning from inside his body.'

He lay the skin back on the surface and took another hide from under the table to cover the dissected limb.

'That will do for now. We will continue our dissection tomorrow and work down his leg to the knee.'

Herophilus washed his arms and hands in a bucket of water and vinegar as the student physicians filed out.

'I received your message before I began my lecture to my students,' Herophilus told them, while he examined his nails to ensure he had removed all traces of gore. 'I am afraid that my colleague Erasistratus is unwell today. He sent word to me that he has been suffering from an upset stomach since last night. I believe he attended a symposium in the Brucheum.'

'I was there, too,' Hanufer replied. 'There was an abundance of food and wine.'

'Ah!' Herophilus replied with a slight disapproving shake of his head. 'My colleague Erasistratus enjoys a symposium, and the more Dionysian it is the better.'

'As did Diomedes, whose body was brought here this morning,' Hanufer added.

The anatomist frowned, reverting to his usual serious demeanour after his implied rebuke about his absent colleague. 'I had it taken next door, to our inner dissecting room. There are students from several of the city's noble families, and I did not wish them to be shocked by seeing the body of a distinguished poet being brought in.' He shook the water from his hands and reached for a towel to dry them. 'Especially not when he was in such a mutilated state.'

He beckoned for them to follow.

The body of Diomedes lay naked upon a wooden table in a smaller chamber, illuminated by light streaming in from high clerestory windows.

Hanufer described how the body had been found, including the message that had been written on the boundary wall of the villa beside the gate.

'I had heard about it already,' Herophilus said. 'As I said, many of the students come from wealthy families and live in the Brucheum. All sorts of whispers are circulating around the Medical School, the Musaeum and the Library this morning. They say that Sotades the poet is abroad and seeking revenge.'

He bent over the body and started to examine the many wounds. 'You can see the teeth marks where flesh has been torn out. I am no expert on eels, but I do know that they have two sets of teeth. One set to hold their prey and another set further back to help pull their prey down their throats. You would need to talk to someone like Philitas of Cos for more information. He is the expert on such creatures. But to me it looks as if these are straightforward bites. They have taken his eyes, nose, ears and most of his tongue.'

'He smells of vinegar, do you not agree?' Hanufer said.

Herophilus sniffed and nodded his head. 'And wine. But why? Was it bad wine? That would account for Erasistratus's ailment.'

Hanufer shook his head. 'I don't think there was anything wrong with the wine. I did an experiment while we were at his eel pond. Eels are driven into a frenzy by vinegar.'

The anatomist straightened and pointed to the gory mess where his genitals had been. 'It looks as if they in their frenzy like to feast on softer tissues.'

Sabu snorted with disgust and looked away. 'I'll never eat these creatures again, my lord.'

Hanufer patted his sergeant's shoulder. Then, looking back at Herophilus, he went on, 'From looking at his body, can you tell how he died?'

'Do you mean, can I tell whether he died by drowning or from these bites?'

Hanufer stared straight into his eyes. 'Or if there could be another cause.'

The anatomist nodded shrewdly. 'The Medical School does not usually receive bodies from the nobility. I wondered why you had him sent here. We receive criminals when they have expired.'

'And not only when they have died?' Hanufer replied. 'As Erasistratus said the last time we were here, Pharaoh Ptolemy Philadelphus permits condemned criminals to be —'

Herophilus was quick to cut him off. 'The pharaoh is the highest authority and his decisions are final. He has others who are able to carry out his direct orders.'

*Is this what Obelius implied to Erasistratus last night? Are these the supplies he talked of for the Medical School? And from the audience Patroclus and I had this morning, it is clear that none may challenge the pharaoh when he speaks.*

It had not been an easy audience, either with the pharaoh or his queen. Both were clearly angered by the death of Diomedes, but especially when they saw the message that Hanufer had copied. As Patroclus had told him before, it was his task to uncover who had written those messages and why. The royal couple affirmed that in no uncertain manner.

'I have no wish to take a scalpel to this body if it will anger the pharaoh,' said Herophilus. 'I am not even sure that I can tell by opening him up.'

'Then let us turn him over,' Hanufer suggested. 'You can do this under my authority.'

Herophilus's eyes opened wide. 'Are you thinking of the way the slave was killed?'

Hanufer nodded, and with Sabu's help the anatomist rolled the body over. The Overseer of Police pointed to the puncture wound that he had felt as the body lay by the pool.

'Did you explore it?' Herophilus asked.

'I did not. I thought I would leave that to you in case I made it worse.'

Going over to a smaller table laden with dissection instruments, the anatomist picked up a probe. Returning, he inserted it into the puncture wound and advanced it. He nodded. 'It travels up a channel through the tissues. You are right, this seems to be the cause of death. The encephalon has been punctured.'

'Then to be sure, can you dissect the brain free?'

Herophilus again nodded and asked Sabu to help him draw his table with his instruments close. Then, just as Erasistratus had done, he started to dissect the neck in order to reach the base of the skull. Hanufer and Sabu watched him peel back the fascia of the scalp, then saw the back of the cranium so that he could dissect out and remove the brain, which he placed in a large metal basin.

Carefully bisecting it and separating the two halves, Herophilus was able to show the conical-shaped space full of blood where a murder weapon had been inserted and rotated to macerate the brain to a pulp.

'So, Diomedes has been murdered by the same method as was used on the slave who was found in the bull pen,' Hanufer said.

'But do you know who that person was, other than that he was a slave?' Herophilus asked. 'Is this even of importance?'

'Oh, I think we have a better idea of who he is now, and it may be of the greatest importance,' Hanufer replied. 'But I must now have your oath that you will talk to no one other than Erasistratus about these cases. And he must not talk to anyone either.'

'I shall tell him as soon as he recovers. And I swear by the oath I took to Hippocrates and Aesculapius that I will talk with no one else about this.'

Hanufer clapped his hands. 'So now I must go, but it is important that I see Erasistratus today. At the start of the symposium last night, he said he would study the encephalon that he removed from that slave, as he said he would do when he removed it the other day.'

He pointed to the bloody grey pink organ of the poet. 'I would like you and he to study both brains and send a report to me at my office today.'

The senior anatomist raised an eyebrow, as if unused to being given what amounted to an order from an official. But he merely nodded. 'I shall see to it. I will start by making a comparison of the two organs.'

Hanufer nodded. 'And now, tell me whose body is in your anatomy amphitheatre, the one you are dissecting to show your students?'

Herophilus looked at him with narrowed eyes. 'He is just a criminal or another slave,' he replied slowly. 'I cannot recall which, as Erasistratus arranged it all. He had been dissecting the body for the students and it was only because he was unwell today that I took over.'

'That scar you showed your students and the damage to the muscles and the thigh bone — what do you think caused it?'

'Almost certainly a spear, I would say.'

'That is what I thought you were implying, when you said he had been lucky to live. And you said it was an injury that had healed a long time ago. But let us go back and see his remains. Do you know how he died?'

Herophilus shook his head. 'There was no obvious sign of violence, and I think Erasistratus thought it was from natural causes. But after the murder of Diomedes, I suppose you want me to look —'

Hanufer nodded and the three of them returned to the now empty anatomy amphitheatre. The two police officials watched as the anatomist rolled the hides around the lower limbs and the abdomen and trunk, from which the organs had already been removed. Again, with Sabu's help, he turned the body over and then searched under the hair.

'There is nothing there,' he announced.

Hanufer harrumphed. 'So we do not know if this man was murdered. Yet if he was, it was not by the same means as the slave and Diomedes.'

It was not until they were outside in the fresh air, walking towards the Musaeum, that Sabu ventured to ask his boss a question.

'Do you think we now know what became of Sergeant Kraspar, my lord? Is his the body in the anatomy amphitheatre?'

Hanufer nodded. 'We do, and it is undoubtedly him. We know that he had a limp, having received a spear through the thigh at Macedonia. And I think we also know that the bull pen slave's name is Zalmoxis, and that he was a Dacian. Somehow they are linked through the poet Sotades.'

'And the eels, my lord?'

'Indeed. That is one of several things I need to ask Philitas of Cos about.'

# CHAPTER 20

A young scholar of the Musaeum told Hanufer and Sabu that Philitas of Cos had gone to the Royal Zoo early that morning after breaking his fast.

'He was much excited,' the scholar said. 'He has been making observations on some of the creatures there and thought that something amazing was about to happen. He was not prepared to tell us what, but said that we would all know soon enough.' The young man beamed. 'But we hear there has been much excitement at the Brucheum this morning. The poet Diomedes is drowned. Can you tell me more so that I can —'

'The poet drowned in a pond after drinking too much at a symposium,' Hanufer said, cutting him short. 'Are you a natural philosopher like Philitas, or a scholar of literature?'

The young man shook his head. 'My name is Ajax, my lord *Archiphylakites*, and I am a mathematician.'

'You are named after a Greek hero, one of the heroes in Homer's *The Iliad*?'

Ajax smiled, held out his arms and looked down at his slight frame. 'Named after him, yes. But sadly I have neither his strength nor his bravery. I have not yet made the discoveries that will cause my name to be sung down the ages, but one day I hope that men will rank me alongside Pythagoras or even my former teacher Euclid. Until then, my meagre claim to fame is that Sotades the poet thought me worthy of a line in his imitation of *The Iliad*.'

His interest piqued, Hanufer asked, 'How did he immortalise you?'

Ajax suddenly looked anxious. 'I am not sure if I am permitted, sir. His Majesty Ptolemy Philadelphus ordered that —'

'He ordered that the works of Sotades should be burned, I know. Yet I am intrigued to know what lines he wrote about you.'

Reassured, Ajax smiled coyly. 'It was not a large part, but he wrote:

*'Ajax was a figure puny, as beauteous as aged Hipponax.*
*He figures smaller than a flea, his wick but a twist of flax.'*

Sabu snorted. 'That is nonsense.'

Ajax nodded. 'But he thought enough of me to insult both my intellect and my manhood.'

'Did you know Sotades well?' Hanufer asked.

Ajax was hesitant. 'We had known each other well when I was younger.'

They left the young mathematician and walked on to collect the horses from the stable in front of the Musaeum. 'I want to know what Philitas can tell me about the eels and their teeth, as Herophilus suggested,' Hanufer said. 'Had Ajax been a natural philosopher I might have asked him more, but we have learned something about Sotades from him.'

'That he probably slept with younger men, my lord?'

'That and the fact that being insulted by him was something that people might have thought gave them prestige. It may be even more so now that his works have been destroyed and yet are being passed on by word of mouth.'

'So where are we going now, my lord?'

'We must interrogate everyone who saw Diomedes last night, which means the people at the house of Obelius. The men who attended the symposium with me, and also those women who talked with the poet before he came to the symposium.' Hanufer explained how the women, who wanted him to tell their fortunes, had detained the poet. 'I want you to go back to Diomedes's villa and question everyone who lives there. I believe he lived alone and the household consisted of his house slaves only. Get your two least favourite constables to wash the messages away from the wall and from the *temenos*. Once they have done that, find something else for them to do.'

'And where are you going, sir?'

'I want to find out some more about Sotades the Obscene. And perhaps another matter.'


Hanufer made his way to the Jewish quarter and to the street of the publishers. He had always had a good sense of direction, and the way that Alexandria had been set out and built by the Divine Alexander's architects on a parallel grid system made it a simple matter to find Saul Sofer's establishment. He looked up admiringly at the large wooden sign above the door with its writing in Greek, Hebrew and hieroglyphics.

As before, the establishment was busy with copyists hard at work at desks. The smell of fresh papyrus, inks and paints pervaded the air and made Hanufer, who had himself trained as a scribe before he became an official of the Medjay police, feel quite at home.

'*Archiphylakites* Hanufer of Crocodilopolis,' called out Saul Sofer, weaving his way through customers and his workers to meet him. He bowed and steepled his fingers in greeting. 'I thank you for honouring my humble establishment. What can I do for you?'

At the sound of the greeting, many of the workers looked up.

*Some of them seem alarmed, which is interesting*, thought Hanufer.

'Perhaps you would like to take some spiced wine or some fig beer with me?' the proprietor asked, also noting the reaction amongst his workers.

Hanufer accepted the offer of the fig beer and followed Saul Sofer through a curtain to what was obviously his inner sanctum. It had racks of papyrus scrolls, bundles of fresh papyrus and a large desk covered in tally sticks and piles of works that the publisher was himself working on. A simple glance told Hanufer that the bulk of his work was in Greek and Hebrew, and to a lesser extent in the Egyptian demotic script of *sekh shat*, traditionally used to write documents.

Mere moments after they had sat down on either side of the desk, a youngster came in with a jug of beer, two mugs and a small plate of figs. Saul Sofer poured the beer and leaned across to place it and the plate of figs beside Hanufer.

'Have you heard about the tragedy this morning?' Hanufer asked.

'About the sad death of the poet Diomedes? Indeed, *hefsed merubah*, a great loss to us all. And such a tragic way for one so young and talented to die. But if it is God's will —' Saul Sofer's voice trailed off and he closed his eyes.

'I understand that Obelius the banker and merchant was going to publish his latest poem.'

Saul Sofer nodded. 'Indeed, my lord. His house was going to publish first, but if needed he may well have used my business to copy the work if it was successful.'

'Is that a common arrangement?'

'Yes, my lord. You have seen how many skilled copyists I employ. As I mentioned when you first visited my business, we publish and copy most of the works for the Library and for many of the literary figures in Alexandria. We are not always the first to publish, though.'

'Had you published Diomedes's work before?'

'We had, although his output was not great. He saw himself as a developing poet.'

'Was he a good poet? I ask as an Egyptian who has much to learn about the many different forms of Greek poetry.'

Saul Sofer laughed. 'As do I, *Archiphylakites* Hanufer. I am Hebrew and no scholar. My expertise is in reproducing the works of the great. If you wish for an expert view, then you should go to the Musaeum and talk with the great Philitas of Cos, or to the Library and see Callimachus himself. Or even the great Librarian Zenodotus.'

'I have seen Philitas of Cos, but have not yet spoken with Callimachus or Zenodotus. When I spoke to Philitas I wanted to know about Sotades, who was also a great poet, as I understand.'

Saul Sofer had just taken a sip of his fig beer and almost choked. 'Forgive me. But did Philitas of Cos say that Sotades was a great poet?'

'He was careful with his words, but told me that he was a paradox. Seemingly he insulted many people, including the royal couple.'

'Indeed, if insulting people was a measure of greatness, then he was by far the greatest of them all, even including Hipponax of Ephesus.'

'Philitas of Cos and a young mathematician called Ajax mentioned this Hipponax to me. Indeed, Ajax said that he was himself the object of Sotades's wit in his imitation of *The Iliad*. It was something like this:

*"Ajax was a figure puny, as beauteous as aged Hipponax.*
*He figures smaller than a flea, his wick but a twist of flax."'*

'Yes, that was Sotades,' said Saul Sofer with a smile. 'He was insulting his mathematical prowess when he said "figures" and his twist of flax was a reference to his manhood. Typical Sotadic wit.'

Hanufer reached into the pocket in his chiton and took out three small papyri rolls. He unfurled them and selecting one, passed it across the desk to Saul Sofer.

'This is a copy of the writing that was left on the altar at the *temenos* the other night. It caused the sacrifice to be abandoned. As you can see, there are hieroglyphs and Greek writing.'

Saul Sofer studied them, then looked up and nodded. 'It is the famous Sotades poem, sir. The one that so insulted Queen Arsinoe and Pharaoh Ptolemy and led to the poet's downfall.'

'Had you actually published the poetry of Sotades?'

'Yes, sir, I had published virtually all of his work. But I also had to destroy every single piece on the orders of the pharaoh.'

'So you have none left? Not a single papyrus?'

'I would risk losing my business, such as it is.' He looked suddenly pained. 'Worse, I would risk the wrath of the pharaoh or his queen — whichever is worse!'

'An odd thing to say, Master Saul.'

The publisher looked slightly embarrassed. 'I meant no offence, but it is well known that Queen Arsinoe has a temper and is not a person to cross. I destroyed every piece of papyrus that had a Sotadic verse on it.'

'And yet people can quote his works. Like the mathematician Ajax. It seems to me that being insulted and written about by Sotades was regarded as a measure of one's importance.'

'Perhaps. The more important one was, the more the poetry stung. The less important one was, the greater the pride in being insulted. I suppose that is part of what Philitas of Cos meant by Sotades being a paradox.'

Hanufer nodded and slid another papyrus across the desk. 'And what about this? It is the message found on the wall outside Diomedes's villa this morning.'

This time, Saul Sofer frowned as he read it. 'It is different, perhaps not his finest work, but like the lines you quoted about the mathematician Ajax, it seems to refer to Sotades's *Iliad*.'

'How so?'

'Hector is another of the characters in the Trojan Wars.'

Hanufer nodded. 'Of course. I have read both *The Iliad* and *The Odyssey*, but not in detail. I was selective with the pieces I studied.'

Saul Sofer shuddered. 'But it sounds as if Sotades has returned from his watery grave and has sought revenge upon Diomedes for the vision he had.'

'You mean for the vision he said he had from the god Harpocrates?'

The publisher nodded. 'All Alexandria has heard about it.'

'And what do you make of these hieroglyphs?'

Saul Sofer smiled. 'You would be more qualified than I to venture an opinion, Hanufer of Crocodilopolis.'

'Indulge me with your opinion.'

Saul Sofer shrugged. 'They appear to be hieroglyphic palindromes. The eyes on either end and the mouth spitting between them. That could indeed be representative of Sotades.'

Hanufer drank half of his fig beer and placed the mug on the desk. 'You mentioned your business a moment ago. You said "such as it is." What did you mean?'

Saul Sofer gave a short laugh. 'Simply that business could always be better, sir.'

Hanufer passed the last papyrus across the desk to him. 'This is a petition that I received. You will see that it is from Zachriel Cohen, a scholar and scribe of the Tribe of Simeon.'

He saw Saul Sofer visibly start, then sit forward and snatch his mug of beer and take a good mouthful. He picked up the papyrus and read.

'As you will see, he says that he is dwelling in the Mansion of the Clerics upon the Island of Pharos,' Hanufer said. 'I visited and talked to him yesterday afternoon.'

Saul Sofer was silent, so Hanufer continued. 'He knew nothing about it and said that neither he nor any of the seventy-two Jewish scholars on the Island of Pharos have ever visited this part of the city.'

Casually, as Saul Sofer continued to study the petition, Hanufer reached across the desk and tapped a papyrus that lay beside a writing set, which clearly the publisher had just been using.

'I see that you did not try to disguise your writing style, Saul Sofer. Now tell me, why this subterfuge? This was a message to me, was it not?'

The publisher laid the papyrus down and swallowed hard. 'Please forgive me, my lord. I knew of no other way that I could safely approach you without others knowing. I thought that if you could work out that I had sent it, then I could explain the concerns that I and my fellow Jewish citizens have. About our persecution in this city.'

Hanufer held out his hands to show the two rings bearing the images of Maat and Sobek. 'Maat is the goddess of truth. I hold this above everything else and I will uphold the truth and the law with the ferocity and power of Sobek.'

Saul Sofer tugged pensively on his lower lip and then sat forward and hit his right fist into his left hand as if to emphasise that he had made a powerful decision. 'If you can help us, Hanufer of Crocodilopolis, then I will do whatever I can to help you.'

From the Jewish quarter Hanufer rode to the Temple of Isis in the Brucheum. After leaving his horse in the care of a temple worker, he entered the temple grounds and was led by a handmaid through a gate that opened into the small garden where Nefrit had taken him before. To his delight she was there, sitting under a canopy, studying a papyrus.

Upon hearing their approach she stood up, a smile spreading across her face.

'My lord, Hanufer,' she began, her face suddenly clouding. 'I am sorry to hear about —'

'About Diomedes. Yes, it is indeed a tragedy.' He looked around him to ensure that they were alone and would be unheard. As they sat down together on the bench, he felt his heart quicken at their proximity to one another.

'I was sorry that we could not talk last night.'

'As was I.'

'I need to ask about what happened after I left. Diomedes seemed to be taken aside by several of the Lady Eupheme's guests.'

'Bilistiche and Didyme both flirted outrageously with him, as did Lady Eupheme and Ambrosia. And he with them all.'

'Did you talk to him?'

'No, I was just there as an entertainer. Less than a courtesan, less than a guest.'

'You could never be that, Nefrit,' Hanufer said quickly. He wanted to say more, but his professional sense took over and instead he asked, 'How much did he flirt?'

'A lot. They all wanted him to tell their futures and he insisted that he did so individually, taking them on their own into a room that Eupheme made available.' She looked at him intently. 'Each one took *several minutes*!'

'Long enough to —?'

'Long enough for many things, Hanufer. Almost all of them were giggling and blushing when they came out.'

'Could they … could they have arranged an assignation afterwards, if they had so desired?'

Nefrit bit her lower lip. 'All things are possible, Hanufer. As I said, he particularly flirted and was many minutes with Bilistiche, Didyme, Eupheme and Ambrosia.'

'But never with you?'

'As I said, I was the musician, the entertainer, not a guest. Besides, I was not attracted to — him.'

Hanufer reached out and touched her hand, and she looked down and closed hers over his fingers.

Staring into each other's eyes, they found themselves drawn together for their first kiss.

# CHAPTER 21

It was with a light heart that Hanufer left the Temple and rode to the villa of Obelius. He could not help but find his eyes drawn to the shrine to the god above the door, with the finger raised to its lips. The sightless eye sockets seemed to be staring directly at him, and he wondered whether the conversations that had taken place at the symposium could in some way be connected with the sudden murder of the poet Diomedes.

Obelius himself was waiting in the agora of the villa as Erasmos, his head slave, opened the door for him.

'I wondered when you would visit us, Hanufer,' the banker said after they had exchanged courtesies. 'We are all shocked to lose such a fine intellect in such tragic circumstances. Come, I have just admitted some other guests.'

Erasmos led the way, opening doors and discreetly closing them behind them, skirting ahead again to open the next door so that Obelius did not have to break step at all.

'How is your head?' Obelius asked as they walked down the marble-tiled corridors. 'Mine feels as if a horse has kicked me. I fear that Erasmos did not obey my wife's orders to water the wine down enough.'

'The wine was most excellent, I thank you,' Hanufer replied diplomatically as Erasmos threw open the doors to the hall in which the Lady Eupheme had been entertaining her guests the night before. Hanufer noticed straight away that there were several doors leading off from it and wondered which of them Diomedes had used to do his fortune-telling for the ladies.

The Lady Bilistiche and Hilarian the playwright were siting talking with Eupheme.

'Why, *Archiphylakites* Hanufer, what a surprise to see you on this sad day,' said Eupheme.

'Hilarian and I were given the news when we were getting ready to exercise our chariot horses on the hippodrome,' said Bilistiche. She was dressed beautifully and almost regally. Clearly she had taken time to change out of her charioteer garb.

'I feel that I should not be wearing colours on a day such as this,' said Eupheme, a hand going to her hair, which was again in a large bun secured by the silver hairpin with the lapis lazuli gem that matched the one in her ring.

Hilarian sighed and rubbed the bridge of his well-chiselled nose. 'I confess that my memory of last night is hazy, but I can scarcely believe that we will not hear the end of Diomedes's fine poem.'

'And yet, what is the significance of the writing and the Egyptian hieroglyphics?' Obelius asked.

'Is Sotades alive?' Bilistiche asked. 'Or is this a ghost at work?'

'The message was from no ghost, Lady Bilistiche,' Hanufer replied. 'It is as yet a mystery.'

'Indeed,' agreed Hilarian. 'How would anyone know that Diomedes lay dead — unless he was murdered?'

Eupheme gasped. 'Is that what you think too, *Archiphylakites* Hanufer? Surely not?'

'Perhaps because Diomedes was there when Sotades was himself murdered?' suggested Hilarian.

'You mean executed,' Obelius corrected. 'Admiral Patroclus is vizier to Ptolemy Philadelphus, and Sotades was already under sentence of death.'

'Had any of you seen the writing?' Hanufer asked.

'I did,' Obelius replied. 'I did not think it was something my wife should see.'

'And we both did,' Bilistiche said, indicating herself and Hilarian. 'We were told about it and visited straight away, but saw that the gates were closed and guarded by your men.'

The doors opened and Stratonicus strode in. 'My apologies, Father and Stepmother, and honoured guests; I was in my studio painting and only just heard that you were all here.'

'Overseer Hanufer was telling us about the tragedy of Diomedes,' Obelius said.

'And of the strange message on his wall,' said Bilistiche. 'We were wondering if it could be that Sotades has returned, or whether it could be a ghost.'

Stratonicus raised his hands and gave a short laugh. 'A ghost? Surely that is not a serous conjecture, Overseer Hanufer?'

'It was not my suggestion, Stratonicus,' Hanufer replied. 'The simple fact is that a message in Greek and in hieroglyphics was found on the wall. Someone put it there. And it was put there in the knowledge that Diomedes was dead. Whoever wrote it made no attempt to rescue him. The body was taken out of the pool by his slaves.'

'Such a waste of a talented young man,' said Bilistiche. 'He was inspired by the Muses and could talk to Harpocrates and see into people's futures.'

Hanufer sat forward on his seat. 'I understand that at the party last night he did just that. He told several fortunes, including your own, Lady Bilistiche.'

The courtesan's lovely eyes narrowed. 'He did, in that room there,' she said, pointing to a door at the end of the hall.

'And he told them for me, Didyme, Ambrosia and four or so others,' volunteered Eupheme.

'Did he tell you anything of interest?' Stratonicus asked with a laugh. 'Or was it all just gossip? He gave us some juicy tastes of the poem he was writing about Sotades.'

'I don't think he revealed any dangerous secrets, though,' said Obelius. 'He said he was still waiting to talk to the sculptor Hecataeus of Caunus.'

Hanufer thought he detected a slight emphasis on the word dangerous.

They talked further and he asked more questions, none of which he felt advanced his investigations overmuch. When he left the cool of the villa and returned to the blistering heat of the day, he looked up again at the shrine of the god of silence and wondered whether there were secrets among the group that were still being guarded by the god.

Sabu had arranged with Cario for food and beer to be ready for Hanufer when he returned to his office.

'Filemon gave those two fish merchants a severe dressing down for their treatment of Cario,' Sabu told his boss when Cario had served them food at their desks and left.

'Did they tell him who they sold their eels to?'

'They could not remember, my lord. And Filemon said he could not persuade them either with words or the threat of arrest, so he believed them. They just took exception to being questioned so persistently by a *demosios*.'

'What of the constables Sidvain and Rhoglos?'

'I ordered them to remove the messages on the *temenos* and the wall of Diomedes's villa. Then I sent them to check the mirrors on the Pharos lighthouse. They are to stay until the fires are lit and they can see that there is plenty of fuel.'

'Why there?'

'To keep them occupied and out of the way, my lord.'

Hanufer smiled approvingly. As they ate, he told Sabu of his own discussion with Saul Sofer. He smiled inwardly as he thought of his meeting with Nefrit and of how they had kissed in the temple garden before seeking the privacy of her home behind the garden. What had happened there was not for the telling.

'The petition I had been sent, purportedly from one of the Jewish scholars who are translating their holy book into Greek, was actually written by Saul Sofer.'

'Why so, my lord?'

'As a test to see if we would follow up on a petition from the Jewish scholar Zachriel Cohen, and also to see if I would work out that it was from him.'

'But why?' Sabu asked, mystified.

'Because his whole community, and possibly others too, have been subjected to extortion by the police. It has been going on for some years.'

Sabu thumped the table with his fist.

'Shh!' Hanufer hissed. 'I am sure this has something to do with the money that you found at Gryton of Salamis's house and why it is of different currencies.'

'You mean that *Archiphylakites* Gryton and Sergeant Kraspar were in it together?'

'No. The amount of money that you found was a lot, but it was not a huge amount. It was of different currencies — and especially Hebrew coins — to make anyone who should find it suspicious.'

'Then you think —'

'That Gryton was investigating this. Indeed, I think he had discovered who was extorting money from the community, probably a great deal of money. His death was too convenient. I think he was murdered.'

'As was Kraspar. Gryton was cremated and Kraspar was —'

'Taken to the Medical School and dissected as a criminal or as a derelict, yes. And you know who I suspect?'

Sabu nodded. 'Shall I arrest them both and make them talk, my lord?'

'No. We dare not yet. We do not yet know who else may have been involved. There may be many others, and we need to know upon whom we can depend.'

They suddenly became aware of a commotion from one of the offices outside. A few moments later there was a knock on the door, and Cario opened it upon Hanufer's order to enter.

'My lord, one of the Royal Palace guards is here. He says that Pharaoh Ptolemy Philadelphus orders that you are to go to the Royal Zoo without delay. The guard will lead you.'

Hanufer and Sabu thought that the guard was either a mute or he had been ordered to say nothing. It did not surprise them overmuch, for if the pharaoh said to say nothing, only a brave man would risk their tongue. When they arrived at the entrance to the Royal Zoo, they were greeted by an officer who was only slightly more communicative.

'His Majesty will attend once you have investigated,' he said, as he and two guards marched quickly through the zoo to the step pyramid structure of the King Djoser House.

Behdet the Keeper of the Bull was outside the entrance, leaning over the Keeper of Snakes, Weneg, who was sitting on the ground with a rough, bloodstained bandage round his head.

From inside the King Djoser House came the hissing of a multitude of snakes.

'What has happened? Have you been attacked, Weneg?' Hanufer asked.

The Keeper of Snakes did not immediately reply, so Behdet answered for him. 'I found him lying in his own blood inside the snake house, my lord. I made sure that he was alive and then ... then I tried to enter, but I dared not. The ... the creature was —'

Weneg looked dazed, but as he looked up and realised that Hanufer was standing before him, he struggled to his feet. He pointed into the snake house and turned towards it.

'Please, my lord, follow me,' he whispered. 'But make no noise ... and do not move suddenly.' He half staggered and was saved by Behdet promptly stepping forward and putting the snake keeper's arm over his shoulders to support him. 'Come quietly,' Weneg whispered again.

Alarmed at what they might find, Sabu drew his sword and followed Hanufer inside. The officer and the two guards nervously prepared to enter, but gratefully refrained when Sabu held up a hand to stop them.

Many of the snakes sounded agitated, and Hanufer and Sabu looked around anxiously to ensure that none of the cage doors were open. They slowly mounted the steps after Weneg and Behdet, and they spiralled upwards until they came to the last flight.

And there Hanufer saw Apophis, the python's whole enormous length lying on the stairs, his great head resting on the lowest step.

Sabu immediately stepped in front of Hanufer, his sword raised ready to slash downwards.

'No!' Weneg hissed, almost imitating one of the reptiles. 'Look!'

Holding on to Behdet, he put out a foot and prodded the head, which instantly collapsed.

'It's only its skin. Master Philitas was here.' He raised his finger to his lips and gestured for them to follow up the stairs, stepping carefully as they passed the giant python's skin.

Hanufer felt perspiration drip down his face, but followed the two keepers.

Upon the floor there was a message written in large hieroglyphics and Greek script. Hanufer only fleetingly looked at it, for he was more concerned about ensuring that the snake itself was not free.

Weneg patted Behdet's chest and removed his arm from his shoulders. 'My lord, look at Apophis.'

The huge python was lying transformed in its vast cage. Its skin shone and its eyes glistened where they had previously been dull and milky.

Sabu gasped at the size of the creature.

'But where is Philitas of Cos?' Hanufer asked, staring at Weneg, who now stretched out a trembling hand and pointed to the huge bulge in the body of the snake.

The giant snakeskin was dragged out so that Pharaoh Ptolemy Philadelphus and his vizier, Admiral Patroclus, could mount the stairs to see the python and the message on the floor for themselves. Hanufer told Sabu to stay outside with the guards.

'What do you make of this outrage, Hanufer of Crocodilopolis?' the pharaoh asked, as he stood looking into the cage of his beloved python.

'I have only made a preliminary collection of the facts, Your Majesty, but this is the situation so far. Behdet the Keeper of the Bull tells me that it was he who discovered Weneg after he had fed and cleaned out Apis's pen. The two have struck up a friendship, for Weneg is the oldest of all your keepers and Behdet is the youngest. They had established a habit of meeting and Weneg had been teaching the younger keeper about the snakes. In return, Behdet was telling him all about the bull that you spared. Behdet had been scared when he saw the discarded snakeskin and thought, as did I when I first saw it, that it was the real snake.'

The pharaoh nodded. 'Indeed, I know that Philitas has been waiting for Apophis to shed his skin, as he said the other day.'

'Philitas had come this morning as usual, as I found out from the guards at the gate. A scholar from the Musaeum came soon after him with some papyrus scrolls that he had forgotten. They say that he left after a short while.'

'I do not like the sound of this,' said Patroclus as he stood looking into the cage where the great python languidly lay.

'Weneg told Behdet that he had been struck by an unseen assailant. Fearing for Philitas they mounted the steps, realising that someone had taken the newly shed skin and arranged it to deter anyone from going up the steps. There they found Apophis in the cage, but no sign of Philitas of Cos. The only other thing they saw in the cage was some blood just inside it.'

Ptolemy Philadelphus pointed to the python. 'Weneg has told me before that after a shedding, a snake may be hungry.' He took a deep breath, as if striving to control his emotions. 'Do you think that … that —'

'That Philitas of Cos has been devoured? Yes, Your Majesty, it looks likely.'

'Should we have the snake killed and slit it open, Your Majesty?' Patroclus asked.

The pharaoh's reaction was unexpected. He flew into a rage. 'No! Such a thing could only be a sign. Someone may have struck my old teacher down, but only the gods could have allowed it to happen. To kill this mighty creature, surely touched with divinity and linked to the celestial Apophis, the actual serpent of the Nile, would undoubtedly risk releasing destruction and chaos in Egypt. Worse, it could interfere with the nightly journey of the sun god Atum through the underworld. If Apophis was so angered, then Atum may be defeated and never rise in the morning. And forget not that our divine Serapis is also at times a snake.' His voice had risen with each sentence until he stopped and closed his eyes, willing his anger to subside. Then he asked, 'Has Weneg said how long it will take for whatever that lump is to pass through the snake's system?'

Hanufer swallowed hard, being in part taken aback by the pharaoh's ire and his wholehearted faith in the Egyptian legends of the gods, and partly feeling a wave of nausea at the idea that the poet could have been swallowed by the snake. 'It could be several days, Your Majesty.'

'Apophis is going to be the star attraction in the procession to worship Alexander and to install Patroclus,' Ptolemy stated.

The vizier spun round. 'Are we still going to hold it, Your Majesty?' he asked in astonishment. 'Especially after this message?'

They all turned and looked at the hieroglyphics and the message beneath it:

*What lies inside the Trojan snake*
*What lies and poison does it make*
*Hector's foe will vanquished fall*
*The poet's words will conquer all*
*Die those who kill and treasures take*

'Well, Hanufer, what do you make of this?' Ptolemy asked. 'Does my vizier need to quake so? Is this from Sotades?'

'Sotades is dead, Your Majesty!' Patroclus stated, striving to keep a truculent note from his voice. 'I quake for no one.'

Footsteps sounded on the stairs, the hard tread of boots, but ahead of them came the sound of delicate sandaled feet.

Moments later Queen Arsinoe appeared, coming up the last flight of stairs, and a few deferential steps behind her were two officers of the royal guard.

'My maidservants told me of the commotion,' she said, ignoring Hanufer and Patroclus, who had dropped to their knees and bent their heads. 'I heard you shouting in anger, brother-husband. And now I see this daub on the floor. I can make out two snakes and a horse. What do they mean? And this poem? Is it the dog Sotades, again?'

Her voice had an edge, but she did not lose her temper.

'There is worse, sister-wife,' Ptolemy replied, pointing to the great bulge in the resting python. 'Philitas of Cos is missing.'

At this, the queen clapped a hand to her mouth and seemed to teeter on her feet. The pharaoh immediately strode to her and slid an arm about her waist.

'I ... I am well, brother-husband, but I shall retire. I trust you will take care of this?'

Standing straight, she looked down at Patroclus and Hanufer. 'Rise, both of you, and deal with this.'

They did as she ordered and stood with heads still bowed as the two guards made way for her to descend the steps again.

The pharaoh turned and spread a hand in the direction of the cage. 'You can see how I and my sister-wife feel,' he said calmly, his rage having subsided. 'Both of us are angered by this and obviously deeply saddened, but we have grown tired of these messages. Find whoever is behind them, Hanufer. I shall go to talk with and console my sister-wife, who I am sure has been more shocked by this than she will allow anyone but myself to know. But speak not of this to anyone! That is a command.'

'It shall be done, Your Majesty,' Hanufer replied, aware that saying he would do his best would be insufficient.

'It looks as if our old teacher Philitas has been murdered, consumed by Apophis, yet we do not know for certain,' the pharaoh continued. 'My keeper Weneg was also attacked and could have been killed. Make it known that whoever is responsible for these atrocities will suffer the most lingering and painful of punishments. Find out if Philitas yet lives, for if he has indeed been slain and consumed, then Pharaoh Ptolemy Philadelphus himself will carry out the execution.'

'I understand, Your Majesty,' Hanufer said, prostrating himself as the pharaoh and his vizier descended the steps without another word.

Corporal Filemon was waiting for Hanufer and Sabu when they eventually came out of the Royal Palace and the zoo.

'We have found another of those hieroglyph and writing messages, my lord. It was written on papyrus and nailed to a wall of the Soma. I have left a constable there to guard it rather than removing it. I hope that was correct, sir? I thought that since you have left the other ones for some time, it would be better to do the same.'

They went quickly to the Street of the Soma where it was crossed by Canopus Street. An assorted crowd was gathered round, many to make votive offerings and others just to look at the message.

None were allowed too close to it, but as Hanufer in his pectoral of office approached, flanked by Sabu and Filemon, they moved aside. Hanufer saw that it was exactly the same as the message that had been drawn upon the floor of the snake house.

The crowd was quite animated and there was anger and much speculation as to what the hieroglyphics and the Greek message meant.

'It's a prophesy. There's going to be a plague of snakes.'

'They'll eat horses. No one will be safe.'

'No, it's the Trojans again. It means there'll be war.'

'The gods won't like it.'

Hanufer was listening with half an ear, aware that for many the messages would have no apparent meaning and could be freely interpreted. Then among the crowd he started to hear the name Sotades repeated again and again.

'He's alive and he's coming for them.'

'Did you hear that the poet Diomedes drowned?'

'The pharaoh's snake ate the scholar, Philitas,' a voice called out loudly.

Hanufer turned to Sabu and whispered, 'Find who said that about Philitas!'

Sabu and Filemon pushed into the crowd, but the remark about the philosopher was not repeated. Some minutes later they returned. They had not been able to find out who had called out about Philitas, but by then they could hear whisperings in the crowd that the philosopher was dead, eaten by the sacred snake Apophis.

'Leave the papyrus where it is for a while, then send one of the constables for it before nightfall,' Hanufer ordered before he turned and led Sabu and Filemon away.

*Who in that crowd said that about Philitas, and how did they know?* Hanufer thought. *There can be only one answer. Someone wanted to plant the seed in the crowd. It is almost certain that it was the murderer or an accomplice. But who could it be? I am not even sure whether it was the voice of a man or a woman.*

As they moved away, they heard further murmurings about Sotades the Obscene. This time, the name of Admiral Patroclus was also being opined about.

Ptolemy Philadelphus was feeling unsettled. He did not like it when Arsinoe was upset, and indeed she was deeply upset by the suggestion that Apophis had consumed their old tutor, Philitas of Cos. She had shown the utmost control when they were with their children and when they ate together. It was only later when they were alone in her apartments that she allowed her emotions to show.

'Sotades is alive, isn't he, Ptolemy?' she asked, suddenly dashing a hand at the senet board that had been set upon a table, ready for them to play.

Rather than calling for a servant to come and pick up the playing pieces, the pharaoh knelt down and started to gather them up himself. 'Patroclus is confident that he drowned, Arsinoe.'

'Then he is a ghost. Is it his *ka* or his *ba* that is writing these messages? They are from him, you know.'

'I have commanded the Overseer of Police to find whoever is responsible. I shall personally deal with them.'

'When? Once there has been another murder?' She stood and pointed at a wall as if nothing existed between her finger and the python's cage in the Royal Zoo. 'Philitas is dead, Ptolemy! Why not cut the snake open and at least have his body given the respect it is owed? Have it mummified, or cremated, but not just left as food for that monster of yours.'

Ptolemy stood with his arms folded. He shook his head. 'I know what must be done, Arsinoe, and I am the pharaoh.

Apophis must live. To kill him would be more dangerous than we could imagine.'

Arsinoe raised her hands in despair. 'And I am your queen. And your sister! Your *older* sister!'

'It is a sign from the gods.'

'Which gods? Are you blind to these messages, Ptolemy? This last one shows that Sotades is set on revenge. He is coming for Patroclus. If any of this is a sign from the gods, then that god can only be Seth, don't you see that? Seth the red-haired demon. Red hair, just like Sotades!'

'What would you have me do?' he asked.

'Get the gods — all of them — the Egyptian, Greek and Jewish — get them to stop Seth and find Sotades so that we can see him dealt with finally and forever, before our eyes.'

'We shall do this. Leave it with me.'

Arsinoe cast her headdress aside. 'I have a headache, Ptolemy. I should not have to endure these outrages. I must lie down.'

The pharaoh felt anger bubble up inside him. He was a living god, but he was being dismissed, which was not to his liking. It was only because he loved his sister-wife so much that he permitted such insolence. He bid her sleep well and left.

As he marched to his own apartment, every door being opened for him, he debated which of his mistresses to send for, Bilistiche or Didyme. He needed someone to take away his cares and calm his inner rage. Someone who would listen to his worries and who would do whatever he desired.

# CHAPTER 22

Hanufer barely slept that night, as the atmosphere had become so hot and sticky. The morning was little better, and at times the air was more reminiscent of the humid conditions in the delta than the climate of the coast. From time to time, an incongruous breeze bearing the smell of the desert rather than the usual tang of the sea from the direction of the Royal Harbour gave momentary ease.

Hanufer was pleased to get indoors again after the relatively short walk from his villa. Back behind his desk, he went over the events of the previous day with Sabu.

'So, we have several murders here, yet we are in a delicate situation because we are unsure how reliable the men under our command are.'

'I am certain that Pylyp and Filemon are trustworthy, my lord.'

'So am I, and as we were discussing before we were called to the Royal Zoo, I am sure that Gryton of Salamis, my predecessor, was investigating extortion by members of the police. No one was able to identify any of the officers involved, as they always wore masks and visited people in their homes after dark. He did not know whether the senior officials were involved or not. More than ever I suspect that Gryton was investigating rather than being involved and that he was murdered, probably by being poisoned.'

Sabu nodded. 'And we know that Kraspar was also murdered, or at least he supposedly fell ill and resigned. Then his body was disposed of by being taken to the Medical

School.' Sabu cringed as he said it. 'Where he has been cut to pieces.'

'I need to talk to Erasistratus about the procedure they have for accepting bodies for their dissection. Herophilus said that Erasistratus had dealt with it, but he is unwell. Still hungover from the wine at the symposium.'

Hanufer took out the rolls of papyrus from his pocket. Unfurling the ones that he had made of the messages, he lay them side by side on the desk.

'We have three messages, all of which I have copied.'

Sabu rose from his desk and stood behind his boss to look over his shoulder.

'First we have the one that was left on the altar at the *temenos*. I showed it to Philitas of Cos, and he confirmed that it was the poem that Sotades had written and which was the cause of his downfall.

*'In the land of the Nile where dogs are gods,*
*A king stuck his prick in an unholy hole.*
*In that unholy hole a king's prick stuck,*
*Where gods are dogs to the vile of the land.*

'When I asked him about the hieroglyphs, he thought they were typical of Sotades. A palindrome, an invention of his where things can be read one way or the other: *mw-ib-mw*. Yet as you said, in our language it is meaningless. Everyone who has seen it thinks it is to do with Sotades having been drowned in a jar. They have thought the middle hieroglyph was a jar, when in fact it is the *ib*, the heart. This makes one conclude that they have just been used as pictures. Now, let us compare the second message from the villa wall of Diomedes:

*'The gods grew angry at his poisoned visions,*
*and even the eels spat out his vicious poisons.*
*Treacherous dogs beware for revenge is sweet,*
*Soon the poisonous toad will lie at Hector's feet.*

'Here the hieroglyphs show eyes and in between a spitting snake. The lines refer to poisoned visions, and eels. Does this refer back to the eels at the *temenos*? Treacherous dogs — who are they? Is this a message from Sotades?'

'Could poisonous visions be the soothsayer's poisonous predictions, his visions from the gods, my lord?' asked Sabu.

'Possibly. It could mean that he is being fed to the eels. But the poisonous toad will lie at Hector's feet. Who is Hector? Is this the Hector in *The Iliad*?'

'I do not know *The Iliad*, my lord,' Sabu said apologetically.

'Then what about this last one from the snake house, which I copied after the pharaoh and his queen had seen it?

*'What lies inside The Trojan snake*
*What lies and poison does it make*
*Hector's foe will vanquished fall*
*When the poet's words will conquer all*
*Die those who kill and treasures take.'*

'Snakes again, my lord. But the hieroglyphs mean nothing.'

'Not as a word, but snakes surrounding a horse. The term used is Trojan snake, not Trojan horse. There is a riddle here. I did not understand it, but notice also that Hector's foe will vanquished fall. The pharaoh asked if Patroclus should quake, be fearful. It is *The Iliad* and *The Odyssey* again.'

'I still do not understand, my lord.'

Hanufer did not reply immediately, but kept on his train of thought as he ran his finger over the last line. Then he went on, "*'The poet's words will conquer all.'*" That is surely referring to Sotades and his words. You see, in *The Iliad*, Hector's foe is called Patroclus. He is the friend of the hero Achilles. As I recall, Patroclus put on Achilles's armour and was killed by Hector. These messages seem to be warnings. Although his name is not mentioned, this is clearly a warning to Patroclus. The pharaoh saw and understood that, and actually asked me whether Patroclus had need to quake. I am sure that Patroclus must also have construed the meaning of the message. The fact is that Philitas has been murdered, but we don't know whether he was dead before the snake swallowed him. And if he was, then how was he killed? Horrific to think, but perhaps he was not dead, merely unconscious.'

Sabu was not a squeamish man, but he shivered and took a sharp breath. 'But why all this about *The Iliad* in the messages, my lord?'

'Because Sotades wrote his own version of *The Iliad* and *The Odyssey* in his type of poetic form, but it has been destroyed. All of his poetry was destroyed on the orders of the pharaoh. Yet this warning implies that Patroclus will die. The question we have to ask is whether this is all to do with the revenge of Sotades.'

Again Hanufer sat in thought for a moment before shaking his head. 'No. I think there is still more in these messages that I cannot yet fathom. So, let us look at the other murders. First the slave, Zalmoxis, and then Diomedes. Both killed by having their brains punctured. Then both deaths disguised. In Zalmoxis's case, he was put in the bull pen and the bull was goaded to trample his features and make him unrecognisable. Diomedes was put in his eel pond to be savaged by his flesh-eating eels. And lastly, we think Philitas of Cos was devoured by the pharaoh's python.'

'Can we not —?'

'Kill the snake and open it up? No, Patroclus actually suggested that to the pharaoh, but Ptolemy Philadelphus believes that python is linked to the snake demon that he is named after, or he is actually the embodiment of the god Apophis. It is to be a main feature in the procession to open the Temple of Alexander and install Patroclus as the high priest. If it is indeed Philitas that is inside the serpent, then why has he been despatched? What would Sotades have had against him? I can see that Sotades would want Diomedes dead and Patroclus, too, for they put him in the leaded jar and supposedly drowned him.'

'But if it is not him that the python has devoured, then where is he?'

Hanufer stroked his chin. 'It is a question that needs answering urgently. Pharaoh Ptolemy said that I need to discover who has written the messages as soon as possible. Certainly before this procession. There is an interesting point about this last message, though.'

'It all baffles me, sir.'

Hanufer tapped the papyrus before him. 'The message I have here I copied from the floor of the snake house, yet it is not the only copy. The person who put whoever is inside the snake into the cage — and who knocked out Weneg the snake keeper — left this message. If it was just a warning to Patroclus, why was the copy put up on the Temple of Alexander wall — one of the most visited places in the city? And when was it put there?'

'So that it would be public knowledge?'

'Exactly. And it could hardly have been put there when people were passing, which they do from dawn. That means it must have been in the night.'

Sabu stared back at his boss. 'You mean *before* the first message was left in the snake house?'

'Yes, before the murder, if murder was committed. In other words, it was carefully planned.'

'So where do we start, my lord?'

'With Diomedes. You will recall that the Lady Didyme was entering her villa this morning as we were returning from the Necropolis prison. I want to know where she was returning from. I shall return the horse that Pylyp commandeered from her.'

'Shall I accompany you, sir?'

'No, I want you to go to the Musaeum and see whether Philitas of Cos has by chance returned there. You must go into his office and do an errand for me. Then go to the Royal Zoo and meet me at the gates. While you do that, I shall pay a courtesan a visit.'

The Lady Didyme gave Hanufer every impression that she was astonished to hear about the death of Diomedes. He did not tell her of the events at the Royal Zoo.

She erupted into tears when he described how the poet's body was found face down and savaged in his own eel pond.

'I … I am heartbroken. As you know, I … I only saw him last night at Eupheme's party. He told my fortune.'

'But he clearly did not see his own,' Hanufer replied. 'Did you come straight home after the party?'

She wiped the tears from her cheeks and nodded. 'Eupheme was rather lavish with her wine and food. I felt I needed to get to bed.'

'Did you rise early?'

She nodded. 'I always do. I went to take the air by Lake Mareotis, as is my custom. It reminds me of a place where I was happy as a child. I had not long returned when one of your constables came and asked for the horse that you have brought back.'

'You were an urn carrier at the intended sacrifice the other night. Were you shocked by the message on the altar?'

'I was upset for Admiral Patroclus and upset for the queen.'

'For Queen Arsinoe? Why so?'

'She is not as popular as she would like to be. The poet Sotades showed that, much to his own misfortune.'

'Why do you think she is not popular, my lady?'

'Because she displaced our Queen Arsinoe, whom Ptolemy divorced. In case you did not know it, the royal children are not her own, but Queen Arsinoe the First's. Arsinoe the Second adopted them. I am sure you know that her own children were killed.'

'It is my intention to learn more about that,' Hanufer replied. He also recalled what Nefrit had said at the house of Judge Thespos and his wife Ambrosia. 'I understand that Arsinoe the First is now living in Coptos, near Thebes, where she is the high priestess of the Temple of Min and Isis.'

Didyme flashed him a wide smile. 'You are well-informed, my lord.'

Hanufer returned her smile. 'In the short time I have been in Alexandria, I have found that there is much that I need to be informed about. So tell me, do you often visit Lady Eupheme?'

'She has not been in Alexandria all that long. She is Obelius's second wife and is originally from Thrace. His first wife, Stratonicus's mother, died years ago. But she is a good friend to me now. She is so widely travelled and so kind.'

'And she seems to be very friendly with the Lady Ambrosia, Judge Thespos's wife. Have you known her long?'

'Everyone of note will get to know Ambrosia. She sees to that and she is very skilled at wheedling any secrets, scandals or gossip from them. She is also very free with her tongue, so she can make or break a person's reputation by spreading good things or ill about them.' She flashed another smile. 'Take yourself, for that matter. You shared a meal with her, the high priest of Serapis and with the high priestess of Isis. You may be pleased to know that you made a favourable impression upon her.'

Hanufer had not expected that he himself would become the subject of gossip in Alexandrian society quite so soon. Mention of Nefrit, however, made his cheeks feel warm and he had to force her from his mind, as he was intent on gaining information from Didyme.

'And the Lady Bilistiche, is she too a friend?'

Didyme looked up sharply, a glint of anger in her eyes, which was quickly replaced by yet another devastatingly lovely smile. 'We share some interests, but not many. She likes to ride chariots and things, whereas I like more artistic pursuits.'

Hanufer noted her emphasis on the word 'things.'

'Do you know about the next procession? The installation of the new high priest of Alexander?'

She nodded. 'I shall be an urn bearer once more. Just as Bilistiche will be the basket carrier.' She shook her head with a trace of petulance. 'Why she is the basket carrier is known only to His Majesty.'

Hanufer was in no doubt that there was some animosity between the two courtesans.

But there was something else that Didyme had said that troubled him, although he was not sure why it should.

Weneg and Behdet had carefully folded the python skin and were about to heave it into a chest when Hanufer and Sabu arrived at the snake house.

'It saddens me that Philitas will not be able to study Apophis's old skin as he had intended,' the Keeper of Snakes said, shaking his head sadly. A fresh bandage had been applied to his head and he was no longer dizzy. 'Behdet is going to help me take it to the Musaeum tomorrow. If noble Philitas returns, then the skin will await him.'

'Do you think that Philitas has been eaten by Apophis?' Hanufer asked.

The Keeper of Snakes hung his head sadly. 'I do, but Pharaoh Ptolemy will not allow harm to come to Apophis, which I am thankful for. Philitas of Cos was a kind man, and I wish that I could find out soon instead of having to wait days or even weeks before —'

'Can you calm Apophis?' Hanufer asked. 'I mean, can you keep him under control and get close to him?'

Sabu shot his boss an alarmed look.

'He permits me to get close to him, and I think that he would permit one other in his cage, but no more. He would sense fear if another approached.'

'I would not fear him,' Behdet said. 'Apis, the bull I look after, is like that with me. I do not fear him and I have faith in the gods to protect me if I step into the cage of Apophis. If they choose not to —' He simply shrugged.

Weneg nodded. 'I also put my life in the hands of the gods, Renenutet and Apophis.'

'You are good men, both of you,' said Hanufer. He nodded to Sabu, who reached into his chiton and drew out the lodestone that Philitas of Cos had shown Hanufer, and which the sergeant had retrieved earlier from the philosopher's study.

The Overseer of Police held his hands out to show the two keepers of animals his rings. 'I also have faith in the god Sobek and the goddess Maat.' He cupped his palms and held them towards Sabu, who placed the lodestone in them.

'I ask the god and goddess to help us with this globe. If you can,' he instructed Behdet and Weneg, 'hold this over the great bulge in Apophis to show us the truth. If the philosopher Philitas of Cos has been consumed, then this polished stone which belongs to him will try to go to him.'

The two police officials watched as the older man and the younger unbolted the cage and with a mixture of humming and singing, gingerly entered. The great serpent followed them with its eyes, its long, split tongue flicking in and out.

Hanufer watched through the latticework of wood slats as the two keepers approached the bulge and gently stroked the great body. Then Weneg let the lodestone dangle from its chain above it.

Nothing happened.

'Lower it gently,' Hanufer said, aware that both he and Sabu had beads of perspiration on their brows, which were mirrored by the patina of sweat on both keepers' bare torsos. 'Then move it along its length.'

The lodestone quivered and then started to oscillate.

'It moves, my lord,' Weneg said in his strange hissing voice. 'It is pulling towards Apophis.'

Indeed, as they watched, it looked as if the lodestone was a living thing on a leash, trying to reach out to the snake. The closer Weneg dangled it, the more taut the chain became and the greater its seeming need to rush towards the serpent's body. As he moved it further along the pulling subsided, only to start again just as strongly.

'That proves it,' Hanufer whispered to Sabu. 'The lodestone is attracted by the iron rings that Philitas wore on his wrists and his ankles.'

Fighting back a wave of nausea, he signalled for the two keepers to come out.

'Have the gods answered you, my lord?' Behdet asked as they emerged and Weneg closed the cage door behind them.

'They have. The gods will be pleased with you both, but they demand your silence. You must say nothing of this to any of the other keepers.'

Tears were streaming down Weneg's cheeks. 'I will not talk, my lord. I … I am ashamed of what has happened. And I fear for what will happen. I … I have a bad feeling.'

Almost as soon as he had said it, a strong breeze blew through the snake house and the air suddenly smelled of the desert again.

Hanufer felt a strange shiver run down his spine.

Pylyp and Filemon raised their mugs of beer to Sabu. On Hanufer's orders, his sergeant had taken the two corporals for a drink at a beer shop near the western harbour.

'Your health, Sergeant,' said Pylyp. 'It has been a pleasure working with you and *Archiphylakites* Hanufer. And this beer is welcome in this blasted heat.'

'Which is not to say that it wasn't with *Archiphylakites* Gryton and Sergeant Kraspar,' Filemon was quick to add. 'They were both good and honest men.'

'But not everyone in the force thought so, did they?' Sabu asked, taking a hefty swig of his beer. 'My boss is concerned about those who didn't respect them.'

'You know who they are, Sergeant, don't you?' Pylyp asked.

'Sidvain and Rhoglos and their followers. The thing is, we don't think we can trust them. My boss thinks —'

Pylyp slapped his hand on the table. 'He is right, Sergeant. They are crooked. I know it, Filemon knows it, and so do the decent constables, but in earlier days when we even tried to raise the matter with Kraspar — well, he was a Thracian like them. We never got far.'

'Overseer Hanufer thinks these rogue constables were extorting money from people around Alexandria. Especially in the Jewish district.'

'That's likely,' said Filemon. 'So what are you going to do about it, Sergeant Sabu?'

'That depends on how many of the force we can trust. Apart from you two.'

'Half of the force, then,' said Pylyp.

Sabu grimaced. 'That's what we were worried about.'

He gulped some beer and wiped his mouth with the back of his fist. 'What do you think about the deaths of Overseer Gryton and Sergeant Kraspar?'

The younger of the two corporals shook his head and grimaced. He looked at Pylyp, who nodded for him to proceed. 'We didn't believe it possible, sir. But what could we do?'

'We know they were murdered,' Sabu said. He told them about finding the money in Gryton's house. 'The boss is convinced it was planted there in case anyone grew suspicious. You do know the house was burned down a couple of days ago?'

Both men nodded.

Sabu did not tell them about their discovery of Kraspar's disposal, as he knew that Hanufer had gone off to investigate matters further himself.

'I want you two to make sure that we can trust your comrades if it comes to it.'

Again the two corporals looked at one another and then nodded.

'You can depend on us, Sergeant,' said Pylyp. 'Have another beer, and this time it is on me.'

# CHAPTER 23

Everyone connected with the Musaeum and the Library had heard about the disappearance of Philitas of Cos. On his way to the Medical School, Hanufer was accosted by the head librarian Zenodotus of Ephesus and Callimachus of Cyrene as he crossed the exedra of the Musaeum, where many of the *philologoi* were sitting debating or individually studying.

The two scholars could not have been more dissimilar. Zenodotus was a gruff-looking man of middle years with shaggy grey hair and a large spatulate beard, while Callimachus was a lithe young man with deep olive skin, cropped black hair and a clean-shaven face. It was common knowledge, Hanufer had been told, that Callimachus was the more intellectual of the two, an innovator who was busy cataloguing the library, essentially proposing a system that was the opposite of the one that Zenodotus had spent twenty years developing.

'Is ... is it true about our dear friend Philitas?' the head librarian asked.

'Has he been devoured by the pharaoh's precious serpent?' Callimachus queried.

Hanufer saw that many of the scholars had looked up as they waylaid Hanufer and had started getting up to gather round.

'I think perhaps we should discuss this somewhere more private,' Hanufer suggested.

Zenodotus was quick to hold out a hand towards the Library entrance. 'Indeed, if you will follow me, we can have a goblet of white wine in my office.' He looked askance at his colleague and added, 'If you have work to do on your system, Callimachus, please do not let us stop you. I can always —'

'By no means. I must know about my friend, my teacher. I feel sick to my very soul with worry about him.'

Zenodotus gave an unenthusiastic smile and gestured for Callimachus to lead the way and for Hanufer to precede him from the exedra into the Library.

Thankfully, it was cooler inside the building, although the air still had that strange stone- and sand-like odour.

It was the overseer's first proper visit to the great institution, and he looked around in awe as they entered through a *peripatos*, a broad corridor with high slit windows. Off this were numerous tall alcoves, wherein scholars were working at desks, or standing to study books on high pedestals. Then they entered the main reading hall with its huge Doric columns and magnificent dome. Huge racks from floor to ceiling were filled with scrolls and papyri, each shelf labelled in Greek. Ladders were leaned against walls for the scholars to reach the higher shelves.

The wall spaces that were not covered in racks either bore murals depicting scenes of the great intellectuals of the past imparting their knowledge, or they had shrines carved into them containing Greek or Egyptian gods. Callimachus and Zenodotus explained the murals to Hanufer as they walked, keeping their voices hushed so as not to disturb the many scholars studying or consulting books or scrolls. Hippocrates was shown under a plane tree teaching his students the art of medicine, Pythagoras sat at a table covered with geometric patterns, Plato was staring at a far-off island, and incongruously, Socrates, surrounded by weeping men and women, was drinking a cup of hemlock.

'Our great philosopher was found guilty of corrupting the youth of Athens,' Zenodotus said.

'And of impiety,' Callimachus added. 'He did not believe in the gods, so he was sentenced to death and permitted to take his own life by drinking a mixture containing hemlock. It paralysed him until he could not breathe.'

Hanufer pointed to a shrine with a statue of the ibis-headed Thoth. 'Our god of writing, medicine and mathematics. And there, Isis, the goddess of healing, wisdom and magic.' Immediately, his thoughts turned to Nefrit and the memory of those kisses, which kept intruding on his consciousness.

Zenodotus pointed to a door and Callimachus stood aside to let the head librarian lead the way into his office. Like the rest of the library it was crammed with papyri, scrolls and books in racks, each of which was labelled.

Hanufer asked casually which publishing houses they used for copying manuscripts.

'Mainly a fellow called Saul Sofer in the Jewish quarter. Him or some of the other publishing houses there.'

'Do you use Obelius of Pella or his son Stratonicus's publishing house?'

Both librarians shook their heads. 'They do more commercial work and look after the private publication of their friends. We reproduce intellectual works and have to have our manuscripts and books done quickly and to a high standard. Saul Sofer and his colleagues suit our needs.'

Hanufer took a proffered seat beside Callimachus while Zenodotus sat behind his large desk. He adroitly answered their questions about Diomedes and Philitas, without mentioning that he had used the philosopher's lodestone to confirm in his mind that the philosopher and his iron bands had been swallowed by the pharaoh's snake.

'It may be days before the snake passes whatever is left of Philitas of Cos,' he concluded.

The two librarians looked stunned, so he quickly took the initiative and asked, 'You will both have heard about the messages that have been found at the *temenos*, at the villa of Diomedes and by the Soma. I had talked with Philitas about the work of Sotades, and he was evasive with his opinion about his worth as a poet.'

'It is quite simple,' said Callimachus, haughtily. 'He was totally worthless.'

'That is true,' Zenodotus agreed. 'He had the temerity to give his version of the great Homer. I say this as one of the foremost scholars of our great bard.' He looked at his colleague for confirmation, which Hanufer noted was instantly given.

'Did you perceive meanings in those messages, either of you?'

The two librarians looked at each other, then shook their heads.

'Are you asking whether we believe they were written by Sotades, as the rumours say?' Zenodotus asked.

'Do you?' Hanufer asked. He produced his copy of the latest message, including the hieroglyphs and the Greek script, and showed them.

'It is possible that they were his words,' Callimachus conceded after he had studied the papyrus scrap for a few moments. 'Yet I do not see that he could personally have put them there if the accounts of his execution by drowning are true.'

Zenodotus winced. 'He was an arrogant fool, but no one deserved to be killed like that.' He sighed. 'And I agree, they could have been Sotades's words. None of them have any real poetic value.'

Hanufer nodded. 'What do you think was meant by the Trojan snake?'

Zenodotus shrugged. 'That would be the typical sort of thing Sotades would say. He thought it clever to use Homer's concepts. That is surely what is meant — that the Trojan snake contains poison that will do its enemies harm, like the Trojan Horse in *The Odyssey* contained a force of elite trained soldiers.'

'Was there anything in particular that you wanted, some text or other in the library?' Callimachus asked.

'Actually, I came for two reasons. Firstly, to consult Manetho of Sebennytos and then the anatomist Erasistratus.'

'Then you had better consult the anatomist, for Manetho was urgently called to the palace by the pharaoh himself.'

Hanufer stared in surprise. 'Pharaoh Ptolemy wanted him?'

'And apparently all the other high priests and priestesses. From what we heard, it is something to do with the procession and the installation of Admiral Patroclus as the new high priest of Alexander.'

As he left the cool interior of the Library, the heat and humidity immediately struck Hanufer again and he ran a finger under his pectoral at the back of his neck. He was starting to feel quite unsettled, especially when he had been told that all of the priests and priestesses had been called to the Royal Palace by the pharaoh himself. When he'd last seen the ruler, he had commanded him to find out who was responsible for the messages and the death of Diomedes and the suspected one of Philitas. This emergency meeting the pharaoh had called clearly meant that things were becoming more urgent.

The fact that neither Herophilus nor Erasistratus had sent a report of their findings to his office had irritated him, and he was determined to demand why they had not done so, when matters were so important.

At the Medical School he was told by a young physician who was leading a group of even younger students towards the anatomy theatre that Erasistratus was still ill and had been moved from his quarters in the Musaeum to a bed in the hospital.

'He is too ill to talk,' Herophilus told Hanufer when he was shown to the special room where the younger anatomist was being treated.

'I thought it was simply an excess of wine and food from the symposium?' Hanufer queried.

'It is much more serious than that. He may have had an apoplectic attack. He cannot move his legs, and he is vomiting and unable to talk because he has great difficulty breathing.'

Hanufer looked at Erasistratus, who was lying naked on a bed apart from a small sheet over his pelvis to his knees, and a wet cloth applied to his forehead. He was lathered in perspiration and his breathing was laboured and stertorous. When he saw Hanufer, his face became quite anxious and he tried to push himself up on his elbows.

'The ... br-brain!' he managed to say, before falling back unconscious.

Herophilus snapped his fingers at a young attendant and pointed to a basin of water and a cloth. 'Keep swabbing him — we must break the fever. Prepare the instruments for me to bleed him.'

He moved away, gesturing for Hanufer to follow. Once out of earshot, he said, 'He has had apoplexy, but I am not sure what the underlying ailment is. He seems to have an excess of blood and of black bile. I need to remove some of the stagnant fluid.'

He explained to Hanufer that according to Greek medicine as taught by Hippocrates of Cos two centuries before, it was believed that most illnesses were the result of an imbalance in the four vital fluids, or humours, as Hippocrates had called them.

'I will open a blood vessel and remove blood from him, and we will give him a purgative to loosen his bowels to remove the black bile.'

'He looks very ill,' Hanufer commented.

The older physician's face creased with anxiety. 'I fear he might die.'

'He is paralysed?'

'Both legs, and he is getting worse.'

Hanufer's mind took him back to the mural of the philosopher Socrates in the Library. Callimachus had said that the hemlock he had been made to drink had caused paralysis.

He told Herophilus of his visit to the Library and about the mural. 'Could he have been poisoned, as the philosopher Socrates was?' he asked. 'With something like hemlock?'

Herophilus almost staggered back and he looked aghast. 'Why did I not consider that? Why, yes, indeed he could have been. Being unable to move both legs rather than one side of his body is certainly suggestive. I must examine him again. Yet I must still bleed him, for poisons also work by causing stagnation of body humours. If poison is the case, then I will also get bezoar stones and make up a remedy. You will excuse me, *Archiphylakites* Hanufer, but I must begin treatment immediately.'

'He was trying to say something about the brain, I think. Was that the brain of the dead slave?'

Herophilus shrugged. 'I will have to see if I can save him first. Tomorrow will be the earliest that I will know. Come then.'

Feeling frustrated, Hanufer left the hospital and once more went out into the uncomfortable heat. He touched the ring with the image of Sobek and silently asked the god for help. There were still things troubling him that he had wanted to ask the younger anatomist.

At about the same time in one of the private villas in the Brucheum, two people were meeting.

He had seldom seen the Magnificence so perturbed. At first he wondered if it was the heat, which had been quite unbearable. Then, watching the movements and the restlessness, he understood it was more than that. It was frustration and anger.

'Have you found out if it worked?'

He nodded. 'It works. We know that from when two of the minions used it to eliminate the last overseer.'

'They took risks. Can you still vouch for them?'

'They are useful. Many of the others follow them like camels. When the time comes, they will do exactly as I command.'

He noted the contemptuous twist of the mouth. 'As *you* command?'

'Your pardon. As I deliver *your* commands, Magnificence.'

'That is better. But is this one dead? I did not give the order to kill, just to make it seem like a sudden illness. There must not be another death until I am ready and give the order. They must suspect that something is coming after all of these signs, but they will not know when. It must be as if it is the will of the gods.'

He bowed and tried to sound reassuring. 'The whole of Alexandria knows about the messages. You can almost taste the fear in the air. The name Sotades is whispered everywhere, and the words have everyone guessing what is to happen next.'

'What do you think of this heat?'

He was surprised at the sudden change of conversation. 'It is oppressive, Magnificence.'

'What do you smell in the air?'

He looked puzzled, but sniffed. 'Sand, Magnificence.'

'It is more than that. It is a sign of Seth.'

'Seth the Egyptian god of —?'

'Of degradation, disorder and revenge!'

'But I didn't think you believed —?'

His words tailed off as he saw the fire of lust in the eyes. He felt himself perspire as the eyes of the one they referred to as the Magnificence strayed over him. He was conscious of how his chiton clung to him. He recognised the look. When the voice spoke again, it had become huskier and there was hunger in it that he knew it was his job to assuage.

'Enough talk. You know what must happen next.' A finger pointed at his chiton. 'Disrobe and make yourself ready!' Then a smile. 'Let us begin with a little distraction this afternoon. A little degradation.'

As he obeyed, he wondered why he did not feel remotely guilty at his latest betrayal.


The air was stifling as Hanufer walked along the Canopic Way. The great wide street was busy, and it was noticeable that more people were covering their mouths and noses with neckcloths, or even improvising as best they could by covering their lower face with a hand or the crook of an elbow. He was glad to reach Saul Sofer's establishment, where he was ushered into the proprietor's inner sanctum and offered a refreshing drink of fig beer.

'Let me get straight to the point,' Hanufer said, as he leaned forward after slaking his thirst. He placed his mug on Saul Sofer's desk. 'I need to know more about Sotades. I have talked with Zenodotus and Callimachus at the Library and before them with Philitas of Cos.'

At the name of Philitas, Saul Sofer closed his eyes and mumbled a blessing. '*Zikhrono livrakha*, he was a great and learned man. Our whole community mourns him, if it is true what they say and he has been consumed by the pharaoh's pet monster. I myself heard about the message placed on the Soma.'

Hanufer shook his head. 'Philitas of Cos is missing and may be dead, that is all I can say.' He reached into his chiton and drew out the papyrus scraps. He unrolled the latest one that he had copied from the Soma wall and slid it across the desk.

'They look like the sort of thing Sotades may have written,' the publisher said after a few moments of consideration.

'That is what Zenodotus and Callimachus both said. They were very disparaging about him as a poet. Indeed, I have not yet heard anyone say anything particularly flattering about him.'

Saul Sofer smiled. 'That is possibly because you have asked the wrong people, my lord.'

'Really? The only remotely positive things were said about him by Philitas of Cos, and even they were not the words of an admirer.'

'May I ask what he said?'

'He said he was an influencer. He could persuade people through his poetry.'

'Last time you were here, I think I told you that he deliberately provoked people. He delighted in it and liked to see just how far he could go. And then of course he went too far.'

Hanufer took some more beer and then wiped the perspiration from his forehead with the back of his hand. 'Yes, indeed. In fact, I talked with the librarians at your suggestion, but I am really no further forward. I do not think that I know the man behind the poet. That is partly why I am here; I would like to know what you thought of Sotades as a person.'

Saul Sofer leaned forward. 'I liked him, sir. Oh yes, he was a man with few morals. He drank excessively. He fornicated with both men and women. He was a seducer and a rogue. But he had humour, sir. When you talked with him, he had a twinkle in his eye; there was mischief in his words and in his mind. He said and wrote things that were hurtful, but in actual dealings with people he was gentle.'

'Would he have been a vengeful man?'

'Only with words, my lord. He was a physically strong man, a swimmer, I believe, but he was not known for acts of violence.'

'Someone struck down the pharaoh's Keeper of Snakes, and it looks as if that same person did violence to Philitas and then put his body in the cage of the python.'

The publisher's eyes widened in shock. 'That is not the Sotades that I knew. But who knows how a man may feel if others had attempted to kill him?'

Hanufer sipped some more beer to take away the sand taste at the back of his throat. 'Look at the hieroglyphs. What do you make of them?'

Saul Sofer hummed thoughtfully. 'As I said, my lord, my knowledge of the hieroglyphics is fairly basic. We will copy Egyptian texts, including hieroglyphics, but I am not a scholar. They suggest that a horse is floating in the water.'

'And the message refers to a Trojan snake?'

The publisher looked blank. 'It is a mystery to me. I do not understand it.' Saul Sofer shrugged and passed the papyrus back to Hanufer.

Hanufer nodded. 'A puzzle indeed.'

'There is another matter. Men with covered faces have been demanding money in order to protect me and others in the community from harm.'

'How long has it been going on?'

'Over a year. They come irregularly, and they come to individuals, not to their businesses. They … they come to my home, when my family are there.'

'Have people been hurt?'

'Yes, my lord. I was beaten in the early days, as were friends. None of us would dare to stand against them.'

'And you never reported these attacks?'

'We tried early on when your predecessor was here, but we were not even permitted to get as far as the office. Then we were persuaded not to try again. That is why I tried that subterfuge with the scholars.'

'Who did you think was behind it?'

'We think the police were involved. But how far up, who knows? Perhaps…' He bit his lip hesitantly. 'Perhaps even the very top, your predecessor *Archiphylakites* Gryton.'

'Or the *Hyparchiphylakites*, Sergeant Kraspar?'

Saul Sofer shifted uneasily in his seat. 'It is not for me to say, my lord. Except … except —'

Hanufer picked up the papyrus, rolled it up with the other pieces and stowed them in his chiton pocket. 'Except that it is still going on?'

'It is, my lord.'

'Just as I thought it would. But tell me, is it only your community that is targeted?'

The publisher reached forward and picked up his mug. He looked down into it and swirled the contents around. 'No, my lord. I know Nabataeans, Egyptians and Nubians who have been similarly made to pay.'

'In coins?'

'Coins, silver and gold, my lord. All small businesses across Alexandria, Pharos and Rhakotis. Yet we Jews have been most affected, as far as I know.'

'And yet none of them have reported it to the police either?'

'For the same reasons, my lord. When you are used to being treated thus, as we all are, then one does what one can for a peaceful life.'

'And yet you contacted me?'

'There always has to be hope, my lord. That is fundamental to my religion.' He finished swirling his mug and took a gulp.

Hanufer nodded and unconsciously stroked his rings. 'I do not know a great deal about your religion, except that you only have one god. This is strange to Egyptians like myself. When I talked with Zachriel Cohen, who you know to be one of the elders of the Tribe of Simeon, he said that they are translating your laws about purity, idolatry and how sacrifices should be prepared and made. He told me it is so different from the ways of both the Greeks and the Egyptians. He implied that it was emotional and difficult for them all. Why is this?'

Saul Sofer smiled thinly. 'To us, there is only one true God and all others are false. Our laws, which we call commandments, and of which there are a great number, came to us directly from God to the prophet Moses. They tell us how to live and properly worship God. For one thing, we must have no other gods and we must not worship any statue or idol. All of the Greek and Egyptian statues and shrines are anathema to us. And so too are the laws about sacrifices. The ways of the Greeks and the Egyptians are strange and primitive to us.'

*And the temenos was defiled, so that a sacrifice could not be made*, Hanufer thought.

'Do you think that Pharaoh Ptolemy Philadelphus knows this?'

'I am neither a scholar nor an elder, my lord.'

'But what do you think about our local god, Serapis? Do you think that he can protect you, as the pharaoh thinks?'

Saul Sofer closed his eyes. 'Only our God can protect us, if we live correctly and He chooses to. He may have other purposes for us.'

'Are you aware that priests and priestesses across Alexandria have been summoned to the Royal Palace today?'

'I had heard rumours, my lord. I also heard that one scholar from each of the twelve tribes on Pharos have been sent for.' He wiped his brow. 'It is so hot, my lord. And the air feels so heavy.'

'A sandstorm is on the way. We had them often in Crocodilopolis.'

Saul Sofer shivered. 'I think you are right, sir. But there is something more. It is as if ... as if something is stirring. Something evil.'

Hanufer was once again aware of a strange tingle running down his spine.

*That is exactly my feeling*, he thought.

# CHAPTER 24

Cario was limping along the corridor as Hanufer came in.

'What happened?' he asked.

Startled to hear the Overseer of Police behind him, Cario spun round and almost dropped the armfuls of documents he was carrying. 'Your pardon, my lord, Pollio told me to take these cases for copying. I think I must have twisted myself when I was out buying bread for him. I caught my foot in a gutter and it went one way and I the other.' He forced a smile. 'It will be fine, sir. But what can I do for you?'

'Come to my office once you have finished and bring those eels.'

'Of course, my lord. But may I warn you, they stink now.'

Hanufer shook a hand in front of his face, as if to fan himself. 'In this stifling heat, I don't think an additional smell will bother me overmuch.'

Back behind his desk, he took out the papyri with the copied messages from his chiton pocket and laid them side-by-side in front of him. Sitting forward and holding his head in both hands he started to ponder, mentally asking and answering questions of himself.

*Where have these messages appeared?*

*First, at the desecrated temenos. Second, at Diomedes's villa and, lastly, at the snake house.*

*No one was killed at the sacrifice, why was that?*

*Because it was a way of making an effective announcement.*

*And what announcement was that?*

*Possibly that Sotades, who was thought to be drowned, is back and very much alive.*

*What features make one think that Sotades is the author?*

*The palindromes in hieroglyphics, even though they make no sense as words. They look like a jar in water, but the middle hieroglyph is actually a heart, the ib. And the eels, with their tails shoved into their throats, which Philitas himself said he thought were like palindromes. The first poem written in Greek was the infamous Sotades poem. But we do not have any written poems by Sotades, as Ptolemy Philadelphus ordered them all to be destroyed.*

*What is there about the poem that so offends?*

*The poem insults the pharaoh and his queen and it insults all of the gods of Egypt.*

*So, what makes you think it couldn't have been Sotades?*

*The testimony of Diomedes and of Admiral Patroclus, who both stated that he had been tossed into the sea in a leaded pithos jar. Surely not even an Olympian swimmer could escape and swim back, especially when he was shackled at the ankles? Unless of course he was picked up by another boat?*

*The second message was found at the villa of Diomedes. There was a body there. So what can this message tell us?*

*First, the hieroglyphs are nonsense, again. It looks like a spitting snake in water. Or perhaps they thought it was a spitting eel? That is possible. The poem itself seems to be in two parts. The first says that the gods grew angry with his poisoned visions. That must mean Diomedes. And even they spat out his poison. Perhaps they spat as they ate his face. Then the second part suggests that a poisonous toad will lie at Hector's feet. That must be a reference to Hector's foe, Patroclus.*

*And lastly, the message near the snake that seems to have swallowed Philitas. The message as repeated at the Soma. Why?*

*As Sabu said, it is clear. To show it to the people. So that the people of Alexandria will know about it and not just the few people who are permitted inside the Royal Zoo.*

*Who was the scholar that followed Philitas into the Royal Zoo? The guards on the gate could barely give a description, except that it was a scholar in a white himation.*

*So, what does lie inside the Trojan snake? Does it mean Philitas? And what about that last line, 'Die those who kill and treasures take' — what treasures?*

*This really worries me. It suggests that Patroclus is next to die. Is it a challenge to stop this?*

*Yet there is a problem with all this. Why should Philitas be killed? He had no part in Sotades's drowning and was not as explicit a critic of the poet as others, like Callimachus and Zenodotus, or Theocritus of Syracuse.*

*It does not make a great deal of sense, unless it was to silence him. In which case, why?*

*This I do not know. And then there are the other murders. Two of them. First the public slave, whom we know to be called Zalmoxis. He was murdered in the same way as Diomedes, that much I already know. Erasistratus examined the brain of the slave Zalmoxis and Herophilus that of Diomedes. Yet there is another curiosity. Erasistratus may have been poisoned, but why?*

*Perhaps to stop further examination of Diomedes?*

*Then there is the murder of Sergeant Kraspar. He was not killed in the same manner, so was his murderer the same person? And Gryton of Salamis, he died suddenly.*

*Gryton and Kraspar may have been close to unmasking the extortionists.*

*So, is there a link between them all?*

*The slave Zalmoxis was Sotades's guard in the Necropolis prison. He and Kraspar were both Thracians, but does that mean anything? One question just leads to another.*

A knock on the door pulled Hanufer from his reverie and he called out to enter. Cario came in with the jar of eels. Despite the covering, they smelled terrible.

'Shall I take them out, my lord?'

'No. But tell me, when you were out, what was the talk about in the streets?'

Cario sucked air through his lips. 'There was much talk about the philosopher Philitas, my lord.'

'What of him?'

'That the pharaoh's monster snake had killed him. There … there seems to be much anger, my lord.'

'Anger at whom?'

Cario seemed reluctant to reply.

'Out with it, Cario. Tell me what you heard, without fear of speaking.'

'People were saying it was a sign of the gods' anger, sir.'

'Which gods?'

'The Greek gods, my lord. Anger about the pharaoh and his sister marrying, sir. But also people are saying that the Egyptian gods were angry, especially Seth, because it is so hot and the air is stifling and smells.'

'Anything else? Speak truthfully.'

'There … there is anger that you and the police are not doing anything to stop these deaths. I am sorry, sir.' He pointed to the jar of eels. 'They say that Sotades lives and that he is seeking revenge. There are rumours that he was saved by a great swarm of eels sent by Poseidon himself. Sotades is being praised as a hero, my lord. As some sort of prophet.'

Hanufer pursed his lips and stared at the jar of eels. 'I was worried that this might happen. Eels!' Then, pinching his nostrils, he waved at them. 'You are right, Cario. They stink of death. Throw them away.'

Hanufer devoted his attention over the following hour to his basket of petitions and administrative duties.

Pollio knocked on his office door and entered at Hanufer's command. He held out a scroll with an official seal.

'A messenger from the Royal Palace just arrived, my lord. He said these are orders from Admiral Patroclus's office about the arrangements that are required for the procession tomorrow.' He shivered. 'The winds are getting stronger and the messenger said that the streets are becoming deserted.'

The noise of the wind had increased in the time that Hanufer had been working, and he was conscious that it had become markedly cooler.

'I will be leaving soon, Pollio. You can go too, when I do. It is not an evening to be out if a sandstorm actually comes.'

'I thank you, my lord. I have many matters still to attend to in the office, but as usual I will be here in the morning before daybreak.'

Left to himself again, Hanufer unrolled the scroll with the orders from the vizier, Admiral Patroclus. It detailed the arrangements for the procession that was to take place the next day. This was to include all of those who had attended the first procession, plus the seventy-two Jewish elders and any priests who had not attended the one to the *temenos*. Admiral Patroclus and then Pharaoh Ptolemy and Queen Arsinoe would lead, followed by a great cage on wheels containing Apophis.

The vizier's own installation as the high priest of Alexander would be performed, before the procession made its way across the *Heptastadion* to the Island of Pharos. There, at the foot of the lighthouse, Patroclus, in his first role as the priest of Alexander, would perform a symbolic filling of a large pithos jar with rocks and an effigy of the poet Sotades, along with some dead eels. This would then be placed on a small boat and sailed out of the harbour into the open sea, where, within sight of the watchers, it would be ceremonially cast into the water.

It would then end with Pharaoh Ptolemy and Queen Arsinoe giving thanks in the Temple of Isis on the Island of Pharos before the procession returned and did a circuit of the city, when the priests and priestesses at every temple would perform purification rituals.

'And so that will be the end of it all,' Hanufer sarcastically mused to himself. 'I just have to arrange for the security along the way.'

He took out his writing set and was preparing an ink block to make notes when Pollio again knocked on the door.

'Judge Thespos would like to see you, my lord,' the scribe said. 'Shall I ask him —'

He did not finish because a hand on the scribe's shoulder shoved him gently aside and the judge walked in.

'Ah, Hanufer, I hoped you might be here, although not for long if you want to avoid being caught in this foul weather. I need to have a word about how we are going to punish the dog responsible for these disgusting messages. If it is Sotades himself, then it will not be my responsibility. If it is someone else, then I need to consider whether I try them under Greek or Egyptian law.'

Hanufer waved for Pollio to leave them, as Judge Thespos lowered himself into a seat opposite. 'Surely it will have to be Greek law, Judge Thespos.'

'But why? If it is a Greek behind it, then yes, of course. But it could equally be an Egyptian, since half the messages have been in your hieroglyphics.'

'Not half, Judge Thespos,' Hanufer replied. He was surprised and wondered whether the judge had actually seen the messages himself.

'Enough to suspect an Egyptian as much as a Greek. Are you close to finding the villain?'

'I am investigating several paths,' Hanufer replied, unwilling to be drawn further.

The judge gave him a sour look. 'But there is another concern. What if this situation gets out of hand?'

'Meaning what, exactly?'

'Meaning that if this really is due to the ghost of Sotades, how do we find and then try a ghost?'

At that point, Hanufer wondered just why the judge had called on him. It seemed a strange time to make such a bizarre enquiry.

Sabu had drilled the constables all afternoon in the heat. The wind had at first been something of a relief, cooling them down, but then it changed. Where before there had merely been the smell of the desert, gradually everyone became aware that it was actually blowing sand. It got worse and worse until it started to irritate bared flesh and made the eyes sting. When he finally dismissed them to the barracks, there was much relief to get indoors.

As Sabu was walking towards the city centre, he was hailed from behind. He was surprised to see Sidvain and Rhoglos coming quickly after him.

'Sergeant Sabu,' Rhoglos said, smiling ingratiatingly. 'Could we have some words? My friend Sidvain and I would like to buy you a jug of beer.'

'Have you not had enough of my orders?' Sabu returned, forcing a grin.

'We are professionals, Sergeant,' said Sidvain. 'We are used to taking orders, especially when we respect our superiors.'

'I'll take that as a compliment, Constable Sidvain. All right, I accept.'

'Come with us, Sergeant. We know a quiet beer shop where we can talk. We have something that we would like to tell you in private.'

Sabu nodded and they walked down through the gridwork of streets towards the Lake Harbour, where the boats on Lake Mareotis came and went. He had been there before on one of his own exploratory walks. They went into a beer house and each drank a jug. They talked generally about the police and the difficulties of controlling a city where there were many petty criminals. Sabu let them lead the conversation, knowing full well that they would get round to the subject they wanted to discuss once they had all drunk several beers.

'Let's go to another beer house that we know,' said Rhoglos, draining his jug.

Sabu drained his and nodded. He thought he must be getting old, for the beer seemed to have affected him more than usual. He felt somewhat drowsy.

It was extremely windy when they emerged from the beer house and it was starting to get dark. The Pharos lighthouse fires had been lit, sending beams of light high overhead and out to sea, and also over Lake Mareotis. But down on the now quiet streets where they walked it was quite dark.

'It's up this alley, into the older part of the city,' Sidvain said, leading the way.

Sabu laughed. 'Lead on. And these jugs will be on me, so you can tell me what —'

They had gone some cubits up the alley when he heard a noise behind him that he recognised immediately. A weapon had been drawn swiftly from its sheath. He instinctively dodged sidewards, but not quickly enough as he felt a searing pain on the back of his neck and he was propelled forward to smash his head into the wall. He felt himself blacking out as he slid down the wall.

A brutal kick in his abdomen caused him to gasp and he realised the danger he was in. There were two against one, and he was already on the ground at their mercy.

'Take that, you Egyptian bastard!' he heard as a boot was stomped on his back.

'And that!' He was struck again on the side of the head with the pommel of a sword.

Unable to focus or even move while further blows were rained down on him by one of his assailants, he felt the other drag him by his collar along the ground. It was too dark to see much, and the winds seemed to swirl from all directions.

'Time for a ducking,' said the one dragging him. Sabu recognised it as Rhoglos.

'Hope you breathe like a fish,' sneered the other. 'If not, you'll be dead when they fish you out of the canal.'

He knew that the pummelling had just been to soften him up enough to dispatch him by whatever means they had planned. It sounded as if they intended to drown him. He tensed his muscles against another frontal blow to his stomach and lashed out with his legs, catching the limbs of one assailant in a scissors move. He kicked hard and felt the man tumble and curse as he fell. The hands on his collar released him. Half expecting a blade to either slash at his throat or stab at his chest, Sabu immediately twisted and in one movement drew his short sword and lashed out sideways.

A scream of agony told him that he had struck home, so he was at slightly less of a disadvantage. Except that he was still on the ground and could not see his assailants clearly for the swirling sand-laden wind. Sweeping his sword the other way, he found it blocked by a metal blade.

Reaching out with his other hand, he grabbed the leg of the one he had struck and yanked it hard, toppling him. So now all three were on the ground.

'The dog cut me,' Sidvain's voice said through gritted teeth. 'Stab him, let's —'

But it was enough for Sabu to know where to strike with his fist, and as he punched in that direction he heard the constable's nose crunch.

Rhoglos proved more wily and more adept with his sword. In the dim light they exchanged sword blows until Sabu brought a knee up to connect with the other's genitals. Then his sword pommel smashed into the constable's head and all went quiet apart from the moaning of Sidvain.

Sabu struggled to his feet, blinking hard against the wind. And then he heard the sound of two lots of footsteps. One from each end of the alley.

# CHAPTER 25

The sandstorm raged all night and only abated at daybreak. When people with their animals ventured out, they saw the trail of devastation that it had caused. There was sand everywhere. It was only a fingerbreadth deep on the roads and streets, but where it had drifted against walls and monuments it could have been several cubits. Many trees had been uprooted, and crude sheds and other wooden structures had collapsed.

Hanufer had a frugal breakfast, before which he patiently listened as Timon told him of how the two maids Delia and Ophelia had been as frightened as mice during the sandstorm and had requested to sleep in his chamber at the foot of his bed.

'I told them tales throughout the night to keep their spirits up, my lord. Why, I even made them both laugh. They particularly liked one I told them about Thalia. She was one of the Nine Muses, sir.'

Hanufer did not want to waste time by telling him that he had seen the statue to her in the Temple of the Muses at the Musaeum, so he merely nodded and let the butler tell his tale.

'Well, Ophelia and Delia knew that she was one of the Nine Muses, but they didn't know that she was also one of the Three Graces. Among other things it was her role to tend to the goddess Aphrodite's hair. Thalia is a mischief-maker, you see, and once when Zeus the king of the Gods threw a feast for all of the other gods and the Nine Muses, she thwarted his plan to seduce the goddess Aphrodite by making a wig from hundreds of eels...'

Hanufer listened and wondered why the two maids found this especially amusing and concluded that it was not Timon's delivery of the tale, more their state of panic during the storm. He felt relieved when the butler retreated to leave him in peace, all the while chuckling.

When Hanufer left, he saw that an army of *demosioi* — those public slaves whose lives revolved around clearing dung from the streets, clearing cesspits and tending to the parks and boulevards — had already been despatched to clear the sands that had been blown from the deserts. He hoped that no one had been hurt during the sandstorm, and his mind immediately turned to Nefrit, who was now rarely far from his thoughts. It had been his intention to call upon her the night before, until the ferocity of the sandstorm had persuaded him to seek the shelter of his villa instead.

Walking along he heard passers-by talk about the displeasure of the gods and in particular of Seth, the storm-bringer. Even the Greeks were convinced that it was his doing.

Cario eagerly met him at the door. 'Sergeant Sabu is still sleeping in your office, my lord.'

'Has he been here all night?'

'He has news, my lord. He said I am to meet you and bring you to the office as soon as I see you.'

Much perplexed, Hanufer followed the limping *demosios* to his office, where he found Sabu lying on the floor, covered by a blanket. About his head he had a bandage. At the sound of their entry he immediately roused himself, threw off the blanket and leaped up. Then he winced as he touched the back of his head.

'Are you wounded, Sabu? Did you have an accident in the storm?'

'I was wounded, but it was no accident, my lord. I was only half-prepared for an attack, but I probably drank too much beer and took a blow on the head, and then another when I collided with a wall. Then the villains began on me.'

'The villains?'

'As we thought, my lord. Rhoglos and Sidvain. Fortunately, I was able to turn the tables somewhat and broke Sidvain's nose and wounded his knee, and I knocked Rhoglos out. I thought there were more of them, but it was actually my two bodyguards, Pylyp and Filemon. We had expected some such thing after I had drilled the men in the afternoon. They were therefore trailing me but keeping some distance. Apparently they lost us temporarily as the sandstorm and darkness started to descend, but together we hauled the wretches into a cell down below us.'

'Did you interrogate them?'

'I did, my lord, with help from Pylyp and Filemon, although we did not hurt them too much.'

Hanufer frowned. He did not approve of torture, but when matters were as important as this, he had no doubt that he might have to sanction more.

'I did not get a great deal from them,' Sabu went on, 'except they admitted that they and others under their command had been extorting money from local businesses, mainly Jewish ones.'

'Did you ask about Sergeant Kraspar?'

'That's when they went quiet, my lord. But I'm sure they did it. They were planning to drown me and dump my body in the Canopic Canal. There was an animal trough just a few cubits from where they attacked me. They had chosen the part of the city well. I had to hold Filemon and Pylyp back at that point, they were so angry.'

'Anything about *Archiphylakites* Gryton?'

'They wouldn't say anything about his death, sir, but they admitted they planted money at his house and burned it down, because we were getting too nosey. They thought we would just assume that Gryton and Kraspar had been doing the extorting themselves. They said they were only acting under orders for somebody else, and that there were others a lot higher up than them.'

Hanufer nodded. 'This is a murky business. Let's go and see them.'

Sabu led the way down to the cells, the corridor illuminated by oil lamps. None of the cells were occupied, and in the last one the two constables were lying on crude trestle beds.

'Wake up, you two!' Sabu commanded as he unlocked the door and went in. He roughly shook Rhoglos and then gave Sidvain the same treatment. When he turned to look at Hanufer, his face was shocked.

'They are dead, my lord. Both of them.'

Cario had heard Hanufer and Sabu going down the stairs to the cells. He was in one of the side rooms where trays of ostraca for making notes were kept when he saw Pollio creeping along the corridor. Tiptoeing across the room, he watched the head clerk push the bolts on the door at the stop of the stairs, then turn to come back.

'Why have you bolted the door, Pollio?' he asked, stepping into the corridor ahead of him, blocking his way.

Pollio glared angrily at him. 'Get back in that room,' he ordered, reaching inside his chiton and bringing out a dagger. 'Don't make a noise or you'll get worse than that kicking I gave you.'

'But why have you locked *Archiphylakites* Hanufer and Sergeant Sabu down in the cells?' Cario asked as he backed into the room.

'I said not a sound!' Pollio came towards him.

Then he lunged, aiming his dagger straight at the heart of the *demosios*.


Hanufer joined Sabu and felt both constables' necks. There was no pulse and when he bent closer and put a hand near their faces, he felt no breath of life.

It was then that he saw the small bottle lying on the floor. He picked it up and smelled it, immediately wincing.

'Poison of some sort,' he said, rising with it in his hand.

'Why would they have such a thing?' Sabu asked. 'Unless it was meant for me, perhaps? I must admit that last night I felt unusually drowsy and wondered if it was just a strong brew of beer. Now I wonder if they had given me this? Although where they had it I don't know. We disarmed and searched them thoroughly.'

Hanufer held it to his sergeant's nose. 'While they may yet have given you some powerful drug to dull your senses, I don't think it was this.'

'I think you are right, my lord. This smells disgusting, and I think even the tiniest amount would not have been masked in a beer.'

'Which makes one think that this must have been a deliberately strong poison, meant to kill quickly. A skilled poisoner would know how to concoct such a thing.'

'What shall we do with the bodies, my lord?'

'Nothing as yet. Let us go to my office.'

They left the cell and went back along the corridor and then up the stairs to find the door bolted from the outside.

'Pollio!' Sabu called out loudly. 'Who bolted this door?'

There was the sound of sandaled feet coming along the corridor, then through the grille in the door they saw Cario hobbling towards them. He was clutching his arm and blood was streaming down it, dripping on the floor as he walked.

'He is up here, sir,' he said through gritted teeth as he managed to pull the bolts back.

'What happened?' Hanufer demanded as they followed him along the corridor to the side room.

'I am sorry, my lord,' Cario said, standing at the entrance so they could see in. 'I saw Pollio bolt the door to the cells.'

The office scribe was pinioned to the floor by several trays of ostraca. Blood ran from an ugly gash between his eyes and he lay groaning and barely conscious.

'He tried to kill me, sir,' Cario said, pointing to the bloody dagger lying on the floor by the wall. 'He stabbed at me, but I managed to throw an ostracon at him. He fell and I pushed two of the trays on top of him. They are very heavy, but as I was bending over him he managed to slash my arm. So I kicked it from his hand and I put more trays on top of him. I am sorry if I have crushed him, sir.'

Sabu patted Cario's good shoulder. 'You did well. I'd have been tempted to do more.'

Hanufer told him to go and sit in his office, then he and Sabu removed the trays from the scribe, who took a sudden breath and opened his eyes.

'My lord, the slave tried to murder me. I tried to stop him. He had a dagger.'

'He had a dagger and yet he threw a piece of ostraca at you?' Hanufer said. 'Why would he do that?'

'I … I think I disturbed him, my lord. He must have wanted to stop you coming for him after you found he had murdered —'

'How did you know anyone had been murdered, Pollio? Unless you had just poisoned them.'

The office clerk looked anxiously between them and started to get up, only to be restrained by Sabu, who put a sturdy knee on his chest, pinning him down.

'They are not dead long, are they, Pollio? You came here before daybreak and discovered that Sergeant Sabu was here and Constables Rhoglos and Sidvain had been arrested. You couldn't release them and so you had to silence them.'

Pollio shook his head vigorously, blood tracking down both cheeks. 'No! It was the slave. He —'

'So how did you persuade them to take the poison? Fear of torture? Fear of death by impalement?'

Hanufer nodded to Sabu. 'Toss him in a cell, but not the one next to the dead constables. Just make sure he has no convenient little bottle to take.' He addressed Pollio as Sabu dragged him up and bent his arms behind him. 'We will ask more questions soon. And you will talk!'

Corporals Pylyp and Filemon were among the first to report for duty. Hanufer called them both into his office where he and Sabu had been going over the events. Cario had told them exactly what had happened and also confessed to them that Pollio had regularly beaten him and warned him against telling anything he had seen. And there had been many things, including all of the petitions that had disappeared during Gryton's days and meetings between Pollio, Rhoglos, Sidvain and other constables. Thanking him, Hanufer despatched him to a surgeon to have his wound treated and stitched closed.

'As you know, these two constables were criminals,' Hanufer said now. 'But they have not just been extorting money. I am sure that they murdered both *Archiphylakites* Gryton and Sergeant Kraspar. They almost certainly drowned him as they were trying to do to Sergeant Sabu.'

Both corporals were horrified to hear that they had disposed of the body by taking it to the Medical School, where it was still being dissected.

'All this we believe to be part of a far more sinister plot, and it involves the poet Sotades. We know that a public slave, a Dacian called Zalmoxis, was murdered, although probably not by them. He was the jailor who helped Sotades escape from the Necropolis prison. His body was disposed of in the bull pen of the Temple of Poseidon, where he was trampled beyond recognition.'

Pylyp shook his head in disbelief. 'What is this plot that you speak of, my lord?'

Hanufer clicked his tongue. 'That is just it, we do not yet know. Since it involves Sotades, we have to assume that it is a threat to harm the vizier, Admiral Patroclus. And since this day at noon there is to be a procession in which he will be installed as the high priest of Alexander, we have to make sure he is completely protected.'

'And that means we have to be able to depend on the constables,' said Sabu.

Filemon frowned. 'But sir —?'

'I know,' replied Hanufer. 'This is why we need you two to help Sergeant Sabu get those constables that you can trust to disarm, arrest and imprison those we cannot trust.'

'But how, my lord?' Pylyp asked doubtfully.

Sabu explained. 'We will do it in the barracks. You two will order all of them back there, saying they are to receive instructions about the procession later today. Before that, make contact with the trusted ones and inform them of the plan. Take them all into the barracks and assemble them in the mess hall for a weapons inspection by me. Get each good man to stand beside one of the others. When I order them to lay their weapons on the floor, our men will take the opportunity to arrest and then manacle them.'

The two corporals smiled.

'And where shall we imprison them, sir?'

'In the hall,' said Sabu. 'There is no way they can escape from there.'

'This will mean that there are perhaps only half of the men needed for the procession, but at least they will be the ones we can trust to protect the vizier. Now go — we have not much time, for the procession starts at noon. Sergeant Sabu will give the instructions once you have arranged the arrest of the corrupt constables.'

The corporals saluted and left.

'Shall I go with them, my lord?'

'No, Sabu. I need you to help me interrogate Pollio.'

Sabu cracked his knuckles. 'It will be a pleasure, my lord.'

# CHAPTER 26

Hanufer disliked using torture, but in the case of the scribe Pollio he had been prepared to do so. Yet the physical presence of Sabu and Hanufer's skilful interrogation technique had made it unnecessary. Pollio admitted that he had given constables Rhoglos and Sidvain poison to prevent them telling more than he dared risk. He had intercepted many petitions and had given the two constables their orders. They in turn had instructed the other corrupted constables in their nefarious dealings. He had also covered up the suspicions about Gryton and Kraspar's deaths on the orders of his boss. On whom that was, however, his lips were sealed.

Hanufer had further questions, but rather than torturing Pollio, he thought he might obtain answers more swiftly from other sources. Besides, Sabu had to get to the barracks to oversee the arrest of the renegade constables.

Erasistratus was conscious but looked deathly pale when Hanufer came to see him.

'He has vomited copiously and is being purged,' Herophilus explained as they stood by his bed in the hospital. 'I have bled him thrice, just a small amount at a time, because I must not risk removing too much of his vital humours. He has also had a bezoar stone applied to him and is having a nostrum containing a bezoar from a bull that has been blessed.'

'The brains...' Erasistratus said upon seeing Hanufer. He grasped the blanket that covered him and tried to sit up, but had not sufficient strength.

'Ah yes, the brains,' Herophilus said. 'He has been most anxious that I should examine them, which I have done this very morning.'

'And the drawings … show him…' Erasistratus said.

Herophilus patted his colleague's shoulder. 'I will take him and show him now, my friend. You rest and I will return shortly.'

They went to the anatomist's office in the Medical School. Like the dissecting rooms it smelled strongly of old blood, vinegar and natron. Upon a desk were two basins each containing a bisected brain floating in vinegar.

'The two cavities are almost identical,' Herophilus said, pointing to a pile of papyri at the end of the table. 'I found Erasistratus's drawing of the first brain, plus his one of the tattoo on the first body. I also made a drawing of this second brain for you.'

Hanufer picked up the papyri and examined them, admiring the skill of the two anatomists in depicting the organs. 'This tattoo is most certainly a delta, which is the brand of a *demosios*, a public slave.'

'But this might interest you more,' the anatomist said. He opened a small wooden box and took out a small finger bone. He handed it to Hanufer.

'Whose bone is this?'

'Ah, it is just one that I use to show the students. But it is not the bone, but what I have wrapped round it.'

'Hair!' Hanufer exclaimed. 'Two strands of long hair.'

'Exactly,' agreed Herophilus. 'From the same head, but neither match the hair of the two victims.'

From the Medical School Hanufer went to the Library, where he asked a young librarian to take him to see Manetho of

Sebennytos.

'Overseer Hanufer, have you news of my old friend Philitas?' the high priest of Serapis asked as Hanufer was shown into his study.

'No more than I expect you have already heard, Manetho. But it is not for that reason I come to see you. I need your help as a historian and expert on the Egyptian royal house of the Ptolemies.'

Manetho looked hesitant. 'I will be leaving soon, I am afraid. The procession is due to start at noon.'

'This should not take long, I hope. I called to see you yesterday, but you had been called with the other priests and priestesses to the Royal Palace. You told me when we met at Judge Thespos's home that you are compiling a biography and a list of all the pharaohs of Egypt and of their families.'

The high priest smiled. 'Ah yes, my book, *The Aegyptiaca*.'

'Pharaoh Ptolemy Philadelphus instructed you to do it?'

'He did, and I have been doing it these past five years.'

'So, when you started, there was a different Queen Arsinoe on the throne. Tell me about her.'

Manetho gestured to a seat opposite him.

'She was the daughter of King Lysimachus of Thrace. Pharaoh Ptolemy Soter, our present pharaoh's father, and Lysimachus arranged the wedding to form an alliance of the two nations against Seleucus Nicator, the Basileus or King of Asia Minor and Mesopotamia. She had an older brother called Agathocles and a sister called Eurydice. Arsinoe and the pharaoh seemed happy and had three children together, Ptolemy, Lysimachus and little Berenice. Then when the Arsinoe that is now our queen came back to Egypt, Ptolemy repudiated Arsinoe the First and married Arsinoe the Second, who is his sister.'

Hanufer nodded and took out his writing set and a fresh papyrus from his chiton pocket. 'I think I need to make notes,' he said

Manetho pushed an already prepared ink block across the desk, which Hanufer accepted with a smile. He selected a reed pen and began to write.

'Hence the pharaoh took the name Ptolemy Philadelphus, and they are together as living embodiments of gods called *theoi philadelphoi*, "brother and sister gods",' Hanufer said as he wrote. 'This I knew. Lady Nefrit also told me that Arsinoe the First was banished to the town of Coptos, near Thebes, where she herself is now the high priestess of the Temple of Min and Isis.'

'But her children, Ptolemy's children, were adopted by Arsinoe the Second.'

'Why did the pharaoh repudiate the first queen Arsinoe?'

'I am told she had plotted against her husband.'

'Now tell me about Ptolemy and Arsinoe the Second. They are full brother and sister?'

'They are. There was a similar happening with Ptolemy Soter, the first of their dynasty. As you know, he was one of the *diadokhai*, the divine Alexander's generals. He had several children with a mistress before he married Eurydice, the daughter of Antipater, another of Alexander's generals. She bore him three children: Ptolemy Keraunos, Meleager and Lysandra. Then he repudiated Eurydice and married her cousin Berenice, who bore him Ptolemy, who is now pharaoh, and Arsinoe.'

Hanufer stopped writing and looked up at the priest of Serapis. 'Surely Ptolemy Keraunos should have become pharaoh, not Ptolemy?'

'Ptolemy Keraunos was ill-tempered and Ptolemy Soter did not consider him fit to be pharaoh. He left court and went to Lysimachus's court.'

'And Arsinoe the Second was married previously to Lysimachus?'

'That is correct, and when Lysimachus was killed she fled and married Ptolemy Keraunos, her half-brother, who had her two children put to death in front of her. She fled again and came to Egypt where, as I said, she became Queen Arsinoe the Second.'

'And what of her other half-sister, Lysandra?'

Manetho smiled. 'This is where it gets even more complex. She was married to Agathocles, the first son of Lysimachus.'

'So Arsinoe became her older half-sister's stepmother?'

'She did, until Agathocles was put to death for treason.'

'That is what I thought. And I understand that there was talk that Arsinoe had plotted against Agathocles and Lysimachus had him executed for treason.'

'That will not appear in my history, of course,' Manetho said, meaningly. 'But Lysandra then fled to the court of Seleucus Nicator.'

Hanufer shook his head and resumed making notes. 'The royal history is like a spider's web.'

'It is. Yet there are other strands in this cobweb. They had another half-brother called Magas. He was Berenice's son by a previous marriage, and he was adopted by Ptolemy Soter when he married Berenice. He is now King of neighbouring Cyrene.'

'And no friend of Egypt,' Hanufer added. 'I had not realised that he was also related.' He lay his pen on the desk and blew on the papyrus. Then, looking up at Manetho, he asked, 'Now, what do you know of the poet Sotades? Philitas told me that he had been court poet in almost all of the empires of the Levant.'

Manetho nodded. 'He had. I know of no other person who made such a successful life out of spreading malice and deceit. From what I can gather he was welcomed everywhere, and in each court he would spread rumours about the other courts he had visited. He was so skilled at it that it is said that rulers were prepared to wage war on the basis of his information, tales of intrigue and rumour-mongering.'

'Until he wrote that salacious poem about Ptolemy Philadelphus and Queen Arsinoe the Second,' Hanufer remarked. 'But from what I have learned, he also insulted many people in Alexandria. Nobles, courtesans and scholars. People like Diomedes and Bilistiche?'

Manetho gave a curt nod of agreement. 'That is true, but regarding scholars, he was selective with the ones he insulted. He only seemed to do it to the less honoured, rather than those with high reputations.'

Hanufer thought of Ajax the young mathematician, who felt honoured to have been singled out by Sotades.

'I understand that he had written a version of *The Iliad* and also of *The Odyssey* in what he called his palindromic poetry — is that correct?'

'It is. Some parts of it were quite witty, but he did his usual trickery and used it to poke fun at people in it.'

Hanufer picked up his pen. 'Yes, I am aware that in it he belittled Patroclus, for Patroclus is one of the main characters in Homer's *Iliad.*'

'He belittled him because they had been lovers. Someone came between them.'

'Ah, I had heard that Sotades was promiscuous.'

The high priest tapped the side of his nose meaningly. 'There is something else that will not find its way into my history.

Queen Arsinoe hates the fact that her brother-husband has mistresses.'

'The Ladies Bilistiche and Didyme?'

'He has a child with Bilistiche. When Arsinoe discovered this, she is said to have taken lovers herself. Very secret ones. But there are few secrets that are not discovered by priests and priestesses. She had two lovers. Men who had been promiscuous with both men and women. I cannot and will not mention names, Hanufer. As the Overseer of Police, perhaps you should muse on that.'

*It all falls into place, yet at the same time it falls apart*, Hanufer thought as he walked through the sands that had not yet been swept from the path leading to the Musaeum. In the pocket of his chiton he had the drawings of the brains of the two murdered men, Zalmoxis and Diomedes, and the small box with the finger bone and the hair strands that Herophilus had given him.

He rubbed his rings and silently asked Sobek and Maat for enlightenment. But no idea suddenly struck him.

*Perhaps this problem is too Greek and I need to muse on it? Muse on it! That's what Manetho, who is also an Egyptian, suggested I do. That is a Greek expression.*

And at the thought he snapped his fingers as he walked on.

He recalled the half listened-to conversation with Timon as he broke his fast that morning. It was about Thalia, the muse of comedy and bucolic poetry. *He was telling me a tale about Zeus and Thalia, and how she had thwarted Zeus's attempted seduction by making a wig of eels.*

He quickened his pace and entered the Musaeum, walking past all the scholars in their white himations and heading for the Temple of the Muses at its centre. He strode into the

305

empty circular hall with its huge dome and the figurines of the Muses under it. Pulling a few coins from his pocket, he tossed them into the offering bowl and crossed to the curtained cubicle under the figurine of Thalia.

As he reached for the curtain, he felt a sudden excruciating pain from a blow to the back of his head. A hand shoved him through the curtain into the dark interior of the cubicle and it seemed as if a myriad of bright lights flashed in front of his eyes.


Sabu and Corporals Pylyp and Filemon had managed the plan to perfection and without a single injury to any of their trusted constables. Four of the renegades had resisted, resulting in one wounding and three cracked heads. All were manacled and imprisoned in the mess hall until further instructions from Hanufer.

In addition to Corporals Pylyp and Filemon, there were twenty-one trusted constables and they had secured seventeen of the renegades.

'When will you interrogate them, Sergeant Sabu?' Pylyp asked.

'As soon as *Archiphylakites* Hanufer says to. They are to be kept here until then, but will be moved to the Mareotis and the Necropolis prisons.'

'They are scum, all of them,' said Pylyp distastefully. 'But at least now we are rid of them we can build a trustworthy force.'

'We knew that Rhoglos and Sidvain were mean-spirited men, but we never thought they would stoop to murder,' agreed Filemon. 'Especially not ones of their own.'

'The question is, how many of the others would also be capable of it?' Sabu asked. 'I am just happy that we will not be depending on them in any way for the procession. It will be up to us to protect Admiral Patroclus.'

'Do you know what Sotades looked like, Sergeant?' Filemon asked Sabu. 'Because we don't.'

The sergeant nodded. 'Overseer Hanufer told me. Admiral Patroclus himself told him. He was powerfully built, like a swimmer. Red hair, beard and blue eyes. A sarcastic smile all the time.' He shrugged. 'But if he appears, it is unlikely that he will look like that. I expect he will be disguised, which means we have to expect anything and be suspicious of everyone. None must be allowed too close to the admiral.'

He patted his chiton and felt the scroll inside. 'So now, let's assemble the men and I will give them Overseer Hanufer's instructions for the procession.'

Some while later, as Sabu was reading the arrangements, the sound of horns being blown came from the gates of the Royal Palace. It was followed by the sound of marching feet and an officer barking commands.

*It's too far too early for the procession*, Sabu thought. *That is the royal guard. They must have been sent on some task nearby.* He returned to instructing the men.


'I was told that your meddling had to stop,' a voice grunted as the curtain was closed behind him.

Hanufer was stunned by the blow and felt a surge of nausea, but the voice indicated that he was in extreme danger.

A hand grabbed his wig. 'There's one quick way to stop asking questions. By letting some air into your throat.'

The hand yanked upwards and Hanufer realised the intention was to bare his throat enough for a blade to slit it.

His wig came free instantly and the assailant was momentarily put off balance. Hanufer spun round and

307

punched straight upwards under the kilt of the priest Pappus. The man gasped and dropped both the wig and the knife on the floor as he grasped his injured genitals. Hanufer headbutted him in the stomach, then as he doubled over he brought his head up to drive it into the priest's face.

Righting himself, Hanufer grabbed the priest's pectoral and drove a fist into the face that was already bleeding from a smashed nose. This time teeth flew out as the priest was hurled into the Temple of the Muses, where he skidded on his back to land splayed out under the dome.

Some scholars came running in upon hearing the noise and stood staring down at the bloodied high priest. Hanufer came out, shaking the fist he had grazed on Pappus's teeth while he replaced his wig with his other hand.

'I am *Archiphylakites* Hanufer and this man tried to slay me. He is under arrest. One of you fetch me rope immediately.'

One of the scholars was the mathematician Ajax. He nodded his head enthusiastically and immediately ran to the cubicle whence Hanufer had just ejected Pappus. He pulled away a rope that was used to hold the curtain back.

'Can I help you, Overseer Hanufer?' he asked. 'I am an expert with ropes and knots, and often contemplate them here as I think of divine Alexander and the Gordian knot.' With a foot on Pappus's chest, the young mathematician bound the priest's wrists together.

Hanufer was adjusting his wig when he again thought of the story Timon had been telling him about the muse Thalia having used a wig made from eels. That and the small box in his chiton suddenly gave him the answer he needed. He now knew who had killed both the slave Zalmoxis and the poet Diomedes.

As he looked up, he imagined that he saw the figurine of the muse Thalia smile.

In a nearby study room Hanufer interrogated Pappus, who proved to be fiercely resistant to his questions until the threat of torture loosened his tongue.

Ajax was happy to remain with the priest until a constable could be sent back for him.

Hanufer ran to the Musaeum stables and commandeered a horse. If what the priest had told him was correct, almost a quarter of the priestly class were in on one of the most audacious plots ever.

The words of the last poetic message were now horrifyingly clear to him.

# CHAPTER 27

Before the sandstorm had fully arrived, Pharaoh Ptolemy had informed a select number of the priests and priestesses of his intentions to worship together with Queen Arsinoe and receive the purification and protection of Isis before the procession itself started.

Thus, as *theoi philadelphoi*, 'brother and sister gods,' Ptolemy Philadelphus and Arsinoe his second wife had left the Royal Palace on foot, rather than being carried on a litter or palanquin surrounded by their personal guards. Arsinoe had always liked the position of the temple on the raised platform between the Small Harbour and the Royal Harbour, with the little island of Antirhodos creating the protective god-like hand in the water. She liked to think of it as the hand of Isis. They mounted the steps and passed the twin statues of the goddess by the great door. There the guards were instructed to wait as the brother and sister walked through the colonnaded court of the *purgatorium*, through which passed the little stream diverted from the Canopic Canal.

The sound of sistrums drifted from the temple, accompanied by the voice of a praise singer.

Two temple handmaids, covered in veils and with long peplos gowns were waiting by the entrance to the *naos*, which contained the great statue of Isis. They were already bowed from the waist, diverting their eyes from the divine couple. They turned as Ptolemy and Arsinoe mounted the marble steps, and then they followed the royal couple in and silently closed the doors after them.

They were in the sacred space, dominated by the brightly painted image of the goddess. Kneeling in front of it with her back to them they saw the high priestess, skilfully shaking a sistrum in each hand as she sang.

'She sings beautifully,' Arsinoe said softly to her brother as they approached.

Suddenly the sistrums stopped, as did the singing. Instead, the royal couple heard a ripple of soft laughter.

'What is the meaning —?' Ptolemy began.

The high priestess turned slowly round, her laughter getting louder.

'Do you really think I sing well, Arsinoe?' she asked, slowly raising her veil. 'Hello Ptolemy.'

Almost simultaneously clubs struck the pharaoh and the queen and sent them sprawling on the floor before the giant statue of Isis.

Hanufer dismounted by the Temple of Isis and approached the officer of the royal guards, who acknowledged his pectoral of office with a bow. He confirmed what Hanufer suspected — that the royal couple were at that moment inside the temple.

Knowing what he did from Pappus, Hanufer dared not enter through the main doors, or risk the noise of the guards accompanying him with their clanging metal, leather chest pieces and heavy cothurnus boots.

He left them with orders to remain in place until the doors were opened. Treading silently, he entered the purgatorium and circumvented the temple itself, moving into the garden. From there he used the side door of the temple, through which Nefrit had previously taken him.

His heart skipped a beat when he saw three women lying on the floor, bound and gagged. They were all conscious and he

311

immediately went to Nefrit. As he did, he could hear a woman's voice from the *naos*.

He put a finger to his lips and gently untied first her gag and then her bonds. He held up a reassuring hand to the two temple handmaids.

'It is a woman who says she is the sister of Ptolemy and Arsinoe,' Nefrit whispered.

'Her name is Lysandra and she is their half-sister, the daughter of Ptolemy Soter's first wife, Queen Eurydice.'

Hanufer signalled for her to follow him. Removing their sandals, they tiptoed through to the anteroom that led to the *naos*. Looking round the corner they could see the pharaoh and the queen on their knees, each bound and gagged and with two veiled figures standing behind them. In front of them stood a remarkably beautiful woman, who bore a striking resemblance to both the pharaoh and the queen. This confirmed Hanufer's suspicion that it was Lysandra.

'So here we are, brother and sister of mine. This is not how it was first planned before it was replanned and then replanned again. Our good friend and the former court poet of my father Lysimachus of Thrace and Macedon, Sotades, was to have been our means of bringing war and defeat to your door. He was to be our Trojan Horse, who would have been welcome at any court except yours. There we had several choices, for you have made enemies of all of your neighbours and Sotades's influence would have spurred them to war with you. Especially with the information we had given him.'

She laughed again. 'But I have you at a disadvantage. I am sorry for the lumps on your royal heads, but you needed to be subdued quickly. We will remove your gags so we can talk, or rather so you can listen while I talk first. Then you may respond — if I permit it.'

She signalled to the two veiled figures, who each produced a sacrificial knife and placed it against each of the couple's throats. 'Any attempt to summon your guards, by either of you, will result in both throats being cut. Do you agree to my terms?'

With eyes full of fear, they both nodded. The gags were pulled down.

'Why, Lysandra?' Arsinoe gasped.

'Why am I here? Don't look so astonished. I have been here for months, living in the Brucheum, just a short distance from the palace where we all once lived and played together. I have been planning this end to your dynasty and a new beginning. Quite simply, I am here for revenge, sister of mine. Upon you for effectively murdering my husband, the brave and good Agathocles. And for displacing my sister-in-law, the real Queen Arsinoe, in our brother's affections and for stealing her children.'

*It is as I suspected*, Hanufer thought as he listened. *The final lines of the last message. 'The poet's words will conquer all / Die those who kill and treasures take.'*

Lysandra shook her head. 'But all that was ruined when that buffoon Patroclus and his lover Diomedes drowned poor Sotades.'

'So those messages, those deaths, were nothing to do with Sotades?' Arsinoe asked in disbelief.

'A subterfuge, that's all. I knew his poems and I passed them on to my friends. It was not difficult to do. Some deaths were regrettable, others they found necessary to safeguard themselves against discovery.'

'And what did you hope to achieve?'

'Why, isn't it obvious? I was going to get rid of you and your lapdog Patroclus during this ridiculous procession of yours. My friends and I have been working on this for some time, although you did not know it. We have half the police force in our power, and they were to surround you at the Soma and assassinate you. Oh, it might have cost a few of our friends' lives, but not many would stand in our way. You have only to hear what the Greeks already say about you behind your backs.'

The couple muttered curses, which only made Lysandra laugh further.

'Our friends had little difficulty in rallying people to our cause after you so besmirched yourselves in the Greeks' eyes by marrying each other. We have many of the priestly class on our side, all just waiting for an opportunity to get rid of you and have what they would consider a good, honest pharaoh and a good Greek queen.'

'But we are your kin,' Ptolemy protested.

'Kin? You have no respect for family. You had my brother, dear Ptolemy Keraunos, banished by our father, and our stepbrother Magas, too.' She laughed again, this time an obvious, hollow laugh. 'But I give thanks to this wonderful sandstorm that has been threatening to come and which finally arrived last night. It frightened you into arranging this worship this day, and you told that select little group — which included our friend Kleitos, the high priest of Poseidon. It gave me the perfect opportunity for a neat and relatively bloodless transfer of power. My son lives with Antiochus Soter of the Seleucid Empire in Mesopotamia. Once you have gone, he will be sent for and crowned pharaoh, and there will be peace with the Seleucid Empire.'

She stood aside and pointed to the pedestal on which the great statue of Isis stood. Another message had been painted on it.

'There are many who believe that Sotades's ghost has been at work. So, I have given Sotades the final word.'

They saw first some hieroglyphs and then the poem in Greek.

*From the deserts Seth came and blew*
*And the murderous unholy thieves he slew*

Lysandra laughed again. 'It may not be thought of as Sotades's best work, but it will be taken as a sign from the gods. And, of course, Patroclus will be thought to be behind all of this. After all, they will think that he brought Seth's rage in the form of the sandstorm upon Alexandria and the destruction of the royal incestuous couple, by murdering Sotades. Even a buffoon like the Overseer of Police will have enough wit to arrest the vizier.'

'You are mad and this will never work. Our guards are outside this temple. So release us and you will be spared,' Ptolemy said defiantly.

Lysandra merely sneered. 'It is not me that is mad, or who has a knife at their throat. *I* decide who may be spared.'

Arsinoe swallowed hard. 'So what are you going to do, have our throats cut?'

'Oh, not as crude as that,' Lysandra replied. She reached into her peplos and took out two small bottles. 'I have become adept at poisoning, which has been useful to my friends. You shall both drink this and hope that you can pass the tests in the Hall of Truth, or else have your hearts gobbled up by the Ammit monster.'

'We will not!' growled Ptolemy.

'Then it shall be the blades across your throats.'

'Wait!' said Arsinoe. 'It does not have to be like this, sister.'

'Sister, is it now? I don't think so. I shall ask Isis to bless this divine poison for you.'

Holding the two bottles in her raised hands, she turned and started to mumble something to the statue.

Hanufer signalled to Nefrit to pick up her lute, which was resting against the wall with her other instruments. He made a couple of gestures, which she understood, and together they crept round the corner and sneaked up on the two assistants while Lysandra's back was still turned.

Hanufer grabbed the wrist of the one holding the blade to the pharaoh's throat and pulled it away, at the same time spinning the figure round and smashing a fist straight into the veiled face. The person went crashing to the floor, and their head made a sickening crack upon striking the marble. Immediately blood started to pool around them.

At the same time Nefrit had smashed her lute over the head of the other, causing the knife to drop as the body slumped to the floor with a gasp of pain.

Hanufer immediately reached down and pulled away the veil and headdress of the one he had felled to reveal the face of Stratonicus. He was staring sightlessly at the roof.

'This is the son of Obelius of Pella, Your Majesty,' he said, feeling his neck to check for signs of life. 'He is dead. His skull has cracked open.'

He moved to turn the other person over and grabbed the veil. 'And here, unless I am mistaken, is the murderess, the Lady Eupheme.'

Nefrit gasped and pointed at Lysandra, who had spun round and looked aghast at what had happened.

'Isis has forsaken me,' she said. 'But I will not give my brother and sister a say in my fate. I'll meet the Ammit monster myself.'

Before Hanufer could reach her, she had unstoppered both bottles and swallowed the contents.

Her eyes suddenly bulged, her cheeks puffed out and her face turned purple. Then she fell at the foot of the statue of the goddess, writhing in agony for a moment, before she started to shake and froth at the mouth in the throes of a convulsion. Seconds later she was dead.

Together Hanufer and Nefrit unbound the pharaoh and his queen and helped them to their feet. They stood and rubbed their wrists, while Hanufer used the ropes to bind the Lady Eupheme.

'Is it true what she said? That they have the police force under their control?' Ptolemy Philadelphus demanded.

'They did have renegades, Your Majesty. But I am confident that my men will have already nullified any threat and imprisoned the renegades.'

'Is Patroclus safe?' Queen Arsinoe asked, concernedly.

'I have taken measures to protect him, Your Majesty.'

The queen looked noticeably relieved, Hanufer thought. He pointed to the now stirring Eupheme. 'I shall interrogate her later, with your permission, Your Majesty. Eupheme personally murdered both a slave called Zalmoxis and the poet Diomedes, which I can prove.'

The pharaoh looked down at her, as if her very presence disgusted him. 'Pull her teeth out and do whatever you must do to get all the information from her. Then my sister-wife and I shall decide how she must die.'

Nefrit stifled a gasp and covered her face with her hands upon hearing this.

'Most importantly, no one must know of any of this,' Ptolemy said. 'You have done well. Both of you will be rewarded. But you must make sure that not a word of this outrage becomes known to the people.'

'Our sister is no longer kin of ours,' said Arsinoe. 'Her body must be disposed of without embalming, burial or ceremony, so that her name will disappear, and she will never enter the afterlife.'

The pharaoh nodded and took his queen's hand. 'The procession will take place at noon as planned.' He pointed to the message on the pedestal. 'Have this desecration removed so that we have an end to all of this Sotades nonsense once and for all.'

Hanufer and Nefrit bowed before the royal couple and stared in disbelief as they, seemingly without emotion or reaction, turned and left the temple.

# CHAPTER 28

The procession went exactly as planned, with the installation of Admiral Patroclus as the high priest of Alexander. The people of the city cheered the royal couple and marvelled at the great python Apophis as it was drawn in its huge cage at the end of the procession. When the effigy of Sotades was loaded into a pithos jar and sailed out from the tip of the Island of Pharos to be tossed symbolically into the sea, it seemed as if a curse upon the city had been lifted.

No one seemed to notice the curious bulge in the python's long body.

Few people paid any attention to the vessel that passed the boat from which the effigy and pithos jar had been tossed. It sailed into the harbour, where some time later a great crate containing the statue carved by Hecataeus was manhandled ashore.

The sculptor, upon giving his name, was surprised to find himself taken into custody and brought to the office of the Alexandrian police, along with the ship's Captain Nestor. They were both kept in the cells until Hanufer had dealt with all of the matters that had arisen that day.

After arranging the arrests of all of the priests who Pappus had told him were involved in the conspiracy, Hanufer organised the transfer of the renegade constables to the prisons.

Then he interrogated Eupheme.

In the same cell in the Necropolis prison once occupied by the poet Sotades, her wrists manacled to great rings in the wall, he questioned her, having first told her that the pharaoh had

319

said she should have her teeth pulled out. To his relief, the threat was enough to make her talk.

'What do I care, now that my love Stratonicus and my Magnificence, the Princess Lysandra, are no more? I would do it all again,' Eupheme said.

Sabu sat listening uncomfortably in a corner of the cell as his boss posed questions and the prisoner responded candidly.

'I was one of Princess Lysandra's ladies at the court of King Lysimachus. I knew Queen Arsinoe — the real and true Queen Arsinoe, before she was sent to marry Ptolemy. She was a kind and good woman and did not deserve to be repudiated, not after she gave the pharaoh his three children. That woman, Arsinoe the whore, who now sits on the throne stole her crown and her children from her. Just as she poisoned Lysimachus's mind against his own son, the good Prince Agathocles, who was put to death. I would have followed Princess Lysandra to the Seleucid court in Mesopotamia had I not caught the attention of Obelius of Pella, when he was on a trading visit there. He asked me to marry him, which I did.'

'And how long was it before you were unfaithful to him? With his own son?'

She glared at him. 'Is it any surprise, when Obelius looks as he does and Stratonicus was like a god? Within weeks we had bedded each other.'

'And as a merchant, Stratonicus was presumably able to get messages to and from Lysandra in Mesopotamia?'

'He ran most of the family businesses, while Obelius sat and counted money and had symposia to impress the great of Alexandria, like Patroclus.'

'So your husband had no part in your affairs?'

She shook her head. 'Stratonicus was able to smuggle Princess Lysandra, she who we called our "Magnificence", back into Alexandria. He set her up in one of the finest and most private villas in the Brucheum, and with her we began to plan her revenge. Revenge because Arsinoe the whore had her husband murdered.'

'And this plan included the poet Sotades?'

'Yes, but we had to wait until we were able to get him out of this hellhole that you have me in now.'

'Your lover Stratonicus bribed the jailor Zalmoxis?'

Her eyes opened wide in surprise. 'You know that? Yes, he released Sotades and we arranged for him to be taken to Caunus, until we could arrange for one of the other empires to take him. Macedon, Seleucia, Cyrene, or Thrace. Any would have welcomed him, and there he would have been able to persuade them to take up arms against Ptolemy and Arsinoe the whore. Especially when they were told that Princess Lysandra was in Alexandria already.'

'This sculptor, Hecataeus, what part did he play?'

'None! He was just a piece in the game. He knew there was some intrigue to get Sotades to safety away from Ptolemy, but that was all. He didn't need to know anything of our plans.'

'And the ship's captain, Nestor?'

'The same. He was just a man with a ship. A ferryman for a poet.'

Hanufer shook his head. 'So the *demosios* Zalmoxis, where did he go?'

'We took him in as a house slave, with the promise that he would be safe until we smuggled him out of Alexandria. Unfortunately, he saw my lover and I together in a bedchamber. I had to silence him in case he told my husband, Obelius.'

'You did it by getting close to him, embracing him?'

Again she looked surprised. She nodded. 'A noble woman can easily seduce a slave. I allowed him to embrace and kiss me.'

'And then you used that lapis lazuli hairpin of yours and slid it rapidly into his skull.' Hanufer reached into his chiton and produced it. 'And once in his head, probably as he was fitting, you swivelled it round and round.'

'How … how do you know?'

'I found the puncture wound at the base of his skull, and I had the anatomist Erasistratus remove his brain. He split it open and it showed how you had pulped it.'

To Hanufer's amazement, Eupheme smiled. 'Men can be such fools when they are running their hands all over you.'

'Just as Diomedes was doing on the night of the symposium?'

'He had tried to make love to me earlier, when he was telling fortunes. Since he had been with Patroclus when they drowned Sotades, we knew that he could be dangerous and might reveal things we needed to be kept secret. We didn't know what he had talked about with Hecataeus, for one thing. Stratonicus was worried by how much you might have taken in at the symposium. So afterwards, as Diomedes was leaving, I arranged to meet him. I told him he could have me if he still wanted.'

'At his villa? And you killed him in the same way?'

She nodded. 'And Stratonicus covered him in vinegar and held him in the eel pond until the creatures had started to feed on him.'

'I discovered the puncture wound at the base of his skull, just as I did on the slave Zalmoxis. The anatomist Herophilus removed his brain under my authority and we found the same cone-shaped mush of brain.'

She sniffed. 'Stratonicus was right. You were more dangerous than we thought you to be.'

'The body of Zalmoxis — I presume that Stratonicus and the renegade priest Kleitos put him in the bull pen together, so that his body would be trampled and made unrecognisable?'

She nodded.

'And Stratonicus followed Philitas of Cos into the Royal Zoo, knocked out Weneg the Keeper of Snakes and killed Philitas before he slipped his body into the python's cage?'

'He did, again because we could not risk you going back to him and asking more about Sotades. It suited us that our whole ploy with the false messages was convincing people that Sotades was alive and seeking revenge.'

'Revenge on Patroclus and Diomedes?'

'Yes, to divert anyone from suspecting that the real target was Arsinoe the whore and Ptolemy.'

'Why do you call Her Majesty a whore? Because of her marriage to her brother?'

Eupheme smirked. 'Partly that, but also because she is a whore. She took lovers, as did Ptolemy. Patroclus and Sotades both enjoyed her bed. There are probably others.'

'Sotades?' Hanufer repeated in surprise.

'Of course, why else do you think that pathetic little poem would cause so much offence? He eventually spurned her, maybe even for Patroclus. You know that he has a liking for men and women?'

*Ah, those will be the two names that Manetho refused to divulge,* thought Hanufer. *That also explains why the queen seemed so concerned that Patroclus was unharmed. Perhaps they are still lovers?*

'Stratonicus made a mistake with his hieroglyphics. They were meaningless as words, and he also used the wrong glyph for a jar. He used one that meant the heart, the *ib*. I presume that was to make it seem as if an Egyptian could have done it?'

'That is correct.'

'That was another mistake, because why would Sotades, a Greek, use hieroglyphics?'

'May the Ammit monster eat your heart, Hanufer of Crocodilopolis!' Eupheme muttered.

Hanufer took out the small box containing the finger bone from his pocket. 'When the anatomists examined the brains of the two dead men, they found these,' he said, unwinding two long red hairs. 'Your hair, from your hairpin.'

Again Eupheme laughed. 'Then our Magnificence was right to tell Stratonicus to use one of her poison vials on Erasistratus at the symposium. She was concerned when he told her that you had arranged for Zalmoxis's body to be taken to the Medical School. She told him not to give so much that it would kill him.'

'Just as he gave some to Pollio the police office scribe to silence Sidvain and Rhoglos, the two constables who murdered *Archiphylakites* Gryton and Sergeant Kraspar.'

'You seem to have worked everything out, Hanufer of Crocodilopolis.'

'Not everything. Why did you arrange to extort money from the people of the Jewish community? And the Nubians and some of the small Egyptian businesses?'

'Simply to make them all distrust the authorities. The more the people distrusted, the easier it would be to sew discontent about the pharaoh and his whore queen.' She smiled. 'And now you know all of our secrets, tell me, what have the royal dogs planned for me, apart from taking my teeth?'

Hanufer stood up. 'That I do not know. Perhaps that is something to ask Harpocrates the god of secrets and silence about.'

Sabu interviewed the sculptor and Nestor the ship captain, ensuring that he was officious enough to scare them and make certain that they would never talk about their association with the poet Sotades.

Patroclus was as good as his word and introduced Hecataeus to the royal couple so that he could present them with his gift of the statue of Tyche, which they realised at once was based upon Queen Arsinoe herself.

It was a sadness to them when Apophis eventually passed the skeletal remains some days later, along with the iron rings that Philitas of Cos had worn for several decades. Ptolemy gave them to Hecataeus the sculptor to have them melted down and incorporated into a life-size statue of the philosopher that he commissioned him to complete. This was to be placed at the entrance to the Library that he had graced for so long.

The official story was to be that Philitas of Cos had returned to his native island, to live his final days as a recluse as he struggled with the many paradoxes that were food to him rather than food itself.

The meeting with Patroclus was not as difficult as Hanufer had imagined it would be. The vizier and high priest of Alexander had listened to the whole story, interrupting only occasionally. He had offered his thanks for saving the royal couple and himself, and for preventing whatever chaos and bloodshed that would have inevitably followed.

Much to Hanufer's relief, he informed him that he would personally deal with the errant priests and organise their gradual replacement.

'Had you heard about Obelius?' Patroclus asked as their meeting came to an end.

'No, sir,' Hanufer replied.

'His wife Eupheme has run away with his son, Stratonicus.' He waited a moment, then added, 'That is what poor Obelius is going to be told. The less he knows, the better.'

# EPILOGUE

Hanufer and Nefrit sailed out to sea and lay back in each other's arms, watching the beams of light from the Pharos lighthouse cutting through the evening darkness.

'So much pain, deceit and killing, my love,' she said.

'I know. Such a beautiful city, yet with so many secrets that must remain so.'

'Poor Obelius, he must be heartbroken to think that his own son and his wife ran away together.' She squeezed his hand. 'I feel guilty about knowing the truth.'

Hanufer raised her hand and kissed it. He had not the heart to tell her the real secrets behind the other murders and what Lady Eupheme's fate had been.

Apart from her usual cow horn and moon headdress, Nefrit was wearing gardenias in her hair. She pulled one out and tossed it onto the surface of the water.

'That is for Sotades,' she said. 'I never knew him, but I am so sad that he died as he did.'

They watched the flower as it bobbed up and down on the waves, until it suddenly disappeared. As if plucked downwards by an unseen hand.

# HISTORICAL NOTE

*Death of a Poet* is a work of fiction set in Alexandria, the capital of Ptolemaic Egypt during the reign of Pharaoh Ptolemy II, known as Ptolemy Philadelphus. He was the second pharaoh in the dynasty, having been appointed co-ruler with his father Ptolemy Soter, then as pharaoh in his own right.

The background to this novel is the fascinatingly complex family history of the Ptolemies and of the dynasties of the other empires that arose after the death of Alexander the Great. He had five generals, known as the *Diadochi*, meaning the successors, who carved up the known world that was his empire. Wars broke out as the power struggle ensued. Ptolemy Soter shrewdly took Egypt as his own and thus established the Ptolemaic dynasty that would last for 275 years, from 305 to 30 BC. The most famous of the Ptolemies was Cleopatra VII, the last ruler of this dynasty, who was immortalised by William Shakespeare in his play *Antony and Cleopatra*.

The city of Alexandria was designed on the Hellenistic model, reputedly on the instructions of Alexander the Great himself. It had a regular grid structure to maximise the cool north winds during the summer and it was a truly cosmopolitan city. Its main streets were extremely wide, constructed so that a chariot could be turned in them.

Ptolemy Philadelphus oversaw the construction of the famous Pharos lighthouse on the nearby Island of Pharos. It was reached by a causeway called the *Heptastadion*, which divided the crescent shape of the coast into two harbours. A scholar himself, he also oversaw the development of the Library of Alexandria and the Musaeum, which was effectively the world's first university. As part of this it had a Medical School where two famous physicians and anatomists, Herophilus and Erasistratus, carried out ground-breaking research by anatomical dissection. According to the later Roman historian Celsus they were permitted to use living people, such as condemned criminals, in vivisection.

The mind baulks at this, but whether it is true or not, Herophilus was responsible for many discoveries about anatomy. He described parts of the brain, the intestinal tract, the lymphatic system, the liver, the genitals and the eye, and amazingly, he described the pump action of the heart, showing that it was responsible for the pulse. He also showed that arteries were six times thicker than veins.

Erasistratus is regarded not only as an anatomist, but also as a physiologist, for he differentiated sensory from motor nerves and he described the anatomy and function of the trachea (the windpipe), the epiglottis (the flap of tissue which prevents food entering the windpipe when one swallows), the heart and the vascular system.

The scholars who flocked to study and work in the Library and the Musaeum under Ptolemy's patronage were legion. Several of them are mentioned in this novel: Manetho the historian and high priest of Serapis, whose history of Egypt written in Greek was commissioned by Ptolemy II; Callimachus, who developed a system to catalogue the Library; Zenodotus, the great Homer critic and scholar; the great poets Theocritus and Hermesianax, and Philitas of Cos, who reputedly wore heavy weights to stop himself from being blown over by the wind. He had been a tutor to both Ptolemy and his sister when they were children. He was a philosopher and poet, who taught many of the other scholars in his time.

History is unclear when, or if, Philitas left Alexandria, but the poet Posidippus describes how a life-size statue of him was commissioned by Ptolemy Philadelphus and constructed by the sculptor Hecataeus. The Alexandrian poet Hermesianax also described a statue that was erected for him under a tree on his native island of Cos.

Ptolemy invited seventy-two Jewish scholars, six from each of the twelve tribes, to translate their holy books — the Septuagint — into Greek. This was a monumentally important moment in history.

He also had a huge private zoo, full of exotic creatures from all over the known world. He had a giant python, which he had sent an expedition to Ethiopia to obtain. This is documented in history, and it may have been one of the largest snakes ever found.

Alexandria was a Greek city in Egypt. The Ptolemies were Macedonian Greeks, but adopted Egyptian ways and did much to integrate the two cultures. Significantly, at the crux of this novel, Ptolemy II married his full sister Arsinoe, after having repudiated his first wife, also called Arsinoe. Incestuous marriage was anathema to the Greeks, but perfectly acceptable to the Egyptians. But it divided the opinions of the city and many Greeks were disparaging about the union. Most notable among these critics was the poet Sotades the Obscene. His infamous poem landed him in trouble with the royal couple and he was thrown in prison. He escaped to the Island of Caunus, but was found by Admiral Patroclus, Ptolemy's vizier, who sealed him in a pithos jar or a lead cage or coffin and tossed him into the sea.

This much is known. What happens thereafter is fiction!

# A NOTE TO THE READER

Dear Reader,

If you have enjoyed the novel enough to leave a review on **Amazon** and **Goodreads**, then I would be truly grateful. I love to hear from readers, so if you would like to contact me, please do so through my **Facebook** page or send me a message through **Twitter.** You can also see my latest news on my **Website.**

Keith Moray

**keithmorayauthor.com**

**Sapere Books** is an exciting new publisher of brilliant fiction and popular history.

To find out more about our latest releases and our monthly bargain books visit our website:
**saperebooks.com**

Made in the USA
Las Vegas, NV
25 March 2023